J

7

J

Howard Jacobson

W F HOWES LTD

This large print edition published in 2015 by
W F Howes Ltd
Unit 4, Rearsby Business Park, Gaddesby Lane,
Rearsby, Leicester LE7 4YH

1 3 5 7 9 10 8 6 4 2

First published in the United Kingdom in 2014
by Jonathan Cape

A CIP catalogue record for this book is available
from the British Library

ISBN 978 1 47128 683 4

Typeset by Palimpsest Book Production Limited,
Falkirk, Stirlingshire
Printed and bound by
www.printondemand-worldwide.com of Peterborough, England

To Jenny – here, now, always

ARGUMENT

THE WOLF AND THE TARANTULA

A grey wolf fell into conversation with a tarantula. 'I love the chase,' the grey wolf said. 'Myself,' said the tarantula, 'I like to sit here and wait for my prey to come to me.' 'Don't you find that lonely?' the wolf asked. 'I could as soon ask you,' the tarantula replied, 'how it is that you don't get sick of taking your wife and kids along on every hunt.' 'I am by temperament a family man,' the wolf answered. 'And what is more there is power in numbers.'

The tarantula paused to crush a passing marmoset then said he doubted the wolf, for all the help he received, would ever be as successful a huntsman as he was. The wolf wagered a week's catch on his ability to outhunt the tarantula and, returning to his lair, told his wife and children of the bet.

'You owe me,' he told the tarantula when they next met.

'And your proof?'

'Well I expect you to trust my word, but if you don't, then go ahead and search the wilderness with your own eyes.'

This the tarantula did, and sure enough discovered

that of all the wolf's natural prey not a single creature remained.

'I salute your efficiency,' the tarantula said, 'but
it does occur to me to wonder what you are going
to do for sustenance now.'

At this the grey wolf burst into tears. 'I have
had to eat my wife,' he admitted. 'And next week
I will start on my children.'

'And after that?'

'After that? After that I will have no option but
to eat myself.'

Moral: Always leave a little on your plate.

BOOK I

CHAPTER 1

THE BIG IF

i

Mornings weren't good for either of them. 'Here we go again,' Ailinn Solomons said to herself.

She swung her legs out of the bed and looked at her feet. Even before Kevern's insult she had disliked them. The broad insteps. The squat scarab toes, more like thumbs, each the same length as the others. She would have liked Pan pipes toes, beautifully graduated, musical, such as a Sylvan god might have put his lips to. She slid them into slippers and then slid them out again. The slippers made them look, if anything, worse. Hausfrau feet. The same old graceless feet, carrying her through the same old graceless life. No wonder, she caught herself thinking . . . but couldn't finish. No wonder what?

In reality there wasn't much that was 'same old' about her life, other than the habit of thinking there was. By any objective measure – and she could see objectivity, just out of reach – she was living adventurously. She had recently moved into a new house. In the company of a new friend. In a new village. For the move she had bought herself new clothes. New sunglasses. A new bag. New nail polish. Even her slippers were new. The house, though new to her, was not new to itself. It felt skulkingly ecclesiastical, which Ailinn had reasons of her own to dislike, as though a disreputable abbé or persecuted priest – a pastor too austere for his congregation or a padre too fleshly for his – had gone to ground there and finally forgotten what he was hiding from. It had stood stonily in its own damp in a dripping valley, smelling of wild garlic and wet gorse, for centuries. Neither the light of hope nor the light of disillusionment made it through its small, low windows, so deep into the valley. It deferred expectation – was the best you could say of it. Whoever had lived here before her, they had been, like the vegetation, neither happy nor unhappy. But though she shrank from its associations, it was still an improvement on the square slab of speckled concrete she had latterly grown up in, with its view that was no view of a silted estuary – the dull northern tide trickling in from nowhere on the way to nowhere – and the company of her frayed-tempered parents who weren't really her parents at all.

And – *and* – she had met a new man. The one who had insulted her feet.

True, he was no Sylvan god, and would not have put her feet to his lips even if he had been – but

4

that was no consolation for her having probably lost him. He had – he'd had – promise.

As for the rest – including the new friend, who was much older than her and more a sort of guardian (funny the way she attracted guardians) – they struck her as incidentals, a rearrangement of the furniture, that was all. In every other regard she was still herself. That was what was cruel about superficial change: it exposed what could never change. Better to have stayed where she was and waited. As long as you are waiting you can't be disappointed. I was all right when I was in suspense, she thought. But that wasn't true either. She had never been all right.

Her heart, periodically, fluttered. Arrhythmia, the doctor called it. 'Nothing to worry about,' he said when the tests came back. She laughed. Of course it was nothing to worry about. Life was nothing to worry about. In the place she had come from people said that your heart fluttered when someone you loved had died.

'What if you don't love anybody?' she had asked her adoptive mother.

'Then it's the anniversary of the death of someone you loved in a previous life,' the older woman had answered.

As though she wasn't morbid enough on her own account without having to hear nonsense like that.

She didn't know who her actual mother and father were and remembered little about her life before her faux parents picked her out from the orphanage like an orange, except for how unlike the way she thought a little girl was supposed to be she felt. Today, whatever she could or couldn't remember, she seemed older to herself than her twenty-five years. What about twenty-five hundred? What about twenty-five thousand? 'Don't exaggerate, Ailinn,' people had always told her. (Twenty-five thousand years?) But it wasn't she who exaggerated, it was they who reduced. Her head was like an echo chamber. If she concentrated long and hard enough, she sometimes thought, she would hear the great ice splitting and the first woolly mammoths come lolloping down from central Asia. Perhaps everybody – even the abridgers and condensers – could do the same but were embarrassed to talk about it. Unless infancy in the company of real parents had filled their minds with more immediate and, yes, trivial sensations. Our birth is but a sleep and a forgetting – who said that?

Ha! – she had forgotten.

It was a good job that history books were hard to come by, that diaries were hidden or destroyed and that libraries put gentle obstacles in the way of research, otherwise she might have decided to ransack the past and live her life backwards. If only to discover who it was her heart periodically fluttered for.

A sodden old snail appeared from under her bed, dragging a smear of egg white behind it. It was

6

all she could do not to crush it with her bare, ugly foot.

Before chancing his nose outside his cottage in the morning, Kevern 'Coco' Cohen turned up the volume on the loop-television, poured tea – taking care to place the cup carelessly on the hall table – and checked twice to be certain that his utility phone was on and flashing. A facility for making and receiving local telephone calls only – all other forms of electronic communication having been shut down after WHAT HAPPENED, IF IT HAPPENED, to the rapid spread of whose violence social media were thought to have contributed – the utility phone flashed a malarial yellow until someone rang, and then it glowed vermilion. But it rarely rang. This, too, he left on the hall table. Then he rumpled the silk Chinese hallway runner – a precious heirloom – with his shoe.

The action was not commemorative in intent, but it often reminded him of a cruelly moonlit night many years before, when after a day strained by something – money worries or illness or news which the young Kevern gathered must have been very bad – his sardonic, creaking father had kicked the runner aside, raised the hem of his brocade dressing gown, and danced an enraged soft-shoe shuffle, his arms and legs going up and down in unison like those of a toy skeleton on a stick. He hadn't known his son was on the stairs, watching.

Kevern pressed himself into the darkness of the

7

stairwell. Became a shadow. He was too frightened to say anything. His father was not a dancing man. He stayed very still, but the cottage thrummed to its occupants' every anxiety – he could sense his parents' troubled sleep through the floorboards under his bed, even though he slept in a room below theirs – and now the disturbance his fear generated gave his presence away.

'Sammy Davis Junior,' his father explained awkwardly when he saw him. His voice was hoarse and dry, a rattle from ruined lungs. Because he spoke with an accent even Kevern found strange, as though he'd never really listened to how people spoke in Port Reuben, he released his words reluctantly. He put two fingers across his mouth, like a tramp sucking on a cigarette butt he'd found in a rubbish bin. This he always did to stifle the letter j before it left his lips.

The boy was none the wiser. 'Sammy Davis Junior?' He too, religiously in his father's presence – and often even when his father wasn't there – sealed his lips against the letter j when it began a word. He didn't know why. It had begun as a game between them when he was small. His father had played it with his own father, he'd told him. Begin a word with a j without remembering to put two fingers across your mouth and it cost you a penny. It had not been much fun then and it was not much fun now. He knew it was expected of him, that was all. But why was his father being Sammy Davis Junior, whoever Sammy Davis Junior was?

8

'Song and dance man,' his father said. 'Mr Bo Jangles. No, you haven't heard of him.'

Him? Which him? Sammy Davis Junior or Mr Bo Jangles?

Either way, it sounded more like a warning than a statement. *If anybody asks, you haven't heard of him. You understand?* Kevern's childhood had been full of such warnings. Each delivered in a half-foreign tongue. You don't know, you haven't seen, you haven't heard. When his schoolteachers asked questions his was the last hand to go up: he said he didn't know, hadn't seen, hadn't heard. In ignorance was safety. But it worried him that he might have sounded like his father, lisping and slithering in another language. So he spoke in a whisper that drew even more attention to his oddness.

In this instance his father needn't have worried. Kevern hadn't only not heard of Sammy Davis Junior, he hadn't heard of Sammy Davis Senior either.

Ailinn would not have said no to such a father, no matter how strange his behaviour. It helped, she thought, to know where your madness came from.

Once Kevern had closed and double-locked the front door, he knelt and peered through the letter box, as he imagined a burglar or other intruder might. He could hear the television and smell the tea. He could see the phone quietly pulsing yellow, as though receiving dialysis, on the hall table. The silk runner, he noted with satisfaction, might have been trodden on by a household of small children. No sane man could possibly leave his own house without rearranging the runner on the way out.

He had a secondary motive for shuffling the rug. It demonstrated that it was of no value to him. The law – though it was nowhere written down; a willing submission to restraint might be a better way of putting it, a supposition of coercion – permitted only one item over a hundred years old per household, and Kevern had several. Mistreatment of them, he hoped, would quiet suspicion.

At the extreme limit of letter-box vision the toes of worn leather carpet slippers were just visible. Clearly he was at home, the fusspot, probably nodding in front of the television or reading the junk mail which had in all likelihood been delivered only minutes ago, in the excitement of collecting which he had left his tea and utility phone by the door. But at home, faffing, however else you describe what he was doing.

He returned to the cottage three times, at fifteen-second intervals, looking through his letter box to ascertain that nothing had changed. On each occasion he pushed his hand inside to be sure the flap had not stuck in the course of his inspections – a routine that had to be repeated in case the act of making sure had itself caused the flap to jam – then he took the cliff path and strode distractedly in the direction of the sea. The sea that no one but a few local fishermen sailed on, because there was nowhere you could get to on it – a sea that lapped no other shore.

Nothing had changed there either. The cliff still fell away sharply, sliced like cake, turning a deep, smoky purple at its base; the water still massed tirelessly, frothing and fuming, every day the same. Faffing, like Kevern. More angrily, but to no more purpose.

That was the great thing about the sea: you didn't have to worry about it. It wasn't going anywhere and it wasn't yours. It hadn't been owned and hidden by your family for generations. It didn't run in your blood.

He did, however, have his own bench. Not officially. It didn't have his name on it, but it was respected by the villagers of Port Reuben as they might have respected a wall against which the village idiot kicked his heels. *Coco sits here. The silly bleeder.*

They didn't think he was simple-minded. If anything they thought him a little too clever. But there are times in the history of humanity when cleverness might as well be simplicity.

At this hour, and especially at this season, when visitors were infrequent, he usually had the cliffs and the sea that went nowhere to himself. Sometimes Densdell Kroplik, his closest neighbour, would venture out of the reclaimed cowshed he called his bachelor pad and join Kevern briefly on the bench to complain, in the manner of a prophet without honour in his own country, about the madness of the world, the sunken condition of the village, and, by way of proof of both – for he was a self-published chronicler of the times and of this place – his plummeting sales figures. An itinerant barber and professional local, he policed the cliffs and public houses of Port Reuben, barring it to interlopers with his eyes, dressing like a landowner, a fisherman, a farmer, or a fool, depending on what clothes were uppermost on the pile on his floor – sometimes dressing like all of them at once – interposing his tuberous frame between Port Reuben and outside influence. Not so much the gatekeeper, Densdell Kroplik, as the gate. Though history, as another form of over-cherishing the past, was discouraged, he got away with being unofficial custodian of Port Reuben's secrets and teller of its tales, by keeping the narrative short and sweet – certainly shorter and sweeter than his conversation which, especially when he was cutting hair, boiled like the sea. Port Reuben, originally Ludgvennok, had once been an impregnable fortress of the old ways, and now it wasn't. THE END. This was the essence of Densdell Kroplik's *A Brief History of Port Reuben*, with a few maps and line drawings, done in his hand, and a number of comical footnotes, citing himself, thrown in.

No more, strictly speaking, than a pamphlet for visitors he would rather have stayed away, *A Brief History of Port Reuben* was for sale by the till in every tourist shop. What few tourists there were bought it with their fudge. But for its author it stood between prosperity and ruination, and by that he meant the village's no less than his own. He checked his outlets every day to see how many had been sold, topping up stocks with signed copies from a sinisterly bulging rucksack that also contained combs, scissors, clippers, and shampoos and conditioners made to a secret formula from heather and thistles and wild flowers that grew in his scruffy clifftop garden. This he lugged, with exaggerated effort, as though making a sacrifice of his health to humanity, from shop to shop. Rather than have him engage them in conversation about his sales, which he never considered satisfactory, the shopkeepers kept out of his way, allowing him to load as many of his pamphlets on them as he thought appropriate. A number of them even bought multiple copies for themselves. They did as birthday presents to relations they didn't like. Anything not to have him fulminating against the bastardisation of the times in their shops, blowing out his weather-beaten cheeks, pulling at his knotted polka-dot neckerchief in sarcastic rage, as though that was all that kept his head attached to his body.

On some mornings, in return for the opportunity to rattle on, Densdell would shave Kevern free of charge. Afraid for his throat – because he was sure Densdell saw him as the incarnate proof, if not the prime cause, of Port Reuben's ruin – Kevern made noises of assent to everything he said. But he understood little of it. Once his razor was out, Densdell Kroplik gave up all pretence of speaking a language they shared. He dropped into a dialect that was older and wilder than the cliffs, coughing up sounds as though they were curses, using words Kevern had never heard before in his life and which he believed, half the time, did not actually exist. Rather than make an effort to decipher any of it, he would concentrate on the idea of the wind picking up the invisible hairs Densdell barbered from him, and spiralling them out to sea in clusters, like dandelion spores.

Little by little the sea claiming him.

This morning, to Kevern's relief, Densdell Kroplik didn't put in an appearance, so he could sit and fret without company. The very seagulls, smelling his anxiety, kept their distance.

He was a tall, skinny, golden-mopped man (though his hair was thinning now), who moved as though apologetic of his height. He was considered, for all his strangeness, to have kind eyes. He unwound himself on to the bench and looked up at the sky. 'Jesus Christ!' he exclaimed, the moment he was comfortable, for no other reason than to pit his voice against those he heard in his head.

Better a voice he could control than a voice he couldn't. He was no visionary, but there were times when he would mistake the sound of a seabird or the distant laughter of fishermen – he didn't doubt it was a mistake – for a cry for help. 'Kevern!' he thought he heard. The two syllables pronounced with equal lack of emphasis. His dead mother's voice. A sick woman's voice, anyway. Quavering and reproachful, having to make itself heard above a jealous, jostling multitude of cries, detached from the person to whom it had belonged. 'Key-vern!'

He hadn't been close to his mother so he guessed this was a trick of longing. He would have liked her to be calling him.

But he recognised a danger in granting this primacy to his imagination: would he know the difference if one day someone really did cry out for his help?

He was not happy, but he was as happy here in his unhappiness, he accepted, as he was ever going to be. The sea confers a grandeur on the smallness of man's dissatisfactions, and Kevern Cohen gratefully accepted the compliment, knowing that his dissatisfactions were no bigger than most men's – loneliness and sense of lost direction (or was it the sense of never having had direction?) – of early-onset middle age. Nothing more. Like his father before him, and he had felt a deeper bond to his father than to his mother, though that wasn't saying much, he turned and carved wood for a living – spindles, newels, candlesticks, bowls, love-spoons for the tourist industry which he sold in local shops – and turning wood was a repetitive and tedious business. He had no family alive, no uncles, nieces, cousins, which was unusual in this part of the world where everyone was as an arm joined to one giant octopus. Kevern was joined to no one. He had no one to love or be loved by. Though this was to a degree occupational – like the moon, a woodturner turns alone – he accepted that it was largely a fault of character. He was lonely because he didn't take or make calls on his utility phone, because he was a neglectful friend, and, worse, an easily dismayed, over-reflective lover, and because he was forty.

Falling in love was something he did from time to time, but he was never able to stay in love or keep a woman in love with him. Nothing dramatic happened. There were no clifftop fallings-out. Compared to the violence with which other couples publicly shredded one another in Port Reuben, his courtships – for they were rarely more than that – came to an end with exemplary courtesy on both sides. They dissolved, that was the best way of putting it, they gradually came apart like a cardboard box that had been left out in the rain. Just occasionally a woman told him he was too serious, hard-going, intense, detached, and maybe a bit prickly. And then shook his hand. He recognised prickly. He was spiny, like a hedgehog, yes. The latest casualty of this spininess was an embryo-affair that had given greater promise than usual of relieving the lonely tedium of his life, and perhaps even bringing him some content. Ailinn Solomons was a wild-haired, quiveringly delicate beauty with a fluttering heart from a northern island village more remote and rugged even than Port Reuben. She had come south with an older

16

companion whom Kevern took to be her aunt, the latter having been left a property in a wet but paradisal valley called, felicitously, Paradise Valley.

No one had lived in the house for several years. The pipes leaked, there were spiders still in the baths, slugs had signed their signatures on all the windows, believing the place belonged to them, the garden was overgrown with weeds that resembled giant cabbages. It was like a children's story cottage, threatening and enchanting at the same time, the garden full of secrets. Kevern had been sitting holding hands with Ailinn on broken deckchairs in the long grass, enjoying an unexpectedly warm spring afternoon, the pair of them absent-mindedly plugged into the utility console that supplied the country with soothing music and calming news, when the sight of her crossed brown legs reminded him of an old song by a long-forgotten black entertainer his father had liked listening to with the cottage blinds down. 'Your feet's too big.'

On account of their innate aggressiveness, songs of that sort were no longer played on the console. Not banned – nothing was banned exactly – simply not played. Encouraged to fall into desuetude, like the word desuetude. Popular taste did what edict and proscription could never have done, and just as, when it came to books, the people chose rags-to-riches memoirs, cookbooks and romances, so, when it came to music, they chose ballads.

Carried away by the day, Kevern began to play

at an imaginary piano and in a rudely comic voice serenade Ailinn's big feet.

Ailinn didn't understand.

'It was a popular song by a jazz pianist called Fats Waller,' he told her, automatically putting two fingers to his lips.

He had to explain what jazz was. Ailinn had never heard any. Jazz, too, without exactly being proscribed, wasn't played. Improvisation had fallen out of fashion. There was room for only one 'if' in life. People wanted to be sure, when a tune began, exactly where it was going to end. Wit, the same. Its unpredictability unsettled people's nerves. And jazz was wit expressed musically. Though he reached the age of ten without having heard of Sammy Davis Junior, Kevern knew of jazz from his father's semi-secret collection of old CDs. But at least he didn't have to tell Ailinn that Fats Waller was black. Given her age, she was unlikely to have remembered a time when popular singers *weren't* black. Again, no laws or duress. A compliant society meant that every section of it consented with gratitude – the gratitude of the providentially spared – to the principle of group aptitude. People of Afro-Caribbean origin were suited by temperament and physique to entertainment and athletics, and so they sang and sprinted. People originally from the Indian subcontinent, electronically gifted as though by nature, undertook to ensure no family was without a functioning utility phone. What was left of the Polish community plumbed;

what was left of the Greek smashed plates. Those from the Gulf States and the Levant whose grandparents hadn't quickly left the country while WHAT HAPPENED, IF IT HAPPENED was happening – fearing they'd be accused of having stoked the flames, fearing, indeed, that the flames would consume them next – opened labneh and shisha-pipe restaurants, kept their heads down, and grew depressed with idleness. To each according to his gifts.

Having heard only ballads, Ailinn was hard pressed to understand how the insulting words Kevern had just sung to her could ever have been set to music. Music was the expression of love.

'They're not really insulting,' Kevern said. 'Except maybe to people whose feet are too big. My father never insulted anybody, but he delighted in this song.'

He was saying too much, but the garden's neglect gave the illusion of safety. No word could get beyond the soundproofing of the giant cabbage-like leaves.

Ailinn still didn't comprehend. 'Why would your father have loved something like that?'

He wanted to say it was a joke, but was reluctant, in her company, to put two fingers to his lips again. She already thought he was strange.

'It struck him as funny,' he said instead.

She shook her head in disbelief, blotting out Kevern's vision. Nothing to see in the whole wide world but her haystack of crow-black hair. Nothing else he wanted to see. 'If you say so,' she said, unconvinced. 'But that still doesn't explain why you're singing it to me.' She seemed in genuine distress. 'Are *my* feet too big?'

He looked again. 'Your feet specifically, no. Your ankles, maybe, a bit . . .'

'And you say you hate me because my ankles are too thick?'

'Hate you? Of course I don't hate you. That's just the silly song.' He could have said 'I love you', but it was too soon for that. 'Your thick ankles are the very reason I'm attracted to you,' he tried instead. 'I'm perverse that way.'

It came out wrong. He had meant it to be funny. Meaning to be funny often landed him in a mess because, like his father, he lacked the reassuring charm necessary to temper the cruelty that lurked in jokes. Maybe his father intended to be cruel. Maybe he, Kevern, did. Despite his kind eyes.

Ailinn Solomons flushed and rose from her deck-chair, knocking over the console and spilling the wine they'd been drinking.

Elderflower wine, so drink wasn't his excuse.

In her agitation she seemed to tremble, like the fronds of a palm tree in a storm.

'And your thick head's the very reason I'm perversely attracted to you,' she said . . . 'Except that I'm not.'

He felt sorry for her, both on account of the unnecessary unkindness of his words and the fear that showed in her eyes in the moment of her standing up to him. Did she think he'd strike her?

She hadn't spoken to him about life on the chill northern archipelago where she had grown up, but he didn't doubt it was in all essentials similar to here. The same vast and icy ocean crashed in on them both. The same befuddled men, even more thin-skinned and peevish in the aftermath of WHAT HAPPENED than their smuggler and wrecker ancestors had been, roamed angrily from pub to pub, ready to raise a hand to any woman who dared to refuse or twit them. *Thick head?* They'd show her a thick fist if she wasn't careful! Snog her first – the snog having become the most common expression of erotic irritation between men and women: an antidote to the bland ballads of love the console pumped out – snog her first and cuff her later. An unnecessary refinement in Kevern's view, since a snog was itself an act of thuggery.

Ailinn Solomons made a sign with her body for him to leave. He heaved himself out of the deck-chair like an old man. She felt leaden herself, but the weight of his grief surprised her. This wasn't the end of the world. They barely knew each other.

She watched him go – as at an upstairs window her companion watched him go – a man made heavy by what he'd brought on himself. Adam leaving the garden, she thought.

She felt a pang for him and for men in general, no matter that some had raised their hands to her. A man turned from her, his back bent, ashamed, defeated, all the fight in him leaked away – why was that a sight she felt she knew so well, when

21

she couldn't recall a single instance, before today, of having seen it?

Alone again, Ailinn Solomons looked at her feet.

ii

A score or so years before the events related above, Esme Nussbaum, an intelligent and enthusiastic thirty-two-year-old researcher employed by Ofnow, the non-statutory monitor of the Public Mood, prepared a short paper on the continuance of low- and medium-level violence in those very areas of the country where its reduction, if not its cessation, was most to have been expected, given the money and energy expended on uprooting it.

'Much has been done, and much continues to be done,' she wrote, 'to soothe the native aggressive-ness of a people who have fought a thousand wars and won most of them, especially in those twisted knarls and narrow crevices of the country where, though the spires of churches soar above the hedge-rows, the sweeter breath of human kindness has, historically, been rarely felt. But some qualities are proving to be ineradicable. The higher the spire, it would seem, the lower the passions it goes on engendering. The populace weeps to sentimental ballads, gorges on stories of adversity overcome, and professes to believe ardently in the virtues of marriage and family life, but not only does the old brutishness retain a pertinacious hold equally on rural communities as on our urban conurbations, evidence suggests the emergence of a new and vicious quarrelsomeness in the home, in the work-place, on our roads and even on our playing fields.'

'You have an unfortunate tendency to overwrite,' her supervisor said when he had read the whole report. 'May I suggest you read fewer novels.'

Esme Nussbaum lowered her head.

'I must also enquire: are you an atheist?'

'I believe I am not obliged to say,' Esme Nussbaum replied.

'Are you a lesbian?'

Again Esme protested her right to privacy and silence.

'A feminist?'

Silence once more.

'I don't ask,' Luther Rabinowitz said at last, 'because I have an objection to atheism, lesbianism or feminism. This is a prejudice-free workplace. We are the servants of a prejudice-free society. But certain kinds of hypersensitivity, while entirely acceptable and laudable in themselves, may some-times distort findings such as you have presented to me. You are obviously yourself prejudiced against the church; and those things you call "vicious" and "brutish", others could as soon interpret as expres-sions of natural vigour and vitality. To still be harping on about WHAT HAPPENED, IF IT HAPPENED, as though it happened, if it happened, yesterday, is to sap the country of its essential life force.'

Esme Nussbaum looked around her while

Rabinowitz spoke. Behind his head a flamingo pink LED scroll repeated the advice Ofnow had been dispensing to the country for the last quarter of a century or more. 'Smile at your neighbour, cherish your spouse, listen to ballads, go to musicals, use your telephone, converse, explain, listen, agree, apologise. Talk is better than silence, the sung word is better than the written, but nothing is better than love.'

'I fully understand the points you are making,' Esme Nussbaum replied in a quiet voice, once she was certain her supervisor had finished speaking, 'and I am saying no more than that we are not healed as effectively as we delude ourselves we are. My concern is that, if we are not forewarned, we will find ourselves repeating the mistakes that led to WHAT HAPPENED, IF IT HAPPENED, in the first place. Only this time it will not be on others that we vent our anger and mistrust.'

Luther Rabinowitz made a pyramid of his fingers. This was to suggest infinite patience. 'You go too far,' he said, 'in describing as "mistakes" actions which our grandparents might or might not have taken. You go too far, as well, in speaking of them venting their "anger" and "mistrust" on "others". It should not be necessary to remind someone in your position that in understanding the past, as in protecting the present, we do not speak of "us" and "them". There was no "we" and there were no "others". It was a time of disorder, that is all we know of it.'

'In which, if we are honest with ourselves,' Esme dared to interject, 'no section of society can claim to have acquitted itself well. I make no accusations. Whether it was done ill, or done well, what was done was done. Then was then. No more needs to be said – on this we agree. And just as there is no blame to be apportioned, so there are no amends to be made, were amends appropriate and were there any way of making them. But what is the past for if not to learn from it—'

'The past exists in order that we forget it.'

'If I may add one word to that—'

Luther Rabinowitz collapsed his pyramid. 'I will consider your report,' he said, dismissing her.

The next day, turning up for work as usual, she was knocked down by a motorcyclist who had mounted the pavement in what passers-by described as a 'vicious rage'.

Coincidences happen.

iii

Ailinn, anyway – whatever the state of things in the rest of the country, and others were now openly saying what Esme Nussbaum had said in her long-suppressed report – had sported a bruise under her right eye when Kevern saw her for the first time, standing behind a long trestle table on which were laid out for sale jams, marmalades, little cakes, pickles, hand-thrown pots and paper flowers.

'Fine-looking girl, that one,' a person Kevern didn't know whispered in his ear.

'Which one?' asked Kevern, not wanting to be rude, but not particularly wanting to be polite either.

'Her. With all the hair and the purple eye.'

Had Kevern been in the mood for conversation he might have answered that there was more than one among the women selling preserves and flowers who had a purple eye. But yes, the black hair – thick and seemingly warm enough to be the nest of some fabulous and he liked to think dangerous creature – struck him forcibly. 'Aha, I see her,' he said, meaning 'Leave me alone.'

Impervious, the stranger continued. 'She'll say she walked into a door. The usual excuse. Needs looking after, in my humble opinion.'

He was dressed like a country auctioneer – of pigs, Kevern thought. He had a pleated, squeeze-box neck, which rippled over the collar of his tweed hacking jacket, and the blotched skin of someone who'd spent too much time in the vicinity of mulch, manure and, yes, money.

'Aha,' Kevern said again, looking away. He hoped his unfriendly demeanour would make it clear he didn't welcome confidentiality, but he mustn't have made it clear enough because the man slipped an arm through his and offered to introduce him.

'No, no, that's not necessary,' Kevern said firmly. He started from all strangers instinctively, but this

26

one's insinuating manner frightened and angered him.

The introduction was effected notwithstanding. Kevern was not sure how.

'Ailinn Solomons, Kevern Cohen. Kevern Cohen . . . but you know each other now.'

They shook hands and the go-between vanished.

'A friend of yours?' Kevern asked the girl.

'Never seen him in my life. I can't imagine how he knows my name.'

'I ask myself the same question.'

They exchanged concerned looks.

'But you're from here, aren't you?' the girl said.

'Yes. But I too have never seen him in my life. You obviously are *not* from here.'

'It shows?'

'It shows in that we have never before met. So you're from where . . .?'

She flung a thumb over her left shoulder, as though telling him to scoot.

'You want me to go?'

'No, sorry, I was showing you where I'm from. If that's north, I'm from up there. Forgive me, I'm nervous. I've been spooked by what's just taken place. I haven't been here long enough for people to know my name.'

She looked around anxiously – Kevern couldn't tell whether to get a second look at the man or to be certain he had gone for good. In deference to her anxiety he made light of his own. (He too had been spooked by what had just occurred.) 'You

27

know these village nosey parkers. He's probably an amateur archivist.'

'You have archives here?'

'Well, no, not officially, but we have the occasional crazy who enjoys hoarding rumours and going through people's rubbish bins. I have one as a neighbour, as it happens.'

'And you let him go through yours?'

'Oh, I have no rubbish.'

He enjoyed the sensation of her looking through him. He wanted her to know that any secrets he had, she was welcome to.

'Well I don't think our man was an archivist,' she said. 'He looked too interested in himself. I'd say he was an auctioneer of pigs.'

Kevern smiled at her.

'Which doesn't explain . . .'

'No, it doesn't . . .'

She *was* a fine-looking girl, delicately strung, easy to hurt despite the dangerous thicket of her hair. He thought he detected in himself an instinct to protect her. Absurdly, he imagined rolling her in his rug. Though what good that would have done her, he couldn't have said.

'You don't have an "up there" accent,' he said.

'And you don't have a "down here" one.'

They felt bonded in not sounding as though they were from either place.

Emboldened by this, he pointed to her bruise. 'Who did that to you?'

She ignored the question, going behind the stall

28

to rearrange the flowers. Then she looked him directly in the eyes and shrugged. It was a gesture he understood. Who'd done that to her? It didn't matter: they all had.

Years before, he'd been a choirboy at the church and, because he had a flutey tenor voice ideally suited to Bach's Evangelist, still sang there every Christmas when they performed the expurgated version of the *St Matthew Passion*. He didn't normally attend fetes – he was not a festive man – but several people from the church had urged him to attend. 'Why?' he'd asked. 'Just come along, Kevern,' they'd said, 'it will do you good.' And more flyers publicising the event were popped through his letter box than he could recall receiving for similar events.

On the morning of the fete, the vicar, Golvan Shlagman, even rang to make sure he was coming. Kevern said he was undecided. He had work to do. All work and no play, the Reverend Shlagman quipped. He hoped Kevern would try his best. It wouldn't be the same without his presence. Kevern didn't see why. Why was his presence a matter of significance suddenly? 'We can't do without the Evangelist,' the vicar laughed, though no Mass or Passion was being sung.

Thinking about it later, Kevern thought Shlagman's laughter had been only just the sane side of hysterical.

Had he hysterically laughed Ailinn into coming to the fete, too?

Seeing as they mistrusted strangers equally, didn't speak in the accents of where they resided, and knew a pig auctioneer when they saw one, he asked her out.

She took a minute or two to decide. He, too, was a stranger, she seemed to be reminding him.

He understood. 'A little walk, that's all,' he said. 'Nowhere far.'

On their first date he kissed the bruise under her eye.

He was not a man who raised his arm to women and hadn't been stirred to anger when Ailinn called him thick-headed. He only nodded and smiled lugubriously – it was that dopey-eyed, lugubrious smile that had earned him the nickname Coco, after a once famous clown who sometimes re-appeared, accompanied by apologies for the cruelty visited on him, in children's picture books. She was right, when all was said and done. He was a lolloping unfunny clown with a big mouth who didn't deserve her love. And now – she made no attempt to stop him getting up and leaving – he'd lost it.

He reproached himself for being too easily put off. It didn't have anything to do with Ailinn; he lacked the trick of intimacy, that was all. On the other hand, the thickness of her ankles relative to the slenderness of her frame – especially the right one, around which she wore a flowery, child-of-nature anklet – did upset him, and on top of that, like every other village girl, no matter that she came from a village at the other end of the country, she smelt of fish.

But then there *were* other girls in the village, and although they had always treated him with that degree of watchfulness they reserved for people to whom they weren't related, their availability took the edge off his desolation. He was alone, but on any evening he could drop by the Friendly Fisherman and fall into conversation with one or other of them. And at least at the bar the smell of beer took away the smell of fish.

He sat on his bench absent-mindedly, watching the seals flop, enjoying the spray on his face, thinking about everything and nothing, exclaiming 'Jesus Christ!' to himself from time to time, until the sun sank beneath its own watery weight into the sea. It became immediately chilly. Feeling the cold, he rose from the bench and decided to try his luck. Company was company. He called by the cottage first and peered in through the letter box. All was almost well. He was still in, still reading his mail in his carpet slippers, still watching television. And his rug was still rumpled. But his utility phone was flashing vermilion, which meant somebody had rung him. Perhaps Ailinn saying she was sorry, though she had done nothing to say sorry for.

After the falling-out, the saying sorry. That was the way. They had all been taught it at school. Always say sorry.

If it was she who had rung him, should he ring her back? He didn't know.

In agitation, because the knowledge that he'd been rung – no matter by whom – distressed him, he let himself in, discovered the caller had left no message – though he thought he detected the breath of someone as agitated as himself – and locked up again. Fifteen minutes later he was in the Friendly Fisherman, ordering a sweet cider.

iv

The inn was more than usually noisy and querulous. That fractiousness which was being reported as on the increase throughout the country was no less on the increase here. There'd been an incident earlier in the village hall and some of the bad feeling had spilled out into the inn from that. It was Thursday, Weight Watchers day, and one of the village women, Tryfena Heilbron, had refused to accept that she'd put on a pound since the last time she'd been weighed. Words had been exchanged and Tryfena had lifted the scales and dashed them to the ground. 'Next time bring scales that work,' she'd shouted at the weigher who shouted back that it was no surprise to her that Tryfena's husband preferred the company of sweeter-tempered, not to say more sylphlike, women.

By the time news of the altercation reached the Friendly Fisherman the men were involved. Breoc Heilbron the haulier, a dangerous brute of a man even when sober, was drunkenly defending the honour of a wife he didn't scruple at other times to abuse. It struck Kevern Cohen as a sign of the times that men who would once have steered clear of Breoc Heilbron's temper were prepared tonight to needle him, not only man to man, by impugning his capacity to hold his drink, but by referring to his wife's notorious temper and even to her weight. Was he imagining it or did he actually hear someone describe her as a heifer? That heifer, Tryfena Heilbron.

That was how people had begun to talk of one another. That heifer, Tryfena Heilbron. That lump of lard, Morvoren Steinberg.

Followed by an apology to Morvoren's husband.

And no doubt, that idiot Kevern Cohen.

Kevern tried to remember whether the village had ever in reality been the placid haven pictured in its brochures by New Heritage, that body to which every taxpayer in the country was expected to contribute in return for an annual weekend away from the growing turmoil of the towns. Had it? He didn't think so. Most of the teachers at the village school he had attended had been free with the cane or the slipper before saying sorry. The boys had brawled viciously in the playground. So had the girls. Tourists on their annual weekend breaks were laughed at behind their backs and made to feel unwelcome in the inns, for all that their custom was indispensable to the local economy. But he thought there had been some days when everything was quiet and everyone rubbed along. Whereas now it was never quiet, and no one rubbed along.

He joined in an ill-tempered game of darts with a group of sullenly drunken men, including Densdell Kroplik, failing to hit a single number he was required to hit and having to buy a round of drinks for his team as a consequence.

'Up yerz,' Kroplik said, raising his glass. Kevern laughed, not finding it funny. He wondered again what possessed him ever to let the barber near his throat with a razor.

The other men apologised.

'Not necessary,' Kevern told them.

Densdell Kroplik didn't think it was necessary either. 'Don't yez go apologising for me,' he said, spitting on the floor. 'I do my own, when the time'z right, and thiz izn't.'

Kevern walked away. He wanted to leave, but didn't. His cottage was quiet and he needed noise. A little later, he accepted a challenge to play pool from a handsome, broad-shouldered woman who ran the mug and tea-towel shop in which he sold his lovespoons. Hedra Deitch.

She scattered the balls with an alarming vehemence, called Kevern 'my lover', and made derogatory remarks to him about her husband who was slumped at the bar like a shot animal, coughing out the last of his blood into a pint pot of brown ale.

'That's how he looks when he finishes himself over me,' she said, in a voice loud enough for him to hear.

Kevern wasn't sure what to say.

'Eat shit!' her husband called across to her.

'Eat shit yerself!'

Kevern thought about leaving, but stayed.

'You think he'd be only too glad to give me a divorce,' Hedra Deitch went on. 'But oh, no. We must stay together for the children, he says. That's a laugh. He doesn't give a flyin' fuck for the children and suspects they're not his anyway.'

'And are they?' Kevern asked.

'What do you think, my lover?'

'I can't imagine you passing off another man's children as his,' Kevern said.

She choked on her laughter. 'You can't imagine that, can't you? Then you doesn't have a very vivid imagination.'

Kevern tried imagining, then thought better of it. He went home alone, after submitting briefly to one of Hedra Deitch's muscular snogs. Forcing brutish kisses on people you neither knew well nor cared much for wasn't confined to men. Both sexes broke skin when they could.

A sharp-edged moon lit his way. Once upon a time he'd have been able to hear the sea on a night such as this, the great roar of the ocean sucking at the rocks, breathing in and then breathing out, but the din of voices raised in brawling throughout the village drowned out all other sounds. A quarter of a mile up the road to his cottage he passed the Deitches kissing passionately in a doorway. To Kevern they resembled a single beast, maddened by the need to bite its own mouth. Great fumes of beer and fish rose from its pelt. If Kevern's ears didn't deceive him, Hedra Deitch was alternately telling her weasel husband to eat shit and apologising to him.

The unseasonably warm wind of earlier in the day – smelling of seals and porpoises, Kevern thought – had turned cold and bitter. Something far out to sea was rotting.

He could have done with company, but he knew it was his own fault he had none. 'Company is always trouble,' his father used to say, laughing his demented solitary laugh. But he didn't have to listen to his father. Taking after your father was optional, wasn't it?

He knelt on one knee and peered in through the letter box of his cottage. Shocked by what he saw, he staggered backwards. The cottage had been ransacked. There was blood on the carpet. In the two or three seconds it took him to recover himself, he wondered why he was surprised. This was no more than he'd been expecting. And now the knife between his shoulder blades . . .

He looked again, not afraid of what he'd see. Relieved, he thought.

At last.

But everything was, after all, exactly as he'd left it – the disrespected rug, the teacup, the slippers. There was a blue glow from the television. All was well. He was in. Alone.

It was his utility phone that was flashing the colour of blood.

It sounded like singing. Not a choir, something more random and impatient, a hubbub set to music. He could smell burning but saw no fire, only smoke. Then an enormous rose of flame opened briefly as though, with one supreme effort, it meant to enfold the charred sky in its petals. Against the flame he was able to make out the silhouette of a figure, a slight boy, falling from a high wall. Even before the boy reached the ground the singing grew ecstatic, as though the singers believed their chanting was responsible. 'Down with the enemies of—!' they cried. He couldn't make out the word in the frenzy of its delivery. Life, was it? *Down with the enemies of Life*? Or mice? *Down with the enemies of Mice*? Down with them, anyway. He thought he recognised the keep from whose tower the boy, like a doll with no weight, continued to float and lightly fall to earth. Yes, he knew it. Inside those walls, inside that fire, he had knelt by the body of a mother – he couldn't say, after all this time, if she were his. Her eyes were open but unseeing. Her clothes had been torn from her body. Where her throat was cut a scarlet rose flowered, smaller than the one that had briefly illuminated the sky, but no less remarkable. Its loveliness flowed from it in a stream, running down her breast. He dipped his finger in it, as though it were wine, and put it to his lips. Down with me, he thought.

CHAPTER 2

TWITTERNACHT

Friday 27th

Ho, hum . . .

For anyone opening my diary for the first time – and it's for futurity in all its misty uncertainty that I write – ho hum denotes the sound of my mind whirring, not cynicism.

It would appear that he learnt to take these Byzantine precautions from his parents, as they, perhaps, had learnt to take them from theirs, otherwise they denote nothing other than an uncommonly anxious disposition . . .

So concluded the first report on Kevern 'Coco' Cohen I ever wrote. I have a copy in front of me in a black folder. Always wise to keep a copy. I was guessing, I admit that much, but guesswork is an important part of what I have been entrusted to do. Guesswork informed by a knowledge of the ways of men, I mean, a trustworthiness of intuition and a shrewdness of observation, which I flatter myself I possess in as great a measure as any person. Perhaps more. I work – I don't call my observations of Kevern Cohen 'work' – in one of the most trustworthy and ophthalmically demanding professions, as a teacher of the Benign Visual Arts. I am also a painter myself. Landscapes, naturally. Hence their giving me far west Bethesda as my territory. Bethesda with its long history of naive art – spirituality apprehended in the everyday – and of course St Mordechai's Mount which I can see from my studio window and walk to when the tide is out. Modesty should forbid me mentioning my *Seventeen Sketches of St Mordechai's Mount In All Seasons* which enjoy prominence in the Parochial Beauty Rooms at the New National Gallery, but they are my best work to date and I am proud of them. I would have preferred to stay in the Capital, for all its troubles – if only to enjoy the illusion of being at the centre of things and eating a little better – but the position I occupy in the Bethesda Art Academy has its consolations. Head of painting within a department as dedicated to feeling as any in the country is not a job you sniff at. I've heard it argued that Bethesda found it easier than most art colleges to make the journey back from insentience to feeling because for us, feeling never really went away. Conceptualism, or mind-machine art as historians now call it, had always been more of a city than a country fad. It had been practised down here but without any real zest or instinct for it. A few local potters defied the tradition of their craft, forgot or simply refused to remember that a pot's job was to express, in silence and slow time, a flowery tale with sweetness, and set about throwing misshapen objects that had no utility except to offend whoever looked on them by virtue of the obscene acts they depicted. The art, they explained, when they could be bothered to explain anything, lay precisely in the offence. But the joke never took. Obscenities don't shock country people who practise them without thinking twice. And as for the ironies of installation art, you needed department stores all around you to appreciate those, just as you need the colours of a big sky and the changeability of a turbulent sea to understand why painters have to paint. The pursuit of beauty is no mystery when you wake to it each day. And I have always argued that the real sentimentality is not the indulgence of colour but the denial of it. It went missing, anyway. Three genera-tions lived and died without seeing colour except in its lipstick-pink and electric-blue manifestations, flashing tubes and the like, ironic statements about colour and its production, denying the naked sensuousness that makes true lovers of painting believe they are seeing the face of God. But enough of that. You will find my thoughts on the subject – much extended – in many a volume of *Sublime Quarterly*, Bethesda's own art magazine, which can be ordered from any gallery shop in the country and also a good number of the better newsagents. I write under my own name – Edward Everett Phineas Zermansky (Everett to my friends, Phinny to my family) – and am told that I am highly readable.

Well, my wife tells me so, anyway.

Or at least she does when she isn't telling me the opposite. Phinny the Palaverous is how she refers to me to her girlfriends. Who know, of course, she doesn't mean it.

I don't say we fight. But we are not immune to malign influences beyond our kitchen and bedroom. How could we be? Are we not all one family?

That the dry, embittered colourlessness of the conceptual – to return to my theme – helped harden the nation's heart is accepted as a truism by artists of today. Art wasn't the cause or centre of the great desensitisation, for which, of course, all artists apologise, but WHAT HAPPENED, IF IT HAPPENED – or TWITTERNACHT, as I like to call it when I am feeling skittish, by way of reference to . . . well to many things, one of them being the then prevailing mode of social interaction that facilitated, though can by no means be said to have provoked it – WHAT HAPPENED, IF IT HAPPENED, I say, happened, if it did, because as a people we'd anaesthetised the feeling parts of ourselves, first through the ugly liberties with form taken by modernism and second through the liberties taken with emotion by that same modernism in its 'post' form. I say 'we' because there is nothing to be achieved by saying 'they', indeed there is much to be lost, given that 'they' is a policed pronoun today, but when I am certain no one is looking (I mean this figuratively) I poke a finger at the alien intellectualism that brought such destruction first on itself and then, as an inevitable consequence, on all of us. Thus, again, the felicity of my TWITTERNACHT *jeu d'esprit*, twitter like much else in the same vein that was then the rage, having proceeded from the alien intelligences of the very people who were to lose most by it. Call that irony, a concept of which they, in particular, were overfond, which is an irony in itself. Let's

43

be clear: no one behaved well, but there is such a thing as provocation. The largest beast can be maddened by the smallest parasitic mite. (Especially when it's clever . . . the mite, that is.) I will say no more than that.

Except . . . No, I'll stick to my guns and shut up. 'You talk too much,' Demelza is always saying to me. And I'm a man who listens to his wife.

Perhaps future generations will describe what we do now as a cult of feeling, but better to feel than not to, better to experience love than its opposite. Better, in short, to live now than to have lived then. If the cost of not allowing ourselves to return to that inglorious past, or anything resembling it, is a certain mistrustfulness and vigilance, I happen to think it's a price worth paying. Hence . . . well, hence my doing what I do. My ho humming, as the Divine Demelza calls it. I don't spy on my students or my colleagues. I keep an eye open, that's all. For what? Well, for anything or anyone – how can I best put this? – *left over*. For business dangerously unfinished. For matter out of place, as a famous anthropologist once described dirt. For recidivism. In any of its guises, recidivism is what we fear most. Hence a job of this sort falling to someone teaching at an art college. Because art, for all its adventure-someness, is also capable of being the most recidivist of human activities, forever falling back in reaction to what was itself a reaction to something else. People can behave like savages when they are allowed to, but only in art do they go so far as to call themselves primitivists. And when the primitivist urge doesn't seize them, the psychoaesthetic urge, the study of human evil – itself another form of primitivism, when you come to think about it – does. So portrait painting is a further recidivism that's frowned on and discouraged – that's in so far as one can discourage anything in a free society. In the main, prize-culture does the job for us. When all the gongs go to landscape, why would any aspiring artist waste his energies on the dull and relent-less cruelties of the human face? While not wanting to affect modesty, I suspect I wouldn't be enjoying the favour and seniority I do – I omitted to say that I am Professor Edward Everett Phineas Zermansky, FRSA – had I not from an early age followed nature's laws in the matter of beauty. There are painters who paint more experimentally than I do, without doubt, but of my more troubled colleagues – those who still hanker secretly for the alien and the grotesque, even the degenerate (though they wouldn't dream of pronouncing that term aloud) – I cannot think of one who hasn't had to wait a long time to be given recognition, and even longer to be given tenure.

But to return to the point from which I began, and I don't apologise for my vagrant style – 'Keep up!' I tell my students when I sense they are losing me; 'Keep up!' I even have to tell my wife on those occasions when I catch her glancing at her watch – I don't claim more for what goes into my black folder on Kevern Cohen than it's worth. I say 'I keep an eye open' but I do so only at the lowest level – code name Grey. Think of those I watch as birds, and I am no more than a Sunday twitcher. The work of serious, scientific ornithology is done by others. For which reason, while I am conscientious in my observations, I have never imagined that what I see or what I miss matters a great deal. Until now. Suddenly, I am conscious of having to deliver. It is as though the common house sparrow, on which – to nobody's interest – I've been keeping an eye for some time, has overnight become an endangered species and I am at a stroke indispensable to the species' protection. I won't pretend to knowledge I don't have. All my reports are now more scrupulously monitored than they were before, so I can't say with any certainty that Kevern 'Coco' Cohen – one of the common house sparrows in question – has risen to the top of any pile. I have a feeling about him, that's all. Or rather I have a feeling that *they* have a feeling. I like the man, I have to say. He has for several years been coming in one day a week to the academy, teaching the art of carving lovespoons out of a single piece of wood. I admire his work, which is exquisite, but there are some who find him a little too good to be true. Not the students; they love his air of grumpy probity as much as I love what he makes, and I am sure that when their opinions are canvassed they will speak of him only in the most glowing terms. But it goes against him with senior members of the college that he doesn't drink with them, spends too much time in the restricted section of the library – not reading a great deal, according to Rozenwyn Feigenblat, our librarian, just staring into space the minute he is a page or two into what he *does* read, as though wondering what he came here for – and is rarely heard to apologise. I don't, of course, mean for reading books, I mean for anything – an act of carelessness or forgetting, a brusqueness, a contradiction. The reason he gives is that as he lives on his own, works in isolation, and so rarely has occasion to lose his temper, he has nothing to apologise for. Not an argument well calculated to win him friends in the common room, because the truth is none of us really think we have anything to apologise for. But the way an institution works is that you go along with the prevailing fiction. And generally – if not individually – the habit of delivering brisk, catch-all apologies is much to be preferred to morbid memory which embalms the past in the Proustian fluids of the maudlin. (Though Proust is no longer read, we still retain the adjective.) My authority for this is the media philosopher Valerian Grossenberger, author of *Seven Reasons To Say Sorry*, whose series of daily lectures for National Radio some years ago can be said to have changed the way we all think. Modern societies had spent too much time, according to Grossenberger, rubbing the twin itches of recollection and penance. In the bad old days, 'never forget' was a guiding maxim – you couldn't move, I've heard tell, for obelisks and mausoleums and other inordinately ugly monuments exhorting memory – but this led first to wholesale neuroticism and impotence and then, as was surely inevitable, to the great falling-out, if there was one. Rather than go on perpetuating the neurasthenic concept of victimisation, Grossenberger argued, the never-forgetters would have done better carving 'I Forgive You' on their stones. In return for which, we might have forgiven them. But that chance came and went. And now who, today, is going to forgive whom for what? Only by having everyone say sorry, without reference to what they are saying sorry for, can the concept of blame be eradicated, and guilt at last be anaesthetised.

Saying sorry, Grossenberger concluded, when he came to address the Bethesda Academy recently – an old man now, but still possessed of his silky powers of reasoning – releases us all from a recriminatory past into an unimpeachable future. We stood and applauded that, not least as it struck us that he was delivering a last eulogy to his own distinguished, emollient career. But if you ask me whether Kevern Cohen stood along with the rest of us, I have to say I don't recall his being present.

I make nothing of it. He might indeed be a man who is so equable of temper that the idea of apology mystifies him. Or he might not yet have got past the 'never forget' stage in his own life. Let us hope that the latter is not the case and agree simply that he's a queer one. 'I find him weird,' my wife said only the other day, after we'd had him over for dinner. 'With those droopy eyes and all that hand washing and tap checking. It's like having What's-he-called over.'

'Lady Macbeth?'

'I said *he*.'

'Pontius Pilate?'

'Yes.'

'As in that fine Dürer—'

'Spare me the lecture, Phinny. Him, yes. But if he's like this in our house, what must he be like in his own?'

'Pontius Pilate?'

'Kevern, you fool.'

'Worse, I don't doubt. Much worse.'

'What I don't understand is how he knows when to stop. While he was helping with the washing-up he kept wandering over to the stove to make sure the gas was off. "I've checked that," I told him, but he said he feared he might have brushed against the taps when he was drying up and it was better to be safe than sorry. But at what point does he decide it's safe?'

'You should have asked him.'

'I did. But his answer was unilluminating. "Never," he said.'

'Never?'

'Never. Isn't that terrible?'

'Yes. But he has to stop sometimes. The man sleeps, for God's sake.'

'I asked him about that, too. Presumably you sleep, I said. So when do you call it a day? At what point are you able to close your eyes? And his answer to that was more unilluminating still. "When I can't stand it any more," he said. And how do you know when that is, I asked. "I just know," he said.'

'Maybe it's when he gets tired. He has the air of a man who tires easily. Men do, you know.'

This irritated her. 'And women don't?'

Which irritated me. 'Of course they do, but we aren't talking about women,' I snapped. 'Or about you.'

We stared angrily into each other's faces.

Why did she, I thought, have to bring her sex into everything?

Why did I, I saw her thinking, have to be so critical of her?

Why were her eyes, I thought, so quick to water up?

Why were mine, I knew she thought, so quickly fierce?

Why did I marry her, I wondered. What had I ever seen in that pallid skin and impertinently, stupidly, retroussé little nose? How could I stop myself, I wondered, from striking her?

Why did she accept me, the witterer I was, I heard her ask herself. How had she let those ugly crossed teeth of mine ever nibble at her breasts? Why had she ever allowed any part of me to come near any part of her? How much more would it take for her to strike me?

I slunk away.

She followed me into my studio.

I wondered if she was carrying a knife from the kitchen. The carver she'd recently had sharpened. I closed my eyes.

'I'm sorry, Phinny,' I heard her say.

I turned around abruptly. She started. Was she afraid of what I might be carrying? A trimming knife? My razor? A hammer?

'Me too, Demelza,' I said.

We were both sorry, and made love whimpering how sorry we were into each other's ears. I kissed her lovely little nose. She gave me her breast to nibble. Sorry. Sorry. Sorry for what, exactly? Neither of us knew. But without doubt a baseless irascibility had begun to be a fact of our marriage. Had we fallen out of love? I didn't think so. Friends of ours were reporting the same. A querulousness that appeared suddenly from nowhere and vanished just as inexplicably, though each time the period it took for lovingness to return extended itself a little more. We had a formulation for it: things just seemed to be getting on top of us. But why? Why, when we lacked for nothing, when beauty accompanied us wherever we went, when every source of discord had been removed?

It was shortly after this particular exchange of unpleasantries, anyway, that the file code for Kevern Cohen changed from grey to purple. Purple isn't vermilion. We weren't in danger territory. But others, I was now to understand, were reliant on what I knew as a sort of confirmation, let's even say – to be plain about it – as a cognitive intensification, of what they knew or didn't know themselves. Kevern Cohen was becoming a precious commodity.

CHAPTER 3

THE FOUR DS

i

It *was* Ailinn who had been ringing him. Against her own instincts. But in line with her companion's, though her companion thought she could go a little further and actually leave a message. 'Even just a hello,' she said.

'When you know me better, Ez,' Ailinn told her, 'you will discover I am not the sort of woman who leaves hellos on men's phones. They pick up or they lose me.'

'And when you know *me* better,' Ez told her, 'you will discover I am not the sort of woman to egg people on to do what they don't want to do. But this is different. You aren't yourself. I've never seen you so down in the mouth.'

'That's because you haven't seen me often. Down in the mouth is not what I do, it's who I am.'

'That isn't true. You were hopeful when you met him. You said you thought you might just have met your soulmate.'

'I did not!'

'Well you said you thought you'd met someone you could possibly get on with.'

'I think that's rather different.'

Brittle-boned and careful with herself, a woman who seemed to Ailinn to quiver with mutuality, Ez leaned in very close. 'Not for you it isn't,' she said, as though the strain for Ailinn of being Ailinn was sometimes more than she could bear for her. 'A man has to be your soulmate before you'll give him the time of day.'

Ailinn raised an eyebrow. She and Ez were not well enough acquainted, she thought, to be having this conversation. She wasn't sure they were well enough acquainted for Ez to be bringing her tea in bed, fluffing up her pillows and patting her hand either, but she put that down to the older woman's loneliness. And consideration, of course. But offering to know so much about the kind of person Ailinn was, her ways with men, what made her happy, when she was and wasn't *herself*, the errands on which she sent her soul, for God's sake – all that seemed to her, however kindly it was meant, to be a presumption too far.

She wasn't angry. Ez didn't strike her as someone who would go through her clothes, or read her letters, or otherwise poke about in her life. She was pretty sure she wouldn't, for example, dream of ringing Kevern to tell him what she'd just told Ailinn. And besides, an older woman could be permitted a few liberties a younger one could not. Wasn't that their unspoken contract – that Ez needed the company of someone who could be almost as a child to her, and Ailinn . . . well she surely didn't need another mother, but all right, someone who could be what she'd never had, an older sister, an aunt, a good friend? Yet even allowing for all that, there was an anxious soulfulness about Ez, a taut emotional avidity that made Ailinn the smallest bit uncomfortable. Why was she sitting on the end of the bed, her body twisted towards Ailinn as though in an act of imploration, her eyes moist with woman-to-woman understanding, the phone in her hand? What in the end did it matter to Ez whether or not she left the village woodturner a message?

She knew she was lucky to be with someone who cared about her happiness. She wasn't used to it. Her mother by adoption meant well by her but lost interest quickly. She would have had no attitude, or at least expressed no opinion, in the matter of Kevern Cohen. She never spoke of Ailinn's future, a job, possible husbands, children. It was as though she'd given Ailinn a life by rescuing her from the orphanage and that was that. Satisfying her conscience, it felt like, needing to perform a charitable act, and once performed, her responsibility was at an end. What, if anything, followed, was of no consequence or interest to her. So there were levels of concern Ailinn accepted she had still to learn about. Maybe her mother was the way she was with her because Ailinn made her so. Maybe she lacked a talent for being liked.

She certainly lacked the talent for being liked by herself. In which case she was grateful to Ez.

And in which case shouldn't she make an effort with the clumsy man who at first had treated her with such gentleness, smiling softly into her face, inclining his head to kiss the bruise under her eye? He was sufficiently unlike the others, anyway, to be worth persisting with.

To hell with it, she thought – though she didn't tell Ez she'd changed her mind; she didn't want her to think it had been her doing – *to hell with it*, and instead of putting down the phone this time when no one answered, she chanced her arm.

Hello. It's Ailinn. You remember? Thick ankles – ring a bell? To be brief about it, because she was sure his time was valuable, she wanted him to know she had inspected herself front on and sideways in the mirror, and OK – she was too thick. And not just around the ankles. Her waist was too thick as well. And her neck. She had become, she realised, as overgrown as the garden in which he'd been rude to her and told her it was a joke. She was grateful, by the way, for having the principles of comedy explained. She hoped she would be better able to get a joke the next time he was rude to her.

Anyway, if it was of the slightest interest to him – and why should it be? – she had decided to take herself off to Weight Watchers on whatever day they set up their scales in the village.

That's me. And now you. What do you intend to do about the thickness of your head?

She didn't laugh in order to make it plain that she too had comic ways. She wasn't going to make herself easy for him. If he couldn't read her, he couldn't read her. She didn't want to be with a man who insisted she got his jokes but wouldn't make the effort to get hers. Nor did she want to be with a man who didn't hear how much she was risking. Without risk on both sides, why bother?

Goodbye, she said. Then feared that sounded too final. Or should that be adieu? Unless that came over as desperation. No, goodbye, she said. And wished she'd never bothered.

What good came of love, when all was said and done? You fell in love and immediately thought about dying. Either because the person you had fallen for had a mind to kill you, or because he exceptionally didn't and then you dreaded being parted from him.

That was a joke, wasn't it?

And she got that well enough.

Kevern picked up her message. Relieved and reluctant at the same time – mistrustful of all excitement – he rang her back. He was surprised when she answered.

Oh! he said.

Oh what?

Oh, I never thought you'd be there.

Good, she thought. He imagines I am out and about.

They could hear each other swallowing hard.

Don't go to Weight Watchers, he told her. It's a free-for-all. And besides, you are fine as you are.

Fine? Only *fine*?

More than fine. Perfect. Lovely. She should take no notice of what he had said. There was something wrong with him.

Something wrong in the sense that he said what he thought without thinking through its consequences, or something wrong in the sense that he saw what wasn't there?

He thought about that. Both, he said. And in many more ways besides. Something wrong with him in every possible regard.

So my ankles aren't thick?

No, he said.

And would it matter to you if they were?

This he had to think about too. No, he said. It wouldn't matter to me in the slightest bit. I don't care how thick your ankles are.

So they *are* thick! You have simply decided that to humour me you will turn a blind eye to them at present. Which is generous, but it might mean you will mind them again in the future when you aren't feeling generous or you are in the mood to be funny. And then it will be too late.

Too late for what?

She had said too much.

He waited for her reply.

Too late for us to part as friends.

I promise you, he said.

You promise me what?

59

That we won't ever part as friends? No good. *That we won't ever part, full stop?* Too good. That I won't mind your ankles in the future, was what he decided to say. Promise.

And now?

Kevern sighed. You win, he said.

I've won, she thought.

She's going to be hard work, this one, he thought.

His other thought was that she was just the girl for him.

ii

The morning after the call he sat on his bench and wondered if he was about to experience happiness and, if so, whether he was up to it. He could have done with someone to talk to – his own age, a little younger, a little older, it didn't matter, just someone to muse with. But enter someone you can muse with and enter, with her, heartbreak. They were as one on this, he and the girl whose ankles he would never again object to, although they didn't yet know it: to think of love was to think of death.

He rarely missed his mother, but he did now. 'What's for the best, Mam? Should I go for it?' But she had always been negative. *What was for the best?* Nothing was for the best – for her the best was not to go for anything, just stay out of trouble and wait to die.

That was the impression she gave Kevern anyway.

In fact she lived a secret life, and though that too was wreathed around in death, the very fact that it was secret meant she saw some risk as worth the taking. Was it because she loved Kevern more than she loved herself that she didn't recommend risk to him?

A funny sort of love, Kevern would have thought, had he known about it.

As for his father, any such conversation would have been equally out of the question. 'You always hurt the one you love,' his father had said the first time Kevern was jilted by a girl. Kevern took that to be an allusion to one of the old songs his father listened to on earphones. His father did not normally have that much to say.

'But she's the one who's hurt me,' he answered.

His father shrugged. 'Bee-bop-a-doo,' he said without taking off his earphones. He looked like a pilot who knew his plane was going down.

'I'll go for it, then,' Kevern said to himself, as though after considering all the sage advice no one had given him. But he still wanted to run it all over in his mind.

It infuriated him when Densdell Kroplik appeared up the path, singing to himself, a countryman's trilby pulled down over his eyes, heavier boots on than the weather merited, swinging his rucksack full of unsold pamphlets and nettle conditioner.

'If you want the bench to yourself I'll clear off,' Kevern said. 'I've got work to do.'

'If I'd wanted a bench to myzelf I'd have found un,' Kroplik said.

I see, playing the yokel this morning, Kevern thought. That wasn't his only thought. The other was 'Up yours', though he was not normally a swearer.

His mouth must have moved because Kroplik asked him what he'd said. In for a penny, in for a pound, Kevern decided, taking a leaf out of Ailinn's book. 'I said, "Up yours." I was repeating what you said to me in the pub last night.'

The barber rubbed his face with his hand. 'Yeah, I sayz that sometimes,' he conceded. 'And a lot worse when the mood takes me.'

'I don't doubt it,' Kevern said.

'Like khidg de vey. If you knowz what that means.'

Kevern nodded, saying nothing. It was a way of getting through life: nodding and saying nothing.

'You don't know, though, do you,' Densdell Kroplik went on, enjoying his own shrewdness. 'But I'll give yerz a guess.'

'No doubt it means something like go fuck yourself.'

Kroplik punched the air. 'We'll make a local of yerz yet. Go fuck yerzelf is spot on.'

'I didn't bring up your abusive language to me last night so you could abuse me further,' Kevern said. He heard how pious he sounded but there was no going back now. 'I'd rather not be spoken to like that,' he went on.

'Oh, you'd *rather not.*'

'I'd rather not.'

'Pog mo hoin.'

'Don't tell me . . . Your mother's a fucker of pigs.'

'Close, close. Kiss my arze.'

'You are a mine of indispensable information,' Kevern said, getting up from the bench.

'That's what I'm paid to be. Do you know who the first person was to say pog mo hoin in these parts?'

'You.'

'The *first* person I sayz.'

'No idea. I wouldn't have been around.'

'No, that you wouldn't. So I'll inform yerz. The giant Hellfellen. That's how he kept strangers out. He stood on this very cliff, right where you're standing now, made a trumpet of hiz fist, stuck it in hiz backside and blew the words "kiss my arze" through it, so loud they could hear it three counties away, and you had to have a very good reason to come here after that.'

Kevern was not a folklore man. Mythology, with its uncouth half-men, half-animals, frightened him. And he hated talk of giants. Especially those who used bad language. If there were going to be gods he wanted them to be supreme spiritual beings who didn't fart, who employed chaste speech and otherwise kept themselves invisible.

'We've always known how to extend a warm welcome down here, that's for sure,' he said.

63

'*We?*' Kroplik made a trumpet of his own fist and belched a little laugh through it. 'Well yes, in point of fact *we* do.'

'So when you tell me to go fuck myself you intend nothing but friendliness by it.'

'Nothing whatsoever, Mister Master Kevern Cohen. Kiss my arze the same. I'm being brotherly, and that's the shape of it. And to prove it I'll give you a free shave.'

On this occasion Mister Master Kevern Cohen declined. 'Pog mo hoin,' he thought about saying, but didn't.

His detestation of swearing amounted almost to an illness. At school, although Latin wasn't taught, one of his classmates told him that the Latin for go fuck yourself was *futue te ipsum* which, for all that it sounded nicer, still didn't sound nice enough. Kiss my arse the same. It wasn't only that he didn't want to kiss anyone or have anyone kiss him there – least of all those to whom it would have been most appropriate to say it – he recoiled from the sound of the word. *Arse*! Even cleansed of Kroplik's brute enunciation it made the body a site of loathing. Swearing was an act of violence to others and an act of ugliness to oneself. It had no place in him.

With one exception he had never heard either his mother or his father swear. The exception – single in type but manifold in application – was his father's deployment of the hissing prefix PISS before words denoting what he most deplored. As, for example, his transliteration of WHAT HAPPENED, IF IT HAPPENED into the raging, jestless jest-speak of THE GREAT PISSASTER or THE PISSFORTUNE TO END ALL PISSFORTUNES or simply THE PISSASTROPHE. Accompanied always by a small, self-satisfied whinny of triumph, as though putting PISS before a word was a blow struck for freedom, followed just as invariably by a stern warning to Kevern never to put a PISS before a word himself, not in private, and definitely not in public.

Otherwise the worst his father ever let drop in his hearing was 'I think I've forgotten to rumple the bloody hall carpet.'

And even for that his wife reproved him. 'Howel! Not in front of the boy.'

It was something more than distaste for bad language. It was as though they had taken an oath, as though the enterprise that was their life together – their life together as the parents of *him* – depended on their keeping that oath.

They were elderly parents – that explained something. Elderly in years in his father's case, elderly in spirit in his mother's. And this made them especially solicitous to him, watching and remorseful, as though they needed to make it up to him for being the age they were, or the age they felt they were. At the end of his life his father had admitted to a mistake. 'We would have done better by you had we let you be more like the rest of them,' he said. 'We wanted to

65

preserve you but we went about it the wrong way. May God forgive me.'

His mother had died a month earlier. She had been dying almost as long as he'd known her, so her exit was expected, though the means of it was not. In circumstances that could not be explained she had suffered multiple burns while taking a short walk only yards from the cottage. As she didn't smoke she had no use for matches. The day was not hot. There was no naked flame in the vicinity. Either someone had set fire to her – in which event she would surely, since she remained conscious, have pointed a finger of blame – or she had combusted spontaneously – and what counted against that theory was that her torso was not burned, only her extremities. She lay quietly on her bed for three days without complaining and seemingly not in pain. Her final words were 'At last.'

But his father died – aged eighty though looking older – in a slow burn of ineffective rage. On the faces of some old men the flesh sags from lack of expressive exercise, the feeling man behind the skin having no more use for it; but on his father's it grew tighter with approaching death as though the skull beneath could not control its grimaces. On his last night he asked Kevern to dig out an ancient music system he kept hidden under the stairs in a box marked Private Property and got him to play the blind soul singer Ray Charles singing 'You Are My Sunshine' over and over. He shook his fists while it was playing, though Kevern couldn't tell whether at him, at Ray Charles, or at the cruel irony of things. 'What a joke,' his father said. 'What a joke that is.'

He had to unclench his father's fingers when the bitter light finally went out of him.

He let the music go on playing.

Kevern had always known about the box marked Private Property. Its futility saddened him. Would the words Private Property deter burglars? Or were they meant to deter him and his mother? What he hadn't known was how many more boxes marked Private Property – some of them cardboard and easy to get into, others made of metal and fitted with locks, but all of them numbered – his father had secreted under his bed, on the top of the wardrobe, in the attic, in his workshop. Hoarding was proscribed by universal consent – no law, you just knew you shouldn't do it – but he didn't think this could be called hoarding exactly. Hoarding, surely, was random and disorganised, the outward manifestation of a disordered personality. His father's boxes hinted at a careful, systematic, if overly secretive mind. But he'd read that people who kept things, whether they ordered them or they didn't, were afraid above all of loss – the fear of losing their things standing in for their fear of losing something else: love, happiness, their lives. Well he didn't need proof that his father was a frightened man. The only question was what he had all along been so frightened of.

Kevern knew the answer to that while maintaining that he didn't. You can know and not know. Kevern didn't know and knew. There were books in the redacted section of Bethesda Art Academy library with pages torn from them. Kevern sat in what appeared to Rozenwyn Feigenblat, the academy librarian, to be a concentration of profound vacancy, reading the pages that were no longer there.

One of his father's boxes was marked for his attention. Another was marked for his attention only in the event of his considering fatherhood. What he was meant to do with all the others he had no idea. Hoard them, he supposed.

Going through the papers and letters in the box marked for his attention, Kevern discovered a shocking truth about his parents. They were first cousins. That fact wasn't documented or brazenly trumpeted, but it was evident to anyone capable of reading between the lines, and Kevern lived between the lines. He couldn't have failed to gather, from his mother's and father's misery and from remarks they let drop over the years, that they didn't belong down here, that they lived in Port Reuben not out of choice, because they loved the sea or sought a simple way of life, but under duress; but he had never understood the nature of that duress, who or what had brought them and why they stayed. Now he knew. Down here no one would care about their incest (as Kevern considered it to be) even had they got wind of it.

Cousins? So bleeding what! We are all one big happy family here. We don't care, my lovelies, if youz is brother and sister.

Kevern didn't miss out on wondering about that too. Was it worse than the letters intimated? Was 'cousins' a euphemism?

Such easy-goingness as Port Reuben and the surrounding villages exercised in the matter of consanguinity was not shared by the rest of the country. Blood needed to be thinned not thickened if there was to be none of that dense, overpopulated insalubriousness that had been the cause of discord. The county was allowed to make an exception of itself only because the authorities didn't take it seriously. A cordon sanitaire could easily be drawn across the neck of the county, cutting it off from the rest of the country; and the existence of an imaginary version of that line – beyond which few aphids (as tourists and even visitors on business were contemptuously known) had ever wanted to stray – already prevented any serious cross-pollution. It was in the overheated towns and cities, where people talked as well as bred too much, that cousins needed to be kept apart. And it hadn't escaped the attention of Ofnow that in acknowledging and encouraging nationality-based group aptitude – popular entertainment and athletics in this corner, plumbing in that – it ran the risk of allowing steam to build up in the enclaves once again. But that didn't apply to Bethesda. The Bethesdans could mate with their own animals as far as the authorities were concerned.

In this, as in so many other matters, Kevern Cohen was not able to be as insouciant as his neighbours. Learning that his parents had been first cousins – if not closer – shook him profoundly. It had nothing to do with legalities: he didn't know whether they'd done wrong in the eyes of the law or not. But their hiding away suggested that they felt they had. And to him it was an animal wrongness: first cousins! – it was too hot, like rutting. They'd run away to breed, and he was the thing they'd bred. Engendered in the steaming straw of their cow-house. Inbred.

He wondered if it explained the oddity of his nature. Was that the reason he had never married and had children of his own? Was he possessed of some genetic knowledge that would ensure his contaminated line would die out?

They'd always been too much of another time for him to feel close to them in the way other sons were close to their parents, so he found it difficult to attribute sins of the flesh to them. What they'd done they'd done. What he couldn't forgive them for was not taking their secret to the grave. Why had they left incriminating documents behind? Shouldn't they have kept him in the dark about what they'd done, as they'd kept him in the dark about almost everything else in their past – where they'd come from, what sort of family theirs was, who they *were*? There were few other

70

papers for him to sort through. Most of the evidential story of their life, other than a number of nondescript notebooks and scrawled-over writing pads he kept for no other reason than that they had kept them, and a locked box which Kevern gave his oath he would open only when it looked likely that he would be a father himself – not before, and certainly not after – had been scrupulously destroyed. So he had to assume that they had deliberately not burned or shredded the handful of letters they had written to each other that proved how closely they were related. But to what end? Did they suppose they were helping him to live a better life? Or were the letters left where he could easily find them in order to give him a reason not to go on living at all? Was it their gift of death to him, like a single silver bullet or a suicide pill?

So much for their delicacy! They had brought him up unable to utter the most commonplace of oaths, a man of refined feeling, a fist of prickles as spiny as a hedgehog, and all along he'd been abnormally sired, a monstrosity, a freak. No wonder he couldn't tell anyone else to kiss his arse or eat shit. He had eaten shit himself.

He made a further unwelcome discovery going through his parents' papers. It wasn't they who had run to this extremity of the country to escape scandal. They had grown up here. Again he was having to read between the lines, but it seemed it was *their* parents, at least on his mother's side, who had bolted. Why that was he couldn't tell. Were they cousins too?

So what, by the infernal laws of genetic mathematics, did that make him? A monstrosity, four or even sixteen times over?

iii

It was Ailinn's adoptive mother's opinion that Ailinn had been abused when she was a little girl. Nothing else quite accounted for her bouts of morose absentness.

Ailinn shook her head. 'I'd remember it, Mother,' she said.

It didn't come naturally to her to call her mother-who-wasn't 'Mother'. And she could see that her mother-who-wasn't didn't care for it either. But she tried. They both did.

'You say you'd remember it, but that depends how old you were when it happened.'

'Believe me, it didn't happen.'

'I believe you that you don't remember, but there's a mechanism in the human heart that helps us to forget.'

'Then mightn't that be because we're meant to forget,' Ailinn replied, 'because it doesn't matter?'

'That's a terrible thing to say.'

Was it? Ailinn didn't think so. What you don't remember might as well not have happened. Remember everything and you have no future. Unless what you remember is mostly pleasant, and it didn't occur to Ailinn to imagine memory as pleasant.

Her own memory went back a long way. She heard the distant reverberations, like echoes trapped in a steel coffin. She just didn't know what it was she was remembering.

'So at the end of your life,' her mother went on, 'when you have little or no memory left . . .'

'That's right, you might as well not have lived it.'

'God help you for saying such a thing. I hope for your sake you won't be feeling that way when you're old.'

Ailinn laughed. 'It could be a blessing,' she said.

But even she knew her cynicism was bravado. Deep within her was a hunger for life to start, to aim herself towards a time when she would not regret having lived. She would outpace memory if she could.

They were at home, drinking tea and dunking biscuits at a scrubbed pine table, looking out over a ploughed field. A crow with a crazed orange eye was hopping with malign purpose from rut to rut. What sort of memory did he have, Ailinn wondered. How many thousands of crows past had it taken to teach him what he knew? And of them, of any of them – what knowledge did he have? Of his own past, even – just yesterday, for example – how much did he know?

Ailinn was nineteen. She had lived in this house how many years now . . .? Twelve, thirteen? It should no longer, whatever the exact computation, have felt foreign to her. But its dry formality: the teapot with its woolly hat, the floral china tea set, the biscuits carefully arranged on the plate, three ginger, three chocolate digestive, the silver tongs for the sugar cubes, the perfectly ploughed field which, by screwing up one eye, she could move from the horizontal to the vertical plane, as though its parallel furrows were a ladder to the heavens, even her weary-eyed, unsmiling adoptive mother who had never quite become her mother proper – all this was to her the setting for some other nineteen-year-old's life. As for where hers was, that she didn't yet know.

She was artistic. A further reason to think she'd been abused. She drew in pastels: the rising field, the scrubbed table, her would-be mother (not her would-be father who found her skills uncanny and disconcerting), the demoniacal crows – great luminous, visionary canvases which her teachers admired for their ethereal, other-worldly atmosphere, though one of them feared her work was a little too reminiscent of Kokoschka's dreamscapes. 'Where do you go to in your head, Ailinn?' he asked her.

'I don't go anywhere,' she said, 'I just draw what I see.'

She knew she was lying. She did go somewhere. She didn't have a name for it, that was all.

And she didn't know why she went there or what it was a memory or a foreboding, or just an idle fantasy, of.

The paper flowers were a sort of peace offering to her adoptive mother. Something nice to show how much she loved her, how grateful she was, how protected and at home she felt. But even the paper flowers looked as though they'd been picked from some other planet.

iv

Kevern had wondered, when he'd first discovered his depraved inheritance, whether it would put him off sex. That it *should* put him off sex, he didn't doubt. But would it?

The answer was no. Or at least not entirely. He knew he had to take precautions. He couldn't bring into the world a being who might show recessive symptoms of a kind which he – so far, at least – had not. And this meant not only being particular when it came to contraception, but going about coitus gently and considerately. Restoring to the act, maybe, something of the sacred. As it happened, such conscientiousness was not difficult for him: it accorded well with his precise, reluctant nature. He had not been put on earth to fling his seed around.

Ailinn didn't mind that he didn't pile-drive himself into her. It made a change.

'Sleepin' with you is like sleepin' with a woman,' she told him.

Though a clean enunciator out of bed, she made a habit of dropping her gs when verbalising sex.

Sleepin', screwin', fuckin', even makin' love. He didn't know why. To rough herself up a bit, perhaps. Or perhaps to rough up him.

'Is that northern speech?' he had asked her.

'Nah. It's *my* speech.' With which she made a triumphant, tarty little fist.

So yes, it was her way of communalising their sex, taking what was special out of it, making it less fragile, putting them both on a more ordinary footing with each other.

Did she find him overscrupulous? Would she have liked him to swear? (Pog mo hoin?)

He unwound himself and sat up. They were in his bed. She had invited him to hers, an altogether more sweetly smelling chamber now that she had got rid of all the spiders and repainted it, with giant paper sunflowers everywhere, but he was uneasy about staying away from his cottage all night. And besides, he lived alone and she didn't.

'So "sleepin'" with me is like "sleepin'" with a woman . . . I'm guessing you mean that as a compliment, though to me, of course, it isn't. Unless you prefer sleeping with women.'

'Never done it,' she said.

'So how do you know it's like sleeping with me?'

'Because sleepin' with you isn't like sleepin' with other men.'

Men! Couldn't she have spared him that?

'How isn't it like sleeping with *other men*?'

'Well you don't seem as though you want to hurt me, for a start.'

'Why would I hurt you? Do you want me to hurt you?'

'No I do not.'

'Then what's the nature of your discontent?'

She slipped out of bed, as though she needed to be upright when he questioned her as hard as this. He tried not to look at her feet.

'I'm not discontented at all,' she said. 'It's hard to describe what I feel. It's as if you don't care, or at least your first care isn't, whether I feel you've entered me.'

'Oh! Would you like me to signal when I have? I could wave a handkerchief.'

He made jokes, she noticed, when he was hurt.

'No, I don't mean that way. I'm really not complaining. It's lovely. I'm not putting this very well but I don't think you care whether you make a difference to me, sexually – *inside* – or not. Most men make a song and dance about it. "Can you feel that? Do you like that?" They want to be sure the conquest of your body is complete. They would like to hear you surrender. It's as though you don't mind whether I notice you're visiting or not.'

'Visiting?'

She took a moment . . . 'Yes, visiting. It's as though you're on a tourist visa. Just popping in to take a look around.'

'That's not how it feels to me. I'm not planning being somewhere else. You need to know that.'

'Good.'

'But it doesn't sound very nice for you.'

'Well it is and it isn't. It's a change not to feel *invaded*. It's nice to be left alone to think my own thoughts.'

'Thoughts! Should you be having *thoughts* at such a time?'

'Feelings, then. You know what I mean – not having to go along with what someone else wants. Not having to be issuing periodic bulletins of praise and satisfaction. But what are yours?'

'What are my thoughts and feelings?'

'Yes. What do you want?'

'Ah, now you're asking.'

'You won't tell me?'

'I don't know.'

'Don't know whether you'll tell me?'

'Don't know what I want.'

But he made her a lovespoon in which the two of them could be recognised, entwined, inseparable, carved from a single piece of wood.

In return for which she made him a pair of exquisitely comical purple pansies, a paper likeness of his face in one, hers in another. She arranged them in a vase on his dressing table, so that they stared at each other unremittingly.

'When you dust them, do it lightly,' she advised.

'I will sigh the dust away.' He pursed his lips and let out the softest emission of air, as though blowing a kiss to a butterfly.

'I love you,' she told him.

Why not, he thought. Why ever not? 'I love you,' he said.

As he'd told her, he wasn't planning to be some-where else.

He should not have judged his parents their sin. When the love thing is upon you there's no one who can break you up. And he wasn't even abso-lutely sure the love thing was upon him – yet.

v

She moved in. Or at least she moved her person in. He cleared space for her to make her flowers in his workshop but she couldn't function in the noise and dust his lathe threw out. So she kept her studio, along with the majority of her posses-sions, in Paradise Valley. There was an argument on the side of sensible precaution for this anyway, though Ez said she wouldn't take it personally if Ailinn moved out. 'Follow your heart,' she said. But Ailinn thought it was still early for that. She'd been alive long enough to know that hearts were fickle.

Didn't her own jump?

She wanted her mail to go on being delivered to Paradise Valley as well. She had her own letter-box neurosis which she didn't want to clash with Kevern's. She feared letters being lost, postmen being careless about their delivery, just tossing them over the wall into Kevern's little garden, or not pushing them properly through the flap. She wasn't waiting for any communication in parti-cular but believed something, that should have reached her in an envelope, was missing from her life: a greeting, an offer she couldn't have said what of, an advantage or an explanation – even terrible news, but terrible news, too, needed to be faced and not forever dreaded – and the idea that she would not discover it when it came, that Kevern would treat it as junk, or that it would blow away, be blown about the world unknown to her, and leave her waiting, never knowing, was one she found deranging. As a little girl she'd read in comics about a time when people wrote to one another by phone but wrote such horrid things that the practice had to be discouraged. She was glad, at least, that she didn't have to 'angst', as they called it in those comics, about losing phone letters as well. So for the time being, at least, her postal address remained Beck House, Paradise Valley.

If she didn't return to collect what was waiting for her for more than two or three days at a time, however, the weight of expectation and dread oppressed her more than she could bear.

Most mornings, after breakfast, she accompanied Kevern to his workroom, kissed him, breathed in the lovely fresh smell of sawdust – it reminded her of the circus, she said – and either went back to bed with a book or walked down into the valley, singing to herself, alone. But occasionally they would leave the cottage together in order to wander the cliffs or just sit side by side on his bench. She had made the mistake, the first time, of straightening his rug after he'd rumpled it. She saw him wince and then, without saying anything, rumple it again. Thereafter she simply stood by, expressionless, her arms beside her sides, as he locked up, confirmed that he had locked up, knelt to look inside the letter box, stood up, knelt down again to confirm that what he had seen he had seen, put his hand inside the flap, took it out, and then put it back again, looked one more time, then put his keys in his pocket. Sometimes he would send her on ahead so that he could do all this again.

'Don't ask,' he said.

And she tried not to. But she loved him and wanted to relieve him of some of the stress he was obviously under.

'Couldn't I?' she asked once, meaning couldn't she make sure *for* him that everything was OK. Share the burden, whatever it was. Pour the tea, rumple the runner, double-lock and then double-lock again, kneel down and lift the flap of the letter box, peer through (check to see if there was anything for her while she was at it). . . . she knew the routine well enough by now.

'Unthinkable,' he said.

'Just try thinking it.'

He shook his head, not liking her suddenly, not wanting to look at her. She knew. And was glad she was wearing trousers so he could not see her ankles.

But that night, in bed, after exhaustively locking

the house from the inside, he tried explaining why she couldn't help him.

'If anything happens it has to be my responsibility. I want at least to know I did all I could. If it happens because of something I have omitted to do, I will never forgive myself. So I make sure.'

'Happens to the house?'

'Happens to the house, happens to me, happens to you . . .'

'But what can happen?'

He stared at her. '*What can happen*. What *can't* happen.' Neither was a question. Both were statements of incontrovertible fact.

They were lying on what she took to be a reproduction Biedermeier bed. He hung his clothes, as now she hung hers, in a fine mahogany wardrobe, two doors on either side of a full-length bevelled mirror, also imitation Biedermeier. It was far too big for the cottage, some of the beam had had to be cut away to make room for it, and she did wonder how anyone had ever succeeded in getting it upstairs. She knew about Biedermeier – it had come back into style. Everyone wanted reproduction Biedermeier. There was a small factory knocking it out in Kildromy, not far from where she grew up. Kildromy-Biedermeier – there was a growing market for it. But she did wonder whether Kevern's furniture wasn't reproduction at all. It looked at once far grander and more worn than anything that came out of Kildromy. Could it be the real thing? Everyone cheated a bit,

82

keeping a few more family treasures than they knew they should. And this the authorities turned a blind eye to. But if these pieces were genuine, Kevern was cheating on a grand scale. She tried asking him about it. 'This Kildromy-Biedermeier?' He stared at her, lost for words. Then he gathered his wits. 'Yes,' he said. 'Kildromy. Spot on.'

So he was lying. She didn't judge him. If anything, it thrilled her to be a silent party to such delinquency. But it explained why he went to such lengths to protect his privacy. No one was ever going to come to so remote a place, so difficult of access, to steal a wardrobe; but what if it wasn't thieves he feared but, she joked to herself, the Biedermeier police?

Once, although she hadn't mentioned her suspicions, he explained that property wasn't the reason he was careful.

'*Careful*!'

'Why, what word would you use?'

'Obsessive? Compulsive? Disordered?'

He smiled. He was smiling a lot so she shouldn't take fright. He liked her teasing and didn't want it to stop.

'Well, whatever the word, I do what I do because I hate the idea of . . . what was that other word you used once, to describe my lack of sexual attack? – *invasion*.'

'I didn't accuse you of lacking sexual attack.'

'OK.'

'I truly didn't. I love the way it is between us.'

'OK. Invasion, anyway, is a good word to describe what I fear. People thinking they can just burst in here, while I'm out or even while I'm in.'

'I understand that,' she said. 'I am the same.'

'Are you?'

'I always locked my bedroom door when I was a little girl. Every time the wind blew or a tree scratched at my window I thought someone was trying to get in. To get *back* in, actually. To reclaim their space.'

'I don't follow. Why *their* space?'

'I can't explain. That was just how I felt. That I had wrongly taken possession of what wasn't mine.'

There was something temporary about her, Kevern thought. Of no fixed abode. Tomorrow she could be gone.

A great wave of protectiveness – that protectiveness he knew he would feel for her when he first saw her and imagined rolling her in his rug – crashed over him. Unless it was possessiveness. Protectiveness, possessiveness – what difference? He wanted her protected because he wanted her to stay his. 'Well you don't have to feel that here,' he said.

'And I don't,' she said.

He kissed her brow. 'Good. I want you to feel safe here. I want you to feel it's yours.'

'Given the precautions you take,' she laughed, 'I couldn't feel safer. It's a nice sensation – being barred and gated.'

But she didn't tell him there was safe and *safe*. That all the barring and gating couldn't secure her peace of mind. That she kept seeing the pig auctioneer, for example, who had known both their names.

'Good,' he said. 'Then I'll keep battening down the hatches.'

She laughed. 'There's a contradiction,' she said, 'in your saying you want me to think of your home as mine, when you protect it so fiercely.'

'I'm not protecting it *from* you. I'm protecting it *for* you.'

This time she kissed him. 'That's gallant of you.'

'I don't say it to be gallant.'

'You like me being here?'

'I love you being here.'

'But?'

'There is no but. It's not you I'm guarding against. I've invited you in. It's the uninvited I dread. My parents were so terrified of people poking about in their lives that they jumped out of their skins whenever they heard footsteps outside. My father shooed away walkers who came anywhere near the cottage. He'd have cleared them off the cliffs if he could have. I'm the same.'

'Anyone would think you have something to hide,' she said skittishly, rubbing her hands down his chest.

He laughed. 'I do. You.'

'But you're not hiding me. People know.'

'Oh, I'm not hiding you from people.'

85

'Then what?'

He thought about it. 'Danger.'

'What kind of danger?'

'Oh, the usual. Death. Disease. Disappointment.'

She hugged her knees like a little girl on an awfully big adventure. In an older man's bed. 'The three Ds,' she said with a little shiver, as though the awfully big adventure might just be a little too big for her.

'Four, actually. Disgust.'

'Whose disgust?'

'I don't know, just disgust.'

'You fear I will disgust you?'

'I didn't say that.'

'You fear you will disgust me?'

'I didn't say that either.'

'Then what are you saying? Disgust isn't an entity that might creep in through your letter box. It isn't out there, like some virus, to shut your doors and windows against.'

Wasn't it?

It was anyway, he acknowledged, a strange word to have hit on. It answered to nothing he felt, or feared he might feel, for Ailinn. Or *from* Ailinn, come to that. So why had he used it?

He decided to make fun of himself. 'You know me,' he said. 'I fear everything. Abstract nouns particularly. Disgust, despair, vehemence, vicissitude, ambidexterity. And I'm not just worried that they'll come in through my letter box, but underneath the doors, *and* down the chimney, *and* out of the taps and electricity sockets, *and* in on the bottom of your shoes . . . Where *are* your shoes?'

She shook her head a dozen times, blinding him with her hair, then threw her arms around him. 'You are the strangest man,' she said. 'I love you.'

'*I'm* strange! Who is it round here who thinks trees are tapping at the window to reclaim what's rightfully theirs?'

'Then we make a good pair of crazies,' she laughed, kissing his face before he could tell her he had never felt more whatever the opposite of disgust was for anyone in his life.

vi

Disgust.

His parents had once warned him against expressing it. He remembered the occasion. A girl he hadn't liked had tried to kiss him on the way home from school. It was the style then among the boys to put their fingers down their throats when anything like that happened. Girls, it was important for them to pretend, made them sick, so they put on a dumb show of vomiting whenever one came near. Kevern was still doing it when he encountered his father standing at the door of his workshop, looking for him. He thought his father might be impressed by this expression of his son's burgeoning manliness. Finger down the throat, 'Ugh, ugh . . .' *Ecce homo!*

When he explained why he was doing what he was doing his father slapped him across the face.

'Don't you ever!' he said.

He thought at first that he meant don't you ever kiss a girl. But it was the finger down the throat, the simulating of disgust he was never to repeat.

His mother, too, when she was told of it, repeated the warning. 'Disgust is hateful,' she said. 'Don't go near it. Your grandmother, God rest her soul, said that to me and I'm repeating it to you.'

'I bet she didn't say don't put your fingers down your throat,' Kevern said, still smarting from his father's blow.

'I'll tell you precisely what she said. She said, "Disgust destroys you – avoid it at all costs."'

'I bet you're making that up.'

'I am not making it up. Those were her exact words. "Disgust destroys you."'

'Was this your mother or dad's?' He didn't know why he asked that. Maybe to catch her out in a lie.

'Mine. But it doesn't matter who said it.'

Already she had exceeded her normal allowance of words to him.

Kevern had never met his grandparents on either side nor seen a photograph of them. They were rarely talked about. Now, at least, he had 'disgust' to go on. One of his grandmothers was a woman who had strong feelings about disgust. It wasn't much but it was better than nothing. At the time he wasn't in the mood to be taught a lesson from beyond the grave. But later he felt it filled the family canvas out a little. *Disgust destroys you* – he could start to picture her.

Thinking about it as he lay in Ailinn's arms, trying to understand why the word had popped out of his mouth unbidden, Kevern wondered whether what had disgusted his grandmother – and in all likelihood disgusted every member of the family – was the incestuous union her child had made. He saw her putting her fingers down her throat. Unless – he had no dates, dates had been expunged in his family – that union didn't come about until after she'd died. In which case could it have been the incestuous union she had made herself?

Self-disgust, was it?

Well, she had reason.

But if his own mother's account was accurate, his grandmother had said it was disgust that destroyed, not incest. Why inveigh against the judgement and not the crime? And why the fervency of the warning? What did she know of what disgust wrought?

Could it have been that she wasn't a woman who *felt* disgust in all its destructive potency but a woman who *inspired* it? And who therefore knew its consequences from the standpoint of the victim?

Do not under any circumstances visit on others what you would not under any circumstances have them visit on you – was that the lesson his parents had wanted to inculcate in him? The reason you would not want it visited on you being that it was murderous.

This then, by such a reading, was his grand-mother's lesson: Be careful not to be on disgust's receiving end. For whoever feels disgusted by you will destroy you.

Had he wanted to destroy the girl whose attempt to kiss him had been so upsetting that he had to pretend it turned his stomach? Maybe he had.

Kevern 'Coco' Cohen got out of bed and religiously blew the dust off Ailinn's paper flowers.

How many men were there? Six hundred, seven hundred, more? She thought she ought to count. The numbers might matter one day. One at a time the men were led, each with his hands tied behind his back, into the marketplace of Medina, and there, one at a time, each with his hands tied behind his back, they were decapitated in the most matter-of-fact way – *glory be to——!* – their headless bodies tipped into a great trench that had been dug specially to accommodate them. What were the dimensions of the trench? She thought she ought to estimate it as accurately as she could. The dimensions might matter one day. The women, she noted coldly, were to be spared, some for slavery, some for concubinage. She had no preference. 'I will choose tomorrow,' she thought, 'when it is too late.' Grief the same. 'I will sorrow tomorrow,' she thought 'when it is too late.' But then what did she have to grieve for? History unmade itself as she watched. Nothing unjust or untoward had happened. It was all just another fantasy, another lie, another Masada complex. As it would be in Maidenek. As it would be in Magdeburg. She looked on in indifference as the trench overflowed with the blood that was nobody's.

CHAPTER 4

R.I.P. LOWENNA MORGENSTERN

i

Ailinn knew even less about *her* family. Kevern thought that Ez, the fraught, angular woman with the tight frizzy hair who had brought her down to share the cottage in Paradise Valley, was her aunt, but she wasn't.

'No relative,' Ailinn explained. 'Not even a friend really. No, that's unfair. She *is* a friend. But a very recent one. I only met her a few months before I came away, in a reading group.'

Reading groups were licensed. Because they were allowed access to books not otherwise available (not banned, just not available), readers had to demonstrate exceptionality of need – either specific scholastic need or, if it could be well argued for (and mere curiosity wasn't an argument), general educational need. Kevern was impressed that Ailinn had been able to demonstrate one or the other. But she told him she had simply been able to pull a few strings, her adoptive mother being a teacher.

Books apart, this account of her relations with Ez explained to Kevern why she had made so little ceremony of introducing them. It was as though she had never been introduced to her herself. He was amazed by how anxious she could be one minute, and how devil-may-care the next. 'And you threw in your lot with a woman you'd met in a reading group, just like that?'

'Well, I'd hardly call it throwing in my lot. She offered me a room in a cottage she hadn't ever seen herself, for as long or as short a time as I wanted it, in return for my company, and some help painting and gardening, and I could find no reason to say no. Why not? I liked her. We had a shared interest in reading. And there was nothing up there to keep me. And I reckoned I could sell my flowers just as well down here . . . probably better, as you get more tourists than we do, and . . . and of course there was you . . .'

'You knew about me?'

'My heart knew about you.'

Her arrhythmic heart.

He couldn't tell how deep her teasing went. Did she truly think they were destined for each other? He would once have laughed at such an idea, but not now. Now, he too (so he hoped to God she wasn't playing with his feelings) wanted to think they had all along been on converging trajectories. But no doubt, and with more reason, his parents had thought the same.

She had no memory of her parents – her actual parents – which made Kevern feel more protective of her still.

'No letters? No photographs?'

She shook her head.

'And you didn't ask?'

'Who would I have asked?'

'Whoever was caring for you.'

She looked surprised by the idea that anyone had cared for her. He picked that up – perhaps because he wanted to think that no one had cared for her until he came along. 'Someone must have been looking after you,' he said.

'Well I suppose the staff at the orphanage to begin with, though I have no memory of them either. Just a smell, like a hospital, of disinfectant. I was brought up by a smell. And after that Mairead, the local schoolteacher, and her husband Hendrie.'

'And what did they smell of?'

She thought about it. 'Stale Sunday afternoons.'

'They'd been friends of your parents?'

She shook her head. 'Didn't know my parents. No one seems to have known them. Mairead told me when I was old enough to understand that she and Hendrie were unable to have children of their own and had been in touch with an orphanage outside Mernoc – a small town miles from anywhere except a prison and a convent – about adoption. When they were invited to visit, they saw me. They chose me like a stray puppy.'

She normally liked to say 'like an orange', but there was something about Kevern that made her think of strays.

'I can understand why,' he said, losing his fingers in the tangle of her hair.

She raised her face to him, like one of her own flowers. 'Why?'

'You know why.'

'Tell me.'

'Because to see you is to see no one else.' He meant it.

'Then it's a pity you didn't choose me first.'

'Why – were they unkind to you?'

'No, not at all. Just remote.'

'Are they still alive?'

'No. Or at least Mairead isn't. Hendrie is in a care home. He has no knowledge of the world around him. Not that he ever had a lot.'

'You didn't like him?'

'Not a great deal. He was a largely silent man who fished and played dominoes. I think he hit Mairead.'

'And you?'

'Occasionally. It wasn't personal. Just something men did. Do. Towards the end, before they put him in a home, it got worse. He started to make remarks like "I owe you nothing", and "You don't belong here", and would throw things at me. But his mind was going then.'

'And you never found out where you *did* belong?'

'I belonged in the Mernoc orphanage.'

'I mean who put you there?'

She shrugged, showing him that his questioning had begun to weary her.

'I'm sorry,' he said. Adding, 'But you belong here now.'

ii

As a matter of course, she woke badly. Her eyes puffed, her hair matted, her skin twice its age. Where had she been?

She wished she knew.

At first Kevern thought it was his fault. He'd been tossing and turning, perhaps, or snoring, or crying out in the night, stopping her sleeping. But she told him she had always been like this – not morning grumpiness but a sort of species desolation, as though opening her eyes on a world in which no one of her sort existed.

He pulled a face. 'Thank you,' he said.

'You're not yet the world I wake up to,' she said. 'It takes me a while to realise you're there.'

'So why such desolation?' he wanted to know. 'Where do you return from when you wake?'

'If only I could tell you. If only I knew myself.'

Mernoc, Kevern guessed. He saw an icy orphanage, miles from nowhere. And Ailinn standing at the window, barefooted, staring into nothing, waiting for somebody to find her.

Pure melodrama. But much of life for Kevern was.

And thinking of her waiting to be found, while he was waiting to find, gave a beautiful symmetry to the love he felt for her.

What she'd told him awakened his pity and pity gave him a better reason to be in love than he'd ever had before. There was rapture and then there was responsibility. Each imposed an obligation of seriousness. But together they made the serious sacred.

He couldn't rescue her from her dreams, but he could make waking better for her. The minute he sensed her stir he would get out of bed and open the windows, so that she would wake to light, the smell of the sea, and the cries of the gulls. But sometimes the light was too harsh and the smell of the sea too pungent and the cries of the gulls a mockery. 'They sound the way I feel,' she'd say.

Did that mean that gulls, too, suffered species desolation?

So he had to make a quick decision every morning: whether to open the curtains or keep them closed.

But when the sea was rough they could still hear the blowhole like a giant mouth sucking in and then expelling water. On wild days they would even see the spittle.

'Reminds me of a whale exhaling air,' she said once. 'Do you remember that passage in *Moby-Dick* describing whale-jets "up-playing and sparkling in the noonday air"?'

He didn't.

'But you've read the book?'

He had. Years ago. *Moby-Dick* was one of the classic novels that had not been encouraged to drift out of print – though most editions were in graphic form – the grounds for its remaining available being the interest felt in it by fishing communities, its remoteness otherwise from the nation's calamitous recent history, and the fact that it was from its opening sentence – 'Call me Ishmael' – that the colossal social experiment undertaken to restore stability borrowed its name.

OPERATION ISHMAEL.

'We should read it together,' she suggested when Kevern told her he could remember little of it beyond Ahab and the whale and of course OPERATION ISHMAEL. 'It's my most favourite book in the world,' she told him. 'It's the story of my life.'

'You've been hunting a great white whale? Could that have been me, perhaps?'

She kissed him absent-mindedly, as though he were a child that needed humouring. Her brow was furrowed. 'It wasn't Ahab I identified with, you fool,' she said. 'That's a man thing. I took the side of the whale.'

'Don't worry, men do the same. The whale is more noble than the whaler.'

'But I bet you don't wake to the knowledge that you're the whale.'

'Are you telling me you do? Is that where you've been all night, swimming away from the madness of Ahab? No wonder you look exhausted.'

'I don't know what I've been doing all night, but it's a pretty good description of what I do all day.'

How serious was she?

'All day? Truly?'

She paused. 'Well what am I signing up for if I say "truly"? If you're asking me if I actually hear the oars of the longboats coming after me, then no. But when people describe having the wind at their back it's a sensation of freedom I don't recognise. An unthreatening, invigorating space behind me? – no, I don't ever have the luxury of that. There might be nothing there when I turn around, but it isn't a beneficent nothing. Nothing good propels me. But I call it a good day when I turn around and at least don't see anything bad.'

He couldn't stop himself taking this personally. Wasn't he the wind at her back? Wasn't he a beneficent force? 'I can't bear to think,' he said, 'that you get no relief from this.'

'Oh, I get relief. I get relief with you. But that's the most dangerous time because it means I've forgotten to be on guard. You remember that description of the nursing whales, "serenely revelling in dalliance and delight"?'

He didn't. He wondered whether she was intending to quote the entire novel to him in small gobbets. Something – and this he did remember – that his father had done when he was small. Not *Moby-Dick* – other, darker, more sardonic books. Until his mother had intervened. 'What are you trying to do to the boy?' he had heard her ask. 'Make him you?' Shortly after which his father locked his books away.

'Well, whenever I feel anything of that sort,' she

went on, 'whenever I feel calm, at rest, loving and being loved – as I do now – I feel I must be in danger. In my universe I don't know how else to account for being loved. Don't kiss me, I used to say to Mairead when she tucked me up in bed at night. I won't be able to sleep. If you kiss me something terrible will follow. Hendrie wanted to send me to a psychiatrist. Or better still, back to the children's home. Mairead said no. She believed the children's home was to blame. She was convinced that something terrible must have been done to me there.'

'And had it, do you think?'

'Oh God, you and my mother. Something terrible's been done to everybody everywhere. Where's the point of hunting down the specifics? Anyway, I think you can tell when a terror has an origin in a particular event. You might not have a name for it but you can date it. A five-year terror, a ten-year terror . . . This is a thousand-year terror.'

He wondered if she overdid the retrospective panic. If she overdramatised herself. Like him. 'A thousand years is a long time to have been hunted by a one-legged nut, Ailinn.'

'You can make fun of me if you like. I know how crazy it must sound. But it's as though it's not just me, as I am now, or as I was the day before yesterday, who's always running. It's an earlier me. Don't laugh. You're just as barmy in your own way. But it feels like a sort of predestiny – as though I was born in flight. Which I suppose

I could have been. It's a pity my real parents aren't around to ask.'

Yes, she overwrote her story. But he loved her. Maybe overloved her. 'We could try to find them,' he said.

'Don't be banal,' she came back sharply, thinking she would have to watch his solicitousness.

He shrank from her asperity. But he had one more question. What he feared when he knelt to check his letter box for the umpteenth time had no features. No person rose up before him. He could weigh the reason for his precautions but he could not picture it. She, though, had Ahab. Was that a way of speaking or did she actually see the man? 'Is he Ahab in the flesh that's coming for you—'

'Wait,' she said. 'Did I say he was "coming for me"? Sounds a bit like waiting for Mairead and Hendrie, doesn't it? Was I waiting for them to "come for me"? You must think my psychology is pathetic, alternating hopes and terrors based on puns—'

'I don't,' he said, afraid that they had begun to judge each other. 'Your psychology is your psychology, therefore I love it. But all I was going to ask was whether Ahab is a generalised idea for you or you actually picture him coming at you with his lampoon.'

'*Lampoon?*'

'Slip of the tongue. You've been making me nervous. *Harpoon.*'

She stared at him. 'You call that a slip?'

'Why, what would you call it?'

'A searchlight into your soul.'

He looked annoyed. 'I let you off your pun,' he said.

She kissed him. 'Yes, you did. But we aren't in a competition, are we, and I'm not making fun of you. It's just that this slip is so you.'

'How so?'

'Well, it's your fear of mockery, isn't it. Your fear of anyone knowing you well enough to poke fun at you.'

She had him here. He had only to deny the justice of the charge to prove it. Touchy? Me?

She had him another way too. Wasn't he her mentor in the matter of a sense of humour? Hadn't he, when she'd been upset with him for teasing her about her thick ankles, lectured her about the nature of a joke? So how much easier-going was he when the joke was on him?

They were in this together, it seemed to her. Skin as fine as parchment, the pair of them. Pride a pin could prick. Hearts that burst when either looked with love at the other.

He could see what she was thinking but decided to be flattered that she offered to penetrate him so deeply. It proved she found him interesting and cared about him.

He excused himself to take a shower. Though he showered frequently, the sounds he made the moment he turned on the water – groans of release (or was it remission?), sighs of deliverance, gasp-ings deep enough, she feared, to shake his heart out of his chest – suggested it was either the first shower he had ever experienced or the last he would ever enjoy. She had wondered, at the begin-ning, whether it were some private sexual ritual, demeaning to her, but later she would sometimes shower with him and he made exactly the same noises then. She couldn't explain it to herself. A shower was just a shower. Why the magnitude of his surrender to it? It could have been his death, so thunderous were his exhalations. Or it could have been his birth.

She was relieved when he stepped back out into the bedroom, dripping like a seal. He appeared exhausted.

'There will be more, you know,' she said.

'More what?'

'More showers.'

He expected her to say 'More life'.

'You never know what there will be more of,' he said, 'but that's certainly more than enough about me and who *I* am and what *I'm* in flight from. We began this conversation discussing whales and you – the least whale-like creature I have ever seen.'

'Despite my thick ankles?'

'Whales don't have thick ankles. As didn't Ahab, as I recall.'

'Well he certainly didn't have two.'

If he hadn't loved her before . . .

Best to leave it at that, anyway, they both thought. But he wanted to be sure that she felt safe with him. Still dripping, he pulled her down into the bed and drew the duvet over them.

Gently, protectively.

But were they overdoing this, he wondered.

She'd have answered yes had he asked her.

iii

It was in his lampoon-fearing nature to wonder whether they would be the talk of the village – the slightly odd woodturner who by and large kept himself to himself, and the tangle-haired flower girl from up north who was several years his junior. But the village wasn't exercised by pairings-off, even when the parties weren't as free to do as they pleased as these two were. People who have lived for aeons within sound of crashing seas, and sight of screaming seabirds spearing mackerel, take sex for granted. It's townspeople who find it dis-arranging.

And besides, the village had something else to yack about: a double murder. Lowenna Morgenstern and Ythel Weinstock found lying side by side in the back of Ythel Weinstock's caravan in pools of each other's blood. By itself, the blood of one would not have found its way, in such quantities, on to the body of the other. So there'd been doubly foul play: not just the murders but this ghoulish intermixing of bodily fluids which was taken by the police to be a commentary on the other sort of fluidal intermingling in which Morgenstern and Weinstock had no doubt been frenetically engaged at the moment their assailant struck.

'Caught in the act' was the phrase going round the village. And no one doubted that it was Lowenna's husband, Ade, who'd caught them. But where was Ade Morgenstern? He hadn't been seen in the village for months, having stormed out of the surgery to which he'd accompanied his wife to have a minor ailment looked at, which ailment, in his view, didn't necessitate the removal of her brassiere. He hadn't seen the brassiere coming off, he had only heard the doctor unhooking it. But his wife had beautiful breasts, as many in the village could testify, and he was a jealous man.

'Breathe in,' he heard the doctor order her. 'And out.' And a moment later, 'Open.'

He was not in the waiting room when his wife emerged fully clothed from her consultation.

Hedra Deitch was less bothered by the question of who was guilty of the crime than its timing. 'If you gotta go, that's as good a moment as any, if you want my view, and that Ythel was a bit of all right,' she told drinkers at the bar of the Friendly Fisherman. 'Rumpy pumpy feels like dying anyway when you've got a husband like mine.'

Pascoe Deitch ignored the insult. 'She always was a screamer,' he put in.

His wife kicked his shin. 'How come you're an expert?'

'When it comes to Lowenna Morgenstern everyone's an expert.'

Hedra kicked his other shin. '*Was* an expert. Who you going to be expert about next?'

Pascoe's expertise, universal or not, caught the attention of the police. Not that he was a suspect. He lacked the energy to be a criminal just as, for all his bravado, his wife believed him to lack the energy to be unfaithful. He masturbated in corners, in front of her, thinking, he told her, about other women – that was the sum of his disloyalty.

'You could feel this one comin',' he told Detective Inspector Gutkind.

'You knew there were family troubles?'

'Everybody knew. But no more than usual. We all have family troubles.'

'So in what sense did you feel this one coming?'

'Something had to give. It was like before a storm. It gave you a headache.'

'Was it something in the marriage that had to give? Did the murdered woman have a lover?'

'Well who else was that lying with her in those pools of blood?'

'You tell me.'

Pascoe shrugged the shrug of popular surmise.

'And did the husband know as much as you know?' Gutkind asked.

'He knew she put it about.'

'Was he a violent man?'

'Ythel?'

'Ade.'

107

'The place is full of violent men. Violent women, too.'

'Are you saying there are many people who might have done this?'

'When a storm's comin' a storm's comin'.'

'But what motive would anyone else have had?'

'What motive do you need? What motive does the thunder have?'

The policeman scratched his head. 'If this murder was as motiveless as thunder I'm left with a long list of suspects.'

Pascoe nodded. 'That's pretty much the way of it.'

That night he went alone to a barn dance in Port Abraham. His wife was wrong in assuming he was too lazy to be unfaithful to her.

iv

Densdell Kroplik generously offered to sell the police multiple copies of his *Brief History of Port Reuben* at half price on the assumption that it would help with their enquiries. Yes, he told Detective Inspector Gutkind, there were violent undercurrents in their society, but these appeared exceptional only in the context of that unwonted and, quite frankly, inappropriate gentleness that had descended on Port Reuben after WHAT HAPPENED, IF IT HAPPENED – see pp. 35–37 of his *Brief History*. Why Port Reuben had had to pay the price – bowing and scraping and saying sorry

– for an event in which it had played no significant role, Densdell Kroplik didn't see. Nothing had happened, if it happened, *here*. WHAT HAPPENED, IF IT HAPPENED, happened in the cities. And yet the villagers and their children and their children's children were expected to share in the universal hand-wringing and name-changing. In his view, if anyone was interested in hearing it, the Lowenna Morgenstern case came as a welcome return to form. In a village with Port Reuben's proud warrior history, people were supposed to kill one another . . . Where there was a compelling argument to do so, he added, in response to Detective Inspector Gutkind's raised eyebrow.

'And what, in your view, constitutes a compelling argument?' the policeman asked.

'Well there you'll have to ask the murderer,' Densdell Kroplik replied.

'And what's this about a proud warrior history?' Gutkind pressed. 'There haven't been warriors in these parts for many a year.'

Densdell Kroplik wasn't going to argue with that. 'The Passing of the Warrior' was the title of his first chapter. But that didn't mean the village didn't have a more recent reputation to live up to. It was its touchy individualism, its fierce wariness, that had gone on lending the place its character and kept it inviolate. Densdell Kroplik's position when it came to outsiders, the hated aphids, was more than a little paradoxical. He needed visitors to buy his pamphlet but on balance he would rather there were no visitors. He wanted to sing to them of the glories of Port Reuben, in its glory days called Ludgvennok, but didn't want them to be so far entranced by his account that they never left. The exhilaration of living in Ludgvennok, which it pained him to call Port Reuben, walled in by cliffs and protected by the sea, enjoying the company of rough-mannered men and wild women, lay, the way he saw it, in its chaste unapproachability. This quality forcibly struck the composer Richard Wagner – if you've heard of him, Detective Inspector – in the course of a short visit he made to Ludgvennok as it was then. In those days husbands and lovers, farmers and fishermen, wreckers and smugglers, settled their grievances, eye to eye, as they had done for time immemorial, without recourse to the law or any other outside interference. Sitting at a window in a hostelry on this very spot, Wagner watched the men of Ludgvennok front up to one another like stags, heard the bacchante women wail, saw the blood flow, and composed until his fingers ached. 'I feel more alive here than I have felt anywhere,' he wrote in a letter to Mathilde Wesendonck. 'I wish you could be with me.'*

* Liebling,
The days go by without my hearing from you and I wonder what I have done to deserve your cruelty. Everything I see, I see only that I might relate it to you. Had I only known how wonderful I was going to find Ludgvennok I would not have allowed you to persuade

Der Strandryuber von Ludgvennok, the opera Wagner subsequently wrote about the village (and dedicated to Mathilde, who had by that time given him his marching orders), was rarely performed; this Densdell Kroplik ascribed not to any fault in the composition but to the lily-livered hypocrisy of the age.

---

me to come on my own. When I think of all I have written about the regeneration of the human race, and all I have done to further its ennoblement, it cheers me to find a people here who live up to everything I have ever understood by nobility of character. It can sometimes, of course, be as much a matter of what one doesn't find as what one does, that renders a place and a people congenial. Whether by deliberate intention or some lucky chance, Ludgvennok appears to have been released from the influence of those whose rapacity of ambition and disagreeableness of appearance has made life such a trial in the European cities where I have spent my life. Even the ear declares itself to be in a paradise to be free, from the moment one wakes to the moment one lies down – without you, alas, my darling – of that repulsive jumbled blabber, that yodelling cackle, in which elsewhere the ----s make the insistence of their presence felt. Here it is almost as though one has returned to a time of purity, when mankind was able to rejoice in its connection with its natural soil, unspoiled by the jargon of a race that has no passion – no *Leidenschaft*, there is no other word – for the land, for art, for the heroical, or for the rest of humanity.

My darling, I do so wish you could be here with me. Your R

'All very laudable,' Detective Inspector Gutkind conceded. As it happened, he had not only heard of Wagner, a composer beloved of his great-grandfather, but kept a small cache of Wagner memorabilia secreted in his wardrobe in fealty to that passion. He could even hum some of the tunes from his operas and went so far as to hum a few bars of the *Siegfried Idyll* to show Kroplik that he too was a man of culture. Nonetheless, 'All very laudable but I have a particularly savage double murder on my hands, not a few high-spirited drunks kicking nine bells out of another,' was what he said.

'Your point being?' Densdell Kroplik wanted to know. He was irked that the detective inspector had heard of Wagner, let alone that he could hum him. He wanted Wagner for himself.

He was sitting in his favourite chair by the fire. In all weathers a fire burned in the Friendly Fisherman. And on most evenings Densdell Kroplik, steam rising from his thighs, sat by it in a heavy seaman's sweater warming and rubbing his hands. He cultivated a take it or leave it air. He knew what was what. It was up to you whether you wanted to learn from him or not.

'My point being that it gets me nowhere to be told Port Reuben is back to doing what it has always done best.'

Densdell Kroplik shrugged. 'It might,' he said, 'if you understood more about the passion for justice and honour that has always burned in the hearts of the men of these parts.'

'I doubt that a passion for justice and honour had anything to do with the murder of Lowenna Morgenstern and Ythel Weinstock.'

Densdell Kroplik pointed a red, fire-warmed finger at the policeman. 'Is that something you can be sure of?' he said. 'There was a famous five-way murder here about a hundred years ago. Two local women, their husbands, and a lover. Whose lover was he? No one was quite sure. Am I hinting at pederasty? I might be. All that was certain was that he was an aphid – which makes pederasty the more likely. Buggers, the lot of them. From the north or the east of the country, it doesn't matter which. Somewhere that wasn't here. A pact was what the coroner decided it had been, a love pact born of hopeless entanglement. They'd gone up on to the cliff, taken off their clothes, watched the sun go down and swallowed pills. What do you think of that?'

'What I think is that it doesn't help me with my case,' Gutkind said. 'A pact is suicide, not murder.'

'Unless,' Kroplik went on, 'unless the villagers, motivated by justifiable disapproval and an understandable hatred of outsiders, had taken it upon themselves to do away with all five offenders. In which case it wasn't a mass suicide but a mob attack in the name of justice and honour.'

'And it's your theory that the whole village could have done away with Lowenna Morgenstern and Ythel Weinstock?'

'Did I say that? I'm just a barber with an interest

113

in local history. All I know, from reading what I have read and from using these' – he made a two-pronged fork of his fingers and pointed to his all-seeing eyes – 'is that people have been subdued here for a long time. They have a proud history of torrid engagement with one another which has been denied expression. There's no knowing what people might do – singly or in a group – when their natures rebel against repression.'

'Well you might call it torrid engagement, I call it crime.'

'Then that's the difference between us,' Densdell Kroplik laughed.

After which, to show he was a man who could be trusted, he gave the policeman a free haircut, humming all the while Brünnhilde's final plea to Wotan to let her sleep protected by flame from the attentions of any old mortal aphid.

v

Kevern Cohen stayed aloof from the malicious speculations. He had flirted with Lowenna Morgenstern occasionally, when they had both had too much to drink, and more recently he had kissed her in the village car park on bonfire night. He was no snogger. If he kissed a woman it was because he was aroused by the softness of her lips, not because he wanted to wound them. Breaking skin was not, for Kevern, the way he expressed desire.

Lowenna Morgenstern had a wonderful mouth for kissing, deep and mysterious, the musky taste of wood-fire on her busy tongue.

'Kissing you is like kissing flame,' he had said, bending over her. 'You should have been a poet, you,' she told him, biting his neck until the blood trickled on to his shirt collar.

And now someone had killed her. The man found dead beside her could just as easily have been him.

Ailinn picked up on his sombre mood. 'Did you know these people well?' she asked.

'Depends what you mean by well,' he said. 'I knew her to say hello to. Yythel I'd heard of but never met. He was a pub singer. Not from here. Lowenna was reputed to have a taste for musical talent. Her husband Ade is the church organist. A discontented, jeering man. A hundred years ago he and his brothers would have stood on the cliffs with lamps and lured ships on to the rocks. Then he'd have laughed as they looted the wreckage. If he killed his wife he was just carrying on the family tradition.'

'But then if he did,' Ailinn said, 'he's only wrecked himself.'

'Don't we all,' Kevern said.

She stopped to look at him. They were walking arm in arm in the valley in their wellingtons, splashing in puddles. The trickle of water called the River Jordan had swollen to the dimensions of a stream. The trees dripped. It would have been the height of fancy to think of it as nature weeping, but Kevern thought it anyway.

'What do you mean *don't we all*?'

'Did I say that?'

'You did.'

'Then I don't know. I suppose I was feeling the tragedy of what's occurred.'

'But it's not your tragedy.'

'Well it is in a sense. It's my village.'

'*Your village*! That's not how you normally talk about it.'

'No, you're right, I don't. Maybe I'm just being ghoulish – wanting to be part of the excitement.'

'I'm surprised it still excites you. Don't you have a lot of this sort of thing down here?'

'Murders, no. Well, a few. But nothing quite as bloody as this.'

'We have them too . . .' She pointed, comically, over her shoulder as she had done the day he met her. As though she were throwing salt. '. . . Up there, if that's north. People are unhappy.'

'I suppose that was all I meant by saying *don't we all*. That we all end up unhappy. You say yourself you walk in fear of unhappiness every hour.'

'Unhappiness? I walk in fear of being hunted to my death.'

'Well then . . .'

'Well then nothing. It's not the same. The whales know who's coming after them, but they still quietly feed their young. You have to risk it. I am still determined to be happy.'

'I was only quoting your own words back to you. *People are unhappy.*'

She put her hands to his face and pulled at his lips, trying to force his melancholy mouth into a smile. 'But we're not, are we? Us? You and me?'

He let her fashion a smile out of him. His eyes burned with love for her. Part protective love, part desire. She could look dark and fierce sometimes, like a bird of prey, a hunter herself, but at others she appeared as helpless as a little girl, the foundling picked out of a children's home in the back of beyond.

'No,' he agreed. 'We're not unhappy. Not you and me. We are different.'

Yes, they were overdoing this.

Later that week he was asked how well he'd known Lowenna Morgenstern.

CHAPTER 5

CALL ME ISHMAEL

Friday 3rd

Suddenly everyone, and I mean *everyone*, is taking an interest in my man. Have I said that already? Suddenly everyone's taking *even more* of an interest in my man, in that case. I can't pretend I'm comfortable with this upsurge of curiosity. One guards one's subjects jealously, as one guards one's wife or reputation. If there was more they needed to know, why didn't they just ask me? I have a nasty feeling I'm being super-seded, which could mean one of two things: either I'm not up to it, in their estimation, or Kevern Cohen's in trouble too deep for me to fathom. I don't care how this impacts on my good name – I have other fish to fry, when all is said and done – but I'm concerned how Kevern will fare, given all his oddities, without a sympathetic person to keep an eye on him. I like the fellow, as I have said. Whatever is actually going on, it strikes me as cruel that someone so predisposed to paranoia should have all his delusions of persecution and incrimination confirmed. And that's just me I'm talking about . . . Ba boom! as my grandfather would say when he made a bad joke. Back in the days when people liked to make bad jokes. Or any kind of joke, come to that. But to return to me . . . I always liked that silly joke, too, when I was small: 'That's enough of me, so what do you think of me?' . . . but to return *seriously* to me, it's hard to tell how I'm regarded 'upstairs'. Certainly no one has – at least in so many words – called my work into question. But 'something a little more definite and up to date wouldn't go amiss' is not exactly the remark of an examiner about to give me an A++ for effort, is it? Tell us something we don't already know, the expressions on their faces said when I first delivered them the news that he had a girlfriend.

I tapped my nose. 'A *regular* girlfriend.'

To whom his intentions, they enquired, after a long, bored silence, are what? It struck me as an odd question. How did I know what his intentions were? Honourable, I guessed, given the man. I was requested, in no uncertain terms, to do better than *guess*. I happen to believe that an intention is a bit like a predisposition to cancer or dementia – essentially genetic. Honourable father, honourable son. Same the world over, even China. Honolable father, honolable son. But families, strictly speaking, are not my territory. To do parents and grandparents you have to have clearance at the very highest level. Mooching about in public records is not generally encouraged. This is a free society, so long as you don't plan to travel – and people are only prevented from leaving the country (or indeed from entering it) for their own good – so access to everything is in principle available to everyone. But the past – especially when it is particularised: the story of you and me and how we got here, the story of Kevern 'Coco' Cohen and whether or not he has inherited the honolable gene – is itself another country. And when it comes to such a country, the powers that be would rather we did not go there. Say sorry and have done is the wisest course, they believe, and I agree with them. Danger lurks in nostalgia. The slogans printed at the foot of the notepaper on which I write my reports – LET SLEEPING DOGS LIE, THE OVEREXAMINED LIFE IS NOT WORTH LIVING, YESTERDAY IS A LESSON WE CAN LEARN ONLY BY LOOKING TO TOMORROW – are reminders rather than threats. So no measures are taken against anyone who does not heed them. Buildings are not barred to you. Doors are not closed in your face. 'Yes, of course' will be the polite rejoinder to any request you make to inspect certificates of birth or death, or voter lists, or even newspapers dating too far back. But the forms you fill in are never read by anyone. Calls are not returned, applications are lost, the person you were talking to in the morning won't be there in the afternoon. If you decide it is easier to forget about it, you will be met with smiles all round. A bottle of champagne tied with a blue ribbon might even be sent to you in the post, together with a note saying 'Sorry we couldn't help. We tried.' But even without these precautions, the consequence of OPERATION ISHMAEL – that great beneficent name change to which the people ultimately gave their wholehearted consent – is that tracing lineage is not only as good as impossible, it is unnecessary. We are all one big happy family now. Zermanskys, Cohens, Rosenthals (that's the head of the academy: Eoghan Rosenthal), Feigenblats (Rozenwyn Feigenblat is the college librarian, and something of a looker I must say) – we acknowledge a kinship which we all tacitly know to be artificial but which works. Apply this simple test: when was the last time anyone was picked on for his name? Precisely. 'We are all Edward Everett Phineas Zermansky!' my students would

121

shout were anyone to persecute me for whatever reason.

We are all Eoghan Rosenthal!

We are all Kevern Cohen!

We are all Lowenna Morgenstern, God save her soul – or at least we were.

If there is anyone alive who is old enough to have an inkling what his parents were called before OPERATION ISHMAEL he will wisely not remember it.

I have heard tell, or at least I have read, that – after an initial period of understand-able reluctance, or misapprehension as I would rather think of it – the renaming turned into a month-long street party, young and old dancing with one another in the parks, strangers embracing, people saying goodbye to their old names as they waited for the official documents that would apprise them of their new. A few lucky ones won the right by televised lottery to choose their own from an approved list. But whether they chose or they were given, people entered into the spirit of the change. It was as though they'd been hypnotised. 'You will sleep,' they were told, 'you will fall into a deep carnivalesque sleep wherein you will dance and make merry. At the count of ten you will awake and while you will remember who you were, you will not remember what you were called. One, two . . .' Not literally that, but similar. A moral hypnosis. For our own good. And as with private memories, so with public records: they have been wiped clean. It is sometimes argued, in lowered voices, that if we can't be sure about our neighbours' antecedents, we expose ourselves to . . .

To what? Alien influences?

Well, it was precisely in order to ensure that such a phrase would never be heard again (and I confess I'm as guilty as any other red-blooded patriot when it comes to itching every now and then to use it) that operation ishmael was instituted. It granted a universal amnesty, dispensing once and for all with invidious distinctions between the doers and the done-to. Time must close over the events, and there is no better way to ensure that than to bring everyone together retroactively. Now that we are one family, and cannot remember when we were anything else, there can be no question of a repetition of whatever happened, if it did, because there is no one left to do to again whatever was or wasn't done.

We are all Rozenwyn Feigenblat!

(We are all at least – I confide to you, dear diary – dying for a piece of her . . .)

While no one is listening, allow me to admit that it took a certain ruthlessness to bring us to this point of unanimity. I neither condemn WHAT HAPPENED nor condone it. Let the fact that I was not yet born prove my impartiality. But it needs to be said that we were not alone in our perplexity. What to do with those about whom something needed to be done; how to put a brake on their ambitions; how to express our displeasure with their foreign policy (bizarre that they should have had a foreign policy given that they were foreigners themselves and had what they called a country only by taking someone else's); how to make safe again a world they'd gravely endangered with their migrations, military occupations, and finally weapons of mass destruction – this was something every other civilised country had to make up its mind about, and it is not without some backward-looking pride that I say we made up ours before anybody else. For which credit must go to my fellow professionals – vice chancellors of conscience-stricken universities and professors of the benign arts, painters, writers, actors, journalists, junior untenured academic staff, without whom the campaign to drive them from the face of the earth, to make of them vaga-bonds and fugitives, a pariah people cursed in every mouth, would not have been conducted in so civilised a manner.

Was there mob violence? I wasn't there, but such a thing does not accord with the view I entertain of this most moderate of countries, home to lyric poets and painters of serene and timeless landscapes. That gross expostulatory rhetoric that has normalised brutality and supremacism in other countries has never disfigured our speech. We do not smudge our canvases in rage. We do not saw at our violins. Whether or not that class of individuals who are the first to throw stones and start fires enjoyed direct acquaintance with the lyric poetry and landscape painting to which they are heirs is immaterial. The effect filtered down to them in language and the habits of contemplation. All of which assures me that, no, there could not have been barbarity. Just the gentle pressure that civilisation itself can exert, the articulated outrage of cultivated people who would not themselves have countenanced, least of all encouraged, inhumanity. Why would they, with so many of the exalted tasks of culture to perform – paintings to finish, lines to learn, lectures to prepare – choose to whip the multitude into acts of ferocity inimical to their own temperaments? Where, apart from any other consideration would they have found the time for it?

'Oh, there's always time,' Rozenwyn Feigenblat bolshily remarked once, when we happened to fall into conversation on this very subject.

I took that to mean that as librarian she knew how much sitting about staring into space we professors and painters are capable of. But then a librarian is not an artist; in her capacity as a filer and notator she will not have grasped the contribution that apparent indolence makes to the creative act.

For an artist, my dear, I wanted to say, to be unoccupied is sacred. What might look like doing nothing is in fact the long wait for beauty to find us. But I could see how that might be misinterpreted. 'If you mean that we sometimes appear bored,' I began instead . . .

She shook her pretty head. 'I'm not talking about boredom,' she said. 'I'm talking about mischief.'

She made it sound like pranks.

'Sexual mischief?' I asked, not wanting to sound too curious.

'Intellectual mischief.'

Not being sure I could trust myself longer in her alluring presence, I let it go at that. Though she left me feeling she had more to say.

What she also left me feeling was that someone should be keeping an eye on her. A position for which, were it vacant, I'd think hard about applying.

126

But back to Kevern Cohen. What it came down to for me, at least, was that the only reliable way of uncovering Kevern Cohen's intentions vis-à-vis his new sweetheart – short of asking him outright, and I wasn't prepared to do that – was to observe him at close quarters. To which end I invited the lovebirds over for dinner. It would be on his day for visiting the college and I suggested, since he'd mentioned her, that he bring Ailinn down with him, which he was wary of doing to begin with – wariness being his first response to everything – but on discussing it with her he changed his mind. No doubt she wanted to meet his friends, of whom he has few and I can just about be counted one. A half-friend, say. A well-wisher, anyway. An extravagantly beautiful woman, Ailinn, with a tumult of dark hair, like charred straw, and darting, watchful, hawk-like features. She called to mind a seirene, one of those bird women who are painted attacking Odysseus and his crew on vases I have inspected in the National Museum. I am not thinking of the most familiar image, which shows a seirene swooping head first at the ship, her talons at the ready, but rather one of the more serenely musical temptresses, striking her drum or plucking at her harp, surprised, if anything, that Odysseus should want to resist. As Kevern plainly didn't.

'Besotted' was the word my wife and I hit on quite separately, though Demelza did accuse me of stealing it from her.

Ailinn brought us a delicate bouquet of her paper flowers. 'Kitsch, I know,' she said, 'but I make them and could find no fresh flowers in the shops.'

I appreciated the thought and the apology. It must have been difficult for her, taste-wise, visiting the house of a professor of the Benign Visual Arts. I told her they were lovely and pretended to smell them. 'Haven't seen you so skittish in a long while,' Demelza said to me as we were making coffee in the kitchen. 'A pretty face and you go as soppy as Petroc.'

Petroc was our Labrador. Petroc Rothschild . . .

Not really, that was just our little off-colour joke . . .

'I am happy for them in their happiness,' was my reply. She pinched my arm. I let out a little cry. 'What's that for?' 'You know what that's for. Being happy for *them* in *their* happiness. Liar! Why don't you just lick her face?' 'Bitch!' I said. 'Prick!' was her retort.

That night, over an acrimonious nightcap of Benedictine and brandy, we discussed divorce. Discussion had always been something we were good at. You could say it was the glue of our conjugality.

Before they left, Ailinn did say one thing that struck me as surprising. 'Sometimes,' she mused, in answer to my asking how she found it down here, 'this part of the country seems full of eyes.'

'Eyes?'

'Watching eyes.'

'Really?' I said, opening my face to her. 'How do you mean?'

Kevern, too, appeared taken aback by her words. 'I don't know,' she said. 'Something about the way they look at you here. It's not disapproval exactly. It's not even suspicion. It's more as though they're waiting for you to make a mistake or show your real nature.'

'Isn't that just because these communities were cut off from the rest of the country for so long?' I said. 'I feel they look at me like that too. They say you have to have lived here for ten generations before they begin to relax with you.'

'I don't want them to relax with me. I'm not looking for friendship,' she said. 'It's the sense you get that someone's always on your heels. Not following you – just *there*. Waiting for you to give yourself away.'

I noted that for later speculation. *Give yourself away*, eh, young lady. So what are you concealing?

Petroc Rothschild must have asked himself the same question because he did not take at all kindly to her, barking when she changed her position too abruptly, and growling most of the time she talked. But then he'd never been overfond of Kevern either.

I enquired whether what she was describing was a recent phenomenon.

'Being here is a recent phenomenon – for me.'

'Of course, of course. I meant did you notice it at once or are you just noticing it now? Has there been a change.'

'I haven't been here long enough to make such fine distinctions,' she reminded me, somewhat sternly, which made me somewhat excited. I like sternness in a woman. Hence Demelza. 'But if you ask me to think about it,' she went on, 'then no, I have not just begun to notice a sense of – I don't know what to call it – *intrusiveness*. Take us' – she put her hand on Kevern's – 'we didn't just meet, we were bundled into each other's arms. Not that I'm complaining about that.'

'I should hope not,' Kevern said, kissing her.

Sweet, but I was more interested, I have to say, in Ailinn's sense of being, as she put it, 'bundled'. Professionally interested.

'So who bundled you?' I asked, but

casually, as though I were merely making polite conversation.

'God knows. Some busybody? The village matchmaker? Nobody I'd ever seen before, or since. I don't know if you've seen him again, Kevern.'

He hadn't.

I asked Kevern if he too felt he'd been pushed into meeting Ailinn. He couldn't of course say yes. He had to say he saw her and was smitten. But yes, now we came to mention it, there had been someone hanging around, egging him on. For which, accompanied by another burning look deep into Ailinn's eyes, he was immeasurably grateful.

Petroc growled so loudly that Ailinn started.

'He doesn't mean you any harm,' I assured her.

'I think he does,' she said.

'You don't like dogs?'

'No, not as a rule. We are as one on this.'

'You and the dog?'

'Me and Kevern.'

I told Kevern that I hadn't on his previous visits noticed he was a dog hater, though I kept to myself my conviction that Petroc hated him.

'I'm not. Just not a dog lover. Or at least not inside the house.'

'Are dogs different inside to out?'

'No but I am.'

Concerned that his curtness of manner might offend me – unless she was concerned it might offend Petroc – Ailinn explained him. 'He doesn't like things moving around his legs,' she laughed. 'Not indoors, anyway.'

'That will make it difficult with children,' I observed.

'Impossible,' they said with some vehemence together. 'Quite impossible.'

I am not without subtlety when it comes to reading behind the words people speak. Why the vehemence, I wondered.

'You don't want children?' I asked, casually. I had the feeling they had not talked it over. But I could have been mistaken.

Kevern, anyway, shook his head. 'I am content to be the end of my line,' he said.

'In this, too,' Ailinn added, 'we are as one.'

I didn't, for what it's worth, believe her. Methinks the lady doth protest too much, methought.

Wherever they were on this subject, I considered it worth noting in my report that Kevern 'Coco' Cohen and Ailinn Solomons shared a detestation of dogs.

I would have bet good money against the powers that be knowing *that*.

CHAPTER 6

AN INSPECTOR CALLS

i

Somebody had seen Kevern kissing Lowenna Morgenstern in the car park on bonfire night.

'That shouldn't make me a suspect,' Kevern told Detective Inspector Gutkind. 'If there's a jealous homicidal maniac on the loose that should make me a potential victim.'

'Unless the jealous homicidal maniac on the loose is you.'

'I'm not on the loose.'

'But you have been on the loose, haven't you? No ties, no responsibilities, free to kiss whoever you like.'

Kevern had never before been presented with such a dashing portrait of his life.

'I'm a bachelor, if that's what you mean. Though I am in a serious relationship at the moment.'

'At the moment? How long have you been in this serious relationship?'

'Three months.'

'And that amounts to serious for you?'

133

'Sacred.'

'Were you in a sacred relationship with Mrs Morgenstern?'

'I don't think a single kiss constitutes a relationship.'

'What would you say it constitutes?'

'A passing thrill.'

'You were aware she was married when you kissed her?'

'I was.'

The policeman waited. '. . . And you had no qualms about that?'

'Not my business. She felt like a kiss, I felt like a kiss.'

'You don't respect marriage?'

'I think it was more that Mrs Morgenstern didn't respect hers. I didn't see it as my job to remember her vows for her.'

'So knowing she wasn't happily married, you took advantage.'

'I don't think, Detective Inspector Grossman—'

'Gutkind.'

'I don't think, Detective Inspector Gutkind, that you can call it taking advantage. You could just as easily say she was taking advantage of my loneliness. But no one was taking advantage of anyone. As I have said – she'd had a few too many tequilas, I'd had a few too many sweet ciders—'

'Sweet cider!' Detective Inspector Gutkind pulled a face.

'And maybe the odd half of lager shandy. I'm sorry if lager shandy disgusts you too.'

'Go on.'

'There's nowhere to go. That's it. She was drunk, I was not entirely sober, she felt like a kiss, I felt like a kiss . . .'

'And whatever you feel like doing, you do?'

Kevern laughed. If only, he thought. 'I think you have a somewhat false picture of me,' he said. 'The clue is in the sweet cider. I am not a man who has a relaxed attitude to pleasure. As a matter of fact, I am not a man who has a relaxed attitude to anything. I have a very unrelaxed attitude, for example, to your being in my house.'

It occurred to him that the picture he was painting was more likely to incriminate him than otherwise. A difficult and lonely neurotic, who laughed where laughter was inappropriate, drank pussy drinks, and was prone to introspection and self-disgust – didn't all murderers fit that bill? And now he was telling the policeman that his presence, here, on the sofa in Kevern's cottage, made him uneasy. Why didn't he just confess to the crime?

'Why do you have an unrelaxed attitude to me being here?' the policeman asked.

'Why do you think? No one likes to be questioned by the police. No one likes to be under suspicion.'

'But you specifically mentioned *your house*. What is it about being questioned specifically in *your house* that upsets you?'

'I'm a very private man.'

'But not so private that you draw the line at kissing other men's wives?'

'I never brought her here.'

'Because?'

'I'm a very private man.'

'And very unrelaxed about a number of things. Did you have an unrelaxed attitude to Mrs Morgenstern's other lovers?'

'I wasn't aware of other lovers.'

'You thought you were special, did you?'

'No. She was known to be free and easy. Nor was I her lover. I didn't think of myself that way.'

'Was that because she repulsed you?'

Kevern laughed. Had he been repulsed? He remembered the bite. It hadn't felt like a repulse.

'It was bonfire night. A few fireworks went off. So did we. It was fun while it lasted.'

'Did you see her go home with Ythel Weinstock that night?'

'I did not.'

'Were you aware that Mrs Morgenstern and Ythel Weinstock were lovers?'

'I was not.'

'Were you aware that he hit her?'

'How could I have been? I didn't know they were intimate.'

'Were you aware that her husband was hitting her?'

'It's something that happens in the village. I wasn't aware of it but I am not surprised. Life in Port Reuben has always been harsh. But now on

136

top of the old cruelties there's frustration. Men are living at the edge of their nerves here. They don't know what they're for. They used to be wreckers, now they run gift shops and say they're sorry. The women goad them. I read that the rest of the country is not much better.'

Worse and worse: now he was painting himself as a moral zealot.

He needn't have worried. Detective Inspector Gutkind also had a dash of moral zealotry in his nature. He believed in conspiracies. It was not permitted to believe in conspiracies (no written law against, of course) but Gutkind couldn't help himself. Conspiracy theorising ran in families and his father had believed in them to the point where he could see nothing else. Gutkind's grandfather had also believed in conspiracies and had lost his job in the newly formed agency Ofnow attempting to root them out. That attempting to root out conspiracies had cost him his job proved there was a conspiracy against him. And behind him was Clarence Worthing, the Wagnerian, Gutkind's great-grandfather who had tasted betrayal to the lees. He fed his resentments and suspicions to his son who fed them to his son who fed them, nicely incubated, to Gutkind. For as far back as the family went, somebody, some group, had been out to get them. Heirlooms in their own way, just as silk Chinese rugs were, romances of family persecution at the hands of conspirators were restricted. It didn't do for any family to be harbouring too many, or indeed any one with too much fervour. Conspiracy theories had fed the suspicion that erupted into that for which society was still having to say sorry. And how could you say sorry when some of the reasoning behind WHAT HAPPENED, IF IT HAPPENED – that conspiracies were sucking the life blood from the nation – remained compelling?

Detective Inspector Gutkind understood why there could be no going backwards in this – and was, anyway, unable to point the finger anywhere but at the odd individual malfeasant, and by its nature individual malfeasance could not amount to conspiracy – but he was a prisoner of his upbringing. He had a careworn build – dapper, the unobservant thought him – lean as though from fretting, with a round face, apoplectic eyes and an unexpectedly wet, cherubic mouth. Had there been a conspiracy to accuse Gutkind of the pederasty that exercised Densdell Kroplik, his mouth would surely have been the basis for it. He looked like someone who pressed his lips where they had no business being pressed.

He smiled at Kevern and wondered if he might be allowed to remove his coat. Kevern could not conceal his awkwardness. It was bad enough that Gutkind was here at all, but a Gutkind without his coat, in his cottage, was more than his nerves could bear. 'Of course,' he said, taking the coat and then not knowing what to do with it, 'that's rude of me.'

He was surprised to see that under his coat Gutkind wore not a jacket but a Fair Isle buttoned cardigan.

Was this to relax the unwary, Kevern wondered. But if that was so, his eyes should have not have looked so combustible as they took in Kevern's person and darted around Kevern's room.

'This Biedermeier?' he asked, running his fingers over the elaborately carved back of the sofa.

Kevern started. 'Imitation,' he said.

'Made down here?'

'Kildromy.'

'That's a long way to go for it.'

'I like the best. I'm a woodworker myself. I appreciate good craftsmanship.'

'It doesn't really go with this cottage, though, does it,' Gutkind went on.

Kevern wanted to say that he didn't think the policeman's cardigan went with his job, but it didn't seem a good idea to antagonise him further. 'It goes with my temperament,' he said.

'And how would you describe that?'

'My temperament? Heavy, ornate and unwelcoming.'

'And out of place?'

'If you like.'

'Would you call yourself a loner?'

'I wouldn't call myself anything. I'm a woodturner, as I think I've told you.'

'Business good?'

'I make candlesticks and lovespoons for the

tourist industry. There isn't a fortune in that, but I get by.'

'Why have local people given you the nickname "Coco"?'

'You'd better ask them. But I think it's ironic. "Coco" was the name of a famous circus clown. It must be evident to you that I am not an entertainer.'

'But you entertain women?'

Here we go again, Kevern thought. He sighed and walked to the window. Not knowing what else to do with it, he was still carrying Gutkind's coat over his arm. Though the sea didn't look wild, the blowhole was busy, fine spray from the great white jet of water catching what there was of sunlight. He thought of Ailinn's whale and suddenly felt weary. 'Get the fuck out,' he wanted to tell the policeman. 'Get the fuck out of my house.' If ever there was a time to let go, let rip, let the bad language out of his constricted system, this was it. But he was who he was. Let's get this over with, he thought. 'Is this about the blood?' he asked, not turning his head.

'What blood is that?'

'My blood. Lowenna Morgenstern bit me the night we kissed after the fireworks. She bit me hard. I don't doubt I was seen afterwards with blood on my shirt. I assume that's why you wanted to talk to me.'

'You don't still have that shirt, do you?'

'Well I must have because I haven't thrown any shirt away in a long time. But I'd be hard pressed to remember which shirt I was wearing that night. And whichever it was, it will have been laundered many times since then.'

Gutkind made a perfect cupid's bow of his transgressive lips. He knew why men washed their shirts.

'Oh, come on, Goldberg—'

'Gutkind.'

Goldberg/Gutkind, Kevern wanted to say, *who gives a damn* . . .

'Oh come on,' he said instead, 'you're not telling me that laundering my shirts indicates suspicious behaviour?'

'It could be if it was Mrs Morgenstern's blood and not yours.'

'Aha, and if, having got a taste of spilling her blood once, I couldn't wait to spill it again.'

'Well that's a theory, Mr Cohen, and I will give it consideration. But to be honest with you it's not Mrs Morgenstern's blood that concerns us right now.'

'So whose is it?'

'Mr Morgenstern's.'

'Ah, well I'm glad he's back in the picture. The village gossip mill has had him down as the murderer from day one. He's already been found guilty and sentenced at the bar of the Friendly Fisherman. All you had to do was find him.'

'You misunderstand. It's not Mr Morgenstern's blood at the crime scene I'm talking about. It's Mr Morgenstern's blood all over Mr Morgenstern.'

Kevern shrugged a shrug of only half-surprise. 'That makes it easier for everyone then, doesn't it?

Husband kills wife and lover and then kills himself. Case closed. Why are you speaking to me?'

'If only it were as simple as that. It would appear that Mr Morgenstern didn't die by his own hand.'

'What!'

'As you say yourself, Mr Cohen, there's a lot of anger and frustration out there.'

'You're telling me Ade Morgenstern's been murdered now?'

'Well if he didn't do it to himself – which given the manner of his death he couldn't – and if it wasn't natural causes – which it wasn't – and if we rule out the hand of God – which I think we must – that's the only supposition I can make.'

Kevern Cohen shook his head. He couldn't quite muster horror or even profound shock, but he mustered what he could. 'Christ, what's going on in this village?'

Detective Inspector Gutkind showed Kevern a philosophic expression. As though to say, well isn't that precisely what I hoped you might be able to answer.

He didn't write this in his report, but what Detective Inspector Gutkind felt in his heart was this: 'Something smells. Maybe not this, but something.'

ii

Kevern thought he'd better prepare Ailinn for what she might hear. He had, some months before they'd met, he mustered the honour to tell her, kissed the murdered woman. He knew not to say it was nothing. He couldn't have it both ways: if he boasted he was no citizen of Snogland, then he couldn't claim a kiss was nothing. Besides, women didn't like to hear men say that things they did with their bodies and which ought to involve their emotions were nothing. If it was nothing then why do it; and if it was something then don't lie about it. But it wasn't a long kiss and if he hadn't thought about it much the day after – he wasn't going to claim he hadn't thought about it at all – he certainly hadn't thought about it since he'd been with Ailinn who drove all trace of memory of other kisses from his mind.

She was disappointed in him. Not angry. Just disappointed. Which was worse.

'I'm sorry,' he said, 'if I've made you jealous.'

'*Jealous*?'

'I don't mean jealous.'

'What do you mean?'

What did he mean? 'You know,' he said.

'Was there something between you I should be jealous of?'

'No, no.' Here it came – in that case why did he bother to kiss her . . .

'What I feel,' she said, letting him off, 'is that it would have been nice to go on thinking of you as a man who doesn't throw kisses around. Who respects himself or at least his mouth more.'

Kevern tried to think of any man he knew who respected his mouth.

'Well it was no disrespect to you,' he said. 'I hadn't met you. Unless you believe one can demean a person in retrospect.'

She thought about it for longer than he would have liked. 'No, no it doesn't demean me in retrospect,' she said at last. 'It demeans you, which reflects on me, and it takes a little from my fantasy . . . but that was always just girlish nonsense anyway. So no, yes, I'm all right about it, and I thank you for being honest with me.'

Kevern felt he'd been kicked in the stomach. She was no/yes/noing him. Yes, no, she was *all right about it*, which was the language of compromise and disillusionment. And he had shattered her fantasy, which meant her hope to live a life above the common. He had brought her low with his honesty – honesty being the kindest yes/no word she could find for his being a man like every other.

A man like Ahab, even. Demoniacally hell-bent on her unhappiness by simple virtue of his being a man. Except that he wasn't. Yes/no.

He asked her to make love to him, on his bed with the sheets thrown back and the windows open, not to remove all trace of Lowenna Morgenstern's kisses from his lips, but to remove all trace of this conversation. She shook her head. It didn't quite work like that for her. In the open air then. On the cliffs. In Paradise Valley. Let Nature do the job. But she wasn't quite in the mood for that either.

She would walk with him, though. A long bracing walk where they could talk about something else. Look beyond them. Not talk about themselves at all. 'We are a bit in each other's heads,' she said.

He knew what she meant but the last thing he wanted to do was walk her out of his.

They walked well together, he thought. Which was a sign of their compatibility. They were always in step. When one put out a hand the other found it immediately. They stopped to look at the same flowers or to admire the same picturesque cottage. They stooped in unison to stroke a cat or pick up litter. Neither started to speak before the other had quite finished, or at the very moment that the other began a sentence. They talked side by side, like instruments in an orchestra. This wasn't only good manners; it was an instinctive compatibility. Their hearts beat to an identical rhythm.

Had his incestuous parents felt like this at the beginning, he wondered.

He laughed, suddenly, for no reason. Threw back his head and laughed at the sky. She didn't ask him why, she simply threw back her head and did the same. A minute later she seized him by the arm and made him look at her. 'This is very dangerous,' she said.

'You think I don't know that?' was his reply.

He proposed a trip away, a few days' holiday from this degrading village. Gutkind had not asked him to stay put, so he believed he was no more a suspect than all the other men in the county Lowenna Morgenstern had kissed. He was more worried about what the policeman might write in his report about the furniture.

They would pack a couple of bags, drive north, find a city where people didn't know them and weren't murdering one another, stay in a nice hotel that had no view of the sea, go to a couple of restaurants, maybe take in a film, reconnect with each other after the Morgenstern business, no matter that they hadn't come apart over it. Ailinn was surprised to discover he owned a car, which he kept under tarpaulin in the public car park. He had never struck her as a car person. Once she saw him drive she realised she was right. 'You drive so slowly,' she said, 'how do you ever get anywhere?'

'Where is there to get?'

'Wherever it is we're going.'

He hadn't told her. He wanted it to be a surprise. To both of them.

'Let's just drive,' he said, 'and stop when we're tired.'

'I'm tired.'

'Already?'

'I'm tired in anticipation.'

Was this, he wondered, a play on his having been unfaithful to her in retrospect?

He stopped the car and looked at her.

She had a suggestion. 'Let me drive. At least that way we'll arrive somewhere.'

He was worried that she hadn't driven in a while, that she didn't know the roads down here, that she wasn't familiar with the vehicle, that she hadn't studied the manual.

'A car's a car, Kevern!'

Fine by Kevern. He pulled on the hand brake, turned off the engine, and changed seats with her. Not being a car person was one of the ways he had always defined his anomalous masculinity. The men of Port Reuben wanted to kill in their cars; they accelerated when they saw a pedestrian, they revved the engines for the pure aggression of it even when their cars were parked in their garages. Then on Sundays they soaped them as though they were their whores. If they reserved such attention for their cars it was no surprise, Kevern thought, that their wives, the moment they had a drink inside them, were eager to kiss him, a man careless of cars.

Ailinn drove so fast he had to close his eyes.

'Anyone would think Ahab's tailing us,' he said.

'Ahab *is* tailing us,' she told him. 'Ahab's always tailing us. That's what Ahab does.'

It seemed to excite her.

'Couldn't we, on this occasion at least, just let him overtake us?'

She pushed her foot harder on the accelerator and wound down the window, letting the wind make her hair fly. 'Where's your sense of adventure?' she asked.

147

Questions, questions. . . Why so many feathers among the splintered furniture and ripped clothes, the broken toys, the smashed plates and fragments of glass, the bricks, the window frames, the pages torn from books holy and profane? Feathers from the mattresses hurled from upper windows, of course, but there are sufficient feathers in this single ruined garden to fill a mattress for every rioter in the city to enjoy the sleep of the righteous on. One feather won't lie still. It curls, tickling itself, tries to float away but something sticky holds it to the child's coat to which it has become attached. And where have all the hooks and crowbars appeared from? If the riots broke out spontaneously, how is it that these weapons were so plentifully to hand? Do the citizens of K sleep with crowbars by their beds? They bring them down with gusto, however they came by them, on the head of a man whom others have previously rolled in a ditch of mud and blood and feathers. A ritual bath. They rolled him and then wrung him out like a rag. The sounds of bones cracking and cries for help mingle with the furious triumphant shouts of murderers and the laughter of onlookers. Which prompts another question: when is wringing a man out like a rag funny?

CHAPTER 7

CLARENCE WORTHING

i

All was not well about the heart of Detective Inspector Gofuckyourself. (It wasn't to be supposed he hadn't registered Kevern Cohen's unspoken contempt. He had good ears. He could pick up an unspoken insult from three counties away. So face to face, and knowing nothing of the other's squeamishness in the matter of obscenities, he was hardly likely to have missed what Kevern wished he would do to himself.)

He was overworked – that contributed to his malaise. In his lifetime, at least, the county had never seen so much serious crime. Murders, attempted murders, robberies with violence, infidelity with violence, a seething resentment of somebody or something that issued in behaviour it was difficult to quantify but which he described to himself as a breakdown of respect, in particular a breakdown of respect to him.

He had his theories about the underlying causes but knew to keep them under his hat.

Home for Gutkind was a small end-of-terrace

house in St Eber, an inland town built around the county's most important china-clay pit. A white dust had long ago settled on every building in St Eber, giving it, though entirely flat and shapeless, an Alpine aspect that the few visitors to the area had always found attractive. Gutkind's cat Luther, who had been spayed and so had little else to do – 'Like me,' Gutkind sometimes thought – rolled around in this dust from morning to night, going from garden to garden to find more. He would be waiting for the detective inspector when he arrived home, his coat powdered as though with icing sugar, his eyelashes as pale as an albino's, even his tongue white. Gutkind, who had no one else to love, sat him on a newspaper in the kitchen and brushed him down roughly, though he knew that he would be out rolling in someone's garden again as soon as he had eaten. As with the cat, so with the man. Gutkind showered twice a day, more often than that at weekends when he was home, watching the particles almost reconstitute themselves into clay as they vanished in a grubby whirlpool down the plughole. It was a form of recycling, Gutkind thought, the clay that had coated his hair and skin returning to its original constituency underground. Otherwise he was not a recycling man. Too many of society's ills were the result of the wrong sort of people with the wrong sort of beliefs finding ways of recycling themselves, no matter how much effort went into their disposal.

Disposal? Detective Inspector Gutkind was not a brute but he believed in calling a spade a spade.

And he was not, in the privacy of his own home, however dusty, a man to say he was sorry.

He had no wife. He had had a wife once, but she had left him soon after they were married. The china clay was one reason she left him, and Gutkind had no desire to move (having to shower so many times a day confirmed his sense of what was wrong with the world), but the other reason she left him was his sense of what was wrong with the world. She discovered for herself what many of her friends had told her – though she hadn't listened at the time – that life with a man who saw conspiracies everywhere was insupportable. 'It's your friends who have put you up to this,' he said as he watched her packing her bags. She shook her head. 'It's your family, then.' 'Why can't it just be *me*, Eugene?' she asked. 'Why can't it be *my* decision?' But he was unable to understand what she was getting at.

Returning home after interviewing Kevern Cohen – yet another person who showed him scant respect – Detective Inspector Gutkind showered, brushed down his cat, showered again, and heated up a tin of beans. He felt more than usually miffed. If I could put my finger on something, he told himself, just *something*, I would feel a damned sight better. But whether he meant put his finger on the motivation of a crime, the name of a criminal, why everything was so twisted from its purpose, why his life was so dusty and lonely, why he hated his cat, he couldn't have said.

He had to have someone to blame. He was not unusual in that. What divided *Homo sapiens* from brute creation was the need to apportion responsibility. If a lion went hungry or a chimpanzee could not find a mate, it was no one's fault. But from the dawn of time man had been blaming the climate, the terrain, fate, the gods, some other tribe or just some other person. To be a man, as distinct from being a chimpanzee, was to be forever at the mercy of a supernatural entity, a force, a being or a collection of beings, whose only function was to make your life on earth unbearable. And wasn't this the secret of man's success: that in chasing dissatisfaction down to its malignant cause he had hit upon the principle, first of religion and then of progress? What was evolution – what was revolution – but the logic of blame in action? What was the pursuit of justice but punishment of the blameworthy?

And who were the most blameworthy of all? Those whom you had loved.

When the sentimental blaming mood was on him – and tonight it roared in his ears the way the sea beside which you had once walked with a lover roared in a treasured seashell – he would climb the stairs to his attic, open an old wardrobe in which he stored clothes he no longer wore but for some reason could not bear to throw away, and pull out a faded periodical or two from the dozen or so which hung there on newspaper sticks, exactly as they had once hung in metropolitan cafés of the sort sophisticated town-bred men and women once patronised in order to drink coffee, eat pastries, and stay up to date with prejudiced opinion. Given that Gutkind kept these periodicals because they contained extended ruminations penned by his great-grandfather, Clarence Worthing, they were, strictly speaking, heirlooms, and exceeded the number of heirlooms – though no one knew exactly what that number was – any one person was permitted to keep. Not being a law exactly, this was not rigorously policed; everyone kept more than they admitted they kept, but, as a detective inspector, Gutkind knew he was taking a bit of a risk and indeed much relished taking it.

He had always dipped intermittently into these publications, enjoying picking up his great-grandfather's thoughts at random, not least because Clarence Worthing had been a cut above the rest of the family, a self-taught thinker and self-bred dandy who had moved in circles of society un-imaginable to Eugene Gutkind. He had never met his great-grandfather but had heard tell of him from his grandmother, Clarence Worthing's daughter, something of a lady herself, and a bohemian to boot, who revelled in the fact that she had hardly ever seen her father, so tied up was he in his affairs – in all senses of the word, if Eugene knew what she meant – a whirl of feckless forget-fulness which she put down to his having been rejected as a young man by the only woman he had ever truly loved – a woman who was not her mother. Eugene marvelled that she was not hurt by this. You could not be hurt by such a man, she told him, so stylish was he even when he let you down. Gutkind yearned to have let someone down stylishly. Taking out the newspapers he bathed in the glorious retrospective reflection of his great-grandfather's irresponsibility . . . and pain. By means of Clarence Worthing, Gutkind too became a person to be reckoned with – a man with a tragic past and a liquid way with words and women.

Over and above this he liked reading the Worthing papers for the clarity of their reasoning and on that account read them, again and again, chronologically and therefore, he surmised, systematically. One train of thought in particular engrossed his attention because it seemed to explain something that was crying out for explanation. And tonight Gutkind was of a mood to peruse it again. In the course of it – an extended essay entitled *When Blood Is Thicker Than Water* – his great-grandfather sought to lay the blame for everything he thought wrong with the world, from the moral, political, ethical and even theological points of view, on 'those' who cultivated a double allegiance which was plain for everybody to see but which good manners forced society to turn a blind eye to. In fact, the phrase 'double allegiance' let them off too easily, he argued, for the question had to be asked whether they considered they owed any sort

155

of genuine allegiance to this, or any country in which they'd found themselves, at all.

Or any sort of allegiance to *him*, Gutkind surmised. He didn't mind that his great-grandfather's reasoning reeked of the ad feminam. How else do you measure a great wrong unless you have been on the receiving end of it? If his great-grandfather proceeded from a position of profound personal disappointment – betrayal even – that made his arguments only the more persuasive to Detective Inspector Gutkind.

'Observe their cohabiting customs,' Gutkind's great-grandfather wrote, 'observe them as a scientist might observe the mating habits of white mice, and you will see that however far outside the swarm they wander to satisfy their appetites, for purposes of procreation they invariably regroup. They choose their mistresses and lovers from those for whom they feel neither respect nor compassion and their wives and husbands from their own ranks. As is often reported by innocents who encounter them without knowing by what rules they live, they can be companionable, amusing, even adorable, and in some circumstances, especially where reciprocal favours are looked for, munificent. But this to them is no more than play, the exercise of their undeniable powers and charm for the mere sadistic fun of it. Thereafter their loyalty is solely to each other. Let one of their number suffer and their vengefulness knows no limits; let one of their number perish and they will make the planet quake for it. To some, this is taken to be the proof of the steadfastness of their tribal life, the respect and affection they have been brought up, over many generations, to show to one another. But it is in fact a manifestation of a sense of superiority that values the life of anyone not belonging to their "tribe" at less than nothing. Only witness, in that country which they call their ancestral home (but which few of them except the most desperate appear to be in any hurry to repair to), a recent exchange of prisoners with one of their many enemies in which, for the sake of a single one of their own – just *one* – they willingly handed over in excess of seven hundred! The mathematics make a telling point. Never, in the history of humanity, has one people held all others in such contempt, or been more convinced that the world can, and will, be organised for their benefit alone. It has been said that were the earth to be laid waste, so long as not a single hair of one of theirs was harmed, they would connive in that destruction. That is not a justification for *their* destruction, though others argue persuasively for it. But it does invite us to ask how much longer we can tolerate their uncurbed presence.'

Gutkind so admired the adamantine and yet heartfelt quality of his great-grandfather's prose that he was at a loss to understand why there had been no published collection of his articles or, come to that, why he had not cut a dash in parliamentary politics. Had his notorious social life taken up too much of his time, or were his words too prophetic for the age he lived in? Gutkind knew for himself what it was to be unappreciated and felt for his great-grandfather's sorrows a scalding agony which there was no warrant to suppose Clarence Worthing ever felt himself.

Part of what Gutkind admired about Worthing's work was its conscientious refinement of argument from one article to the next. The refusal of all talk of destruction with which one essay ended, for example, was picked up again in the next with an allusion to 'self-destruction', that being the course on which 'the arrogant, the forward and the vain', as he called them, appeared, paradoxically, to be hell-bent. 'Some worm of divisiveness in their own souls has impelled them – throughout history, as though they knew history itself was against them – to the brink of self-destruction. Imaginatively, the story of their annihilation engrosses them; let them enjoy a period of peace and they conjure war, let them enjoy a period of regard and they conjure hate. They dream of their decimation as hungry men dream of banquets. What their heated brains cannot conceive, their inhuman behaviour invites. "Kill us, kill us! Prove us right!" Time and again they have been saved, not by their own resolution, but by the world taking them at their own low self-valuation and endeavouring to deliver them the consummation they devoutly wish. Only then are they able to come together as a people, mend their divisions, and celebrate their escape as one more proof of the divine protection to which their specialness entitles them. But it is a dangerous game and will backfire on them one day.'

Gutkind heard in this a personal plea by his great-grandfather, to one he had loved without reciprocation, to beware the dragon's teeth she and hers had sowed. He even wondered if it was a coded message. A last-minute warning to her, perhaps, to escape (he had even used that word), to gather up her things and leave, or to go into hiding, before the first shots were fired.

How many messages of this sort, he asked himself, had been sent in this fashion. Not just by Clarence Worthing but by others who had lost their hearts to apparently charming and companionable men and women who proved, when things turned serious, to have been merely trifling with their affections and who, without once looking back, beat a speedy retreat to the bosoms of their own? How much 'saving', for the sake of brief but never to be forgotten embraces, had been going on? Like all theorists of betrayal and conspiracy, Gutkind was a hyperbolist. From the single example of his great-grandfather he extrapolated a whole underground of the hurt, scheming tirelessly, not to say paradoxically, to give another chance to those they knew – knew from their own experience – did not deserve it.

This seemed so plausible to the detective that he began to question whether WHAT HAPPENED had in the end claimed any victims at all. Had it remained an undescribed crime all these years because it was an unsolved crime, and had it been unsolved because it was uncommitted? That made a great deal of sense to him. It explained why the world was not the happier place it should have been, and no doubt would have been, had what was meant to happen happened.

In the early days of Gutkind's courtship his wife-to-be had sent him a graphic letter, imprinted with her lipstick kisses, describing her desires. 'Read and burn', she wrote at the bottom.

Now that he understood these essays of his great-grandfather's as personal missives to a woman he'd loved, he imagined him advising the same precaution. Read and burn.

But this didn't take from the truth of Clarence Worthing's analysis. If anything – since it was designed to win assent even from those it might have hurt, since it was intended to prepare, alert and warn, not rabble-rouse – it made the analysis more compelling. The empathetic Gutkind did figuratively as he was told. He read and burned.

ii

Tonight, he spread out a few more pages of the silver-tongued Clarence Worthing on the kitchen table, blowing on them reverently, a paragraph at a time, to keep them free of dust. How he admired the undeviating strength of his resolution, not compromised by passion but stiffened by it. How wonderful it must have been to know where the wrongness at the heart of life was to be located and what it looked like. Here were no abstractions; here was flesh and blood. His great-grandfather wrote as though the enemy were in the other room, perhaps falsely playing with his children as he wrote, perhaps seducing his wife as he had once been seduced himself. Gutkind felt that he could touch them. Put his arms around them, submit his cheek to their false kisses. He closed his eyes and believed that he could smell them. It was a kind of love. A hatred born of pure fascination. His noble-hearted ancestor had been their friend. He had allowed them into his heart. He had been betrayed by them. Gutkind felt his own heart swell. He almost swooned with this love which was indistinguishable from hate. He closed his eyes and made a perfect pink circle of his lips. Womanly, he felt. Kiss me!

But when he opened his eyes again there was no one there. Only Luther, rolling in the white dust. He felt as though that very dust obscured his vision, fell like a veil over his face, through which he could make out nothing distinct, no person or group of persons, just his own causeless dissatisfaction.

But he needed features and so he conjured them, not from the family journals but from his own immediate experience of what the features of aloof, cold-blooded superiority looked like. Those features belonged to Kevern 'Coco' Cohen.

CHAPTER 8

LITTLE ST ALURED

i

Ailinn drove adventurously but sweetly, ignoring the routine rage of other drivers. They honked her if she didn't pull over to let them pass, and they honked her when she did; she was too fast for some and too slow for others; she lingered too long at traffic lights or she set off too early for those running the lights in opposing directions. A cyclist hammered on the roof of the car, then seeing she was a woman blew her an enraged kiss.

'I'd have turned back by now,' Kevern admitted. 'I'd have killed or been killed.'

'You get used to this as a woman,' Ailinn said.

'You're not turning this into a gender issue?'

'I don't have to. How many women have wound down their windows to scream at me? How many women have shown me the finger?'

'I haven't been counting.'

'You don't need to count. Would that cyclist have blown a kiss at you?'

'All right, I accept what you are saying. But he

was young. Any crisis in society manifests itself in the behaviour of young men. So let's go home.'

She wouldn't hear of it. Home was no better, remember. At home men weren't just showing women the finger, they were killing them, and Kevern, or had he forgotten, was suspected of killing a woman himself.

'And a man,' he reminded her. 'Indeed a couple of men. Don't minimise my offence.'

'I don't. But your behaviour doesn't constitute a crisis.'

Kevern tightened his seat belt. 'You'll tell me it's a tautology,' he said, 'but the behaviour of men is the proof we're in crisis.'

'That's a tautology,' she said, finally getting on to the motorway.

She drove at her usual speed, confidently, with a narrowed concentration as though driving through a tunnel. Kevern spoke not one word. After about an hour and a half, as much from a charitable impulse as anything else, she left the motorway again and followed the signs to the small cathedral city of Ashbrittle, at one time home to more ecclesiastical dignitaries than any other town in the country, and for that reason a magnet for Christian tourists. But that was before WHAT HAPPENED, IF IT HAPPENED happened. Subsequently, though the church insisted it had not been specifically instrumental in those events, it had allowed its head to drop. Too much saying sorry, Kevern thought, as he realised where she'd driven them.

163

'This do?' she asked.

Kevern wound down his window then wound it up again. 'You can smell the disuse,' he said.

'Shall we drive straight out again?'

'No, let's stay. I need to rest my eyes.'

'You haven't been driving.'

'That's what you think.'

They found a motherly bed and breakfast a mile or two outside the town, away from the smell of disuse, and went immediately to bed. Pencil sketches of details of gravestones, lychgates and stoups, arches and columns seen from unexpected angles, hung above their bed. 'Soft clerical porn,' Kevern called it. 'The kitsch to which religion, when no one any longer believes in it, is reduced.'

Ailinn thought he was making too much of it. They were just pictures. Something had to go on the walls. And how would he have felt had they shown the Saviour bleeding on the cross. He said that would have depended on who'd painted it.

'Let's have a break from judgement,' Ailinn suggested. At least on their first night away. 'We're supposed to be on holiday. Let's just enjoy the relief of not being in Port Reuben. And not being looked at every minute of every day.'

He agreed. 'Or interrogated.'

'Well that's your own fault for kissing married women.'

'You sound like Detective Inspector Gutkind.'

'Did he ask about me?'

'No. Should he?'

'I suppose not. But you'd think I'd be material to his assessment of your character, or at least your circumstances.'

'He was more interested in assessing my furniture.'

She laughed a small laugh then remembered something. 'I was questioned by the police once. Not since I've been with you. Before I left home. I thought they were more interested in my belongings too.'

'What were you questioned about?'

'That was never entirely clear. A burglary, I think. Not for kissing someone in a car park, that I can say. But mainly they wanted the chance to get a look at where I lived. They wondered if I'd held on to any family photographs or letters from before I was adopted. I told them I didn't have any family photographs or letters from before I was adopted for the reason that I had no family. And besides, I knew the law. They said everyone broke the law a bit. I told them I didn't. I told them that if they wanted to know more about me they should try the children's home in Mernoc. And then be so kind as to let me know what they'd found out.'

'And did they?'

'Let me know?'

'Find anything out.'

'No idea.'

She shuddered in his arms, her heart aflutter – 'Someone dear to me has just died,' she said, and then when Kevern sat up in alarm she laughed to reassure him. 'A silly superstition from my part of the world.'

But he was a superstitious man himself. Only a fool, he thought, wasn't. What if her heart had fluttered out of time – an anticipatory flutter – because the someone close to her who had died was him.

A moment later there was a knock on their door. Their hearts leapt together. Who knew they were here?

They needn't have been alarmed: it was only the motherly proprietor wondering if they wanted a hot-water bottle.

They said no.

They had each other.

ii

Ashbrittle was deserted when they went strolling after breakfast. But somehow aflutter too, like Ailinn's heart, as though with affrighted ghosts.

They stared about them. Soul-departed terrace after soul-departed terrace, mocking the moderate, clerical sociability for the expression of which they'd been lovingly designed. Expectant, calling-card residences at which no one called. The stone a melancholy, rusted yellow. The brass doorbells black from never being pushed. A light rain seemed not so much to fall from the sky as rise from the cracked paving stones. A couple of shops selling local-history pamphlets (no one wanted a complete book), pewter goblets, silver spoons featuring the diocesian crest and of course postcards of the cathedral were open, but many more were boarded up. The river had a film of grease on it, like gravy left to go cold. The Bishop's Barn, a one time favourite with tourists, was closed for renovation, but the sign saying so was in need of renovation itself. Graffiti was scrawled on its strong yet quiet Jacobean door. Kevern couldn't read the words or decipher the symbols but to him all graffiti was the language of alienated hate, even when it was urging 'Love'.

They walked in silence under High Street Gate which housed a library, also indefinitely closed for renovation, and found Cathedral Close. 'I have a soft spot for cathedral closes,' Ailinn said, looking around. 'I always feel people must be living such good lives in them.'

'Well maybe they are,' Kevern said. 'That's if anyone is living here at all. It feels as if they've all gone. A plague-bell tolled and they all ran for it. Unless they're on their knees in their cellars, saying sorry.'

Ailinn stopped and told him to be quiet. She could hear music coming from the grandest of the houses. She wanted it to be Bach or Handel but it was only a utility-console ballad wondering where we would be without love.

'In the shit,' Kevern said. To himself. He wasn't going to use language like that to the woman he loved.

She took his arm and moved him on in what,

as a devotee of cathedral closes, she knew to be the direction of the main entrance to the cathedral itself. Her early years had been spent in an orphanage that was an adjunct to a monastery. She knew her way around church architecture.

'The gargoyles have been defaced,' Kevern noted, looking up. 'They have no features. No bent noses, no bulging eyes, no pendulous lips.'

'Years of bad weather,' Ailinn guessed.

'Well that's a kind interpretation. But I bet this is deliberate. They've been smoothed over – made to look like nothing and nobody.'

'Botoxed, you reckon?'

He laughed. 'Morally Botoxed. Rendered inoffensive.'

'Still – isn't that better than the way they looked before?'

'Maybe. But they might as well not be here in that case. If they aren't going to remind you of evil, they have no function.'

Ailinn reminded him that their function was to carry water away from the building.

'I meant spiritual function,' Kevern said piously.

Inside, the light struggled to pierce the dust of the stained-glass windows. Far apart from each other, two elderly ladies, dressed in black, prayed, one with her face in her hands.

'There you are,' Ailinn whispered.

'I'm not sure they count,' Kevern whispered back. 'They look as though they've been here for two hundred years.'

'It can take a long time,' Ailinn said, 'for God to answer your prayers.'

'More time than we have.'

'But not more time than they have.'

'And how does he adjudicate between prayers,' Kevern wondered, 'when they are savagely opposed? What if these two are praying for the destruction of each other? How can he satisfy the desires of them both?'

'With difficulty. That's why it takes him so long.'

'I take comfort at least,' Kevern said, 'in there being so few people making their devotions here. It must mean that the rest of them have what they want.'

'God help them,' Ailinn said.

'God help us all,' Kevern agreed.

They let their eyes wander absently over the crucifixes and Bible scenes, neither of them willing to make the effort to determine if any of the art was distinguished. They paused before an elaborately carved stone shrine, virtually a throne, built over a small slab, no bigger than a pillow, which announced itself as containing the blessed remains of *Little St Alured of Ashbrittle, killed by—*.

Kevern took out his glasses to examine the carving. 'Well whatever else, they were wonderful craftsmen,' he said. 'If I could do this with wood . . . such lightness, you think you're looking at flowers. Don't quote me on this, but I almost fancy I can see the poor little bugger's soul ascending to heaven on a tracery of stone petals.'

169

But Ailinn was more interested in deciphering who the poor little bugger was killed by. 'This hasn't been worn away by time,' she said. 'It's been scratched out.'

'Maybe they decided they had the wrong killer.'

'Then why didn't they replace the name with that of the right one?'

'Could still be investigating. The case might be *sub judice*.'

'After nine hundred years?'

Kevern conceded it was unlikely. 'But then justice, like God, grinds slowly. We should put Gutkind on to it.'

Ailinn knew how Kevern's mind worked. You set it a problem and when it could come up with no answer, it came up with a joke. He had lost interest now in Little St Alured and how he was murdered, and by whom, and why someone or other – an individual with an axe to grind or the depleted might of the church – didn't want anyone to know. She was the curious one. But in the end she too had to admit there were some things that had to remain a mystery.

They took the darkness of the cathedral out with them on to the street.

'This place needs cheering up,' Ailinn said. 'It needs sunshine.'

'It needs something. Pilgrims, I reckon. Believers. Some of the old dogmatism. You can't have a church town without belief and you can't have belief without intolerance.'

'And you think that would liven it up?'

'I do. All this penitential . . .'

'All this penitential what?'

He didn't have the word. 'You know . . . gargoylelessness. If you want God you've got to have the Devil.'

'I'm for neither,' Ailinn said.

'Then this is what you get.'

Glass shatters. They both hear it. She is at one end of the country and he is at another, yet still they hear it. The smashing mania, the shattering of every window in the land. After all the fires, all the beheadings, all the iron hooks and crowbars, the frenzy to kill has not abated. Only now it has become centralised. He is frightened, she less so. She thinks they've done their worst already. He thinks there's always something further they might come up with; he has more admiration for the ingenuity of man; viewing things millennially, he thinks they haven't even started yet. And look, he could be right. This time the mob wears uniforms, and answers to a higher authority even than God. She reads quietly, waiting for the knock. He hides his head. That is how they sit on the train heading east, looking out at the snow, not exchanging a word, she reading, he hiding his head. The train is not a surprise. They were always going to be put aboard this train. There are some among their fellow passengers for whom the train is a relief now that they are finally on it. In the snow everything will be washed away.

CHAPTER 9

THE BLACK MARKET IN MEMORY

i

The following morning, chilled by Ashbrittle's faded faith, Kevern – half hoping she would say no – suggested they leave and drive to the Necropolis. The Necropolis was his father's name for the capital.

'Another of his jokes?' Ailinn wondered.

'You could say that, but he might have been in dead earnest.'

'Well I wouldn't know,' Ailinn said, looking straight ahead.

She meant about jokes – since that had been Kevern's first assessment of her: that she didn't get them. But she meant about fathers too.

Neither had visited the Necropolis before. Singly, they wouldn't have dared. It had a bad reputation. Outside the capital people survived the failure of the banks with surprising fortitude; they even took a grim satisfaction in returning to old frugal ways which proved their moral superiority to those who had lived the high life in the capital for so long, washing oysters down with champagne and living in mansions that had their own swimming pools. It was a sweet revenge. In time the Necropolis recovered, to a degree, but its self-esteem, as a great centre of finance and indulgence, had been damaged. WHAT HAPPENED, IF IT HAPPENED – or, as his father called it, THE GREAT PISSASTROPHE – for the most part happened there, and while no one was blaming anyone, a sort of slinking seediness replaced the old strutting glamour. In the Necropolis the divorce rates were higher than anywhere else. So were domestic shootings. Men urinated openly in the streets. Women brawled with one another, used the vilest language, got drunk and thought nothing of throwing up where the men had urinated. You could have your pockets picked in broad daylight. Put up too fierce a struggle and you might have your throat cut. *Might*. It wasn't a daily occurrence, but people in the country were pleased to report that it wasn't unheard of.

Not allowed to remember the glory that had been, the Necropolis put up a cocksure front, belied by the failure of the once great stores and hotels to live up to the past sumptuousness which their premises still evoked. The shops with the grandest windows were not bursting with expensive items. You could get tables at the best restaurants on the day you wanted them. And there was a thriving black-market trade in memorabilia of better times – even, one might say, in memory itself.

Had they not been in love and on an adventure,

each emboldening the other, Ailinn and Kevern would not have gone there.

Kevern's father must have warned him against going to the Necropolis a hundred times over the years, but when he tried to recall his actual words Kevern couldn't find any; he could only see the prematurely old man opening and closing his mouth, dressed in his oriental brocade dressing gown, arthritic and embittered, his back to the fire – a fire that was lit in all weathers – angrily smoking a cigarette through a long amber Bakelite cigarette holder, listening with one ear to the footsteps of walkers (snoopers, he called them) passing the cottage to get to the cliffs. Except for when he wore a carpenter's apron in his workshop, he dressed, in Kevern's recollection of him, no other way. Always his brocade dressing gown. Had he just arrived and was waiting for the rest of his clothes to follow, or was everything packed in readiness for departure? Had he for the space of one day in all the years he'd lived in the cottage made peace with the idea that it was his home?

His mother the same, though she didn't dress as though to face down a firing squad. They could have been master and servant, so fatalistically elegant was he, so like an item of her own luggage, a bundle of rags – the bare necessity to keep out the cold – was she.

Whether she had formed an independent view of the Necropolis, or ever been there herself,

Kevern didn't know. She didn't talk to him about things like that. The past wasn't only another country, it was another life. But he thought he recalled her seconding her husband, saying, in her weary voice, as though to herself – because who else listened – 'Your father is right, don't go there.'

Kevern suddenly felt guilty realising that he too left his mother out of everything. He put his hand on Ailinn's knee as though in that way, from one woman to another, he could make it up to her – the mother he had trouble remembering.

Ailinn took her hand off the wheel and put it on his. 'Use both hands,' he said, frightened she meant to play pat-a-cake with him while she was driving. 'Please.'

'Well I'm looking forward to this,' she said, hiding her apprehension.

'Me too. I'm looking forward to my first Lebanese.'

'Or an Indian.'

'Or a Chinese.'

'And I can see if I can get my phone fixed,' she said.

'I didn't know anything was wrong with your phone.'

'It rings sometimes and when I answer there's no one there. And occasionally I hear an odd clicking when I'm on the phone to you.'

'How come you've only just mentioned this?'

'I didn't want to worry you.'

'You think someone's listening in?'

'Who would want to do that?'

'Search me . . . Gutkind?'

'Why would he want to listen in to my conversations?'

'Who knows? Maybe he wants to be sure you're not in any danger from me – the lady killer.'

They both laughed.

Kevern didn't mention his crazy thought. That the person bugging her phone might have been his dead father, making sure she was the right woman for his son.

'Is there such a thing as retinal hysteria?' Kevern asked as they approached the city.

Ailinn remembered an old English novel she'd read about a newly and unhappily married Puritan girl visiting Rome for the first time, the stupendous fragmentariness of the pagan/papal city – they were one and the same thing for her – passing in fleshly and yet funereal procession across her vision, throbbing and glowing, as though her retina were afflicted. So yes, Ailinn thought, a person's excited emotional state could affect the way he saw. But why was Kevern's emotional state excited or, more to the point, what did he think he was seeing?

'Zebra stripes,' he said. 'And leopard spots. And peacock feathers. Have we taken a wrong turn and driven into the jungle?'

'You don't think you could be hung-over?'

'You were with me last night. What did I drink?'

'A migraine then?'

'I don't get them. I feel fine. I am just blinded by colour.'

She had been too busy concentrating on the roads, which she feared would be more frightening than any she was used to, to notice what he had begun to notice as they approached the Necropolis. But he was right. The Necropolitans were dressed as though for a children's garden party. The moratorium on the wearing of black clothes, declared in the aftermath of THE GREAT PISSASTROPHE in order to discourage all outward show of national mourning (for who was there to mourn?) was honoured now only in the breach, they thought. Neither Ailinn nor Kevern thought twice about wearing black. But the Necropolis appeared to be obeying it to the letter still, as though seeing in the prohibition an opportunity for making or at least for seeming merry. What neither Kevern nor Ailinn had anticipated was the difference this abjuration of black would make to the look of everything. It was as though the spirit of serious industry itself had been syphoned out of the city.

But it wasn't just the vibrant colours of the clothes people wore that struck them, but the outlandishness of the designs. The further in they drove the more vintage-clothes stalls they passed, until the city began to resemble a medieval funfair or tourney, on either side of the road stalls and pavilions under flapping striped tarpaulins piled high with fancy dress. Kevern rubbed his eyes. 'I don't get it,' he said. 'I've had a policeman snooping around my house in the hope of uncovering a single family keepsake, and here they go about in their great-grandparents' underthings as bold as brass.'

Ailinn laughed at him. 'I doubt the stuff is genuinely old,' she said.

He thought he could smell the mustiness of antiquity on the streets. Mothballs, rotting shawls, old shoes, greasy hats, the forbidding odour of people long forgotten and garments that should have been thrown away. 'What do you mean not *genuinely* old?'

'Like your Kildromy-Biedermeier. I'd say they're fake vintage.'

'What's the point of that?'

'What's the point of your Kildromy-Biedermeier? It's a way of eating your cake and having it. This way they can cock a snook at the authorities without actually doing anything wrong. I think it's fun. Why don't we stop so you can buy me a crinoline and some cowboy boots? And I'll buy you a Prussian officer's outfit.'

'To do what in?'

'Ask me to dance. Take me into the woods. Whatever Prussian officers do.'

'*Did*,' he corrected her. 'There are no more Prussian officers. I hate this playing with everything.'

'Oh, Kevern, where's your sense of fun?'

He smiled at her. It pleased him when she bested him. 'Not everything is amenable to fun.'

179

'You think we should be solemn about the past?'

'I think we should let it go. What's past is past.'

Had she not been driving she'd have rolled her eyes at him.

But she knew now he did not always say what he believed.

ii

Only as they approached the Necropolis proper did the stalls begin to thin out, though even then they did not vanish altogether. And where stores selling better clothes should have been there were mainly holes in the ground and cranes. Had there been more workmen about, the cranes could have been taken as evidence that massive development was under way, but these too had a vintage air, mementoes of busier days. In accordance with the city's musty festivity, the cranes were festooned with tattered bunting and faded decorations from Christmases or other festivals long past.

At Kevern's instigation – he didn't want to be in the car a moment longer – they checked into a hotel in the part of the city once referred to in the fashion and travel magazines as Luxor, in deference to the opulence of the shopping. Luxor was where most of the grand hotels had been, though there was little of the old glamorous traffic in their lobbies or on the streets outside today. Foreign tourism fell off dramatically after WHAT HAPPENED and had never fully recovered. Who wanted to holiday in the environs of Babi Yar? That this was a reciprocal reluctance it suited the authorities to insist. If visitors didn't want to come and holiday in our backyard, we sure as hell didn't want to holiday in theirs. Where hadn't things been done the stench of which remained abhorrent to the misinformed or oversensitive tourist? Nowhere was safe, when you really thought about it. Nowhere was pleasant. What country wasn't a charnel house of its own history? You were better staying home, if you cared about that sort of thing, with your eyes closed and a cold compress on your forehead. You were better advised to keep to your individual fortress, shuttered and bolted against the movement, in or out, of people, infection and ideas. You contained your own conflagrations, that was the international wisdom, or at least that was the international wisdom as explained by Ofnow. Eventually, we'd all grow less nice in our expectations and things would get back to how they'd been.

In the meantime Luxor retained a little of its old exoticism thanks to the convergence of two accidents of history. Many of the oil rich who had been in the Necropolis, feasting on the decline of the banks (which, by some logic that only the most sophisticated economists understood, made them still richer), and gorging on the best of the new season's fashions, found themselves, when WHAT HAPPENED happened, between the devil of abroad and the deep blue sea of home. They were

181

conscious, even without the advice of their embassies, that WHAT HAPPENED, no matter that they'd welcomed and in some cases been instrumental in it, might easily happen to them next; but equally aware that the revolutionary fervour sweeping their own countries was an even greater danger to them, as a hated elite who could afford to spend half their lives in foreign hotels. What was spring to some was winter to them. Anxious about staying but terrified to leave, they spent what was left of their lives in fretful uncertainty, and now their grandchildren and their grandchildren's children resided where they had been marooned, in a sort of melancholy but pampered limbo, some in the very hotels their grandparents had been staying in when the world convulsed. In the absence of anything else to do, they continued to shop, went on raiding the best stores when the seasons and the windows changed, as it was in their blood to do, but the city had ceased to be a centre of fashion, the clothes were shoddier, the jewellery cheaper, and there was nowhere now for them to return to show off their purchases.

It was a new, rare sight to Kevern and to Ailinn – these idly perambulating gold-ringed men in keffiyehs, paler-skinned, Kevern imagined, than their grandparents must have been, but still with those stern, warrior profiles he had been educated to idealise. The noble generosity of the Arab was as much a given in the citizenship classes Kevern had taken at school, as the free spontaneity of the

Afro-Caribbean and the honest industriousness of the Asian. As for the chaste obedience of the women, that was still evident in the modesty of their dress.

'Nice,' Kevern commented, 'to see some black.'

Ailinn said nothing.

As black as ravens, they seemed to her, but nothing like so purposeful, covered from head to foot, only their slow eyes and the gold heels of their shoes visible. She noted with amazement the docility of their bearing as they trailed a step or two behind their men, talking among themselves. Some wheeled perambulators, but in general there were few children. Where was the point in children? And where, anyway, were the nannies? How did it feel, she wondered, to live this privileged life of no design, like a protected species which could forage unimpeded for whatever it liked but with no nest to take its findings back to.

Some of the men smoked hookahs in the lounge of the hotel, morose, looking occasionally at their watches but never at their women who sat staring at their jewelled utility phones, bemused, waiting for them to ring or perform some other once sacred but now forgotten function – totems that had lost their potency. The women allowed their fingers idly to play across the decommissioned keypads. The men too were fidgety, their fingers never far from their prayer beads.

'You should get a set of those, they could calm your nerves,' Ailinn whispered, as they waited for a porter to take their luggage to their rooms. They were travelling light and could have carried their own, but the porters needed employment and where, anyway, was the hurry?

'Are you implying I'm a fretter?'

'You? A fretter!' she laughed, holding on to his arm, then wondering whether, in such a place, it was disrespectful of her to stand so close to a man.

After he'd shown them to their room the porter took Kevern to one side and asked him if there were gramophone records, CDs or videos he was looking for. Bootleg blues bands, rock and roll, comedy – he knew where to lay his hands on anything. Kevern shook his head. What about books that had fallen out of print, bootleg tickets to underground cabarets, souvenir passports of those who hadn't got away before WHAT HAPPENED, IF IT HAPPENED happened, belts and badges worn by the hate gangs of the time, incitement posters, pennants, cartoons, signed confessions . . .?

Kevern wanted to know who would want such things. The porter shrugged. 'Collectors,' he said.

'No,' Kevern said. 'No, thank you,' remembering the amount of contraband music and words belonging to his father that was hidden away in his loft. It hadn't occurred to him any of it could be worth money.

The bedroom was, or at least had been, ornate. The bed was a four-poster. The carpet vermilion and gold, the drapes similar, sentimental photographs of famous department stores with queues outside adorned the wall. A large bath sat in the middle of the bathroom on gilded griffin's claws, now broken and discoloured. It will topple, Kevern thought, if we get into it together. He didn't like the look of the towels either: though they must once have been sumptuous, each one large enough to wrap an entire bath-oiled family in, they now hung, grey and textureless, over rusted rails.

He went to the window and gazed out towards the park. At school he had read descriptions of the Necropolis written by post-apocalyptic fantasists of a generation before. They were published as an anthology intended as light relief for the pupils, a propaganda joke showing just how wrong people could be when they let their imaginations – and indeed their politics – run away with them. But the anthology was later withdrawn, not because the post-apocalyptics had been proved right, but because the truth was not quite the resplendent rebuttal of their vision it should have been. Kevern remembered the gleaming vistas of technological frenzy dreamed up by one of the writers, citizens of the Metropolis of Zog sitting on brightly coloured tubular benches conversing with their neighbours via bubbles of video speech transmitted faster than the speed of sound by satellite. They had given up talking to one another because talk was too cumbersome. Another envisioned the population living in cages underground, dispersing their seed by means of a carefully regulated system of electronic cartridges which travelled through translucent pipes, along with electricity and water. Otherwise they neither enjoyed nor wanted any other form of human contact. The alternative vision was of devastation – open sewers strewn with the debris of a consumer society that no longer possessed the will or the wherewithal to consume, abandoned motor vehicles with their doors pulled off, electricity pylons which seemed to have marched into the city from the country like an invading army and were now uprooted, bent double like dinosaurs in pain or flat on their backs like . . . Kevern couldn't remember what they were *like*, only that everything was like something else, as though what had destroyed the city was not disease or overpopulation or an asteroid but a fatal outbreak of febrile fantasy-fiction metaphor.

One way or another the destruction wrought by electronics haunted all these writers' imaginations. So much ingenuity and invention bringing so little happiness. In their own way, though, they were optimistic and triumphalist, no matter that they pretended otherwise, each recording the victory of the writers' analogical fancy over nature.

What these writers gloomily and even hysterically prophesied, Kevern thought, was in fact a fulfilment of their private wishes.

Nothing gleamed in the city Kevern looked out on. The people on the streets had not turned into walking computer screens, riding translucent vehicles that sped along on tracks of spun steel. But

186

neither was it a wasteland that could at least quicken the heart with horror. Yes, the bedecked cranes appeared melancholy, reminding him of drunks fallen asleep in doorways after a party, and after a while the brightly coloured retro clothing of the pedestrians and shoppers began to show as desperate, as though they were waiting for a carnival that was never going to start, but traffic lights worked and, though the cars looked even older than his, they still had their doors, their lights, their windscreen wipers, and – Kevern could clearly hear them from five floors up and through closed windows – their horns. There was no congestion, no sense of drivers fleeing an infected city in one direction, or rushing to join the techno-mayhem from another, so the horn-blowing must have denoted more indurated irascibility than specific impatience. Over in the park, men hooded like Eskimos – saying what things were 'like' went with the apocalyptic terri-tory, Kevern realised – walked ill-tempered dogs, tugging at their leads, wanting them to do what they had come to the park to do and then be off. Every now and then a dog and his master relieved themselves in tandem. Though only the man appeared to relieve himself in anger. An occasional better-off-looking person walking a better-off-looking dog kept his distance, not afraid exactly, but routinely careful. Neither kind appeared to be taking pleasure in the outing. Kevern kept watch-ing, expecting to see an eruption of hostilities, but nothing eventuated. A quiet moroseness prevailed, that was all. An all-pervading torpor that belied the colours, bored the dogs, and made the very light appear exhausted.

Kevern guessed that if you wanted to see blood spilled you had to wait till it got dark.

The pavements on the main roads were unswept, but they weren't the debris-strewn sewers piled with wreckage he'd read about in his school anthology. It wasn't the apocalypse.

There weren't any powerful similes to be made. Nothing was like anything.

So what was it? It was a city seen through a sheet of scratched Perspex. For all the variegations of hue, it had no outlines. People blurred into one another. Kevern wondered if a wife would recognise her husband if she ran into him anywhere but in their home. Would either miss the other if they never *returned* home? And yet they had passed three cinemas and two theatres on the drive in, all advertising romantic musicals. Love – that was the universal subject. Love to play guitars to. Love to dance to. Love to sing about. Old and young, rich and poor, the indigenous and the children of immigrants – love!

Ailinn joined him at the window. 'Well one thing this does do,' she said, 'is make you miss the Friendly Fisherman.'

He couldn't tell if she was exaggerating.

They decided against going out to eat, ordered the Lebanese they'd promised each other – it turned out to be no more than a cold plate of aubergine mushed in a dozen different ways – and went to bed.

The mattress dipped in the middle.

'Christ!' Kevern said ruminatively, looking up at the flaking ceiling.

Ailinn agreed with him. 'Christ!'

iii

They took a late breakfast – mixed mushed aubergines again – in a room that must once have suggested a pasha's pavilion (mosaic tiled floor, mirrors on the ceiling, carpets on the walls), but now looked bored with itself – a street-corner bric-a-brac shop going out of business. Sensing that the permanent residents of the hotel weren't looking for conversation, Kevern and Ailinn kept their eyes lowered. They were served mint tea which Kevern failed to pour from the requisite height. 'It tastes better if you aerate it like this,' the only other person in the breakfast room not in a keffiyeh called across from a nearby table. He was holding his own glass teapot aloft as though he meant to take a shower from it. 'And you get more foam.'

Kevern, feeling like a country boy, thanked him.

'Where are you two from?' the man asked.

Kevern sneaked a look at Ailinn. How did she feel about talking to a stranger? She nodded imperceptibly. 'Port Reuben,' Kevern said.

189

The man, as broad as a door and dressed like a widely travelled photographer in khaki chinos and a cotton jacket with a thousand pockets, shook his head. 'Never heard of it. Sorry.'

'That's all right,' Kevern said. 'We aren't on the line about it. And you?'

'I'm not on the line about it either.'

If the man was a comedian, Ailinn wondered, how would her thin-skinned lover deal with him.

Kevern worried for her on the same grounds.

He tried a laugh. 'No, I meant where are you from.'

'Me? Oh, everywhere and nowhere. Wherever I'm needed.'

'Then you're needed here,' said Kevern, with a worldly flourish of his arm. 'Should we take sugar with this?'

The man asked if he could join them and joined them without waiting for an answer. The width of him was a comfort to Kevern. You needed a wide man to advise you in a strange place. Ailinn thought the same. He would have made a good father.

It turned out that he was a doctor employed exclusively by this and a number of other nearby hotels to attend to the mental welfare of their long-term guests. 'It keeps me busier than you would imagine,' he said, smiling at Ailinn, as though she, having to deal with the mental welfare of Kevern, would be able to imagine only too easily what kept him busy.

There were questions Kevern wanted to ask but

he wasn't sure about the propriety of asking them while there were guests still eating. Reading Kevern's compunction, the doctor, who had introduced himself as Ferdinand Moskowitz, but call him Ferdie, leaned across the table as though to gather his new friends into his wide embrace. 'No one hears or cares what we're talking about,' he said. 'They're miles away. Depression can do that. It can make you indifferent to your surroundings, uninterested in yourself let alone other people.'

'And those who are not depressed?' Kevern asked.

Ferdie Moskowitz showed him a mouthful of white teeth. Kevern imagined him dazzling the Tuareg with them. 'No such animal here. The only distinction to be drawn is between neurotic depression and psychotic depression, and even then those who start out with the milder form very quickly develop the more serious. Dispossession does that.'

'We're all dispossessed in our way,' Ailinn said quickly. She wanted to say it before Kevern did. She could deal with her own pessimism better than she could deal with his. His slighted her. Slighted *them* – the love they felt for each other.

'Yes, and we're all depressed,' the doctor said. 'But in fact few of us are dispossessed as these poor souls are. You must remember that theirs is a culture that had already fallen into melancholy, long before' – he made an imaginary loop with his hand, from which he made as if to hang himself – 'long before you know what.'

191

'Not what they told us at school,' Kevern said. *'Fierce warrior people,'* he quoted from memory, *'who dispensed largesse and loved the good things in life . . .'*

'Ah, yes – Omar Khayyam via Lawrence of Arabia. *Come fill the cup . . .'*

Kevern closed his eyes, as though savouring something delectable, and tried to remember a line. *'Enjoy wine and women and don't be afraid –* isn't that how it went?'

'We read that at school as well,' Ailinn said, 'only our version was Enjoy but *do* be afraid.'

The doctor made a sound halfway between a cough and a snort. 'As though that was all they ever did,' he said. 'As though, between lying languorously on scented pillows and occasionally riding out to inconsequential battle in a sand-storm, they had nothing to do but wait for us to come and impose our values on them.'

Kevern shrugged. For himself, he wanted to impose his values on no one. He wasn't even sure he knew what his values were.

'Either way,' the doctor continued, 'that's not the real Omar Khayyam. He was a philosopher and a mystic not a hedonist, which of course you can't expect schoolboys – or schoolgirls – to understand. And as for the large-souled warrior of our romantic imagination – he vanished a long time ago, after believing too many lies and too many promises and losing too many wars. Read their later literature and the dominant note is that of elegy.'

'Our dominant note is elegy, too,' Kevern said. 'We've all lost something.'

Ferdinand Moskowitz raised an eyebrow. 'That's an easy thing to say, but you have not lost as the poor souls I treat have lost. At least you can elegise like a good liberal in your own country.'

'I don't think of myself as a good liberal,' Kevern said.

'Well, however you think of yourself, you have the luxury of thinking it in your own home.'

Kevern exchanged glances with Ailinn. Later on they would wonder why they had done that. Other than asking them to call him Ferdie – a name that upset Kevern to an unaccountable degree – what had Moskowitz said to irritate and unite them? Weren't they indeed, as he had described them, people who enjoyed the luxury of home? All right, Ailinn had spent her earliest years in an orphanage and had left the home made for her by her rescuers, but had she not found a new one with Kevern, hugger-mugger on a clifftop at the furthest extreme of the country? 'I cling on for dear life,' Kevern had told her once, making crampons of his fingers, but that was just his exaggerated way of talking. They had found a home in each other. So what nerve had the doctor touched?

'Wherever we live,' Kevern said at last – and his words sounded enigmatic to himself, as though enigma could be catching – 'we await alike the judgement of history.'

Ferdinand Moskowitz rattled his pockets and

moved his lips like a man shaping a secret. 'We do indeed,' he said. 'But there are some things we don't have to wait for history to judge.'

'Such as?'

'Such as our using the people you see here – our grandparents using their grandparents – as proxy martyrs. We said we were acting in their interests when all along we were acting in our own. The truth is we didn't give a fig about their misery or dispossession. It was we who felt dispossessed. They were a handy peg to hang our fuming inferiority on, that was all. And once they'd given us our opportunity we left them to rot.'

'This isn't exactly rotting,' Kevern said.

'You haven't seen inside their heads . . .' He paused, then went on, 'Look, I know what you're thinking. These are the lucky ones, the rich and the powdered, born here to parents who were born here. The bombs didn't fall on them, because they financed the bombs. The banks didn't crash on them, because they owned the banks. They were spared the humiliations to which for years their poorer brothers were subjected. But that doesn't mean they don't feel those humiliations. Observe them at your leisure – their lives are sterile and they don't even have the consolation of being able to hate their enemies.'

This was all getting a bit too close to the bone for Kevern. He wasn't sure what to say. People didn't discuss war or WHAT HAPPENED, or the aftermath of either, in Port Reuben. It was not the thing. Not banned, just not done. Like history. WHAT HAPPENED – if WHAT HAPPENED was indeed what they were talking about – was passé. Was this why his father cautioned him against the Necropolis, because in the Necropolis they were still discussing a war that was long over? Was *Ferdie* Moskowitz the disappointment his father wanted to save him from?

'How so?' was the best response Kevern could come up with. This was like arguing through cotton wool. It wasn't that Kevern didn't have a view on the subject, he didn't know what the subject was.

'*How so*? You can't hate in retrospect, that's how so. You can't avenge yourself in retrospect. You can only smoke your pipes and count your beads and dream. And do you know what they fear most? That *our* history will make a mockery of events, extenuate, argue that black was white, make them the villains, ennoble by time and suffering those who made a profession out of their eternal victimhood, stealing and marauding on the back of a fiction that they'd been stolen from themselves.'

The wool descended further over Kevern's eyes. Soon he would not be able to breathe for it.

'*They* being . . .?' he just managed to ask.

But the doctor had lost patience. No longer a father figure to either of them, he rose, bowed in an exaggerated manner to Ailinn, and left the breakfast room.

A moment later, though, he popped his head

around the door and pulled a clownish face. 'The gone but not forgotten,' he said.

The phrase seemed to amuse him greatly for he repeated it. 'The gone but not forgotten.'

'I don't think Ferdie likes me,' Kevern said, after he disappeared a second time.

It was to become a refrain between them whenever Kevern sniffed a predator – 'I don't think Ferdie likes me.'

And Ailinn would laugh.

iv

That afternoon, with a light rain pattering against the scratched Perspex, they decided they would get Ailinn's phone fixed. The best places, the concierge told them, were in the north of the city and he didn't advise driving.

'Is it dangerous?' Kevern asked.

The concierge laughed. 'Not dangerous, just tricky.'

'Tricky to find?'

'Tricky to everything.'

He offered to call them a taxi but Ailinn needed a walk. They wandered aimlessly for an hour or more – Kevern preferred wandering to asking directions, because asking meant listening, and the minute someone said go straight ahead for a hundred metres then take a left and then a hundred metres after that take a right, he was lost.

Occasionally a tout, dressed like a busker or a master of ceremonials at some pagan festival, stepped out of a doorway and offered them whatever their hearts desired. 'Do you have anything black?' Kevern asked one of them.

The tout looked offended. He was neither pimp nor racist. 'Black?'

'Like a black tee-shirt or jacket?'

The tout missed Kevern's joke. 'I could get you,' he replied. 'Where are you staying?'

Kevern gave him the wrong hotel. He wasn't taking any chances.

Finding themselves in a part of town where there was actually construction going on, they went into a café to escape the dust. A beefy, furiously orange-faced builder in brightly coloured overalls, covered in plaster, raised his head from his sandwich and looked Ailinn up and down. 'Tasty,' Kevern thought he heard him say. But he could have been clearing his throat or referring to his sandwich. The gesture he made to a second builder who entered the café, however, slowly twirling a probing finger in Ailinn's direction, was unambiguous. The new arrival took a look at Ailinn and fingered her impressionistically in return.

'What's that meant to signify?' Kevern asked them, looking from one to the other.

The builder with the inflamed, enraged face made a creaking motion with his jaw, as though resetting the position of his teeth, and laughed.

'Take no notice,' Ailinn said. 'It's not worth it.'

'You tell him, gorgeous,' the second builder said, opening his mouth and showing her his tongue.

The first builder did the same.

These are the gargoyles I missed in Ashbrittle, Kevern thought.

'Come on. Let's leave them to dream about it,' Ailinn said. She took Kevern by the elbow and led him out.

They were both strangers to the city, but Ailinn felt she could cope better in it than Kevern ever would.

Back on the street the rain was falling more heavily. 'Let's just jump in a taxi, get it sorted and then go home,' she said. 'I think we've been away long enough. I have a migraine coming on.'

It was a vicarious migraine, a migraine for him, a man who didn't have migraines.

Kevern felt guilty. His idea to come away, his idea to mooch about looking into the windows of ill-lit shops and see where they ended up, his idea to go into the coffee shop – his idea, come to that, to ask Ailinn out in the first place, his idea to kiss Lowenna Morgenstern, everything that was making life difficult for Ailinn – his idea.

There were few taxis and those that passed were uninterested in stopping. Kevern wasn't sure if their For Hire lights were on or off, but he thought some drivers slowed down, took a look at them, and then sped off. Could they see from their austere clothes, or their hesitant demeanour, that he and Ailinn weren't from round here and did they therefore fear they couldn't pay or wouldn't tip? Or was it simply something about their faces?

Ailinn had turned white. Seeing a taxi, Kevern made a determined effort to hail it, running into the street and waving his arms. The driver slowed, peered out of his window, drove a little way past them, and then stopped. Kevern took Ailinn's hand. 'Come on,' he said. But someone else had decided the taxi was for him and was racing on ahead of them. 'Hey!' Kevern shouted. 'Hey, that's ours.'

'What makes it yours?' the man shouted back.

He was wearing a striped grey and blue cardigan, Kevern noted with relief, as though that made him someone he felt confident he could reason with. And wore rimless spectacles. A respectable, soberly dressed person in his early thirties. With a woman at his side.

'Come on,' Kevern said, 'be fair. You know I flagged it down before you did. Didn't I, driver?'

The driver shrugged. The man in the cardigan was blazing with fury. 'You don't have to yell and scream,' he said.

'Who's yelling and screaming? I flagged the taxi down before you, and I expect you to accept that, that's all. This lady has a migraine. I need to get her back to our hotel.'

'And I have a wife and tired children to get home.'

'Then you can get the next taxi,' Kevern said, seeing no children.

199

'If it means so much to you that you have to behave in this insane manner, then take the taxi,' the man said, raising an arm.

Kevern wondered if the arm was raised to call another taxi or aim a blow. He felt a hand on his back. Was it a punch? In his anger, Kevern wouldn't have known if it was a knife going between his shoulder blades. 'Take your hands off me,' he said.

'Calm down, you clown, you've got what you want. Just get yourself into the taxi and pootle off wherever you belong.'

'Get your fucking hands off me,' Kevern said.

'Hey,' the man said. 'Don't swear in front of my children.'

'Then don't you fucking lay your hands on me,' Kevern said, still seeing no children.

What happened next he didn't remember. Not because he was knocked unconscious but because a great sheet of rage had come down before his eyes, and behind it a deep sense of dishonour. Why was he fighting? Why was he swearing? He was not a fighting or a swearing man. And he couldn't bear that Ailinn had seen him in the guise of either.

It was she who had pushed him into the taxi and got them back to the hotel. 'Your hands are ice cold,' she told him when they were back in their room. Otherwise she said nothing. She looked, Kevern thought, as though made of ice herself.

He didn't know what time it was, but he fell into bed.

'I don't think Ferdie likes me,' he said before he fell asleep.

Ailinn did not laugh.

It was her suggestion, when they woke in the early hours of the morning, that they drive home without even waiting for breakfast. It was clear she didn't want a conversation about what had happened.

'Do you hate me?' he asked.

'I don't hate you. I'm just bewildered. And frightened for you.'

'Frightened?'

'Frightened of what might have happened to you. You didn't know who that man was. He might have been anybody.'

'He was a family man who didn't want his children to hear foul language, that's if there were any children. Though he didn't mind them seeing him pushing a stranger. There was nothing to be frightened of.'

'You don't know that. I was also frightened *about* you. I didn't like to see you like that.'

'Do you want me to explain?'

'No.' She meant no, not now, but it came out more final than that.

'I'm sorry,' he said.

'So am I.'

He couldn't bear leaving right away as she proposed. The thought of driving home in this hostile silence appalled him. You don't leave anywhere like that: it would feel too irresistibly as though they were leaving each other. Better to sit tight, with throbbing temples, and wait for the mood to change. How many marriages might have been saved if only the parties to it had waited – days, weeks, months, it didn't matter – for the mood to change?

'Let's get your phone fixed and then go,' he said.

He wanted to be back where they were before the swearing. And he was anxious to show her that her concerns were foremost in his mind. It was concern for her after all, his desperation to get her back to the hotel so she could sleep off her migraine, that made him fight for the taxi. Unless it was the responsibility he felt for her that had unhinged him. Was he not up to the job of looking after a woman? Did fear of failure unman him?

'I don't care about my phone,' she said.

'But I do. And I'd like an errand to clear my head.'

'To clear *your* head!'

'To clear both our heads.'

'So how do you propose we do this? Go outside and hail a taxi?'

So the punch came, whoever delivered it. But he still refused to capitulate to what it could have meant had he let it.

'I'll get the hotel to call us one,' he said.

He said it firmly. He was not going to allow looking after a woman to emasculate him.

v

It took an hour for a taxi to arrive but when it did the driver swung out of his cab to greet them, bowed low, introduced himself as Ranajay Margolis, looked up at the rain and produced an umbrella as a magician might produce a wand. He insisted on opening the passenger doors for them, one at a time, Ailinn's first.

Struck by his manners, Kevern asked where he was from originally.

Ailinn dug him. He had lived too long in Port Reuben where a black or Asian face was seldom seen. No one had entered the country from anywhere else for a long time. Every person's country of origin – regardless of whether they were a Margolis or a Gutkind – was this one. Wasn't that what made now so much better than then?

Kevern didn't mind the dig. So long as she was digging him they were together.

Ranajay Margolis was amused. He almost danced himself back into his seat. 'I am from here,' he said. 'As for *originally* that depends how far back you want me to go. Where are you from *originally*?'

Kevern held up a hand. He took the point.

Ailinn explained that they wanted to get her phone fixed.

'I'm just the man,' the driver said in his quicksilver

manner, turning round frequently and flashing them his snowy teeth, 'but first I'll give you a tour.'

'We don't want a tour, thank you,' she said. 'Just my phone fixed.'

'There are special places for that,' the driver said. 'I know them all. But they aren't easy to find and some of them aren't very trustworthy.'

'We know, that's why we're asking you to take us.'

He bowed as he was driving. 'You sure you don't want a tour?'

'Certain.'

'In that case,' he said, raising a finger like an exclamation mark, as though to punctuate a great idea that had just come to him, 'we will have to go to where the Cohens lived.'

'The Cohens! I'm a Cohen,' Kevern said. He felt a burst of excitement as he said it. Ranajay Margolis had asked him where he was from originally. What if he was from here? Would he encounter people who looked like him on the streets? Uncles, nieces, cousins? Would they be sitting on benches – so many tall, angel-haired 'Cocos' with long faces – minding their language and wondering what their lives amounted to?

Ranajay studied his reflection in the driver's mirror. 'No,' he explained, 'I mean *real* Cohens.'

Kevern offered to show him his ID.

Ranajay shook his head. 'That changes nothing,' he said.

They drove north for about half an hour, along

tense, surly streets, past stores selling Turkish vegetables, and then stores selling Indian vegetables, and then stores selling Caribbean vegetables, until they came to a suburb of houses built in a bygone, faraway style, Greek temples, Elizabethan mansions, woodland cottages, Swiss chalets, Malibu country clubs. No film set could have suggested lavish living with so little subtlety. But whatever their original ostentation, the mansions housed more modest domestic ambitions now. Indian children played on the street or stared out at the taxi through upper-storey windows. A handful of men in open-necked shirts played cards under a portico that might once have sheltered foreign dignitaries and maybe even royalty as they drank cocktails. Perhaps because no one could afford their upkeep, some of the grandest dwellings had fallen into disuse. Colonnades crumbled. Corinthian columns that must once have glowed with the phosphorescence of fantasy were dull in the drizzle, in need of replastering and paint. Yet this was no slum. Those houses that were inhabited looked cared for, the neat gardens and net curtains, the atmosphere of quiet industry – even the card-playing was businesslike – mocking the grandeur of those who'd originally occupied them. Many of the garages, large enough to take a fleet of Hollywood limousines – one for him, one for her, and something only marginally smaller for Junior – served as electrical or mechanics workshops and even retail outlets, though it was hard to imagine any passing trade. Signs promised prompt and efficient repairs to utility phones and consoles. Black-eyed adolescent boys sat cross-legged on walls, engrossed in their electronic toys, as though to advertise the competence of their parents' businesses.

The Cohens had lived here, Ranajay had said. What did he mean? Had it been a Cohen colony? Cohentown? He was adamant, anyway, that no Cohens lived here now, and that Kevern's family never had. But who was he to say that? How did he know?

Kevern's parents would never tell him where they had come from. It didn't matter, they'd said. It wasn't important. Don't ask. The question itself depressed and enraged them. Maybe it reminded them of their sin in marrying. But his father had warned him off the Necropolis. 'Don't go there,' he had said, 'it will dismay and disappoint you.' But he hadn't said 'Don't go to *Cohentown*, it will disappoint you.' Just don't go anywhere. Just stay in Port Reuben which – he might have added – will also disappoint you.

He didn't see how he could be disappointed when he had no expectations. But he had been excited when Ranajay had said Cohens had lived here. So there must have been some expectation in him somewhere, some anticipation, at least, that he had known nothing about.

Cohentown – why not?

What do I feel, he asked himself, thinking he should feel more.

What he felt was oppressed, as though there was thunder about.

He asked to be let out of the cab so he could smell the air. 'There's no air to smell,' Ranajay Margolis said. 'Just cooking.'

'Cooking's fine.'

Ranajay was insistent. 'Come. I will take you to the best place to have your phone fixed. I can get you a good deal.'

'Just give me a minute. I want to see if anything comes back to me.'

'You were never here,' Ranajay insisted. 'It's not possible.'

'I think that's for me to decide,' Kevern said.

Ranajay blew out his cheeks, stopped the car, got out with his umbrella, and opened Kevern's door. A group of children looked up, not curiously, not incuriously. He bore no resemblance to them but they weren't amazed by his presence. He had a thought. Were they used to sentimental visitors? Did other members of his family turn up here periodically to find themselves, to smell the air and see what they could remember?

This was silly. There were countless Cohens in the world. There was no reason to suppose that the Cohens whose neighbourhood, according to Ranajay, this had been, were *his* Cohens. But he fancied he would know if he stood here long enough. Birds navigate vast distances to find their way home. They must be able to tell when they are getting close. They must feel a pounding in their hearts. Why shouldn't he, navigating time, feel the same?

Most of the houses had long drives, but one had a front door on the street. He wondered if he dared look through the letter box, see if the silk runner was rumpled, see if the utility phone was winking on the hall table. But there were old newspapers stuffed into the letter box. Looking up, he saw that a number of the windows were broken. The disuse of this house suited him better than the subdued occupancy of the others. In the disuse he might reconnect to a line of used-up Cohens past. He closed his eyes. If you could hear the sea in a washed-up shell why shouldn't he hear the past in this dereliction? You didn't begin and end with yourself. If his family had been here he would surely know it in whatever part of himself such things are known – at his fingertips, on his tongue, in his throat, in the throbbing of his temples. Ghosts? Of course there were ghosts. What was culture but ghosts? What was memory? What was self? But he knew the danger of indulging this. Yes, he could persuade himself that the tang of happy days, alternating with frightful event, came back to him – kisses and losses, embraces and altercations, love, heartbreak, shouting, incest . . . whatever his father and mother had concealed from him, whatever they had warned him would dismay and disappoint him were he to recover any trace of it.

His temples throbbed all right. And since he was not given to migraines they must have throbbed with something else. Recollection? The anticipation of recollection? But it was so much folly. He was no less able to imagine fondness or taste bitter loss while sitting on his bench in Port Reuben. So Cohens had lived here once. And been happy and unhappy as other families had been. So what!

And anyway, *anyway* for Christ's sake! – it came as a shock to him to remember – Cohen was as much a given name as Kevern. He didn't know what his family name had really been when Cohens who were really Cohens roamed Cohentown. Cadwallader, maybe. Or Chygwidden. What was he doing chasing a past associated with a name that wasn't even his?

But then that precisely was the point, wasn't it. No one was meant to know who was, or who had been, who. No one was meant to track himself or his antecedents down. Call me Ishmael. Life had begun again.

Ailinn had come out of the cab and was watching him. 'Are you all right, my love?' she asked.

His relief knew no bounds. She'd called him 'my love'. Which must have meant the wretched taxi incident had been forgiven. He wanted to kiss her in the street. He took her hand instead and squeezed it.

He nodded. 'There's a strange atmosphere of squatting here,' he said, noticing a mother coming out to check on her children, and maybe on him too. He was struck by how softly she padded, as though not to wake the dead. 'They have the air of living lives on someone else's grave.'

'That's a quick judgement to leap to,' Ailinn laughed. 'You've been here all of five minutes!'

'It's not a judgement. I'm just trying to describe what I feel. Don't you think there's a queer apprehensive silence out here?'

'Well if there is, it might be caused by the way you're staring at everyone. I'd be apprehensive if I had you outside my door, trying to describe what you feel. Let's go now.'

'I don't know what it is,' he continued. 'It's as though the place is not possessed by its inhabitants.'

This annoyed Ranajay. 'These people live here quite legally,' he said. 'And have done for long, long times.'

'Don't worry,' Kevern said, 'I'm not claiming anything back.'

'It was never yours,' Ranajay said. 'Not possible.'

Never yours, like yesterday's taxi. Like Ailinn's honour in the café. Did ownership of everything have to be fought for in this city?

Ailinn feared that if Kevern didn't back off, their driver would leave them here. And then let Kevern see how unpossessed by its inhabitants it was. She lightly touched Ranajay's arm. 'I don't think he means to imply it was his,' she said.

Kevern suddenly felt faint. 'Let's get your phone fixed and then go back to the hotel,' he said. 'I've had enough of here.'

He climbed back into the taxi, not waiting for her to get in first.

He had heard his mother's voice. 'Kevern,' she called. Just that. 'Key-vern' – coming from a long way away, not in pain or terror, but as though through a pain of glass. Then he thought he heard the glass shatter. Could she have broken it with her voice?

It made no sense that she should be calling him. She hadn't been a Cohen except by marriage to his father, unless . . . but he wasn't thinking along those lines today, so why should he hear her calling to him in Cohentown?

Calling him in, or warning him to turn away? Away, he thought. He could even feel her hands on his chest. Go! Leave it, your father is right, it will dismay and disappoint you.

Such a strange locution: *dismay and disappoint.* Like everything else they'd ever told him – distant and non-committal. As though they were discussing a life that didn't belong to them to a son who didn't belong to them either.

It had always been that way. Even as they sat on the train going east, looking out at the snow, there was no intimacy. When the train finally pulls into the little station other families will be counted, sent this way and that way, and where necessary ripped from one another's arms. How does a mother say goodbye to her child for the last time? What's the kindest thing – to hang on until you are prised apart by bayonet, or to turn on your heels and go without once looking back? What are the rules of heartbreak? What is the etiquette?

Kevern wonders which course his parents will decide on when the time comes and the soldiers subject them to their hellish calculus. Then, as though prodded by a bayonet himself, he suffers an abrupt revulsion, like a revulsion from sex or the recollection of shame, from the ghoulishness of memories that are not his to possess.

Appalled, Kevern hauls himself back from the stale monotony of dreams. Always the same places, the same faces, the same fears. Each leaking into the other as though his brain has slipped a cog. Dementia must be like this, nothing in the right place or plane, but isn't he a bit young for that? So he climbs, so he climbed, so he will go on climbing, back into the taxi taking him away, feeling fraudulent and faint.

Now it was Ranajay's turn to wonder if he'd caused offence. 'I'm only meaning this for your husband's sake,' he said to Ailinn, starting the vehicle up again. 'He could not ever have lived here. There is no one now existing who lived here.'

He looked as though he was going to cry.

'It's all right,' she said, putting an arm around Kevern who seemed to have snapped into a sleep. He hadn't fainted. Just gone from waking to sleeping as if at a hypnotist's command.

Ranajay was beside himself with distress. 'My fault, my fault. I shouldn't have brought you to this part,' he said.

'There is no reason why you shouldn't have

brought us here,' Ailinn assured him. She felt she had spent the entire day making life easier for men. 'We asked you to.'

He inclined his head. 'Thank you,' he said. 'I am sure your husband is mistaken. There is no one left from here. They went away a long time ago. Before memory.'

Shut up, she wanted to scream. Shut up now!

But it pleased her that he had called Kevern her husband. *Husband* – she liked the ring of it. *Husband, I come.* Who was it who said that? How she would have felt to hear herself called Kevern's wife she wasn't sure. But OK, she thought, no matter that he had been half-crazed the entire time they'd been away. Yes, on the whole, OK. There were worse men out there.

They never did get her phone fixed. It would take three to five working days for the parts to arrive. And they weren't intending to stay around that long. She'd buy another.

They drove home to Port Reuben later that afternoon in careful, contemplative silence, neither wanting to discomfort the other with so much as a word or a thought. Every subject seemed fraught. They were both greatly on edge, but were still unprepared for what they found on their return. Someone had been inside the cottage.

'I knew it,' Kevern said before he had even turned the key in the door. 'I have known it the whole time we were away.'

'Are you absolutely certain?' Ailinn asked.

It was late and they were tired. The moon was full and a full moon plays tricks with people's senses. He could have been mistaken.

They had to shout over the roaring of the blow-hole. No, he wasn't mistaken. He had looked through his letter box and what he had seen he had seen.

His silk runner had been interfered with.

How did he know that?

It was straight.

BOOK II

All that most maddens and torments; all that stirs up the lees of things; all truth with malice in it; all that cracks the sinews and cakes the brain; all the subtle demonism of life and thought; all evil, to crazy Ahab were visibly personified and made practically assailable in Moby Dick.

Herman Melville

CHAPTER 1

A CRAZY PERSON'S HISTORY OF DEFILEMENT, FOR USE IN SCHOOLS

i

Had whoever it was who straightened Kevern 'Coco' Cohen's silk runner been looking for something in particular, something corroborative of Kevern's guilt – no matter, for the time being, what the crime – it was unlikely to have been a little book written by his maternal grandmother, Jenna Hannaford, about which Kevern himself knew nothing. It would not anyway have been found. Jenna's daughter, Kevern's mother, destroyed it when she read it, recognising it to be the work of a crazy person. In that she would have met no resistance from its author. *A Crazy Person's History of Defilement, for Use in Schools* was Jenna Hannaford's own title.

'If you think any school is going to teach that, you're crazy,' her husband told her.

She smiled sweetly at him. She was an elegant woman with a long neck and a mass of yellow hair which she put up carelessly, piling it on top of her head like a bird's nest. He was short, suffered from

217

over-curvature of the thoracic vertebrae and had no hair at all. But it wasn't all beauty and beast. She suffered from depression, had trouble buttoning her clothes because her fingers trembled, and dyed her hair. 'Do you think I don't know that?' she asked.

'Then why are you writing it?'

'Because I'm crazy.'

'Just don't let anyone see it.'

'Of course I won't. Do you think I'm crazy?'

Just don't let anyone was her husband's perpetual refrain. Just don't let anyone see, just don't let anyone hear, just don't let anyone know. He told her not to go out. It was just better that nobody knew she was there, or at least, since everybody did know she was there, just better that nobody saw her. He wasn't afraid she'd run off with someone with a straight back. He was just afraid.

'You worry too much about me, Myron,' she told him.

'I can't worry too much about you.'

'What will be will be,' she said.

She never finished her *Crazy Person's History of Defilement*. Work in progress was how she described it to herself. By that she meant she never expected it to be finished because the subject she was addressing would never be finished. But the other reason she didn't finish it was that she disappeared. Walked out one blowy September afternoon with her head held high, after warning her daughter

218

Sibella not to expect too much happiness and telling her husband to cut down on his smoking, and was never seen again.

Off the cliffs into the sea? An accident? A leap? Who knew?

Myron Hannaford never forgave himself. He believed in God but only to have someone to castigate himself to. 'I should have worried about her more,' he told Him.

Sibella kept her mother's papers in a little suitcase under her bed, not daring to read through them in case her mother returned and discovered they'd been tampered with. After her father died she was cared for by the boy she'd been brought up with – a relation ten years her senior, she wasn't sure from which side of the family, who longer ago than she could remember had come to live with them by the sea for his health's sake (though he wasn't allowed to go out and breathe the sea air), a gangling, morose, pale-faced fellow with a talent for woodwork (he took over Sibella's father's lathe as automatically as he took over her) and a secret love of syncopated music. When she was old enough, they married. It was never really discussed; it was simply assumed that that was what they would do. Who else was there for either of them?

And in most regards it made no material difference to the life they'd been living before they married.

She had already, in line with ISHMAEL, changed

her name from Hannaford to Cronfeld, and as her cousin Howel had changed his to Cohen she didn't feel she had to make too big a change a second time.

On the eve of the wedding Sibella crept out of the cottage with her crazy mother's papers and threw them into the sea.

Because she was a little crazy herself she no sooner threw them into the sea than she knew she shouldn't have. What if a page was washed back up into the village on the tide and found by a fisherman? What if it was swept up into the blowhole and spewed out, paragraph by paragraph, for walkers to find? She scrambled down the rocks to see what she could rescue, then remembered she couldn't swim. There was nothing she could do but hope. As far as she knew, no page ever was recovered from the water in Port Reuben. But from that time forward she lived in a sort of half-absent dread of something turning up, still just about legible, on a roller heading for the West Australian coast or on an ice floe in the South Atlantic, the precise consequences of which for her family could not be foreseen, but without question they would be disastrous.

If you want something to be destroyed for ever, her mother had warned her when she was small, you have to set fire to it and watch it burn away to nothing. It was a frightening time, the little girl knew, though she didn't understand what made it so. Her father had never been more agitated. He wouldn't allow the radio to be played and if anyone knocked on their door they didn't open it. Once, when they heard people coming, he held her to him and put his hand over her mouth. 'If you aren't quiet,' he told her, when the visitors had gone, 'we'll have to put you in a drawer.'

She thought she heard her parents crying in the night.

Her mother's words about the finality of fire stayed in her mind. She asked her if fire burned everything.

'Almost everything.'

'So what doesn't it burn?'

Her mother never took time to deliberate. She had an answer to every question ready, as though she knew it was going to be asked. 'Love and hatred,' she said. 'But I might be wrong about love.'

'How can you burn love?' Sibella wanted to know.

'By burning the people who feel it.'

'So why can't you burn hatred?'

'Because hatred exists outside of people. I liken it to a virus. People catch it. Disgust the same. That's another thing that's flameproof. It lives for ever. So my advice to you is never to inspire it.'

'Love or disgust?'

'Ha! The cynical answer is "both". But I am not a cynic. Just a pessimist. So my prayer for you is that you will inspire love, but not disgust.'

'How do I do make sure I don't?'

Her mother looked at her and this time thought a while before answering. Then she laughed her crazy woman's laugh. 'You can't!'

It was because she feared her mother was right and that hatred and disgust were indestructible by flame that Sibella threw the book into the sea. It had disgusted her father, it disgusted her mother even as she was writing it, and in so far as she could understand its ravings, it disgusted Sibella. So the bottom of the sea, where it could disgust the fish, was the best place for it.

As for what her mother told her about fire, she tried to live by it thereafter. She sat on the cliffs above the cottage and burned things – papers, letters, photographs, handkerchiefs, wild flowers. Sometimes, after she was married, she thought she would have burned her jewellery had it been flammable.

She had a lot of time, while her husband worked on his lathe and Kevern was at school, in which to worry and remember, though she couldn't remember ever coming to Port Reuben which was not, her mother had once inadvertently let slip, her place of birth.

'So where was my place of birth?' she asked.

'Somewhere else.'

'Where?'

'Somewhere far.'

'Was it nice?'

'Nowhere's nice.'

'Why did we leave?'

Her mother ran her fingers through her distracted hair. 'It seemed a good idea at the time.'

Her father overheard. 'It *was* a good idea at the time,' he said. 'It still is a good idea. We're alive, aren't we? Just don't answer any questions.'

'What questions?'

'And don't *ask* so many questions either.'

And that was all they told her. Her mother kissed her on the head and returned to the kitchen table to go on writing the book that never could and never would be finished. There wasn't much talking in the house. Her father, too, preferred silence to conversation and work to pleasure. Both her parents seemed never to want to finish what they were doing, as though the moment they finished they'd be finished themselves.

She remembered how her mother worked, with a bright light to ease her depression always shining in her face, surrounded by books (which to Sibella's sense only made the depression more intense), twisting loops of her hair around her forefinger, her head propped between two fists when she was thinking, and then her mouth opening and closing as she wrote, occasionally laughing like a hyena, though whether at something she had read or something she had written, something that amused her or something that made her angry – because crazy people laughed when they were angry as well as when they were amused – Sibella was never sure.

'Don't read over my shoulder, Sibella,' her mother would tell her when she tried to find out, 'you're blocking my light,' but in so absent-minded a manner that Sibella felt it was all right to stay where she was and go on reading. She understood little of it at the time, not even the drawings and photographs her mother glued into the book, and wouldn't have sworn that she understood it later when she had all the time in the world to absorb its meanings. But a few elusive phrases lodged in her mind – 'when they saw a moneylender they saw a bloodsucker, for those two defiled substances, money and blood, circulate alike'; 'whoever cleans bodies is hated irrationally for doing what needs to be done'; 'let my child be brought up to the highest level of civilisation, she will still always be thought of as a divine executioner, the child of divine executioners, and must always live in expectation of execution herself' – and they were sufficient to persuade her that it had to be destroyed.

ii

Aged forty-five, and appearing older – while not growing crooked like her father, she had never possessed an iota of her mother's looks – she tried to inspire love, as her mother had hoped she would, and had an almost affair with Madron Shmukler the village butcher. 'You are nothing to write home about yourself,' she told him when he expressed surprise that she attracted him given that she wasn't at all pretty and not remotely his type. He too was forty-five and looked older. They didn't bother to go through the routine of discussing their otherwise-engaged spouses, it was all so predictable. He would deliver meat to the cottage and when the coast was clear they would climb the cliffs separately, as though going in different directions – though there was nowhere for either of them to go – and then meet on Port Reuben Head, which gave them a good view of anyone approaching. Here they would sit on the grass, surprised to be attracted to each other, and half-heartedly – no, quarter-heartedly, she thought – make companionable if perfunctory contact. He would put his hands on her breasts, which were still surprisingly soft under an item of clothing he was unable to name, and she would put her hands inside his trousers. What she found was surprisingly soft too.

Could you call that an affair? Neither of them thought so but they went on doing it, intermittently, until they were too old to climb the cliffs.

She had picked him out at the start of it because he was a butcher and she wanted someone to talk about blood to. Did he feel it polluted him?

'Do I feel it *what*?'

'What I want to know is whether butchers feel unclean. Do they fear they have dirty hands?'

He took his own hands out of her shirt – was it a shirt? – and examined them. 'Look for yourself,' he said. 'You have to wash a lot in my line of work.'

'No, I mean morally unclean. Spiritually . . .'

'Cutting chops?'

'Slaughtering . . .'

'I don't slaughter. I'm more like an undertaker. The animals come to me already dead, but instead of burying them I cut them up and sell them to you.'

Theirs was first and foremost a commercial relationship, he didn't want her to forget. Though later, as a sign of his maturing fondness, he didn't charge her.

He reached for the worn handbag she carried everywhere with her, though she kept almost nothing in it. 'Same with a tanner,' he said. 'Whoever treated the leather for this old thing didn't actually skin the animal.'

She didn't like the way he handled her bag. 'But you're still a link in the chain,' she said.

He stared at her in bafflement. What did she mean? Who was she? What was he doing with her? She was small and round, with flickering blue eyes and discoloured ping-pong-ball cheeks, and wore old-fashioned clothes. She reminded him of Miss Klug, one of his old primary-school teachers, unless what she reminded him of was how Miss Klug had made him feel – embarrassed to be her favourite, but safe. He was nothing to write home about himself, as Sibella had reminded him, but his butcher's brawn and innocent blue eyes had excited a few women over the years, and but for his being married and having four sons, he wouldn't have been embarrassed to be seen with any of them.

Sibella, though, was not a woman he wanted anyone to know about. Was she crazy?

'A link in what chain?' he asked.

She laughed, reminding herself suddenly of her mother. 'The defilement chain.'

'I don't know what that means.'

'Do you feel that the part you play in killing animals – I know you don't actually *kill* them – I take your point about undertakers and tanners – but do you feel that there's blood on your hands and that people treat you differently because of it?'

He wondered if that was the longest question he'd ever been asked. He flicked away an ant that was crawling up her leg. 'Why would people treat me differently?'

She remembered the Untouchables of India, photographs of whom her mother found in magazines and pasted into her crazy person's history. Their lowly status, according to her mother, had many explanations but none so telling as their original association with blood. They were their society's ritual murderers, and as such considered unclean. The Burakumin of Japan – information about whom her mother had also collected – the same. Butchers, undertakers, slaughtermen, spillers of blood, killers of gods. And the taboo against touching them could never be broken. They had death on them, and whoever had death on him was outcast. Illogical, because someone had to deal with the dead, the tasks they performed were indispensable and even sacred, but logic had nothing to do with defilement.

'Because they can't forgive the blood,' Sibella said.

Madron shook his head. 'Well that's what you say, but they forgive mine fine enough.'

She shrugged but returned to the subject often. It almost became their love talk. Death, defilement, ritual murderers, sacred executioners.

'Put another record on, girl,' he would say to her.

And she would try. Sometimes, lying with her head against his chest, listening to the hungry screeching of the seagulls, looking up at the undersides of their ugly, torpedo bodies, she would almost succeed.

But she was never free of the sensation that she disgusted him. Which was strange because it was he – a man who dabbled in blood for a living – who was supposed to disgust her.

She loved him, after a fashion, nonetheless. And missed him more intensely than she thought she would when he died, more intensely even than she missed her parents. Was that, she wondered, because in their agitated distance from her they had been half dead already. She could barely remember her mother's disappearance. As for how her father died, she realised with shame that she didn't know. Howel told her it had happened. That she did remember. 'I'll be looking after you now,' he said.

Poor Madron had a heart attack, that was all. One of those quiet ones in the bath. She hoped she hadn't been instrumental in bringing it on. Not by making love, which between them had never been strenuous, but by making him feel dirty. Had she talked his heart into stopping?

She would have liked to kiss his perplexed brow one more time but she understood she couldn't see him. She suffered the terrible fate of all mistresses of married men in that she didn't dare show her face at his funeral.

'Don't show your face.' Where had she heard that before?

It was on the seventh anniversary of his death – almost certainly not coincidentally – that she set fire to her fingers.

CHAPTER 2

FRIENDS

i

'We should never have gone away,' Kevern said to Ailinn when they were inside.

She felt he was blaming her, though the trip had been his idea.

'Can you tell yet if anything's been taken?' she asked.

'It's not what's been taken. I have nothing it would be worth anyone's while to take. It's what's been *seen* that concerns me.'

He stood at the window, not wanting to look around, grinding his fists into his eyes.

'Your feet,' Ailinn said. 'I've only just noticed.'

'What?'

'They're too big.'

He stared at her.

'I'm trying to cheer you up with a joke,' she said.

She stood forlorn in the middle of the little sitting room, not knowing where to put herself, how to help, what to say. When Kevern was at a loss he

230

joked, so she thought she should try the same. But the only effect of her joke was to remind him of something and send him flying up the stairs. She heard him banging about, like a wild animal trapped in someone's loft. After ten minutes he came back down, looking ashen. 'Have they been up there?' she asked.

'*They*?'

'Anyone?'

He fell into an armchair and shrugged. 'Must have been. Everything's too neat.'

'So nothing's gone?'

'Hard to say. My father's records are still there. And I think all his books. That's something. If they wanted to get me on an heirloom charge they'd have taken those. But who knows what they've read, or listened to, or photographed?'

She couldn't help herself. '*They*?'

'I think you should go,' he said.

She went over to him and kissed the top of his head. 'I can't leave you alone in this state,' she said.

'I don't know what you mean by "this state". I am how I always am.'

'Then I can't leave you in that state. Come on – discuss it with me. What do you think's happened?'

He sat forward and dropped his head between his knees. 'Ahab's been,' he said.

★   ★   ★

231

One detail he didn't mention: whoever had tidied up his runner had been for a lie-down in his bed.

ii

She didn't want to leave him in any state but she had no choice. 'I need to sleep this one out alone,' he said.

She offered to take the couch but he begged her to go. 'Just for tonight,' he said. 'This is my doing. I was the one who kissed Lowenna Morgenstern.'

'One of the many.'

'You know what I mean.'

'You think this is about her?'

'No. But it's still my fault.'

'You aren't going to do anything silly,' she said.

'Like what? Leave the country?'

She kissed his non-responding lips, noticing for the first time that there were dry serrations in them and that his breath was sour, then she walked back slowly, heavily, through the village to Paradise Valley. I feel a hundred, she thought. A drunken man called out to her. 'I want to bite you,' he said. She laughed. I'm a hundred and he wants to bite me. 'You'll break your teeth,' she dared to call back. But he was too unsteady to take her up on the challenge. A couple snogged violently against a dry-stone wall. Making the beast. A good description of them. A thing of scales and claws. Prehistoric. Kevern and Lowenna, she thought. But she agreed with his assessment that this – supposing he had not imagined it all – was not about Lowenna. As she pushed open the first of the field gates to the Valley a cat ran across her feet. A bad omen according to her adoptive mother. When a cat ran across your feet someone was going on a long journey. And why was that bad? Because you would never see them again.

Her heart fluttered.

Did Kevern's bitter gibe about leaving the country mean anything? Did any of his gibes mean anything? For their own good, people were discouraged from leaving the country – assuming they had any notion of what or where any other country was – but there was always a way if you were desperate, particularly if you lived by the sea and had the money to persuade one of the local fishermen to smuggle you out. You'd never be heard of again. In all likelihood the fisherman would throw you overboard once you were out of sight of the mainland. But at least you'd achieved what you wanted and got away. Why, though, would Kevern want that? He'd told her he loved her. He'd told her he'd never been – and had never in his life expected to be – so happy. So why? And if he wasn't running from the police, who was he running from? Ahab, he'd said. Ahab! Ahab was hers. She felt possessive of him, and angry with Kevern. Before he met her, he had not been troubled by any Ahab. Lampoons, yes.

Harpoons, no. What was he doing purloining her terror?

iii

She found Ez up, playing patience and listening to love ballads on the utility console.

'Heavens,' Ez said, 'what brings you home?'

'Trouble.'

'Did the trip go badly?'

'No, the trip went well. Or at least we went well. What we didn't like we didn't like together. It was what we found when we got back.'

Ez put away her cards. 'I'll make tea,' she said, 'unless you'd like something stiffer.'

'Stiffer.'

The older woman poured them a brandy. Rather ceremoniously, Ailinn thought, as though this was a conversation she'd been expecting, was waiting for even, and the brandy had been bought for just such an event. Brandy – when did they ever drink brandy together?

'So . . .?'

'So . . .?'

'So what was it exactly that you found when you got back?'

'Somebody broke into Kevern's cottage while we were away.'

'Was there damage?'

'No. They'd tidied it up.'

'That's an unusual break-in. Was much taken?'

'As far as I could tell – as far as Kevern could tell – nothing.'

'Could you have been mistaken?'

Ailinn was not prepared to tell Ez that Kevern's rug had been straightened, because that would have necessitated her explaining why it was always left rumpled, and that would have been to betray her lover to her friend. She trusted Ez but that was not the point. You don't trust anyone with another person's secrets.

'He's very alert to the slightest change,' she said. 'He knows if anyone's leaned on his gate or sniffed the scent out of one of his roses.'

'Roses? You never said he was a gardener.'

'He isn't. I was being facetious. I'm sorry, I'm upset.'

'Do you know what I think?' Ez said. She was a *do you know what I think* kind of a woman. She assumed people went to her to hear homilies. As, indeed, they often did. 'I think you were both tired after a long drive. And if Kevern is as sensitive to any vibration in the vicinity of his cottage as you say, he was probably anxious the whole time you were away and simply found what he'd feared finding.'

'You are very sure of everything,' Ailinn said. She felt she'd been forced to take a side and the only side she could take was Kevern's.

Ez, she noticed, coloured. For all her intrusiveness, she tried to take a relaxed attitude to Ailinn's worries, half listening, half humouring, in the way of an older person, a concerned relation or a teacher, who knew that things usually worked out tolerably well in the end. The better a friend you were, the more cheerful a front you presented, was Ez's philosophy. A cup of tea, a moral lesson, a hug. She was doctorly, motherly, and even a touch professorial, at the same time. Ailinn had liked the contrarieties of her personality from the moment she met her in the reading group. She dressed modestly, in button-up cardigans and long skirts but liked hobbling about, for short periods, on high heels. Crimson high heels, as though she kept an alternative version of herself under her skirt. She had the quiet, respectful manner of a librarian, and no sense of humour to speak of, but if anything was said which she thought might be designed to amuse her she would choke with laughter, spluttering like a schoolgirl, or throwing back her head and showing how beautiful, before it lost its smoothness, the arc of her throat had once been. She was on her own now but she hadn't always been, Ailinn surmised. There'd been some personal tragedy in her life. A man she'd loved had run away or died. She carried a torch for someone. She burned a little candle in her heart. That was what the crimson shoes were doing – keeping a spark alive. Ailinn even wondered if this was his cottage, whoever he was, or whether they'd had their affair here, in this dripping corner of Paradise Valley where mushrooms would grow out of your shoes if you didn't wear them for a day. Was that why she'd asked Ailinn along – so that she had reason to hold herself together, so that she wouldn't give way to morbidity? In which case Ailinn's falling in love with Kevern and all but moving out of the Valley was inconsiderate. Did that explain the unwonted attentiveness of Ez's manner tonight, the way she appeared to be counting syllables and listening to pauses? Did she *want* to hear that something was amiss between them?

'No, I'm not sure of anything,' she said. 'I was just looking at the situation from all angles.'

'What if it's the police?' Ailinn wondered aloud. 'What if they really do suspect him?'

'But nothing was taken from the cottage, you say.'

'Well that's what Kevern said. But he didn't exactly give himself time to check.'

'You can usually tell.'

'Can you?'

'You can usually tell when something of your own, something that matters to you, has been taken. You just know.'

Ailinn looked at her. What a lot Ez suddenly *just knew*. She took another sip of the brandy. 'What did you do, Ez?' she asked. 'What did you do before you became book-group police?'

Ez laughed – but not, on this occasion, like a young girl. 'That's an amusing concept,' she said. 'I'm sure you didn't think I was policing any of the meetings you came to. I just chose the books.'

'Exactly. You policed what we read. Were you a different kind of policeman before that?'

'I was an administrator.'

'Administering what?'

'Oh, this and that. I kept an eye open.'

'On whom?'

'Good question. Other people who were keeping an eye open.'

Perhaps it was the brandy talking, but Ailinn suddenly propped her elbows on the table, supported her head in her hands and stared hard into her friend's face. 'What's this all about, Ez?' she asked.

'*This*?'

'Why did you bring me here? Why were Kevern and I thrown into one another's arms? Why did you force me to ring him when we'd broken up? Why did someone break into his house while we were away?'

'A: I brought you here because you were – because you are – my friend. B: I am not aware that you and Kevern were thrown into each other's arms. I thought you said it was love at first sight. C: As for Kevern's house – I have no idea why someone would have broken in, just as you have no idea whether anyone actually did.'

'Then why are you annoyed with me?'

'I am not in the slightest bit annoyed with you.' She reached out to stroke Ailinn's cheek. 'I am concerned about you, that's all.'

'Then why are your hands cold?'

'I didn't know they were.'

'And why are you concerned? You are never

238

concerned for me. Not in this way. How many times have you told me I was someone in whom you had absolute faith? And what did that mean, anyway?'

Perhaps it was the brandy talking again, but she began to cry. Not a flood, just a trickle of soft tears that were gone almost as soon as they appeared.

'You're very tired. I think you should go to bed,' Ez said.

'Yes, I think so too. But I won't sleep. I will lie there all night wondering.'

'Wondering who broke in?'

'Wondering whether he was serious when he spoke about leaving the country.'

'Kevern said he was going to leave the country?'

'Not exactly. But he allowed the idea to float before me, like a threat.'

'We need to talk,' Ez said. And this time had Ailinn felt her hands she would have discovered they weren't just cold, they were frozen.

CHAPTER 3

THE WOMEN'S ILLNESS

Monday 25th

Not normally a diary day, but there are things I have to get down before they escape me.

Bloody Gutkind!

Looking on the bright side, as it is my nature to do, the decline of Gutkind's fortunes, following his most recent act of lumbering zealotry, must herald an improvement in mine. Funny how fate – the divine juggler – balances the fortunes of men with such precision, so that with each rise or fall we vacate space, not just for any old rival, but for someone we have a particular reason for hating. It was to yours truly, anyway, that the powers that be turned to minimise the damage Gutkind was causing. First of all the clown needed to be called off Kevern Cohen, and who better than me, given that I'd taught him briefly (Gutkind, that is) as a mature student, impossible as it is to believe that so unimaginative a man could ever have flirted with the idea of a second career in the Benign Visual Arts, though the Benign Visual Arts, I have to say, did not flirt back – who better, I repeat, than someone with my authority to remind him of the limits of his? Nothing too heavy-handed, just a quiet, *entre nous* suggestion – implicating no one higher up – that he back off. Why break a butterfly on a wheel and all that. Since you're acquainted with him, Professor, you can intimate our disfavour, was the flavour (the flavour of their disfavour is nice, don't you think?) of their communication to me. My knowing Kevern as well, of course, gave me extra ammunition. 'I've been watching Cohen for some time,' I could get away with saying to Detective Inspector Gutkind, 'and nothing I have seen suggests he would harm a hair of a woman's head, let alone do what was done to poor Lowenna Morgenstern, so please don't bother your own pretty little head about him any further. Kevern Cohen? Mr Lovespoon himself! Are you joking? A policeman of all people should know there are some men who are incapable of committing a murder because they know they'd never get the blood off their hands. Can you imagine our friend Kevern "Coco" Cohen scrubbing underneath his fingernails?

He'd be there, crouched over himself, washing until Doomsday. Don't make me laugh, Detective Inspector. The country's crawling with ruffians. Go bag yourself one of those.'

How it was that Gutkind became first an acquaintance and subsequently a student of mine is a story in itself. We met through our wives, is the short of it. They had become friends in the course of attending Credibility Fatigue classes together. And that, too, is a story in itself. It's always the women who go a little wobbly in the matter of WHAT HAPPENED – probably as a consequence of giving or anticipating giving birth, unless it's a more generally diffused hormonal agitation – whereupon some stiffening of their resolve is called for. I can't speak for Mrs Gutkind, who has since left her husband – for which, I have to say, no sane person could blame her – but my wife, Demelza, fell a while back into terribly depressed spirits, questioning the point of saying sorry all the time when by all official accounts (as indeed by mine) there was nothing really to say sorry for, questioning the way we lived our lives, questioning the powers that be, even questioning me, the person who puts food on her table. 'Nothing makes any sense to me,' she'd complain. 'I feel a pall over everything, I

242

feel the children are fed lies at school, I feel I was fed lies at school, I suspect you're feeding lies to your students, we are supposed to have mended what went wrong, except that we are told nothing went wrong, but if it's not safe to go out on to the streets – not safe here, in fucking sleepy Bethesda! – it's as though we're all in a trance, like zombies, pretending, what are we pretending Phinny, what aren't we saying, what aren't you saying, what are these little jobs you say you have to do, other women . . . are you seeing other women? Except I don't feel here' – her hands upon her lovely breasts – 'that you are seeing other women, it feels more as if you've taken to religion or are going out to drink with aliens or someone, is that what you're doing, or are we the aliens, are we from another planet, Phinny, because increasingly I don't feel I'm from this one . . .' And more along such loopy lines.

The doctor, at my instigation, prescribed antidepressants.

Credibility Fatigue classes were my idea too. Between ourselves, dear diary, I'd had a minor professional fling – our both being professors of illusions of sorts – with Megan Abrahamson, the woman who ran the classes in Bethesda, a stern, blue-eyed

243

beauty who'd fallen into a terrible depression herself when she was giving birth to her first child and so knew from the inside exactly what Demelza and others like her were going through. 'What we fear as mothers-to-be,' she explained to me, 'is bringing our child into a dangerous, deceitful world. We see a threat whenever anyone approaches us and we hear a lie in everything that's said. It's the protective instinct gone haywire. So when you learn about what happened, if it happened you are of a mind to say no ifs or buts about it, it happened, and obviously shouldn't have happened, or we wouldn't all still be so cagey about it, saying sorry while insisting there's nothing to say sorry for. You want, you see, the truth and nothing but the truth for your baby. It isn't you who isn't seeing straight, you think, it's everybody else. In your own eyes you are getting to the bottom of a truth that has been obfuscated, no matter that the person doing the obfuscating is you. It's at this point that I find some straight-talking history, painful as it is, is what's required. "OK, you asked for it," I say. I show them classified documents and photographs: this is what those whom you fear were the innocent victims of what happened were responsible for, I say; this is the damage they wrought, this is the weaponry they unloosed on defenceless peoples, these are the countries they laid waste in their baseless, neurotic, opportunistic fear of being laid waste themselves, these are the bitter fruits of their egoistic policy of "never again", this is how they justified it here, in our parliament and in our newspapers, this is the misery of which they were the authors, these are their faces, these are their words, this is their history, repeated and repeated again wherever they set foot, sorrowful to themselves but a thousand times more sorrowful to those whose necks they trod on and who, when they could finally take no more, trod back, that's if they did, and these are their confessions, the expressions of self-loathing, the acts of self-immolation, the orgy of introverted hate they unleashed on one another as a last expression of an ancient culpability for which they knew, better than anyone else, there could be no redemption. Yes, it breaks the heart, but WHAT HAPPENED, if indeed it happened, was at the last visited by them upon themselves . . .'

I could have kissed her.

In fact I did kiss her.

To what degree these classes put Demelza's concerns to rest I have no idea. She has always been an obstinate, at times even a hysterical, woman. But she certainly turned more placid and glazed-eyed once she'd completed the course. Could have been the antidepressants, I accept, but I like to think that demonstrable truth played its part.

Gutkind and I shared a drink at the bar close to the Credibility Fatigue Centre from time to time while waiting for our wives. He was more angry with his than I was with mine. 'Some bleeding heart has got to her,' he said.

I wondered – *de haut en bas*, professor to police constable, which was all he was in those days – in what way someone had 'got' to her.

He was needled by my asking. 'Women talk to each other,' he said.

His eyes could be too fierce for his complexion. When they blazed, as they were blazing now, they burned out the little natural colour he possessed. In fairness to him I should say that most of the men in the pub we were drinking in looked the same. Coals of fire burning in every face. Just possibly they too were waiting for their wives, though they had the air of frequenting such places as this, as indeed did Gutkind, whereas for me pub-going was an exceptional circumstance. Regulars or not, they knew in their bones I wasn't Bethesda born, they could smell the outsider on me.

I came once with Kevern Cohen and I feared there was going to be a lynch party. Two aphids! Why did that make them so angry? If they had to mark their awareness of our difference why didn't they just laugh at us? Or come over to touch our skin? 'Jesus God Almighty, it's skin remarkably similar to ours! Let's be friends.' But no, they snarled and ground their knuckles into the bar, exchanging glances with one another as though each felt it was his neighbour's place to raise an arm against us, and the fact that no one did was a species of betrayal and ultimately shame. Was the impotence they felt another reason for mistrusting us the more? 'Those you don't kill when you should, you end up hating with a fury that is beyond murderousness,' Kevern said as we were urinating in adjoining booths. In fact I was urinating and Kevern was waiting for me to finish. He found it impossible, he confided, to pass water in the presence of another man. 'What about a woman?' I enquired. 'Can any man pass water in the presence of a woman?' he asked, in what was not, I believe, a feigned astonishment. 'Demelza and I do it all the time,' I told him.

I thought he was going to throw up.

It struck me as a good job that no locals were present to witness Kevern's fastidiousness. They would have been still more inclined to lynch him. I have thought about what he said many times. Not on the subject of urinating in company but on the subject of hating those it would have been better that you'd killed. Was he right? And why such murderous hatred in the first place? I could only suppose that the living evidence of someone and somewhere else – the someone and somewhere else those pub regulars could smell on us the minute we entered the room – entirely undermined their confidence in the suffi-ciency of who and where they were. Are we so precarious in our sense of self that the mere existence of difference throws us into molecular chaos? Is it electrical? And was it even possible that Kevern's inability to pass water in my company had a com-parable effect on me? I'm not saying I wanted to kill him on account of his extreme niceness in the matter of a quick piss, but I don't rule out the possibility that I did. Joking. No real danger, of course, because I've read too many poems and seen too much art to be a man of violence – art and poetry being what those troglodytic aphid-haters lacked to turn them from monsters into men.

I didn't convey any of these thoughts to Gutkind, who struck me as a bit of a trog himself, a brooding more than a thinking being anyway. 'She's got it into her head that I see plots everywhere,' he was saying when I returned from my reflections. His wife he was talking about. 'And you've got it into your head that someone's been plotting to get her to think that?' I replied. He eyed me narrowly. I knew what he was thinking. 'Supercilious swine!' But you get that a lot in my profession. The world does not care for professors, even though for a while it was hoped that a number of the worst sort had been thinned out in the purges.

I ordered more drinks and proposed a toast to the course. 'Megan Abrahamson should sort her out proper,' I said, trying to sound like a local. He shook his head, not doubting my confidence but annoyed that a wife of his needed to be sorted out at all. Evidently he took it as a slur on his manhood and position. 'In my line of work,' he said – from which I took him to imply that my line of work wasn't work at all – 'you rarely see an effect without a cause. I don't say every victim has been playing head games with the culprit, but more often than not a crime could have been averted had the victim been more circumspect.' I nodded my approval at his use of 'circumspect'. Fair's fair – if you mark a man down for inconsequence you should also mark him up for vocabulary. 'And if there's a reason why one person's been attacked,' he went on, without showing me any gratitude, 'there sure as hell has to be a reason why a couple of hundred thousand were.'

'If they were.' At any time it seemed necessary to me to throw that in, but with our wives currently receiving corrective instruction from Megan Abrahamson it seemed especially important to be punctilious.

'I grant your if in so far as it relates to eventuation,' Gutkind said, 'but not in so far as it relates to provocation.'

Get him, I thought. But put this sudden turgescence of language down to police school.

I took his point. In the matter of deserts he was an unreconstructed non-iffer. What had happened had had to happen in his little, heretical policeman's book, no ifs about it. Unlike our women, who in their illness feared they were complicit in covering up something terrible, Gutkind believed everyone else was complicit in covering up something grand. No ifs or buts: it had needed to happen and only fell short of a desirable outcome in so far as it could be shown – either on account of faint-heartedness on the one side, or a diabolical cunning on the other – not to have happened at all. That his wife had trouble with the logic of his frustration drove him almost to madness. As I understood it, her comprehension halted at the moment he denied a thing he so patently approved. 'Did it happen or didn't it?' she had screamed at him. Yes, as an idea, he had explained to her, no, as a realisation of that idea. 'So why are we saying sorry?' That was a good question, he agreed. They were saying sorry over the intention. 'Which in that case,' she persisted, 'must have been a bad intention.' No, no, no! It was good intention ineffectively carried out. 'So are we saying sorry for that? Sorry we didn't do it better? That doesn't sound much of an apology to me.' 'Then don't say it for fuck's sake!' Gutkind had exploded. I wouldn't have been surprised to learn he snogged her after that. If only to have something tangible to say sorry for himself.

'All's well that ends well,' I said, as we finished our drinks, more as a way of calming him down than anything else.

'Except it doesn't end, does it?' he said. 'People like our wives won't allow it.'

'I mean it ends well,' I said, 'in that one way or another the thing you desired was achieved.'

I could see he was about to tell me that

it hadn't ended to his satisfaction at all. What the hell did he want, this denier with a broken heart – a rerun? I raised my hand to suggest that I was out of steam. Once a man starts comparing your wife to his wife it's wise to bring the conversation to an end. But he must have liked something about me, or been impressed by the advantage an education in the Benign Visual Arts clearly gave me in our conversation, because about six months later he enrolled as a mature student.

Six months after that I failed him. It wasn't that he wrote badly, just that his conspiracy-theorist's view of art made every artist the victim of some other artist's malevolence, Masaccio dying before he was thirty thanks to the machinations of Fra Angelico, Lautrec having been thrown off his horse by Pierre Puvis de Chavannes, Constable . . . but there was no end of it. 'Art isn't war,' I told him when discussing his papers. 'Isn't it!' he said, storming out of my office.

So no matter how much time had passed it wasn't going to be easy, I thought, taking one thing with another, to persuade him to leave Kevern 'Coco' Cohen to me. But when I got to him he was already apprised of the official view of his breaking into Kevern's cottage. 'I know, I know,' he said. 'I've been a naughty boy.'

'Who told you?'

'None of yours,' he said. 'But since she got to me before you did I assume she must be your superior.'

'She?'

'Ha. I'm glad it stings. Yes, she.'

I was the one now who needed to re-arrange his features. 'Shows the importance of this,' I said.

'Importance my arse. If importance was the measure they'd have let me get on with it. All it shows is that the nancy boy has friends in high places.'

'Nancy boy?'

'You should see his furniture.'

'If he was a nancy boy you wouldn't suspect him of doing away with Lowenna Morgenstern?'

'I don't. Though he does admit to kissing her.'

'There you are then,' I said.

'There I am then what? A kiss doesn't prove you're straight.'

'I agree. Nor does it prove you're a killer.'

'Of course he's not a killer. He hasn't got the courage. Or the strength. His crime is hoarding stuff.'

'What stuff?' I asked. This made me anxious. I should have known about stuff.

'I've just told you. Nancy-boy stuff. Furniture, books, records, pillowcases, tablecloths. You should see his towels. Silk-edged! You should see his bed. If you've been looking after him properly you will have seen his bed. You haven't? There you are then. Some of us aren't doing our jobs.'

'One can do one's job and not be officious,' I answered him, officiously.

'And one can do one's job and not be efficient. He's not right. You should know that. He's not right and his place is not right. And all this pretending to have a girlfriend. If you ask me, his girlfriend is not right either.'

'Not being right,' I reminded him, 'is not your province.'

'I know that. Except that I have to clean up the consequences of couples being wrong. But if those whose province it is insist on keeping their eyes in their backsides . . .'

'We go at a different pace, that's all. We have truth to sieve through. We can't just go on hunches.'

'Well, he's yours again now,' he said with displeasure, 'whatever you go on.'

'There's just one more thing,' I said. He turned his face from me. He didn't care what other things there were. But I had to get an acknowledgement from him. 'Whatever you saw in his cottage must remain between

you and him,' I said. 'It's not public information. And you have to stay away from
him. They don't want him frightened.'

'What – afraid he'll run away?' He tried to
find a laugh but failed.

'He needs not to be startled,' I said. 'That's
all. They aren't playing about with this one.
They want him where they can keep an
eye on him.'

'So, it's as I've been saying all along –
he's not right.'

What I said next I said only to appear I
knew more than he did. 'On the contrary
– he might be only too right.'

But as soon as I said it I realised I knew
more than I knew I knew.

CHAPTER 4

THE CHIMES AT MIDNIGHT

i

He slept badly. Knowing someone had been lying on his bed – perhaps even *in* his bed – took from his already small capacity to rest.

But the real reason he slept badly was that Ailinn wasn't beside him. How quickly he'd come to rely on her being there! How safe, without his realising it, she'd made him feel!

Safety, he thought, could creep up on you as exactly as fear could.

Women sometimes talked of resisting love because it weakened them. Had it weakened him, he wondered, by insinuating safety into his life and seducing him into taking his eye off danger?

He shouldn't have asked her to move in with him in the first place, but nor should he have asked her to leave. He shouldn't have been short with her. It wasn't her fault that he'd deep-kissed Lowenna Morgenstern and brought Detective Inspector Gutkind into his cottage. Except that he knew Lowenna Morgenstern wasn't to blame either. It was Gutkind who had straightened his rug, he had no doubt of that. It was Gutkind who'd let himself in – while he, Kevern, was away from home, telling strangers to fuck off and hearing voices in Cohentown – Gutkind who'd gone searching through his things. But he wasn't searching for a blood-stained shirt. That, too, Kevern knew for sure. Gutkind didn't take him for a murderer. So what *did* Gutkind take him for?

And never mind Gutkind, who was nobody, nothing, just an accident of history – what *was* there to unearth?

He lay on his Ailinnless bed looking up at the ceiling with its low, weevilled beams, and watched the question refuse to take definite form. Like one of those humming patterns in the wallpaper that disturb the nights of feverish children, it twisted and writhed, now coming away from the wallpaper altogether, coming at him, making him wonder if it was truly outside himself at all or merely mimicked in visual form the fragmented evasions of his mind. There were some questions you couldn't ask, even of yourself. There were some questions you couldn't begin to mould from the black chaos of ignorance, for fear of what definition would bring. Because – because once you'd framed the question you'd given a half-shape to the answer. Better it stay amorphous on the ceiling, as much a musical sound as a drawn or sculpted form. As much a lost note from an electronic sonata, a jammed keyboard, as a moving blob of paint.

But tonight, without Ailinn to soothe him into forgetfulness, he couldn't leave it alone. Why, he compelled himself to ask, why this apprehension? Why the years of compulsive letter-box peering? Why the lock-checking?

He knew the psychology. It was displacement, all of it. It stood for something else. But wasn't it also simply a way of practising? A way of accustoming himself, at the very least, to what was not and never would be under his control?

Was that then all that he'd been waiting for – proof positive that he couldn't affect, for well or ill, his own outcome?

But did even that explain the persistence of the apprehension? Never mind whether there was or wasn't something that required an answer, why always this *apprehension* that there was? He felt he needed to hold his head to keep it steady. A clamp would have been a good thing. A brain vice. *Always* was the word that kept slipping in and out. *Always*, because the question itself predated his having to ask it. Why have I *always* been apprehensive? What do I think I've done that cries out for reparation? What do I fear I might do again?

He felt he let his mother and father down enunciating it in the silence of this bedroom which had once been their bedroom. Crude of him. Overwrought. Pusillanimous. And maybe even dangerous. Could this have been the very question, maybe the only question, they had all along been educating him never to ask? Could this have been what they who wanted to get in and take a look around had been waiting for all this time, could this have been what Gutkind had been hoping to lay hands on – the question, or rather the capitulation to the need to ask it? *What do I fear I have done* was like a confession of guilt. And it gave away his location. 'Hey! you who have always suspected someone of something, cast your gaze this way, the someone is me and I am over here. Here, here, come!'

Come and do what?

Take me away.

Another of his father's crazed songs came back to him. Something about them carrying him off, ha, ha! All Kevern could remember was that 'haha' and his mother putting her hands to her ears and shouting 'Shut up, Howel!' Which just made him sing it the more, laughing the laughter of the insanely unamused.

Ha, ha . . .

ii

Whatever Kevern imagined they were expecting to find it was not *A Crazy Person's History of Defilement, for Use in Schools.* When he counted off incriminating evidence on his fingers his grandmother's researches didn't figure. Expunged, the lot of it. For the good of the family. And that meant expunged from Kevern's knowledge too. Generation after generation, expunging this,

259

expunging that. Truth to tell, he had little left to hide. The first thing he had done on discovering that his rug had been straightened was to rush upstairs to see if any of his father's possessions had been touched – the Louis Armstrong and Fats Waller records, the books of poetry, the videos of those fast-talking fatalistic comedians his father had loved (never laughing at them, just nodding his head as though at the wisdom of Plato), the small packets of letters – but rationally he knew these would be of interest to no one, except in so far as his keeping them demonstrated a sentimental hankering for heritage. But the silk runner and the Biedermeier furniture already told that story loud and clear. And anyway, a small fine for clinging on to the past couldn't have been all Gutkind wanted to lay on him.

So why were they sacrosanct to Kevern? And what *did* Gutkind want to lay on him?

'What do I fear I have done?' Kevern lay there repeating to himself. It was the wrong question. 'What do *we* fear *we* have done?' he should have asked – more than *asked*, demanded to be told – remembering his father's breakdown, a nervous collapse for which he wouldn't hear of being treated, in the first place because he didn't want doctors poking around – a terror that was itself, Kevern thought at the time, a symptom of the breakdown – and secondly because he thought there was nothing any doctor could do as he had inherited the propensity from his own father. 'Let's just hope,' he recalled the old man saying from his bed, 'that it will die out with me and we haven't passed it on to you.'

Kevern didn't understand. Hadn't his grandfather, of whom he knew next to nothing, suffered his breakdown after the disappearance of his wife, Kevern's grandmother Jenna, of whom Kevern also knew next to nothing except that one elusive fact – that she'd gone out of the cottage and never returned? Who wouldn't suffer a breakdown after that? In which case there was no genetic disposition to this illness in the family, unless there was a genetic disposition on the part of the womenfolk to disappear.

'A witty distinction,' his father acknowledged, 'but that's your mother's father you're thinking of, so there's nothing genetically I could have inherited from him anyway.'

'What propensity then do you think you inherited from your own?' Kevern asked.

'The propensity to terror, but not, I am ashamed to say, the propensity to courage in the face of it. Nor, come to that, though this is not something I would wish you to have known about me before – but now it doesn't matter, now nothing matters – the propensity to loyalty.'

Kevern asked him what he meant, but he would say no more.

A disloyal coward, then. Well Kevern could enter sympathetically into that. How much loyalty would he show, if ever put to the test? How much resolution in the face of fear, pain, suspicion? When he locked and double-locked his door, wasn't he double-locking himself against faint-heartedness? But it hardly helped to know this. Whatever evidence Gutkind had been hunting for, it surely wasn't evidence of Kevern's inherited feebleness of character.

Then he remembered that just before he died his father grabbed his sleeve and, knocking over the candle that provided the only light he could bear, begged distractedly for his dog.

'You have no dog,' Kevern said.

'You don't have to lie to me,' his father said.

Kevern wondered if that meant his father wanted him to lie to him. But he couldn't produce a dog. He could tell him his dog had died, but where would be the kindness in that? 'You have had no dog for a long time,' he decided to say instead.

His father nodded, seeming to remember. 'Mr Bo Jangles' – he summoned the strength to cross the J, as though for the final time – 'grieved for his dog for twenty years. I've grieved longer.'

Kevern took the hand he hadn't loved. 'Well, he was a fine dog,' he said.

'Not for the dog, you fool!'

Kevern didn't ask 'Then for whom?' It was possible he didn't want to know.

'Forgive me,' his father said after a pause that Kevern thought would be his last.

'I have nothing to forgive you for,' Kevern said. 'You have cared for me.'

'Not you.'

'You have, you cared for me. You and Mam.'

The old man took his hand from Kevern's grasp and waved it across his face, as though to shoo away flies. 'Not you forgive me. *He* forgive me.'

'The dog?'

'What dog? Why do you keep going on about a dog when I'm talking about my brother?'

This was the first time Kevern had heard mention of a brother. Presumably he too, like the dog, was the invention of delirium.

'I'm sure he had nothing to forgive you for, either.'

'What do you know!' Another assault on the invisible flies, then something like a laugh from far away. 'Ha! It'll have to be you, then. You're the only one left, so it'll have to be you. Like the song. 'It had to be you' . . . You forgive me. You do it for him.'

'Can I do that?'

'There's no one else.'

'Then I forgive you,' Kevern said.

They were so secretive a family it didn't occur to him to ask what his father needed to be forgiven for. He didn't think it was any of his business. More to the point, he didn't *want* it to be any of his business. The aesthete in him shrank from such melodrama. He made small, finely crafted objects. A candlestick was the biggest thing to come off his lathe. And even his candlesticks had narrow waists and attenuated necks. If he hung his clothes in a Biedermeier wardrobe it was only in deference to his father's bulking sense of private tragedy. Biedermeier was where he came from, that was all. But where he came from kept rearing up at him, never to be satisfied until it had ripped open his throat. More melodrama. See, he jeered at himself, you are no better than your father. You can go on making all the intricately entangled lovespoons you like, your own entanglements remain gross. Ailinn? No, of course not Ailinn. But hadn't his treatment of her been gross? Shutting her out of his life like a dog?

He hadn't asked his father, ever, about anything because he hadn't ever wanted to hear the answer. But you don't always have to ask to know. And Kevern knew the answer in the way he knew so many things. He knew it and he didn't know it.

His father, then no more than a boy, he couldn't have been, closing the door on a brother, refusing to assist him, refusing his cries for help, leaving him out in the cold like a dog, letting whoever was after him have him, never mind who or why, he knew who and why – this, from innumerable clues, from an accumulation of half-expressed regrets and barely smothered confessions, from a history of hysterical injunctions and prohibitions, from asides and songs and sorrows, from skeletal dances and stillborn jests, from what he knew generally of the human heart and what he

264

knew specifically of his father's shrivelled soul, from logical deduction and common sense and experience, from the frightened life they'd lived in their fortress cottage ever since he could remember, and from what he suspected too well he would do if ever put to the same test – all this Kevern saw and didn't see.

iii

He was out early the morning after these recollections, sitting on his bench chewing over his father's plea, feeling the spittle from the blowhole on his face – submitting to nature's insults – when Densdell Kroplik found him. Kevern had heard the footsteps and hoped they were Ailinn's. Ailinn, with one of her paper flowers in her hair and another in her hand, come to receive his apology and plant a kiss on his brow. Ailinn, the light of his life.

He needed to be embraced. But not by Densdell Kroplik.

'A penny for them,' Kroplik said, employing his civil voice.

He was a strange sight up here against the sky, as though Caspar David Friedrich's Wanderer Above the Mists had suddenly turned around and shown himself. He was not wearing a frockcoat, though, but a smart, tweed, countryman's suit, with a raincoat over his arm. A miracle that anyone so businesslike could emerge from Kroplik's cowshed. It was this that made Kevern wonder if he were seeing things.

A raincoat and no rucksack, as though he'd come down out of the morning mist to meet his solicitor. Even the angry ruddiness of his cheeks was damped down, Kevern noted. Did that mean he could turn it on and off at will – his raging rusticity?

'So what business are you on, looking such a dandy?' Kevern asked.

Kroplik tapped his nose.

It was that gesture, more than anything else – denoting a man who had a hundred secrets of his own and was privy to a thousand more – that inveigled Kevern, who had hardly slept, into confidentiality. Who could say: maybe Kroplik knew something about what was going on.

'I've been away for a few days,' Kevern confided.

'Anywhere interesting?'

Kevern waved that part of the conversation away. 'While I was gone my cottage was broken into.'

'Not guilty,' Kroplik said.

'I would never have thought you were. I just wondered if you'd heard anything on the grapevine.'

'I'm not on the grapevine.'

Kevern had a go at an affable grin. It was that or push the swine into the sea. 'I've yet to hear of anything happening in this village that you haven't heard of first.'

Densdell Kroplik inclined his head before the

compliment. 'I'm the village historian,' he said, 'not the village gossip. Ask me something that occurred here a hundred years ago and I'll tell you. Ask me what occurred yesterday and your guess is as good as mine. I don't deal in yesterday.'

Kevern was grateful that, as befitted his suit and his unruddied cheeks, Densdell Kroplik, though as awkward as ever, was not playing the local this morning. But he still regretted what he said next even as he was saying it. 'That you know of – did my father have anything to hide?'

The historian rubbed both his eyes, as though before a spectacle that amazed him. It was a morning of miracles for both of them. He asked Kevern if he minded his joining him on the bench. He pretended to need time to catch the breath of his astonishment. 'Other than his being an aphid, you mean?'

'Yes, other than that.'

He scratched his head under his hat. 'Well he had you,' he finally answered.

'I assume that's a joke,' Kevern said, smothering the action of putting two fingers to his lips with a cough.

'Joke or not, many a child born round here is a clue to a secret people would rather didn't get out.'

'I'm guessing you're not telling me I'm someone else's child?'

'You wouldn't be the first. It's always hard to prove whose child anyone is, and usually unwise to try.'

My fault, Kevern thought. My own stupid fault. 'So is this a general supposition or do you know something specific?'

Densdell Kroplik put a hand on Kevern's knee. That Kevern could recall, no other man had ever done that. Not even his father. He found it hard to believe it could presage anything but an appalling revelation.

'No, nothing specific,' Kroplik said, noticing that Kevern shrank from his touch, 'though there was a story circulating some years ago – tell me to stop if this is painful – that your mother used to get free meat.'

'What the hell does that mean?'

'What it sounds. A certain butcher from these parts was said to enjoy her company on and off. They'd go for walks together. Up around here.'

'How do you know?'

'I'm a historian.'

'But not of gossip, you said.'

'Give it enough time, brother, and gossip's history.'

'And he'd give her free meat, this butcher?'

'That's my understanding.'

'Free *meat*!'

'Would you have rather she'd paid?'

Kevern rose from the bench. 'OK, enough,' he said.

Kroplik shrugged his shoulders. This wasn't his doing. Kevern had started it. 'I know how you feel,' he said. 'My mother was a slut too.'

'OK, I said that'll do!' Kevern repeated.

'Keep your shirt on. It's just a word. Mine ran off with a tin miner from St Abraham.' *St Abraham!* – he spat the words on to the ground. 'Used to be Laxobre. Lovely name that. Flinty. Like licking a stone. What lunatic would change Laxobre to St Poxy Abraham? Axe-wielding men lived in Laxobre. Not that that excuses them stealing my mother.' He paused to wipe his mouth. 'Anyway the butcher wouldn't have been your father. I don't as a rule do births and deaths, but for you I'd hazard a guess he came into the picture after you were born.'

Kevern wasn't sure it made it any better to imagine his mother – his mother! that bundle of old rags! – getting free meat from the butcher while he was at school. Did the other kids know? Did his father?

'I don't question your historiographical accuracy,' he said, 'but—'

'My what?'

'Don't play the village clown with me. You know what well enough. But this is fantastical. You must have seen my mother.'

'Walking out with the butcher?'

'No. You must have seen what she looked like.'

'Well I only saw her when she was getting on a bit. So that tells me nothing. She might have been a good-looking woman when she was younger. Your grandmother was a beauty, everyone said. Stuck-up, but beautiful.'

269

'I wouldn't know about that. She died before my time.'

'And mine. But you can take it from me she was. I saw a painting of her once. Done from photographs or memory, in my humble opinion. Too proud to pose for anybody, that one. Too private.'

'How do you know that?'

'I don't. But the painting was called something like *So Lovely Yet So Cold*, or *So Near Yet So Far*. Which I reckon is a clue.'

'Where is this painting?'

'Search me. Behind a bar some place. I might have its whereabouts written down, but I wouldn't swear to it. Her husband now—'

'Her husband what?'

'No one wanted to paint him. Nothing beautiful about a hunchback.'

Kevern needed to resume his position on the bench. Was this to be one of those mornings after which a man's life is never the same again? Like the morning you meet the woman you love? Like the morning you forget to lock your door?

'You're going to have to slow down,' he said. 'You're going to have to ease me into this more gently. You're telling me my mother took free meat from a butcher in return for sexual favours. You're telling me my grandmother was reputed to be a beautiful, stand-offish woman which you can confirm because you've seen a portrait of her hanging above a bar you can't remember where.

And now my grandfather was a hunchback. How much of this are you making up?'

For some reason Densdell Kroplik, raincoat or no raincoat, made the decision to revert to being the evil, inconsistently incoherent genius of Port Reuben. 'I never zeed 'im with my own eyes, Mister Master Cohen,' he said. 'So I can only goes on what I've picked up here and yonder. But yes. Nowadays they'd as like as not throw stones at your grand-daddy but in them days they'd 'ave respected him. Hellfellen, the giant, was a hunch-back. Charged people to feel his hump. It was a way of taxing travellers. If you wanted to get in or out of Ludgvennok you had to pay to feel him, which you gladly did anyways 'cos a hump brings you good luck. I doubt if your grand-daddy did any of that. Kept himself to himself, I'd say. And kept his wife to himself too, if he knew what was good for him. But everyone understood it was lucky to have a hunchback in the village. He might 'ave frightened the kids, but a talisman's a talisman. They'd 'ave given him no trouble whoever he was.'

'What do you mean whoever he was?'

This time it was Kroplik who rose from the bench.

'He was an aphid,' he said, wagging a finger. 'Don't you forget that. An upcountry man with no business to be here, hump or no hump. And aphids in those days had to watch their step. Not like now when they've got the run of the place. And then there was all that other stuff going on.

All the killing. All the rumours. Eyes everywhere. But they'd not have allowed anyone to harm him here, I can tell you that. Not a hunchback. Harm a hair on the head of a hunchback and you bring curses on your own head. Villagers don't forget a lesson like that. So they let him be. I'd say you're lucky to be here, Mister Master Cohen.'

'What the hell does that mean?'

'It means whatever you wants it to mean.'

'I'm *lucky to be here*?'

'Damn lucky, I'd say.'

'I was *born* here, Mr Kroplik.'

'That's the luck I'm talking about.'

Saying which, he slung his raincoat over his shoulder, wished Kevern Cohen good day and made his way into the village where a taxi was waiting outside the Friendly Fisherman to take him to his appointment in St Eber with, as it happened, a mutual friend. Detective Inspector Gutkind.

Or Eugene, as Kroplik now felt at liberty to call him.

iv

This conversation so disturbed Kevern's thoughts throughout the day that he almost forgot he had an evening class to give at the academy. He considered ringing and cancelling but his professional conscientiousness wouldn't let him do it. He called a taxi which got him there shaken but just in time.

There was relief in that. It meant he wouldn't be waylaid by Everett who had been quizzing him with more than usual insistence of late, and with more than usual intrusiveness. Why so interested in Ailinn?

It was good to talk to his class about wood. It took his mind off policemen and hunchbacks. 'In wood,' he said, in conclusion, 'is redemption.' Which some of his students thought was taking it a bit far. But it was true for him.

Despite the lateness of the hour he decided to sit in the library for a while. Anything rather than go back to his violated cottage and find Ailinn not there.

Rozenwyn Feigenblat, the very model of a provincial college librarian in a white lacy blouse and long black skirt and boots – she looked, he always thought, as though she'd ridden to work from somewhere far away, side-saddle while not taking her eyes off a book – greeted him with her accustomed ironic warmth. She liked him, he thought. He liked her. There was something of the centaur's wife about her, not half-horse, half-woman exactly, but half belonging to the world of action and half to the world of thought. A rider below the neck, she was a reader, oval-faced and small-eyed, concentrated and inquisitive, above it. She wore her fair hair in a pigtail which hung, tied with rubber bands, somehow sarcastically, over her left shoulder. He wondered if she unwound it when she rode.

He had nearly kissed her once, not a snog, he

doubted Rozenwyn Feigenblat was a snogger, but much as he had kissed Lowenna Morgenstern, out of liking, out of a passing pang of fondness, and because it seemed a shame not to. But something in the way she responded to his cautious advance – a look of near regret, as though she pitied him her unavailability – warned him off. Otherwise engaged, her look said. Would have, maybe, some other time, who knows, but just at this moment . . . can't. And now he gave off the same message. Have Ailinn, so unavailable. Only he didn't have Ailinn, did he?

He sensed a moment of danger. 'You don't normally come in here at this time,' she said. Her little darting eyes had fires in them. Had her circumstances suddenly changed?

'No,' he said, 'but I need an hour of quiet.'

'An hour I can't give you. I close in half.'

A moment of danger, all right.

'So what can I read in half an hour?'

'You want a short story?'

'I am sick of stories. Can you do short and factual?'

She put her finger to her chin, parodying thought. 'How about . . . How about . . . *Beauty and Morality* . . .'

'Everett's latest? I'd hardly call that factual.'

'No, but it's short.'

'Not what I'm in the mood for.'

'Is it the beauty or the morality that's putting you off?'

'Beauty never puts me off.'

'So morality does?'

'No. It must be the conjunction I don't buy.'

'Then you don't buy Everett.'

She gave a little tug to her pigtail, as though it were a coded signal for gossip about those senior to them to begin.

'Everett's fine,' Kevern was careful to say, 'when not in art-exultation mode.'

'You don't believe any of that?'

'I don't believe many things about art.'

'But you're an artist . . .' She almost crooned the word.

Careful, Kevern thought.

'I carve lovespoons,' he said. 'If that makes me an artist then I'm an artist. That's the beginning and the end of it.'

'You have no philosophy?'

'To be an artist is to have the freedom to think anything, and that includes thinking one would rather not think.'

'If you really believe an artist has the freedom to think anything, that must include the freedom to think evil.'

Kevern laughed, as though at his own limitations. 'In principle, yes. But not much in the way of evil thinking goes into carving lovespoons, I have to tell you.'

'You've never made an evil lovespoon?'

He thought about it. 'I suppose I've made what you could call erotic lovespoons. But celebrating the body is hardly evil.'

275

'What about a lovespoon that shows the erotic cruelties the body is capable of. People kill for love – are you unable to conceive a lovespoon depicting that?'

'I can conceive one, yes. But I wouldn't make it.'

'Why not, if an artist is free to think anything?'

'Because that freedom includes the freedom to resist evil.'

'And the freedom to embrace it?'

'Yes, of course. Only why would one embrace evil of the sort you describe?'

She had been leaning against her desk, her booted ankles crossed. Now she straightened up and laughed. 'If you don't know that then you're not really an artist,' she said. 'I'd say you're an ethicist.'

'No, that's Everett. Beauty and morality.'

'Oh, he doesn't believe that. He's a lubricious little devil.'

'Everett?'

'He tried to push his hand up my skirt once, right here in the library.'

Well it is that kind of a skirt, Kevern thought, trying not to show where his mind had wandered. 'Expressing his freedom to think evil, do you suppose?' he finally got around to saying.

She laughed her dangerous librarian's laugh. 'You're not wide of the mark. He likes to play with the idea of wrongdoing. It thrills him. He'd be another de Sade if he had the balls. They all would. There isn't a painter or a potter in this place that doesn't long to do something wicked. But none of them has the balls. In another age they'd have joined illegal organisations, worn uniforms and beaten people with their brushes. Now there's nothing for them to do but say sorry. So they have to content themselves with screwing students and assaulting librarians.'

Kevern thought he ought to stick up for his profession. 'Opportunities for doing evil have always been limited in Bethesda,' he said.

She snorted. 'Don't you believe it. There was a time when this institution was happy to consort with the Devil.'

'I didn't think we went back to the Middle Ages.'

'Shows how wrong you can be. Look there . . .'

She pointed to a blown-up photograph that hung above the Local Topography shelves, alongside a couple of wishy-washy studies of St Mordechai's Mount at low tide by Professor Edward Everett Phineas Zermansky, FRSA. It was a famous, often-reproduced photograph showing about twenty quaintly old-fashioned ice-cream vans lined up, like elephants at a circus, looking at St Mordechai's Mount themselves. Kevern had glanced at it several times without ever knowing what he was looking at. The photograph was renowned for the cute symmetry of its composition, he guessed, and for the idea of long-ago seaside idylls it evoked.

He wondered what Rozenwyn wanted him to see.

'That was taken before they were decommissioned,' she said. 'A month later those vans were going round the country painted with the slogan "Leave Now or Face Arrest". Bethesda Academy did the artwork.'

'Ice-cream vans?'

'Yes.'

'Telling people to leave?'

'Yes.'

'Which people?'

'Come on, Kevern. You know which people.'

He shook his head, as though it were a kaleidoscope, to rearrange the patterns.

'But why ice-cream vans, for Christ's sake?'

'Your guess is as good as mine. Not to frighten the children? Because they had macabre imaginations?'

'They weren't, I assume, selling ice cream?'

'You assume right. But here's the strangest thing . . .'

He waited.

'. . . they kept the chimes.'

'Beethoven's Fifth? *Für Elise?*" "*Greensleeves*"?'

'Exactly. And some forgotten favourites of the period. "Whistle While You Work" . . . "You Are My Sunshine".'

Something twitched, like curtains opening furtively, at the furthest corners of Kevern's mind. He stared at her in perplexity. 'When was this?'

'Well it wasn't the Middle Ages, Kevern.'

'No, but when?' He tapped his forehead.

'You're too young,' she said, understanding his meaning.

'You Are My Sunshine' . . . He began to hum it for her. If he was too young, how come he knew it? Then he remembered the blind soul singer and his father's final bitter laughter, directed he hadn't known where. If I don't sit down, he thought, I will topple over.

'Are you all right?' Rozenwyn asked.

He nodded. 'And you know this for sure?' he asked stupidly, gripping the table behind him, so that his hands were close to hers.

She patted the wrist nearer to her. 'I'm a librarian,' she said. 'A librarian knows where to look.'

But he wanted her to be exaggerating, at least. 'Still and all,' he said, 'painting a few vans is not exactly a criminal act, is it? And it was just a warning. I can imagine the Everetts of the day believing they were acting humanely.'

'I don't doubt it. We always think what we're doing is humane, even when we're secretly relishing the evil of it. But all the warning did was soften the populace up for what came next. As did the defamations and the boycotts in which this institution also played a noble part. Let's not be modest. We did more than paint the vans. We provided them with the fuel. There is this malignancy out there, we said. And left it to others to operate.'

Kevern looked around. Was Rozenwyn Feigenblat

at liberty, he wondered, to be talking like this? He was his father's child. He had been brought up not to show too much expression in a public place. You never knew who was watching.

But he was a man not a boy and needed to show Rozenwyn he had some fight in him. 'You have to make allowances for this being an *academic* institution,' he said with heavy irony.

She rolled her eyes. 'They wouldn't welcome your making allowances for them,' she said. 'They don't like you.'

'Don't they? I didn't know that. Why don't they like me?'

'Uniquely malevolent.'

'Uniquely malevolent! Me?'

'I'm being facetious,' she said. '*Uniquely malevolent* is a quotation from then. I use it now for anyone or anything not approved of by junior academics. The actual reason they don't like *you* is that they have to dislike somebody or they have no occupation. And of course because you hold different views.'

'I don't hold views.'

'There you are then. They are nothing but views. Views I have to listen to them expounding for hours at a time. They think that's my job – answering their requests for books that an idiot would know there's no point consulting, books with unacceptable arguments torn out of them, books that have already silenced argument, cult books, propaganda, justification manuals . . . and then agreeing with their ill-informed conclusions.'

You have nothing to say on the subject, Kevern reminded himself. You are the grandson of a hunchback. You are lucky to have been born here. You Are My Sunshine.

'You're probably more Everett's man than I realise,' Rozenwyn said, noting Kevern's reserve. 'But you tell me when there has ever been a reign of terror that wasn't instigated by intellectuals and presided over by someone possessed of the madness of the artist.'

'You have done a lot of thinking,' Kevern said.

'For a woman, do you mean?'

'Of course not.'

'For a librarian then?'

'No, I don't mean that either.'

But he wondered if he did.

'It's a great intellectual privilege to work in a library,' she reminded him. 'The Argentinian writer Borges was a librarian. The English poet Philip Larkin was a librarian.'

Kevern hadn't heard of either of them.

'All human life is here,' she went on. 'The best of it and the worst of it, mainly the worst. Books do that, they bring out the bad in readers if there's bad already in them.'

'And if there isn't?'

She smiled at him and stroked her pigtail. 'Then they bring out the good. As in me, I hope. I've been able to read a lot here.'

'You should write a book about it yourself,' he said.

'What for? So they can tear the pages out? I am content to know what I know.'

'So why are you telling me?'

She regarded him archly. 'To pass the time.'

He consulted his watch. 'I should be going then,' he said.

'Why don't you look at people when you're talking to them?' she asked suddenly, as though reverting to a conversation they'd been having earlier.

'I didn't know I didn't look at people.' He was lying. Ailinn too would comment on his apparent rudeness. 'But if I don't, it's shyness.'

'Your colleagues think of you as unapproachable,' she went on. 'They think you look down on them. They call you arrogant.'

'I'm sorry to hear it. I carve lovespoons. I have nothing to be arrogant about.'

'There you go . . . the simple carpenter. That's the arrogance they mistrust.'

'I can't do anything about it,' he said. 'I'm sorry if they hate me . . .'

'I didn't say "hate". I said they mistrusted you.'

'For being "uniquely malevolent" . . .'

She laughed. 'No, for being uniquely arrogant.'

He smiled at her. 'That's all right then. As long I'm uniquely something.'

'Well you could do worse. You could be like them. You could read books with pages torn out of them and think you've stumbled upon truth. You could subscribe to a belief system . . .'

'Beliefs kill,' he said.

'Yes, like beauty.'

Their eyes met. She tossed her pigtail from her shoulder – as she must do when she mounts her horse, he thought, or when she climbs into bed. She put a hand out as though to touch his shirt. He thought she meant to move in to kiss him.

'This is the wrong thing to do,' he said.

'I know,' she said in a soft, mocking voice. 'That's why I'm doing it.'

But she was only seeing what sort of an ethicist he was.

'He's more naive than he ought to be,' she wrote the following morning in her report, 'and more fragile. We ought to get a move on.'

They arrived to music, laboured to music, trooped to the crematoria to music. '*Brüder! zur Sonne, zur Freiheit,*' they were made to sing. 'Brothers! to the sun, to freedom.' '*Brüder! zum Lichte empor*' – 'Brothers! to the light.' Followed, maybe, by the Blue Danube in all its loveliness, or a song from *Die Meistersinger von Nürnberg,* not that any of them cared where he was from. Music that ennobles the spirit revealing its ultimate sardonic nature, its knowledge of its own untruth, because ultimately there is no ennobled nature. What was the logic? To pacify or to jeer? Why ice-cream vans, the arrival of which, playing the 'Marseillaise' or '*Für Elise*' or 'Whistle While You Work', excited the eager anticipation of the children? To pacify or to jeer? Or both? Between themselves, the parents cannot agree on the function or the message. The vans, for now, are better than the trains, some say. Shame there isn't actually any ice cream for the children, but be grateful and sing along. Others believe the vans are just the start of it. We have heard the chimes at midnight, they believe.

CHAPTER 5

LOST LETTERS

i

July 8, 201-

Darling Mummy and Daddy,

It was so lovely to be with you last weekend. I am only sorry that you didn't feel the same way about seeing me. I didn't, and don't ever, mean to cause you vexation. What I said came from my heart. And you have always encouraged me to follow my heart. You will say that the opinions of others, especially Fridleif, have made that heart no longer mine, but believe me – that is not true. My decision to take up a secretarial appointment at the Congregational Federation of the Islands is mine alone. It is a purely administrative post and therefore purely secular. I have not left you. Of course I have been influenced by people I have met up here. Isn't that bound to be the effect of an education? Isn't that precisely what an education is for? You, Mummy, said you should never have let me leave home – 'wandering to the furthest ends

285

of the earth like some gypsy', as you chose to put it, though I haven't left the country and am no more than four hours away, even at the speed you drive – but what's happened isn't your fault just as it wouldn't have been your fault had I gone to New Guinea and become a headhunter. I just wish you could consider what I'm doing as a tribute to the open-minded spirit in which you brought me up. My thinking is a continuation of yours, that's all. And I am still your daughter wherever I live and whoever I work with.

Your ever loving
Rebecca

This was the first of a small bundle of letters Ailinn's companion gave her to peruse. 'Don't for the moment ask me how I came by them,' she said, 'just read them.'

'Now?'

'Now.'

The second letter was dated four months later.

November 12, 201-

Dearest Mummy and Daddy,

Up until the final minute I hoped you would turn up. Fridleif had tried to warn me against disappointment – not in a hostile way, I assure you, but quite the opposite. (You would love him if you would only give yourself the chance.) 'You must understand how hard it must be for them,' he said. But I hoped against hope nonetheless. Even as we exchanged our vows I still expected to see you materialise at the church door and come walking down the aisle.

There, it's said. The **church** door.

How did that ever get to be such a terrible word in our family? What did the church ever do to us? Yes, yes, I know, but that was like a thousand years ago. Is there nothing we can't forgive? Is there nothing we can't forget?

Try saying it to each other when you go to bed at night. Church, church, church . . . You'll be surprised how easy it gets. Do you remember the finger rhyme we used to play together? 'Here's the church, and here's the steeple, open the door and see all the people!' The word seemed innocent enough then. No one sent a thunderbolt out of the sky to punish us for saying it.

But if it can't be innocent to you now I'm a big girl couldn't you at least learn to hate it a little less for my sake?

Open the door and see all the people!

Let's get it all over and done with, anyway. I married the man I love in a church. In the presence of God, Father, Son and Holy Spirit we exchanged vows. And I am now Mrs Macshuibhne, the wife of the Reverend Fridleif Macshuibhne. A bit of a mouthful, I agree, but you'd get used to it if you only tried.

Please be happy for me, at least.
Rebecca

'How did you come by this?' Ailinn wanted to know.

'We agreed you wouldn't ask.'

'No, *you* agreed I wouldn't ask.'

'Just go on reading.'

March 24, 201-

Dear Mummy and Daddy,

Still no word from you. Must I accept that you have abandoned me?

What have I done that is so terrible? What shame have I brought on you?

I accept that there was a time when we needed to show solidarity with one another. We were depleted and demoralised. I knew that. Every defection was interpreted as a sign of weakness and exploited – how could I not know that given the number of times I heard it. If they don't even love one another, people said – or we feared people would say, which isn't quite the same thing – why should we love them. But that was a long time ago. No one is trying to exploit us any more. No one even notices us. We are accepted now. We have never been more safe. I know what you will say. You will say what you always said. 'Don't be lulled into a false sense of security. Remember the

Allegory of the Frog."* Daddy, if I remembered the Allegory of the Frog I would never stay anywhere for five minutes at a time. If I remembered the Allegory of the Frog I would never know a moment's peace. And the water isn't hot here any more. It isn't even lukewarm. Yes, I know you've heard that before. I know it was what our grandparents said the last time. 'Here? Don't make us laugh. Anywhere but here.' Until the eleventh hour, until eleven seconds before the eleventh minute before the clocks stopped for us, as you've told me a thousand times, they ignored the warning signs, laughed at those who told them it was now or never, refused what stared them in the face. Here? Not here! 'And you know their fate, Becky.' Yes, Daddy, I know their fate, and I owe it to the memory of all those who suffered that fate – whom you speak of as though they were family though none of our family perished, I remind you – never to forget it. But that was then and now is now. And that was there and here is here. You used to laugh at me when I came home from university – 'Here she is, our daughter, life president of the It Couldn't Happen Here Society.' And I called you, Daddy, 'honorary chair of the Never Again League'. Well, I don't disrespect you for believing what you believe. It is right to worry. But you cannot compare like with unlike. If you could only see how I am treated up here. The kindness! The consideration!

The things you fear are all inside your own heads. And I sometimes think such fears make life not worth living. Is it a life to be in terror every day? To start whenever anyone knocks at the door? To recoil in shock from every thoughtless insult? If those are the conditions on which we hold our freedom to be ourselves, marry, bring up our children, worship, then it is no freedom at all. You cannot live a life forever waiting for it to end.

And it is such a waste when we could be so happy. Heaven knows we were happy as a family for so long. If I was with you now we would be happy again. But I can't be with you again without you accepting Fridleif. And what possible reason do you have not to accept him? He is not the Devil. He is not the end of us. Can't we stop all this sectarianism and just live in peace? All you are doing by rejecting me is making what you dread come true.

Your ever loving daughter,
Becky

PS You are also about to be grandparents.

'This is not going to end well,' Ailinn said. 'Just read.'

September 17, 201-

Dearest Mummy and Daddy,

I will not upset you by sending you a photograph of your grandchild. I accept now, with great sorrow, that there will be no peace between us. But I do owe it to you – and to myself – to explain why I have done what I have done one last time.

Your generation is not my generation. I say that with the deepest respect. I never was and am not now a rebellious child. I understand why you think as you do. But the ship has sailed. My generation refuses to jump at every murmur of imagined hostility. We love our lives. We love this country. We relish being here. And to go on relishing being here we don't have to be as we were before. That's why I have decided to convert. Not as a rejection of the way you brought me up but as a step forward from it. We were always a preparatory people, Fridleif says. And we have done what we were put on earth to do. We have completed our mission and shown the way. We stood out against every manner of oppression, and having conquered it there is no need for all the morbid remembering and re-remembering. I don't say we should forget, I say we have been given the chance to progress and we should take it. It's time to live for the future, not the past. It's time to be a people that looks forward not back.

So why have I decided to embrace my husband's faith? For the beauty of it, Mummy. For the music of it, Daddy. As an expression of the loveliness of life that our grandparents suffered for us to enjoy.

Trust me, I have never been more what you brought me up to be than when I submit to what our people, in their understandably and even necessary touchy sense of separateness, have abjured for centuries – the incense, the iconography, the fragmented light of stained-glass windows, the rapture. We have been accepted and we are ready to join everybody else now. I am, anyway.

Be happy for me.

Your ever loving daughter in Christ,

Rebecca

'I know,' Ailinn said, when Ez told her that Rebecca was her grandmother.

'How did you know?'

'I've been expecting the letter.'

'Is that meant to be funny?'

'No, not at all.'

'So what do you mean?'

Ailinn made a 'leave it' gesture with her hand, wafting whatever she meant away. Wafting it out of the room, wafting it out into Paradise Valley.

'I can tell she was my grandmother, that's all. I can read myself in her. Was there a reconciliation?'

'I'd like you to read the final letter,' Ez said.

Ailinn was reluctant. She couldn't have said why. Maybe it was the word 'final'. But she read it.

May 202-
My Darling Parents,
  I am very alarmed by what I have heard is happening where you are. Please write and tell me you are all right. That's all I ask.
  Yours in fear,
  R

'Now the envelope,' Ez said.
  It was stamped, in large purple letters,

RECIPIENT UNKNOWN AT
THIS ADDRESS
RETURN TO SENDER

*THE ALLEGORY OF THE FROG

A frog was thrown into a pan of boiling water. 'What do you take me for?' the frog said, jumping smartly out. 'Some kind of a shlemiel?'

The following day the frog was lowered gently, even lovingly, into a pan of lukewarm water. As the temperature was increased, a degree at a time, the frog luxuriated, floating lethargically on his back with his eyes closed, imagining himself at an exclusive spa.

'This is the life,' the frog said.

Relaxed in every joint, blissfully unaware, the frog allowed himself to be boiled to death.

CHAPTER 6

GUTKIND AND KROPLIK

i

'How do you take it?'

The policeman Eugene Gutkind pouring morning tea for the historian Densdell Kroplik.

'Like a man.'

'And that would be how?'

'Five sugars and no milk. Is this a cat or an albino dog?'

Densdell Kroplik stroking the ball of bad-breathed icing sugar rubbing up against his leg.

'Don't touch it. You'll never get the stuff off your fingers.'

'Like guilt,' Kroplik laughed, sitting forward on the couch, his legs apart, something heavy between them.

A bolt of disgust went through Gutkind's body. Did he really want *that* sitting on his furniture?

He had invited Kroplik round to his end-of-terrace house in St Eber to show him his great-grandfather's collection of Wagner memorabilia. The rarely played composer had brought the

295

two men together, the decline in the popularity of his music confirming their shared conviction that they were living in unpropitious times. Each believed in conspiracies, though not necessarily the same conspiracies.

'Isn't this against the law?' Kroplik asked, leafing through the photographs and playbills and scraps of unauthenticated manuscript that Gutkind had brought out of filing boxes wrapped in old newsprint.

Gutkind wondered how many more jokes on the theme of legality his co-conspiracy theorist intended to make. 'The law is not so small-minded,' he said. 'It winks at a reasonable number of personal items. It's only when they turn out to be an archive that there's trouble.'

Since Kroplik must have had an archive of some size in order to compile even his *Brief History*, this was meant as a friendly shot across his bows.

'So how are you getting on finding the killer of the Whore of Ludgvennok?' Kroplik asked, that being the context in which the name of Richard Wagner had first come up between them. Just a question. He could have been asking whether the policeman had seen any good films lately.

Gutkind put his fingers together like a preacher and lowered his head.

'I presume you're talking about Lowenna Morgenstern?'

Kroplik snorted. 'How many whores do you know?'

'How many whores are there?'

'In these parts there's nobbut whores, Detective Inspector.'

'Then what makes this one different?'

'She's dead.'

Gutkind parted his fingers. There was no denying that Lowenna Morgenstern was dead. But was she a whore? 'Are you telling me,' he asked, insinuating a note of fine scruple, 'that Lowenna Morgenstern sold her kisses?'

'I'm telling you nothing. I'm asking. You found anyone yet? Got a suspect?'

'The process proceeds,' Gutkind said, rejoining his fingers.

'Maybe I'll have more sugar,' Kroplik proceeded in another direction, helping himself to a sixth cube. 'Would your albino dog like one or does he just lick himself when he's in need of something sweet?'

He was disappointed that the detective inspector had stopped asking him who he thought might have murdered Lowenna Morgenstern, Lowenna Morgenstern's lover and latterly Lowenna Morgenstern's husband. He felt it undermined both his authority and his judgement.

Gutkind passed him a programme for a performance of *Götterdämmerung* at Bayreuth. It had some elegant faded handwriting on the back, a set of initials together with a phone number. Gutkind had some time ago concluded that they were the initials of the woman his great-grandfather had loved to hopeless distraction, and that the phone number was hers. They must have met in the Festspielhaus, perhaps at the bar, or maybe they had even found themselves sitting next to each other, perhaps so transported by the divine music that they rubbed knees though they were each in the company of other lovers. That the woman should have gone to Bayreuth in the first place puzzled Gutkind, all things considered, but the enigma of it made her all the more fascinating, as Clarence Worthing himself must have felt. I too would have fallen for her, Gutkind thought, conjuring the woman's exotic appearance from the archive of his fancy. I too would have been entrapped.

The programme itself was illustrated with several artists' interpretations of the world ablaze. These could have doubled for the state of his great-grandfather's heart. 'I like thinking about the end of the world,' he said. 'You?'

Densdell Kroplik scratched his face. 'We've lived through the end of the world,' he answered. 'This is the aftermath. This is the post-apocalypse.'

Gutkind looked out of his leaded window at the pyramids of grey clay. The land spewing up its innards. The inside of his unloved, unlived-in terrace house no better. Apart from the dusting of clay, there was something green and sticky over everything, as though a bag of spinach had exploded in the microwave, blowing off the door and paintballing every surface – the table, the walls, the ceiling, even the photograph of Gutkind and his wife on their wedding day, she (her doing, not his) with her head scissored off, Gutkind and his headless bride. Then again, it could just have been mould. Gutkind looked between his fingers. Yes, mould. 'You could be right,' he said.

'I am right. It's the twilight of the gods.'

'Wagner's gods? Here? In St Eber?'

'The gods of Ludgvennok.'

'I don't much care about anybody's gods,' Gutkind said. 'I care more about me.'

'Well it's the twilight of you too, ain't it? Look at your fucking dog, man. What are you doing here, in this whited-out shit-heap, if you'll pardon my Latin, trying – unsuccessfully by your own account – to solve murders that never will be solved? What am I doing over at Ludgvennok, excuse me' – here he spat, trying to avoid the cat – '*Port Reuben*, as I have to call it, what am I doing cutting aphids' hair in Port Cunting Reuben for a living? We were gods once. Now look at us. The last two men on the planet to have listened to *Tristan und Isolde*.'

Eugene Gutkind fell into a melancholy trance, as though imagining the time when he trod the earth like a god, a monocle in his eye such as Clarence Worthing must have worn, in his hand a silver-topped cane, on his arm, highly perfumed . . .

In reality there was spinach on his shoes. 'So who or what reduced us to this?' he asked, not expecting an answer.

'Saying sorry,' Kroplik said. 'Saying sorry is what did it. You never heard the gods apologise. They let loose their thunderbolts and whoever they hit, they hit. Their own stupid fault for being in the way.'

'I'm a fair-minded man . . .' Gutkind said.

'For a policeman . . .'

'I'm a fair-minded man for anyone. I don't mind saying sorry if I've done something to say sorry for. But you can't say sorry if you've done nothing. You can't find a man guilty if there's been no crime.'

'Well look at it this way, Detective Inspector – there are plenty of unsolved crimes kicking about. And plenty of uncaught criminals. Missy Morgenstern's murderer for one. Does it matter if you end up punishing the wrong man? Not a bit of it. The wrongfully guilty balance the wrong-fully innocent. What goes around comes around. Pick yourself up an aphid. They're all murderers by association. Hang the lot.'

Detective Inspector Gutkind felt himself growing irritated by Densdell Kroplik's misplaced ire. It struck him as messy and unserious. His own life might have been dismal but it was ordered. It had feeling in it. He offered his guest a whisky. Maybe a whisky would concentrate his mind.

'Let's agree about something,' he said.

'We do. The genius of Richard Wagner. And the end of the world.'

'No. Let's agree about saying sorry. We shouldn't be saying it – we agree about that, don't we?'

Kroplik raised his dusty whisky glass and finished off its contents. 'We do. We agree about most things. And about that most of all. Fuck saying sorry!'

'Fuck saying sorry!'

The air was thick with rebellion.

'Bloody Gutkind!' Kroplik suddenly expostulated.

Gutkind looked alarmed.

'Bloody Kroplik!' Kroplik continued. 'What kind of a name is Kroplik, for Christ's sake? What kind of a name is Gutkind? We sound like a comedy team – Kroplik and Gutkind.'

'Or Gutkind and Kroplik.'

The policeman Eugene Gutkind sharing the rarity of a joke with the historian Densdell Kroplik.

'I am glad,' said Kroplik sarcastically, shifting his weight from one thigh to another, disarranging the cushions on the detective's sofa, 'that you are able to find humour in this.'

'On the contrary, I agree with you. They turn us into a pair of comedians, though our lives are essentially tragic, and for that we are the ones who have to say we're sorry. I find no humour in it whatsoever.'

'Good. Then enough's enough. We are gods not clowns, and gods apologise to no one for their crimes, because what a god does can't be called a crime. *Nicht wahr*?'

'What?'

301

'*Nicht wahr?* Wagnerian for don't you agree. I thought you'd know that. I bet even your dog knows that.'

The cat pricked the ear nearest to Kroplik. '*Nicht wahr?*' Kroplik shouted into it.

'These days we don't get to hear much German in St Eber,' Gutkind said, as much in defence of the cat as himself.

'Pity. But Gutkind's got a bit of a German ring to it, don't you think? *Gut* and *kinder*?'

'I suppose it has. Like *Krop* and *lik*.'

'You see what the aphid swines have done to us? Now we're fighting on behalf of names that don't even belong to us. What's your actual name? What did the whores call you in the good old days? Mr . . .? Mr What? Or did you let them call you Eugene? Take me, Eugene. Use me, Eugene.'

If Kroplik isn't mistaken, Gutkind blushes.

'Whatever my name was then, I was too young to give it to whores.'

'Your father then . . . your grandfather . . . how did the whores address them?'

These were infractions too far for Detective Inspector Gutkind, Wagner or no Wagner. He was not a man who had ever visited a whore. And nor, he knew in his soul, had any of the men in his family before him. It had always been ideal love they'd longed for. A beautiful woman, smelling of Prague or Vienna, light on their arm, transported into an ecstasy of extinction – the two of them breathing their last together . . .

ertrinken . . . versinken . . . unbewußt . . . höchste Lust! . . .

Kroplik couldn't go on waiting for him to expire. 'Well mine was Scannláin. Son of the Scannláins of Ludgvennok. And had been for two thousand bloody years. And then for a crime we didn't commit, and not for any of the thousands we did . . . that's the galling part—'

'For a crime *no one* committed,' Gutkind interjected.

Densdell Kroplik was past caring whether a crime had been committed or not. He held out his glass for another whisky. The high life – downing whisky in St Eber at 11.30 in the morning. The gods drinking to their exemption from the petty cares of mortals. Atop Valhalla, dust or no dust.

Gutkind sploshed whisky into Kroplik's glass. He wanted him drunk and silent. He wanted him a thing of ears. Other than his cat, Eugene Gutkind had no one to talk to. His wife had left him. He had few friends in the force and no friends in St Eber. Who in St Eber did have friends? A few brawling mates and a headless wife to curse comprised happiness in St Eber, and he no longer even had the wife. So he rarely got the opportunity to pour out his heart. A detective inspector, anyway, had to measure his words. But he didn't have to measure anything with Densdell Kroplik, least of all whisky. He wasn't a kindred spirit. Wagner didn't make him a kindred spirit.

303

To Gutkind's eye Kroplik lacked discrimination. Not knowing where to pin the blame he pinned it on everyone. A bad hater, if ever he saw one. A man lacking specificity. But he was still the nearest thing to a kindred spirit there was. 'Drink,' he said. 'Drink to what we believe and know to be true.'

And when Densdell Kroplik was drunk enough not to hear what was being said to him, true or not true, and not to care either way, when he was half asleep on the couch with the icing-sugar cat sitting on his face, Detective Inspector Eugene Gutkind began his exposition . . .

There had been no crime. No *Götterdämmerung* anyway. No last encounter with the forces of evil, no burning, and no renewal of the world. Those who should have perished had been fore-warned by men of tender conscience like Clarence Worthing who, though he longed to wipe the slate clean, could not betray the memory of his fragrant encounter with Ottilie or Naomi or Lieselotte, in the Bayreuth Festspielhaus. For what you have done to me, I wish you in hell, they said. But for what you have done to me I also wish you to be spared. Such are the contradictions that enter the hearts of men who know what it is to love and not be loved in return. The irony of it was not lost on Detective Inspector Gutkind. They owed their lives to a conspiracy of the inconsolable and the snubbed, these Ottilies and Lieselottes who had imbibed conspiracy with their mothers' milk. They'd escaped betrayal, they who betrayed as soon as snap a finger.

So WHAT HAPPENED, in his view, was that NOT MUCH HAD. They had got out. Crept away like rats in the dark. That was not just supposition based on his cracking Clarence Worthing's code. It was demonstrable fact. If there'd been a massacre where were the bodies? Where were the pits, where the evidence of funeral pyres and gallows trees, where the photographs or other recorded proof of burned-out houses, streets, entire suburbs? Believe the figures that had once been irresponsibly bandied about and the air should still be stinking with the destruction. They say you can smell extinction for centuries afterwards. Go to the Somme. You can see it in the soil. You can taste it in the potatoes.

He had done the maths, worked it out algebraically, done the measurements geometrically, consulted log tables – so many people killed in so many weeks in so many square metres . . . by whom? It would have taken half the population up in arms, and mightily skilled in the use of them, to have wreaked such destruction in so brief a period of time. No, there had been no *Götterdämmerung*.

He takes a swig from the bottle and looks at Kroplik with his head thrown back, his mouth open and his legs spread. What the hell is that inside his trousers? He regrets inviting him over. He is ashamed of his own loneliness. But there is so much to say, and no one to say it to.

He feels subtler than any man he knows. No *Götterdämmerung* does not mean, you fool, that there was no anything. First law of criminal investigation: everyone exaggerates. Second law of criminal investigation: just because everyone exaggerates doesn't mean there's nothing to investigate. In my profession, Mr Kroplik, we don't say there is no smoke without fire. Rumour is also a crime. False accusation – you can go down for that. But that said, there *is* always a fire. Somewhere, something is forever burning. That's why no accusation is ever entirely wasted. Eventually we will find a culprit for any crime. So yes, WHAT HAPPENED happened in that there was minor disturbance and insignificant destruction. To win another of their propaganda wars they did what they had done for centuries and put on another of their pantomimes of persecution. Allowed the spilling of a little blood to justify their disappearing, while no one was looking, with their accumulated loot. A sacrificial people, my great-grandfather called them, and as one of their sacrifices himself, he knew. But they also sacrifice their own. There's a name for it but I've forgotten it. You'll probably know it, Kroplik, you unedifying piss-ant. Like a caste system. You probably didn't know they had a caste system, but my word they did. This one can't light a candle, that one can't go near a body. Some can't even touch a woman unless they're wearing surgical gloves. And some know it's their job to die when the time comes. It's not as unselfish as it sounds. Their children get looked after and they go straight to heaven. Not to lie with virgins, that's someone else. This lot go straight to heaven and read books. For the honour of which they put themselves in the way of trouble, announce themselves in the street by what they wear, hang identifying objects in the windows of their houses where they wait patiently to be burned alive. Here! Over here!

The shouting doesn't wake Kroplik who sleeps like the dead.

I, my rat-arsed friend, Gutkind continues, am a policeman. I know the difference between right and wrong. Wrong is burning someone alive in his own house, I don't care if he invited you in and handed you the box of matches. You can always say no. Sure, you were provoked. Criminals are always provoked. An open door, a short dress, a handbag left unzipped. Don't get me wrong – I sympathise. I'm not beyond a provocation or two myself. Right this minute I'm provoked into violent thoughts by the sight of you snoring on my sofa. But I restrain myself from cutting off your balls. That's what makes me not a villain.

But keep wrongdoing in proportion is another of my mottos. Not everything is the greatest crime in history.

He rubs his face and drinks.

No sir!

And drinks some more.

You'll have your own favourite greatest crime in history, Mr Historian of the Gods of Ludgvennok, but I can tell you this wasn't it. And why wasn't it?

Because of this! He smites his heart.

Would he have done what Clarence Worthing did had he been in his position? Would he have assisted in their escape? Tears flood his eyes. The sublime music swells in his ears . . . *ertrinken* . . . *versinken* . . . *unbewußt* . . . *höchste Lust*! . . . Yes, he and Clarence Worthing are one, made weak and strong by love.

Finishing off what is left in the bottle, he rejoins Densdell Kroplik on the couch where, exhausted by the intensity of his own emotion, he falls immediately asleep on Kroplik's shoulder, the convulsing cat, heaving up fur balls coated in clay dust, between them.

It's only a shame no family photographer is in attendance.

ii

It's Kroplik who wakes first, still drunk. It takes him a moment or two to work out where he is. Though it's only early afternoon it's dark already in St Eber, the shabby pyramids of clay, as though each is lit from within by a small candle, the sole illumination.

Is this Egypt?

Then he notices that the cat has coughed up a puddle of china-clay slime on the lapel of his one smart suit. Or is it Gutkind's doing? It smells as though it's been in Gutkind's stomach. Kroplik clutches his own. He lives on a daily diet of indignity but this is one insult he doesn't have to bear. He has brought his razor along to give the detective inspector a close shave as a token of his friendship and regard. But he is too angry to be a friend. Slime! From Gutkind's poisoned gut! On his one good suit!

He is aware that Gutkind has been ranting at him while he slept. The usual subject – villainy. Was he telling him he knew – teasing him, taunting him with his knowledge. I know the difference between right and wrong Kroplik is sure he heard him say through his stupor. Provocation is no defence. This time . . .

Is this why he was invited over?

It amazes him that Gutkind should have the brains to solve a crime. Yes, he'd as good as laid it out for him a hundred times, but Gutkind had struck him as too dumb to see what was in front of his face.

I've underestimated him, Kroplik decides. I've fatally underestimated the cunt. And laughs appreciatively at his own choice of words. Make a good final chapter heading for the next volume of his history – no, not 'The Cunt', but 'A Fatal Underestimation'.

He thinks about taking out his razor, putting it

to Gutkind's throat, and confessing. What would the policeman do then? Throw up some more? Then he has a better idea. He staggers to his feet and closes the curtains. I'll just cut his throat and have done, he has decided.

But it's the cat that gets it first.

CHAPTER 7

NUSSBAUM UNBOUND

i

Esme Nussbaum lay in what the doctors called a coma for two months after the motorcyclist rode the pavement and knocked her down. To her it was a long and much-needed sleep. A chance to think things over without interruption. Regain perspective. And maybe lose a little weight.

She wasn't joking about the weight. She was done with looking comfortable and unthreatening. It was time to show more bone. Splintered bone, she laughed to herself, causing the screen to bleep, though she didn't doubt the bone would mend eventually. It wasn't that she'd been incapable of causing discomfort when discomfort needed to be caused. She was known to be a woman who sometimes asked troublesome questions. But there'd been no real spike inside her. She could annoy without quite inspiring fear. Now she fancied being someone else. No, now she *was* someone else. Someone with sharper edges, all spikes. Broken, she was more frightening.

Already her thoughts were unlike any she'd had before. They flew at her. In her previous, comfortable life she would reason her way to a conclusion, which meant that she could be reasoned out of it in time as well. The motorcycle hadn't really been necessary. There were other ways of making her conformable . . .

Comfortable and Conformable – her middle names. Esme C. C. Nussbaum. Always a wordmonger, an anagramatiser, a palindromaniac, she now saw words three-dimensionally in her sleep. Comfortable and Conformable cavorted lewdly on the ceiling of her unconsciousness, pressing their podgy bellies together like middle-aged lovers, blowing into each other's ears, two becoming one. She smiled inside herself. It really was a pleasure lying here, waiting for what words would get up to next, what thoughts would come whooshing at her. She liked being the subject of their discussions. It was like listening in to gossip about herself. No, she wasn't as Comfortable or Conformable as she blamed herself for being, was the latest revelation. If she'd been that easy to get on with, what was she doing here, lying in a coma, half dead? She must have put the wind up someone. That was one of the most persistent of her winged thoughts: people frighten easily. Another was: people – ordinary people, people you think you know and like – want to kill you.

She was not herself frightened when such thoughts flew at her. She had once watched an old horror film with her parents about a blonde woman being attacked by birds. They had been terrified as a family. They put their hands over their faces as the birds dive-bombed everyone in the blonde's vicinity. 'Avenging some great but never to be disclosed wrong,' her father said. But lying flat with thoughts flying at her was not like that. She didn't feel assailed. There was no more they could do to her – that partly explained her calm acceptance of their presence, even when they swooped so low she might justifiably have worried for her eyes. But it was more than being beyond terror. She welcomed their violence. It was Conformable with how she felt. They were *thoughts*, after all, which meant they originated in her. If this was herself massing above her, screeching, well then . . . she extended all the hospitality she had to offer. It was about time. A good time, yes, in that she had bags of it to give; but *about* time in the sense that she had wasted too much of it thinking thoughts that were less . . . less what? How nice it was having all the time in the world to find the right word. Less . . . less . . . Esme Nussbaum knew more words than was good for her. She had been the school Scrabble champion; she could finish a crossword while others were still on the first clue; she knew words even her teachers thought did not exist. Now she raided her store for a word that had bird in it, that sounded avian, an av word. Avirulent had a ring, but it meant the opposite of what she needed it to mean. She didn't want to lose the virulence, she wanted to store it. Avile was good – to avile, as she'd had to explain to a sceptical Scrabble opponent in the quarter-finals, meaning to make vile, to debase. But there was no adjective to go with it that she knew of. No avilious. And no noun, no aviliousness. Had there been, then aviliousness was exactly the quality her previous, unwinged thoughts had lacked. They had been too moderate. Too sparing. Yes, she had presented a report, for which they'd killed her – in intention, if not in fact – that spoke of the persistent rage she'd found in the course of monitoring the nation's mood. She had not tried to sugar that pill. We cannot, she had argued, glide over the past with an IF. We must confront WHAT HAPPENED, not to apportion blame – it was too late for that, anyway – but to know what it was and why time hadn't healed it. Yes, she had stood her ground, said what had to be said, done her best to persuade the IFFERS with whom she worked, but that best wasn't good enough. She hadn't followed the logic of her own findings. She had been insufficiently avilious. She hadn't made vile, that's to say she hadn't grasped, hadn't penetrated and presented, even to herself, the vileness of what had been done. Not WHAT HAD HAPPENED but WHAT HAD BEEN DONE.

Ah, but had she gone that far they would have had her run over a second and, if need be, a third time.

Were they that ruthless? Ruthless was not the

word Esme Nussbaum would have picked. They were acting out of the best motives. They wanted a harmonious society. Their mistake was not to see that she wanted a harmonious society too. The difference was that they saw harmony as something you attained by leaving things out – contrariety and contradiction, argument, variety – and she saw it as something you achieved by keeping everything in.

Though she had limited access to information that others didn't, she had done no original research into the terrible events which those who did not see as she saw wanted to disown. Research, she thought, had not been necessary. She knew the events to have been terrible simply by their effects. Had they been of less consequence then the aftermath would have been of less consequence too. But the aftermath, of which she too, lying here smashed into tiny pieces, was the bloody proof, brooked no controversy. They could mow her down as often as they liked – and she bore them no malice for it; on the contrary she owed this long reflective holiday to them – but the truth remained the truth. Anger and unhappiness seeped out from under every doorway of every house in every town and every village in the country. Housewives threw open their windows each morning to let out the fumes of unmotivated domestic fury that had built up overnight. Men spat bile into their beer glasses, abused strangers, beat their own children, committed acts of medieval violence on their wives, or on women who weren't their wives, that no amount of sexual frustration or jealousy could explain.

Now that she had the leisure to think, Esme Nussbaum was no longer looking for explanations. You only need an explanation where there's a mystery, and there was no mystery. How could it have worked out otherwise? You can't have a poisoned stomach and a sweet breath. You can't lop off a limb and expect you will be whole. You can't rob and not make someone the poorer, and when it's yourself that you rob then it's yourself you impoverish.

Of the thoughts that flew at her, as the weeks passed, this last was the most persistent, skimming her cheek with its quilled wing, as though it wanted to scratch her into waking – *we are the poorer by what we took away*.

But she was in no rush to come out of her coma where it was warm and silent – she only saw words, she didn't hear them – and declare what she knew. She had no more reports to write just yet. It was good to look at the world slowly and evenly. You don't need to have your eyes open to see things.

ii

Her father blamed her.

'She couldn't have been looking where she was going,' he said.

316

'Esme always looks where she's going,' his wife replied.

'Then if it wasn't an accident . . .'

'It *wasn't* an accident.'

'OK, if you say so, it wasn't an accident. In that case someone must have had it in for her.'

'You don't say.'

'The question is—'

'I don't want to hear that question.'

'The question is what had she done wrong.'

'Your own daughter! How dare you?'

He gave a foolish, thwarted laugh, that was more like a belch. He was a near-sighted, jeering man with a hiatus hernia. 'It feels as though something's balled-up in my chest all the time,' he complained to his doctor who recommended Mylanta or Lanzaprozole or Maldroxal Plus or Basaljel or Ranitidine. He took them all but felt no better.

'It's your opinions,' his wife told him, watching in distaste as he banged at his thorax in the vain hope of dislodging whatever was stuck inside him. 'It's your hateful nature paying you back. To speak like that, about your own daughter!'

'People don't have it in for you for no reason,' he persisted.

'Not another word,' his wife said. 'Not another word or I swear I'll cut your chest open with a breadknife.'

The Nussbaums had been having this argument all their married lives. Their mangled daughter was just another opportunity for them to rehearse it all again, their understanding of the universe, what they did or did not believe. What Compton Nussbaum believed was that what happened happened for the best of reasons, there was no effect that didn't have a cause, what people suffered they had brought upon themselves. What Rhoda Nussbaum believed was that she was married to a pig.

'Have you never been sorry for anyone?' she asked him.

'What good would my sorrow do them?'

'That's not an answer to my question. Do you never feel another person's pain?'

'I feel satisfied when I see justice done.'

'What about injustice? What about cruelty?'

He banged his chest. 'Sentimentality.'

'So if I go out and get raped . . .?'

'It will be your own fault.'

'How so? For being a woman?'

'Well I won't be going out and getting raped, will I?'

More's the pity, she thought.

You don't see your daughter lying as good as dead and blame her for it, Rhoda Nussbaum believed. If I were to kill my husband for what he has just said I would be cleared by any court in the country. The only argument she could see for not killing her husband was that she'd be proving him right – yes, people do get what they deserve.

He'd been a civil servant. '*Servant* gets it,' Rhoda

Nussbaum would say when he refused to hear a word against those who employed him. He was proud when his daughter gained early promotion at Ofnow, but turned against her when she turned against it.

'I'm only asking questions,' she would cry in her own defence.

'Then don't,' was his fatherly reply.

She should have found a man and left home for him. But the men she met were like her father. 'Then don't,' they'd say. And the one thing they didn't say no about, she did.

Her mother encouraged her. 'They're all no good,' she said. 'Stay here with me.'

That suited her. She liked her mother and could see that she was lonely. It helped, too, that she was not sentimental about men.

Her father thought she was a lesbian. Many men thought the same. There was something uncanny about her, the seriousness with which she took her work, her obduracy, her pedantry, the size of her vocabulary, the lack of bounce in her hair, the flat shoes she wore, her failure often to get a joke, her unwillingness to play along, her way of over-doing sympathy as though understanding beat snogging. But only her father hated her in his heart. Her being a lesbian was a denial of him. And also, by his own remorseless logic, meant that he was being punished. He didn't know what for, but you don't get a lesbian for a daughter unless you've done something very wrong indeed.

He'd have preferred it had she not come out of the coma.

'You will not tell her she only got what she deserved,' his wife said on the eve of their daughter's removal from the hospital. 'If you want to live an hour longer you will not say it's your own stupid fault.'

He stood at the front door, waiting for the ambulance to arrive. A ball of something even more indigestible than usual was lodged inside his chest.

'Welcome home,' he belched when she was stretchered in. She raised her hand slightly and gave him a faint wave.

I'm doing well, he thought. I'm handling this OK.

Esme thought the same. Not about him, about her. I'm being good. But she knew she'd never be able to keep it up. She'd have to tell him soon enough how wrong he had always been about everything.

Her mother nursed her like a grievance.

'My little girl,' she crooned over her.

Esme told her to stop. She was getting better. In some respects she felt better than she'd ever felt before. Her mother worried that that meant she was preparing to embrace the life of a permanent invalid. But then there was a secret corner of herself that was willing to embrace the life of a permanent nurse. Feed her daughter soup, kill her husband, put up the shutters, smell him rot and hope not to see daylight again.

Esme had never moved out of her parents' house so she was back in her old room. Yet it felt as though she'd been away all her adult life and was revisiting the sanctum of her childhood for the first time in decades. It was the lying down that did that. Lying down and seeing words jerk about above her head. Can one ever return to bed for a long period and not be reminded of being a child? Even the books on her shelves and the magazines on the chest of drawers, bought just before she was run over, even her newest clothes, seemed to belong to a much younger her. Where had she been in the intervening years?

Her mother caught her weeping once. 'Oh, my little girl,' she cried.

'Cut that out!' Esme said. 'I'm not in pain and I'm not sad. I'm just missing something.'

'What?'

'The last fifteen years of my life.'

'You haven't been here that long, darling.'

'I know that. I just can't think what I did with them before.'

In a few weeks she was able to lever herself up by her arms. It would be longer before she could walk, but there was no hurry. Physiotherapists visited her and were disappointed by her slow progress. 'She's regaining strength,' they told her mother, 'but she doesn't seem to have the will to be up and about.'

She wasn't worried about it herself. She still had a lot of thinking to do. Once she was out of the coma her thoughts did not fly at her. She missed that, as people from the country miss birdsong when they move to town. She had to call words to her now. She had to start at the beginning of an idea and puzzle it out. It was like following one end of a ball of thread, uncertain where it would lead her.

Her mother fretted. 'Why are you so quiet?'

'Thinking.'

'You've had a lot of time to think.'

'You can't have too much.'

Can't you? Her mother wasn't sure.

But her father liked her like this. He took it for remorse. Any minute now he expected her to announce that the accident had killed off her lesbian tendencies.

'What's happening in the world?' she asked one morning.

She had got herself over to the breakfast table to join her parents.

'The usual,' her mother said. 'Births, marriages, funerals.'

'What would you have instead?' her husband asked her.

'Something less horrible.'

'We make our beds, we lie in them,' Compton said.

Esme looked from her father to her mother, and back. How long had marriage been a horror to them both? From the first moment of their marrying, forty years before? Had they recoiled from each other even as they exchanged vows? She had never heard them speak lovingly of a time when they didn't dislike each other intensely. So why had they married, and why hadn't they parted? What was it that kept them together? The very magnetism of horror, was that it? The harmony that there is in hatred?

She suddenly saw them as a pair of evil planets, barren of life, spinning through space, in constant relation to each other but never colliding. Did a marriage obey the same unvarying law of physics as the solar system? And society too? Was this equipoise of antagonism essential?

But when the planets in disorder wander . . . Who said that? Esme knew a crossword clue when she saw one. *Disorder wander – prince among men, 6 letters.*

Then she remembered the rest from sixth-form literature. *But when the planets in evil mixture to disorder wander, what plagues and what portents . . . what commotion in the winds . . .*

By these lights her parents had a successful marriage. They hadn't wandered in disorder. They might not have known a moment's happiness together, but at least the winds had stayed quiet.

Now apply this, she reasons, to that commotion whose abiding after-effects had been her study. A raging wind had been loosed, bearing plagues and portents, proof that the planets had wandered badly off their course. Some equipoise of hatred had been lost. You don't kill the thing you love, but you don't kill the thing you hate, either. You dance with the thing you hate to the music of the spheres. And all remains well – relatively speaking; of course relatively speaking, relative to massacre and annihilation – so long as the dance continues. The madness is to think you can dance alone, without a partner in mistrust. Had her mother left her father as she had so often threatened to, what would have become of either of them? She couldn't imagine her mother without her father, so intrinsic to her character was her contempt for him. She existed to denounce him. But he, oh she could imagine him on the streets wielding a machete. WHAT HAPPENED happened, no ifs or buts about it, not because ten thousand men like her father had been abandoned by their wives – though that must have added to the savour of it for some – IT HAPPENED because they forgot, or more likely never fully understood, that those they were killing performed the same function as their wives. It was a catastrophe of literal-mindedness. You don't kill the thing you hate just because you hate it.

As for *why* the hatred, Esme Nussbaum is not concerned to put her mind to that. Not now. Perhaps later when she has more strength. Should she slip back into a coma, she thinks, she'll have the mental space for it.

She is just strong enough, however, to see this one thought through to the end: an essential ingredient of the harmony of disharmony was lost when men like her father went on the rampage. And now, still, all these decades later, they wander in uncomplemented disorder.

She is no longer employed by Ofnow. When Ofnow kills its employees it assumes them to be off the payroll. Her mother has been trying to get her a pension – an endeavour in which she has not been able to count on the support of her husband who understands Ofnow's reasoning – but without success. She knows what their response will be if she pushes them too hard. They will prove her daughter is no longer on the payroll by killing her again.

Sometimes Esme forgets that she is no longer employed by Ofnow and finds herself preparing a new report to take into the office on Monday morning. It will argue that if the country is to enjoy any sort of harmony again, there must be restitution. Not a crude financial recompense to the descendants of those who vanished in the course of WHAT HAPPENED (there can be no talk of victims) – their whereabouts anyway, supposing some exist, are unknown. What she has in mind is making restitution to the descendants, or rather the *idea* of the descendants, of those who remained (there can of course be no talk of culprits either). *Us*, in other words, the living descendants of the living. Restitution in this sense: *Giving us all back what we have lost.*

There will be considerable relief in the office that she is not proposing financial recompense no matter that it cannot possibly be implemented.

Blood money presupposes an offence and, since there hasn't been one, blood money isn't on the table. But they won't know what in God's name she means by giving us back what we have lost. *What have we lost?* Explain yourself, Miss Nussbaum. And she will. Gladly.

'What we have lost,' she will tell them, 'is the experience of a deep antagonism. Not a casual, take-it-or-leave-it, family or neighbourly antagonism – but something altogether less accidental and arbitrary than that. A shapely, long-ingested, cultural antagonism, in which everything, from who we worship to what we eat, is accounted for and made clear. *We are who we are because we are not them.*'

They stare at her.

'Remove them from the picture and who are we?'

They are still staring at her.

'We must give the people back their necessary opposite,' she will tell them, heated by her own fierceness, the splintered bones in her body a thousand weapons to slay with.

'And how do you propose doing that, young lady?' someone dares to ask.

Ah, she will say. Now you're asking.

iii

At the very moment Esme Nussbaum was knocked down outside her place of work, her mother fell

326

off a chair on which she'd been standing to dust the bookshelves. Mothers and daughters, especially when no man beloved of either is around to break the current, can be attuned like this.

In the time her daughter was in hospital Rhoda Nussbaum never gave up hope of her coming out of her coma because she could hear her thinking live thoughts. And now that Esme was home, back in the room that had been her nursery, back in her care, her mother heard even more of what was going on inside her head. Planets, marriages, collisions, commotion – she heard all that. Some of her daughter's thoughts and phrases she even recognised as her own. How could it be otherwise? If she was attuned to Esme, then Esme was attuned to her. Even in the womb the baby hears its mother's music. And as an essentially companionless woman, with a rich store of anger in her, Rhoda had confided in her daughter, sometimes in words, sometimes silently, earlier and more frequently than was common or even desirable. Necessary Opposites, for example, was the name of a two-girl, two-boy rock band Rhoda had danced to when she was a teenager. She was pretty certain the band vanished at about the time most hard-rock bands were consensually driven underground, and that would have been a few years before Esme was born. How extraordinary that a phrase that had been lying there in pieces in Rhoda Nussbaum's mind, unused and unreferred to, should suddenly reassemble itself in Esme's. But then again, maybe not. Rhoda had tried to dance her brains out to Necessary Opposites because she didn't like what her brains contained. Was it coincidence? The evil thing she wanted to dance out was all trace of a man in pain – or pretending to be in pain – declaring over and over *I am who I am because I am not them* as though it were an incantation, and begging her to kiss him, forgive him, enfold him, make him better. As though he had a better self she could release.

Hearing the words returned to her in Esme's thoughts did not bring back a long-forgotten event because she had never forgotten it – where she was when she heard them, how they made her feel, the feebleness of her response . . .

CHAPTER 8

GÖTTERDÄMMERUNG

i

A blooming, strong-jawed girl of just sixteen, still to meet the husband she can't bear, Rhoda Nussbaum (to be) had a brief affair with a man more than three times her age. Though she called it an affair, there was not much sex in it. Nor much love. It was an affair of curiosity. She was inexperienced, but with a fierce sense of the ridiculous that made her courageous, and he was her schoolteacher. An unattractive man physically, but you don't say no to your teacher. Especially when he wants you to know he's emotionally damaged and you might just be the one to heal him.

'I'm in bits,' he told her when she put her face up to be kissed.

The hands with which he held her shook. At first she thought it was she who was shaking, but she saw the light dancing in his wedding ring like sun on choppy water. 'Make me whole again,' he said, his scraggy beard moving independently of his lips, as though it too was bouncing on a wild, wild sea.

'That's a lot to ask of a pupil you've only ever given B+ to,' she said.

He had no sense of the ridiculous and didn't laugh. He was a folk singer in his spare time and, though they were a long way from any wild, wild sea, sang about fishermen bringing in herrings. The fact that he sometimes brought his guitar to school was another reason Rhoda allowed him to try it on with her. The other girls would be jealous if they found out and Rhoda had every intention of their finding out.

'I just want you to be yourself,' he said.

She swivelled her jaw at him. 'What if I don't know which of my selves to be?'

'You don't have to worry. You're being the self I care best about now.'

Care best about! But what she said was, 'And which self is that?'

'The good and innocent one.'

'Ha!' she snorted. Lacking experience she might have been, but they were in a hotel room drinking cider on the edge of the bed, on the outside of the locked door a frolicsome sign saying LEAVE US ALONE: WE'RE PLAYING, and she knew that while there were many words for what she was being not a one of them was 'innocent'.

'Oh yes you are,' he said, unbuttoning her school shirt. 'Where there's no blood, there's no guilt.'

'There might be blood,' she warned him.

He overcame his surprise to smile his saddest folkie's smile at her. 'That's different. Blood shed

330

in the name of love is not like blood shed in the name of hate.'

She wasn't having any love talk, but she could hardly not ask, 'How do you know? Have you shed blood in the name of hate?'

He let his long horse face droop lower even than usual. 'All in good time,' he said.

He was teasing her, she thought. This was his sexual come-on. *I have done such things . . .* Boys did that but she didn't expect it of a grown man. She liked him less for it and she hadn't liked him much to start with. He shouldn't have supposed she needed him to have terrible secrets. This was terrible secret enough. He was married, her teacher, older than her parents, undressing her, describing the shape of her breasts with his fingers, his touch so intrusively naked he might have been describing them in four-letter words. They were offending against every decency she had been taught.

He thought he guessed what she was thinking. He thought the mention of hate had startled her. But he had guessed wrong. She wanted him to finish a conversation he had started, that was all.

He told her in the end, some three or four visits to the hotel bedroom later. Very suddenly and brutally.

'You'd have been about ten,' he said. They were still dressed, looking out of the window on to a bank of air conditioners. Two pigeons were fighting over a crumb of bread that must have been thrown out of a window above theirs. The room had a worn, padded reproduction of the Rokeby Venus for a bedhead. In the days when the economy boomed and nothing yet had HAPPENED this had been an expensively raffish hotel, softly carpeted for high-heeled assignations. It still spoke knowingly of indulgence and love, but with only half a heart. So great a change in only six or seven years! Now a schoolteacher could afford to bring his pupil here.

A scented candle burned. His guitar case stood unopened in a corner. Was he going to sing to her, she wondered. The sign announcing that they were playing so leave them alone was swinging on the door.

She knew what he was referring to. WHAT HAPPENED, IF IT HAPPENED was the thing that happened when she was about ten. She hadn't known much about it, living too far from any of the centres of conflagration to see anything with her own eyes or hear anything with her own ears. One or two school acquaintances must have been caught up in it because they never showed their faces again, but they hadn't been close friends so their absence didn't impinge on her. Otherwise, apart from her form teacher once bursting into tears, and the headmaster banning all mobile phones and personal computers from the school premises, nothing occurred at school to suggest anything was wrong, and at home her parents remained tight-lipped. There was a blackout imposed by her father, no papers allowed into the house and no serious radio or television, but that had hardly bothered Rhoda aged ten. OPERATION ISHMAEL, however, in which she went, in a single bound, from Hinchcliffe to Behrens, could not be accounted for without reference to the turbulence it was devised to quiet, and so, one way or another, Rhoda learnt what she had never been taught. Namely that something unspeakably terrible had happened, if it had.

For me to think about when I'm older, she'd decided.

And now older was what she was.

'Yes,' she said. 'And . . .'

He gathered her into his arms. She didn't feel as safe there as she imagined she would when it all started. There was something ghostly about him – he was eerily elongated in body as well as face, as though he had grown too much as a consequence of a childhood illness equivalent to those that stopped people growing at all, bony, with a big wet vertical mouth that hung open despite the attempted camouflage of the beard, showing tombstone teeth. It wasn't difficult to imagine him with the skin stripped from his bones.

Why am I doing this, she asked herself. Why am I here? I don't even like him.

'She would have been about the age you are now, had she lived,' he said.

'She?'

'The girl . . .'

She waited.

'The girl I killed.'

'You killed a girl?'

'Come to bed,' he said.

She shook her head. She wasn't afraid. She just thought he was trying to impress her again. And maybe frighten or arouse her into doing something she didn't want to do.

'How do you mean you killed a girl?'

'How did I do it?'

That wasn't really her question, but all right, how did he do it?

'Not with my bare hands if that's what you think. I left it to others. I stood by and let it happen.'

She released herself. 'What others?'

'Does that matter?'

She pulled the face she and all her girlfriends pulled to denote they were talking to a moron. 'Hello!' she said. *'Does that matter?'*

He reached for her cheek. 'What matters is that I loved and killed for the same reason.' He paused, waiting for a reaction. Was he expecting her to tell him it was all right. *There, there – I forgive you.* 'What attracted me,' he went on, as though he was working out his motives for the first time, 'repelled me.'

'You killed because you were repelled?'

'No, I killed because I was attracted.'

She wanted to go home now.

'Stay,' he said. 'Please stay.'

Rhoda stared into his ugly wet mouth and

remembered a skull that had gone round the class during an anatomy lesson. Its mouth, too, though it had once been wired, fell open when the skull was passed from girl to girl.

'You mustn't think I'm going to be violent with you,' he said.

'*She* probably didn't think you were going to be violent with her.'

'I had no choice with her.'

She might only have been a schoolgirl but she knew everyone had a choice. 'That's your excuse,' she said, knotting her tie.

'No, I'm not making an excuse. It just is what it is. Sometimes you have to do something – you can't help yourself – you are drawn into it. You will understand when you're older. You have to destroy to survive. While they live, you can't. Most times it doesn't come to that, but when the opportunity presents itself . . .'

'The opportunity?'

'That's what it was.'

'And she was how old?'

'The girl? I've told you. She'd be about your age now, so then she would have been nine or ten.'

'You went with a girl of nine?'

He had the shakes again, she noticed. 'No, I didn't "go" with her. She was the daughter.'

'Whose daughter?'

'The daughter of the woman I *was* "going" with. It was the mother who attracted me.'

This was getting worse by the second, Rhoda

thought. At sixteen, if the words you like to use don't express contempt, they express disgust. Rhoda allowed her teacher to see her rehearsing all of them in her head.

'Wait a minute. Just listen. Let me tell you how it was before you judge me. The mother went for me, not the other way round. I met her at a print shop where I'd gone to get an invitation printed. She was doing the same, only she was arguing over the invitations they'd done for her. They were for the private view of a painter at a gallery I assumed was hers. She wanted me to agree that they'd botched the job. "Look at the colours!" she said. "Did you ever see a woman's breasts that colour?" They looked all right to me, but I agreed because I thought she was genuinely upset—'

'And because you hoped you'd get a look at the colour of hers.'

'No, yes, maybe. That's cheeky of you, but I deserve it. But that's not the point. I was being supportive, that's all. I didn't know then that dissatisfaction was her hallmark, that arguing with tradespeople was just something she did. Like throwing parties. There was a gallery opening or an engagement party or a ruby wedding every week in her world and she paid for most of them. All lavish affairs. Champagne and lobster canapés. She had money to burn. She had everything to burn. She would have burned me had I let her. So it was poetic justice in the end. If you think I lost my mind you'd be right. I lost my mind from the moment I saw her shouting about her invitations. I'd never been with anybody like her. She was older and knew more of the world than I did. A woman with her own art gallery. She was my opposite in every way – unreserved, voluptuous, selfish, faithless, as wild as a cat. She laughed more than anybody I'd ever met, too, but when she wasn't laughing her face would become a mask of tragedy. She had these great, dark, over-painted, sorrowful eyes, as though they told the whole mournful history of her people. That was her explanation, anyway. "We have experienced too much," she would tell me, holding me to her breast, and ten minutes later she was doing a seating plan. "Does nothing mean anything to you for long?" I'd ask her, and she'd say, "Yes, you," or "Yes, my daughter," and once she even said, "Yes, God." She told me she prayed but when I asked her what she prayed for it was always something material – good weather for the opening, the continued absence of her husband ("So that I can have my way with you all weekend" – as though God would help with that), a lightning bolt to destroy the boycotters who milled outside her gallery, chanting against the country whose best painters she represented – though in their presence she merely guffawed her contempt and called them sanctimonious ghouls. "They'll go when they find some other no-hope cause," she told me in front of their faces. There was no guilt or conscience in her. No beauty or inspiration. Don't get me wrong, she was beautiful to look at herself. Dark and soft. Bewitching. Sometimes when I held her I thought she had no bones, her body was so yielding. Though she was obstinate in all our conversations and fought me over everything, in bed she would be anything I wanted her to be. But there was no spiritual beauty. She gave money to charity but the impulse never seemed charitable to me. It was too easy, too automatic. Before my parents ever gave money they would sit around and discuss it for weeks. Should we make a donation here or would it be better spent there? She just wrote a cheque and never thought about it again. She would go to concerts and openings of shows at other art galleries but I never saw her moved. My music she hated. "Caterwauling about fishermen and bumpkins," she called it. I doubt she'd ever eaten a fish. I doubt she'd ever seen the sea, come to that. Or been out into the country. She looked down on people, imitated the accents of the poor, jeered at me even, sometimes, for not having her advantages. And that included a dinner jacket. "You can't come to one of my family events looking like that," she said the first time she saw me in my corduroy suit.

'I wished I didn't have to go to her "family events" or meet her "people" – I never felt at home with them. Was that because they looked down
on me? I didn't know. But I always felt they tolerated me, that was all. And if I dared to say a word

against them she'd fly at me in a rage. Once she broke two of my teeth. Yet for all the specialness of her "people", for all the superiority of their suffering over anyone else's, she would still affect the airs and graces of a woman who had just taken tea with royalty. These attempts to hide who she was and where she'd come from – her family had sold hats on a street market! – shocked me. And she did it so badly. People laughed at her behind their hands and she didn't notice. No doubt they were laughing at me too. I know what you must be thinking – why did I stay? I was obsessed by her, that's why. The more I hated her the more fascinated I became. I can't explain that. Was she my cruel mistress or my lapdog? I tell you, though you are too young to understand obsession, I was obsessed by the oily sallowness of her skin, her heavy breasts, her swampy lips, the little panting cries she made when I entered her – forgive me – the extravagant way she moved her hands, making up stories, telling lies, transparent fantasies, trying to impress whoever she needed to impress – a room of thirty people or just me, it didn't matter – but it sickened me too.'

He paused as though remembering his manners. Was there perhaps something she wanted to say at this point?

There wasn't. Rhoda thought he was probably right – she didn't have quite the years yet for this.

He took that to be permission to go on.

'There was something ancient about her. I don't

mean in appearance. I mean in what she represented. She went too far back. History should have finished with the likes of her by now. Sometimes when I was making love to her – forgive me, please forgive me, but I have to explain – I felt I was in a sarcophagus making love to a mummy. I thought she would come apart in my hands, under my kisses and caresses, like parchment. Can you be oily *and* dry? Can you be soft *and* brittle? Well she could. That was her power over me. And then she would stir, sit up like someone risen from the dead – Cleopatra herself – and shake her jewellery in my face. That jewellery! She would put those hands up to my cheeks and look at me with longing – or was it loathing? – and I'd hear the jewellery clinking and I wanted to tear it off her. Christ, how badly I wanted to do that! Rip it from her throat and drag it out of her ears. All that false beauty, the impossible way she spoke, her contempt for her marriage, her raving about her precious daughters, her people's tragic past, her pseudo-religiousness, the art she didn't care about – it's a miracle I never did strangle her.'

Rhoda finally found some words. 'So you got someone else to strangle her for you?'

He took a moment to reply. Measuring the silence. 'I let the gallery be burned.'

'With her in it?'

'With the child in it. There were living quarters there. She liked staying there sometimes. It was a treat for her. She could play at shop. Her mother even let her talk to clients sometimes, about the art. She thought it was a great joke. "Out of the mouths of babes," she'd say.'

Rhoda retreated into silence again. *Let the gallery be burned*, did he say? *Let*? She didn't want to know whether that meant he had invited arsonists in or had actually started the fire himself and then failed to put it out. Whatever else, she didn't want to picture him putting a match to the building, knowing there was a child inside. A child who, had she lived, would have been about the age she was now. She didn't want to show her fear.

'It was strange, you know,' he went on, in a different tone altogether now, almost matter-of-fact, 'it was as though it wasn't me doing it. Or if it was me it was me doing it at some other time. Any time in the last, I don't know, two, three thousand years I could have done the same – seen the flames, shaken my head and walked away.'

Very well, he was mad. That somehow made her feel better and even, strangely, less frightened. She had her sanity to defeat him with.

'What do you mean you could have done it two thousand years ago? Are you telling me you're some sort of a vampire?'

'I'm telling you my actions weren't mine alone. I was just repeating what had been done countless times before, and I don't doubt for the same reasons. Would you understand me if I said I'd been culturally primed to do it?'

She brought her hand to her mouth and laughed

bitterly up her sleeve, the way everyone did at school when an elder made a preposterous statement. 'Would you understand me if I said I'd been culturally primed to refuse to do my homework?' she gathered the boldness to ask.

He smiled at her smartness. 'Yes, I'd understand and say I hope that's the worst thing you will ever be culturally primed to do.'

'No you wouldn't. You'd say I was letting myself off.'

'It was a necessity,' he said. 'There are such things. It's you or them. You can't both breathe the same air. Some people are too different. *I am who I am because I am not them*, you tell yourself. That's what you fall in love with at first – this clean break with yourself. Because if you are not them, they are not you. But then you realise it isn't anything about them that you love, it's the prospect of your own annihilation. They say before the executed die they fall in love with their executioner. Maybe had she not told me our affair was over, that she'd found a man more suitable to her needs – a financier, I supposed, or a painter, one of her own, anyway – I'd have accepted death at her hands as my consummation. But her timing was wrong. She missed her chance. The world changed while she wasn't looking. One day the streets were quiet, the next the mob was out, shouting, burning, killing. I see from your expression that you know nothing of any mob. You were too young then and you've been well schooled since. But trust me, the gentlest people were suddenly behaving like animals. Was I part of it? Yes and no. I felt what they felt, they felt what I felt, though I believed then and believe now that I acted alone and for my own motives. But the violence didn't surprise me. You'd think the sight of people behaving so unlike themselves would surprise you but it doesn't. Violence quickly comes to look quite normal. Perhaps what I saw was a reflection of the violence in my heart. Perhaps I saw it as more violent than it was because I wanted it to be so. But I couldn't have made up the things that happened. I didn't join in. I even risked my own skin to get to her, to plead with her. *Give me another chance.* That's what she had reduced me to. *Give me another chance! I'll do whatever you like. I'll change.* As though I could ever change into anything she wanted for more than fifteen minutes. As though I could ever be anything but a convenience to her. I ran to the house but found it closed up. Good, I thought, at least they've got away. But then it occurred to me that they might be at the gallery, which at least had shutters. That was two miles away. I ran the whole distance. The shutters weren't down. The crowds had not got that far yet, though the usual boycotters were outside, noisier and more menacing than ever. With the strength that comes from desperation I pushed my way through them and hammered on the window. Little Jesse appeared. Even at that age she was her mother all over again. Same mournful eyes, same heavy cheeks, same rude flirtatiousness. Same indifference to danger. She was even wearing her mother's high-heeled shoes. "Mum's out," she mouthed. I told her to let me in. I'd wait. She said, "Mum doesn't want to see you any more." "What about you?" I shouted. "Don't you want to see me any more?" She shrugged. Easy come, easy go. I might as well have been a servant or the gardener. A person of no consequence though I'd petted and played with her and bought her presents she didn't need. She eyed me sardonically. Her mother's child. *Don't be pathetic*, I could see she was thinking. I asked who was in the gallery with her. She said no one. She could have been lying but I chose to see her being left alone as proof of her mother's callousness, and as a sign. Nine years old and left to fend for herself. What does that tell you? So should I have cared for her more than her faithless, so-called doting mother did? Whether I could have done anything I don't know. I could have tried to spirit her away. I could have tried to reason with the crowd – *There's only a child in there*. Only an insolent, superior little girl, but a child nonetheless. Unlikely to have made any difference but I could have tried. But the shouts and smell of smoke had a powerful effect on me. I don't say they excited me, but they gave a sort of universality to what I was feeling. *I am who I am because I am not them* – well, I was not alone in feeling that. We were all who we were because we were not them. So why did that translate into hate? I don't know, but when everyone's feeling the same thing it can appear to be reasonableness. Can you understand that? What everyone's doing becomes a common duty. Besides, it wasn't for me to play God. These people had their own God, I thought – let *Him* look after her. So I did nothing when she turned her back on me. Didn't bang on the window. Didn't call her. Didn't warn her. I stood outside for a short while, staring at the inflammatory words painted on the window – GALILEE GALLERIES – as though in a trance. Could have been thirty seconds, could have been thirty minutes, then I walked away.'

He kept his eyes averted from Rhoda's, showing her his long, brittle hands. The hands he hadn't employed to help a child. What did he want her to do – kiss them or break them off at the wrists?

'And now you think it's my duty to let you replace her with me,' she said. She was on her feet, dressed and ready to leave, feeling sick but strong, with her school bag under arm. 'Well you've got another think coming.'

She was relieved to make it out safely on to the street.

ii

She didn't repeat a word to anyone of what she'd been told. There was no point. For one thing, to have spoken of it would have compromised her – what was she doing talking to her teacher about his murderous, obsessional love life in a hotel room? – and for another she didn't expect to be believed. She wasn't sure how much of it she believed herself. He could have made the whole thing up to impress her, or made the second half up to exact an imaginary revenge. You can murder in your thoughts, she knew that. And even if she'd been believed – what then? Where was the crime? What law do you break by walking away? She didn't know much about what had gone on when she was ten, but she'd heard adults talking and knew the slate had been wiped clean. So long as you joined in the chorus of saying sorry, you were in the clear. The past was the past and brought automatic absolution.

As for him, she hoped fervently that he would quit the school, but he didn't. He didn't ask her to go to a hotel with him again either. He just did what he was good at and looked away.

If her presence made him anxious, he concealed it well. She, however, grew morose and began to do badly at school. No one knew why, but she lost interest in her studies and left before she had achieved what had been expected of her. Whereas he appeared, if anything, to prosper. Good divinity teachers were hard to come by.

Not long afterwards, at a concert given by Necessary Opposites, she met Compton who repelled her. The degree to which he made her flesh creep excited her. He was opposite to everyone she cared about, opposite to everything she admired and loved. It was marry him or kill him. And, in anticipation of her daughter's thinking, she saw that it would have been literal-minded of her to kill him.

She didn't tell Compton about her affair with a murderer or a liar or both. She didn't want his hands on her experience, she didn't want to hear him say that the murdered girl got what was owing to her. She was angry enough. Nor did she tell Esme when she was of an age to understand. In Esme's case it wasn't necessary; she picked up the essentials without words needing to be exchanged. There was certainly some rage in her that Rhoda proudly believed was her doing. She'd instilled an appetite for justice that was like a hunger in her own belly. Esme, she was confident, would fight the good fight for her. Esme would show courage where she hadn't. Esme would make someone pay.

CHAPTER 9

THE CELESTIAL BANDLEADER

i

Esme Nussbaum never did go back to her old office. But fragments of it came to her. She hadn't been as alone as she'd thought. They were slow and watchful, but first one and then another of her ex-colleagues took up the challenge implicit in the report she had produced before her accident. She was right. Something had to be done to curtail the quarrelsomeness that was poisoning the family, the workplace, the schoolyard, and society at large. It would be a while before they would catch up with her more recent thinking, but within five years it had become acceptable to admit there was a problem to be solved. Five years after that, though still shaky on her legs, she was leading a team charged with putting back what had been taken away.

At the first meeting she addressed as head of the Commission for Restitution she spelled out the problems that lay ahead.

'We cannot any longer go on deploying euphemisms,' she declared. 'We have to call a spade a spade. If we are to put back what has been taken away we must restore its human name. These were people. How do you put back people who, in whatever circumstances or for whatever motives, were annihilated?'

She thought the question was rhetorical but a couple of hands went up.

'I am not,' she said, 'looking for immediate answers. We have research to do. But I will take a couple of suggestions to kick us off.'

The first was to go looking in other countries where comparable destruction had either not taken place at all, or had been partial. The second was to come up with an alternative necessary opposite – some other ethnic or religious group that could stand in as hate object for that which had been obliterated. 'Couldn't something be done with the Chinese?' someone asked.

In answer to the first, Esme doubted whether, even if such people could be found, they'd be reckless enough to quit the places of safety in which they'd settled. And supposing that some were game, they were sure to be adventurers and chancers, misfits and counterfeiters and opportunists, the last people she thought suitable to fill the void that had been left. What no one wanted were more riots within a generation.

In answer to the second, she was firm that the mutual suspicion needed to restore the country's equipoise of hate was not a moveable feast. Difference, which after all was easy to come by, was not in itself enough. So, with respect, 'no' to the Chinese who, though they had always kept themselves to themselves, and had never, for that reason, won the love of the indigenous population, were too unalike to do the job. She was undeviating on this. Alternative objects of suspicion couldn't simply be plucked out of their fractious society at will, or appointed by diktat, on the assumption that any old hostility or incomprehension would do. She needed her auditors to mark her words and mark them well: You have to see a version of yourself – where you've come from or where you might, if you aren't careful, end up – before you can do the cheek-to-cheek of hate. Family lineaments must be discerned. A reflection you cannot bear to see. An echo you cannot bear to hear. In other words, you must have chewed on the same bone of moral philosophy, subscribed to a similar spirituality and even, at some point in the not too distant past, have worshipped at the same shrines. It was difference where there was so much that was similar that accounted for the unique antipathy of which they were in search. And only one people with one set of prints fitted that bill.

As for the question of whether they – this 'version of ourselves' – would reciprocate our hatred, why it was no question at all. They were the mirror image of our hostility. They too saw the family resemblance and were fascinated and appalled. True, some had been more easily assimilable than

others. They fell in love with those who miscom-
prehended them – the miscomprehension being a
fatal allure in itself. They embraced the culture
that vilified and disfigured them. Melted to the
music and fainted away before the fastidious
beauty of the words. But they had solved their
own problem and in doing so had solved the first
of Esme's. They had disappeared into the landscape, become their opposites, long before the
time that concerned her and her team. For the
remainder, if any could be found, the orchestra
had only to start up for the dance to begin again.

I feel like a celestial bandleader, Esme thought.

A simple reiteration of a previously dismissed
thought was what put Esme's commission on a
new track. The thought that, WHATEVER HAD
HAPPENED, not everyone could have been destroyed.
No operation could have been so successful. Some
would of course have escaped. But some, too,
would surely have hidden. Not all the country had
been up in arms. There were places where feelings
had not run so high and blood had not been so
plentifully spilled. Out of kindness of heart,
principle, godliness, or just the obduracy that
flourishes away from big towns and capital cities
– that dogged refusal to go along with the majority
– people would have offered help, given shelter,
taken at least a frightened child in. There was no
point in being overly optimistic. The chance of
finding entire families living peaceably on rocky

outcrops where they'd been hiding out for generations was slim. But failing that, could it be that there was not a single man and single woman of pure descent to be discovered somewhere in a population of almost one hundred million people? For no more was necessary – just one single man and one single woman, subject to rigorous authentication and in reasonable health, and it could all begin again.

I feel like Noah, Esme thought.

ii

Had she been in better health herself, she'd have remained in charge of the commission. But when her mother died – her poor angry mother who never got to meet a man she liked – Esme knew she had to change the circumstances of her life. She longed for clean air and her damaged limbs needed the exercise of country walks. Working in the field, in both senses, would suit her better, she decided. And by her own logic, the more far-flung that field, the more likely she was to find what she was looking for. Fossil-hunting she called it.

She put her father in a home, reminding him that his senescence was punishment for his nature, and travelled north. The fossil-hunting did not go well at first. She laughed at her own naivety. Did she expect she would find her necessary opposite sitting up in a field, like a hare at dusk, waiting to be seen? Did she think a family of them would roll up at the public house where she liked to drink a tomato juice before going home to make herself a salad, and wonder what had taken her so long? And would she recognise them when she saw them, anyway?

It was in the nature of the problem that she had never, of course – knowingly, at least – met any. She had done a fair amount of reading but wasn't sure about the reliability of the sources she consulted. A children's story from the previous century, for example, cited as distinguishing features the puffy lips, the fleshy eyelids, the low, receding forehead, the large ears like the handles of a coffee cup – *eine Kaffeetasse* – the short arms, the bow-leggedness, the shuffling gait, the jabbering voice, the sickly-sweet odour – I shouldn't have too much trouble noticing if one of those stumbles past, Esme laughed. From more recent publications she learnt about the drooping eyes and jowly faces, the thinning hair, the thick eyeglasses, the large floppy breasts (on the men as well as the women). Best of all – she read – throw a handful of coins in a pool, the person quickest to dive in is the person you're looking for. Well she wasn't going to do that. But then what reason was there to believe they would still look and act as they had two or three generations earlier? If any had survived was it not likely that they'd have taken care to alter their appearance and demeanour, or more likely still that, exiled from their communities, they'd have assumed the manners and lineaments of their neighbours, and not only forgotten what they were supposed to look like but who they were supposed to be? I could be living next to one and not know, Esme realised. I could be living next door to a whole family and *they* might not know.

She wasn't, of course, the only person looking, even in as remote a place as Edenhope where she had decided, in her own words, to set up camp. She debriefed agents on a regular basis, sometimes getting them to report to her in person, sometimes by utility-phone conference call. Some she felt she could rely on more than others, and many had not been told who in fact they were looking for. They were paid to keep their eyes open, that was all. For who? For what? Simply for anyone behaving strangely, out of character with the community, anyone local people thought suspicious, of dubious provenance. For a multitude of reasons, but most of all so as not to set up the wrong sort of expectations, Esme omitted all mention of slanting foreheads and shuffling gait. If these lesser agents supposed they were hunting down such minor infractions against the Present as heirloom hoarding or spending too much time in reference libraries then so much the better. Softlee softlee catchee money. Monkey, beg your pardon. She didn't want any possibles scared off by unsubtle, overenthusiastic investigation. And a reference library, that immemorial refuge of the dispossessed, was not a bad place to be looking, little help as the limited archives available would give those wondering who they were and where they'd come from.

'Another wild goose chase,' she would say wearily to herself, after a trail of clues ended nowhere. Sociologically, it was interesting to discover how many misfits even the smallest hamlets yielded. How many runaway wives or husbands, how many defectors of one sort or the other – from responsibility, from debt, from the law, from careers, from gender – how many were judged, rightly or wrongly, to be foreigners, illegal immigrants, gypsies, visitors from another solar system even. Was there anyone, she sometimes wondered, who wasn't alien to someone else? The surprise, given this degree of social mistrust, was that more hadn't HAPPENED and indeed wasn't HAPPENING now. But this just went to show how right she had been in her analysis: those who had been the object of WHAT HAPPENED weren't just any old, interchangeable excuse for civil riot, they occupied a particular, even privileged, place in the nation's taxonomy of fear and loathing.

After several years of unrewarded endeavour, at the end of which Esme Nussbaum thought she had finally worn out what remained of her energies, an exciting piece of information came her way. The agent responsible for it was precisely one of those who knew nothing of what they were about and were therefore always more likely, in Esme's view, to yield a result. She felt tentatively vindicated. It all came from one or two fairly innocuous questions being asked about boxes of letters found stored in a convent.

A convent! Esme Nussbaum threw her head back and laughed, as she often did at things that weren't funny, like a crazy woman. She found the idea of a convent so ludicrously incongruous she was certain it was going to yield something. Something big or something small she didn't know, but something . . .

She suddenly felt years younger.

Barely two months later, she was to be seen extending her hand and flashing her brightest and most motherly smile. 'Hello, I'm Ez,' she said.

'Hello, Ez,' said Ailinn Solomons.

CHAPTER 10

LOST AND FOUND AND
LOST AGAIN

i

There are times in your life, he thought,
when you need to see an animal. Not a
dog or a cat – they carried too many associations of the humans whose feet they clung to.
Something unconnected. Something wild. Seals,
he decided were the thing. From his bench he
could sometimes see them, their bald heads
bobbing about in the ocean. Were there hunchback
seals whose totemic disfigurement at one and the
same time shamed their progeny and guaranteed
them immunity. Immunity from what? From
whatever vengeance seals meted out to one another
for offences buried deep in seal history. Your
colleagues detest you, the librarian had told him.
In fact the word she'd used was 'mistrust', but to
him that was just splitting hairs. Did seals detest?

They weren't out there, anyway. After an hour
or more of looking, he gave up on them and
returned reluctantly to his cottage. There was no
explaining why he did that. He could have gone

on watching. Or gone for a stiff, dizzying walk. Shaken stuff out of his head. Let the wind blow him about. If there were times in your life when you needed to see an animal, there were also times in your life when you needed to be an animal.

There were no visitors. He had the cliffs to himself. He could have scampered, sniffed the ground, rubbed his nose in droppings, howled, screamed. Beyond a general impression of height and risk and isolation, he didn't know the cliffs on which he'd so often walked. He sedulously avoided looking, as though ignorance of his surroundings, particularly an ignorance of what grew beneath his feet, was a metaphysical necessity to him. Now was his chance. But he didn't take it. Instead, he let monotonous mortal habit claim him. And back down to his cottage he went.

It wasn't even as though he was in the mood for work. On some days his lathe answered every anxiety. The whirl of the spindle shut out his thoughts, all the concentrated frustration in his body vanished at the point where he held the handle of the chisel as gently as he might have held the fingers of a child. The wood curled beneath its blade, like the hair of that same child becoming unloosed from a bonnet. He favoured a light touch, not always knowing exactly what he wanted to make. Let it turn itself, he thought on good days, let it turn out as it chooses. If the bowl was waiting in the wood, then God was waiting in the bowl as surely as love had been waiting – a long, long time waiting – in the spoons he'd carved for Ailinn. But not today. No curls, no God, no Ailinn. It was like waiting for a storm to break.

He was relieved to find his utility phone flashing. If it was trouble, bring it on, he thought. If it was Ailinn, please let her say she was coming over. It had been weeks since he'd seen her. He had not rung her because he was frightened to encounter a hostile voice. 'You threw me out. Drop dead!' She'd have been within her rights to say that and more, then slam the phone down. He'd offered her his bed, his home, his loyalty. You can't do that and then ask someone to leave, no matter how distraught you feel or how temporary you want their absence to be. A life companion is a life companion. It wasn't her fault his cottage had been broken into and his Chinese runner straightened. And if he'd meant it when he'd told her that the little he had was hers, then it was her house that had been broken into, her Chinese runner that had been straightened, too. He had to stop thinking of himself as a man alone, unless that was now what, thanks to his own stupidity, he had once again become. Only this time it would not be the same as before. There was no same as before, not after Ailinn. After Ailinn, nothing.

He wondered whether he should leave the utility phone to flash. All day and all night if necessary. Not rush to find out. Delay the disappointment. Though it was still morning he knew that if he went to bed he would immediately drop into sleep.

Anticipation keeps some men awake. It poleaxed Kevern. He thought of it as a gift. When the terrible time came – it didn't matter which – he would deal with it by passing out. He had warned Ailinn what he would do.

'Good to know I can count on you,' she said.

'Under no circumstances think you can count on me,' he said, just in case she intended her comment as a joke. 'I'm not man enough.'

'I won't make that mistake,' she said.

'I am not your rock.'

'I understand.'

'Should anything happen to you I will fall immediately into the deepest sleep known to man. I might never wake up from it. I'd hope never to wake up from it. That's how impossible I would find life without you. See it as the proof of my devotion. But understand I'd be no use when it comes to getting help or, if you're beyond help, gathering your friends, organising your funeral, arranging the flowers.'

'You'd let me just lie there on your floor.'

'*Our* floor – yes.'

'And what if anything happens to you?'

'I'm not asking you to do any better.'

'I can leave you on our floor?'

'You can leave me anywhere. Dead or dying I won't know anything about it.'

'So ours is a fair-weather love?'

'That makes it sound selfish, but yes if you mean that when we prosper we prosper and when we don't—'

She got the picture. '—we don't.'

It must have been with this conversation in mind that she framed her message – the message to which, when the moment came to run from it, he knew he had to listen.

'It's me,' she said. 'I've been going mad here. Why haven't you rung me? We need to speak urgently. Don't go comatose on me. It's not the something terrible you've told me you won't be man enough to cope with. Or at least I don't think it is.'

ii

A brief nod to the work done in past times by St Brigid's Roman Catholic Convent and Orphanage, Mernoc, is in order here, if only to correct the misconception that every Roman Catholic orphanage was just a workhouse under another name. 'I am not disposed to maintain that the being born in a workhouse is in itself the most fortunate and enviable circumstance that can possibly befall a human being,' wrote that once popular English humanitarian, Charles Dickens, and under his influence a sentimental predisposition against such charitable institutions was, for a century or more, and not just in his own country, the norm. Whatever the justice of this negative view of the workhouse, St Brigid's conformed to another pattern entirely. Children placed in its care were viewed as gifts from God himself, little angels with damaged wings, no less, whose physical and spiritual well-being was the first and last concern of all members of the community, from the lowliest novitiate to the Mother Superior herself.

The reputation of St Brigid's must have reached the ears of Rebecca Macshuibhne, though it was on the mainland, some thirty miles south of the island on which she now lived, and for all that her husband, Fridleif, had taught her to think ill of Roman Catholics. Before she met Fridleif she had made no distinction between Catholicism and Congregationalism. In her home Christianity was Christianity. Such ignorance of fine and not-so-fine distinctions was not intended to be contemptuous. It was just that Jesus was understood to be central to all Christian faiths and wasn't central, except in a negative sense, to hers. Not an immoveable aversion, however, as was attested to by her subsequent marriage to the Rev. Fridleif Macshuibhne, her eager assumption of her pastoral duties as his wife, and the baptism of their daughter Coira.

That this solemn rite, which her grandparents Wolfie and Bella Lestchinsky made no effort to attend, constituted Coira's once-and-for-all initiation into the care of Christ, neither Rebecca nor Fridleif thought to question. They had promised on the child's behalf to reject the Devil and all rebellion against God, to renounce deceit, to submit to Christ as Lord.

The deed was done, the child was a Christian.

And there the matter would have rested had not the final letter Rebecca sent to her parents been returned to her in that chilling fashion.

Rebecca could not stop looking at the stamp.

'It won't tell you any more than it already has,' Fridleif said.

'What do you think it means?'

He showed her his clear, Arctic eyes. 'It's possible,' he said, 'that it was they who returned it.'

'With an official stamp, Fridleif?'

He took the envelope from her and held it to the light.

'I've done that a thousand times,' she said. 'And anyway, why would they send my letter back? They never did before. Not replying is one thing – and I know it hurt you, Fridleif, as it hurt me – but returning my letter unopened is something else again. That's not their way. We don't behave like that in my family.'

Her husband looked at her in a manner she found provoking. But theirs was a proudly peaceable marriage and she wanted it to remain that way. 'It's too much of a coincidence,' she went on, 'that this should happen when there's so much trouble down there. I'm frightened.'

He touched her hand. 'The Lord will protect them.'

She had heard her father invoke the name of the Lord in the face of danger often enough. But with him the invocation had been ironical, angry, disappointed. The Lord should protect them but wouldn't. Hadn't. And wouldn't ever. Which her father took to be a personal affront to him. And yet his had never been a counsel of despair. There was something out there in which he believed, an idea that answered to the name of the Lord no matter that the Lord himself did scant justice to it. Reason. Human resourcefulness. Intelligence.

Of what use to them their intelligence was now, however, she couldn't imagine.

Seeing her eyes fill with tears, Fridleif stretched out his other hand to her. 'Look,' he said in his gentlest voice, 'we don't really know how bad it is down there. These things get blown out of all proportion.'

'*These things?*'

'Rumours, I mean. That's all we have to go on.'

He seemed insubstantial to her, all of a sudden. He was a feathery man – that had been his charm. He had flitted into her life, a creature of light and optimism, so unlike her father. His translucent faith a wonderful release to her after the weighty, frightened sonorousness of her parents and their friends. But it was as though he had never before been tested in her presence, and now that he had – well, he was failing. You have God but you have no gravitas, Rebecca thought.

'Then if rumours are all we have to go on,' she replied at last, 'I must see what's happening with my own eyes.'

He didn't say anything, assuming that having

spoken from her heart she wouldn't think it necessary to act from it.

But the next day she repeated her determination to find out for herself. He shook his head. 'I can't let you go,' he said. 'It's too dangerous.'

'Too dangerous? Yesterday you said it was blown out of all proportion.'

'We don't know what's true or what isn't, but I can't let you put yourself in danger. You have a child. *Our* child. You have a husband. You have the people of Mernoc.'

'I have a mother and father,' she reminded him.

'You could have fooled me,' he said.

'Say that again.'

He knew not to say it again.

'I will take Coira with me,' she said. 'If it turns out they're all right they'll be glad to see her. Grandchildren always do the trick.'

'And if they're not all right?'

'Then we'll come back.'

'Rebecca, I can't allow this,' he said.

She told him he had no choice. He told her he was Coira's father. He couldn't allow her to endanger the child. And as for grandchildren always doing the trick . . . he hesitated . . . not *this* grandchild.

What Rebecca then said, what Rebecca then felt, was a surprise to her. 'They won't see Coira like that.'

'Like what?'

'As lost to them.'

'How will they see her?'

It was her turn now to hesitate. 'As a little bit of both.'

'She isn't a little bit of both. She's been baptised.'

'You make that sound pretty final.'

'It is pretty final.'

'So I've been bypassed, have I?'

'How can you ask that? You too have been baptised.'

'That doesn't change everything, Fridleif.'

'Yes, it does. It changes *everything*. Otherwise it's of no meaning.'

'It doesn't change what's in me, my blood, my genes.'

'Your *blood*?'

'We didn't start at the beginning, you know. By our law Coira remains within the fold. As do I, as the daughter of my mother.'

Fridleif put his hands together and prayed silently. He had never expected to hear the phrase 'our law' on his wife's lips. He felt as though she had struck him in the heart.

Rebecca didn't join him in prayer. She looked out of the window at the featureless grey sea.

'I never thought we would fight over who our child belongs to,' Fridleif said at last.

'I'm not fighting. I know who she belongs to. She belongs to us. You and me.'

'And to Christ.'

She waved the idea away. If it had been beautiful

to her once, it wasn't beautiful to her now. 'She belongs to us, Fridleif. *Us!* And I am half of us.'

'I won't allow you to take her away.'

If it was a threat, it had no menace in it.

The following morning she was gone. She and the child.

But she made a concession to her husband, though she never told him of it. She decided against taking Coira with her. If her parents weren't alive, she would be subjecting her to danger for no reason. If they were alive, God willing, she would make peace with them face to face herself, and then return with the child. Her reasoning was clear. If Coira was her daughter by blood, in direct line of descendancy from her mother and her grandparents and their grandparents before them, then she wasn't safe. No one in whom the lust for murder had been aroused was going to stop to consider the finer points of lineage and conversion; no one was going to care that Coira had been baptised and was, in her father's eyes, the child of Christ. She had heard her parents make the argument again and again – 'When they come to get you, Becky, they won't be making subtle distinctions. They won't spare you because you've changed your name and happen to think differently from us on a few points. They won't release you with a kiss because you think it couldn't ever happen here. It's who you are by blood that interests them, nothing else.' She had despaired of them. Well, for different reasons she was despairing now. But she couldn't leave Coira with her father. Not after the words that had been exchanged. She had made great sacrifices for Fridleif. She had broken the hearts of her mother and father who in her own heart she did not expect ever to see again. She had given him everything else; she would not give him her child.

It was at this point in her deliberations that she remembered what she'd heard of St Brigid's Convent and Orphanage. Fridleif would never think of searching for her there. He would as soon go looking for his child in hell. In the anger that spilled from her she took pleasure from the thought that a Roman Catholic orphanage was an even greater anathema to him than her parents' home.

Though she would have liked to check the nuns out, there wasn't any way she could do so without arousing their suspicions. They might recognise her as the wife of a minister, and she did not want them to connect Fridleif to the child. She pulled at the bell to the orphanage at an hour it was evident there were nuns about, and then fled. What the nuns found when they answered the door was a basket with a baby inside. 'Moses' they would have called her, had there not been a label tied around her neck identifying her as Coira. No surname. Rebecca would have liked to restore her own name to the child but – though she didn't share her parents' suspiciousness, especially of the conventual – didn't think she dare risk it. Coira Lestchinsky! – maybe not. An accompanying note explained that the mother was suffering clinical depression and, though she loved the child with all her heart, did not feel capable of looking after her as she would have wished. She commended Coira, who had been baptised far from here, to the tender Christian mercies of the nuns. 'Love her,' she pleaded.

Towards the early years of Coira's education she made what she hoped was a fair contribution. She would collect the child at a later date when, God willing, she would be in better health, but, if she failed to return, a more substantial donation would automatically be made. She left a parcel of letters with the child's belongings. These, were she not to return, were to be opened only on Coira's majority.

She wasn't sure, at the moment of leaving her, that she could go through with it, but her grief reminded her of what her parents must have felt when she left them, and she knew she had to find them if she could.

She removed the label from Coira's neck and wrote a further message on it. 'Protect her for me. See how small she is – she is more shawl than baby. Pray for her. Pray, if you can, for me. Pray that this has a safe and happy outcome.'

But like many other prayers uttered in these days, the nuns' prayers, if they remembered to say them, were not listened to. Rebecca did not locate her parents nor did she ever return, in safety and happiness, for Coira.

Not counting the letters, all she bequeathed to her bereft daughter was her own sense of being between the devil and the deep blue sea. And the terrible conundrum of not knowing which was which.

iii

In the days he'd been without Ailinn, Kevern had gone again through his parents' papers. He had been tempted to open the box intended for a grandchild, should one materialise, but couldn't bring himself to disobey instructions he had long considered sacred. For a non-believer, Kevern had a highly developed sense of the sacramental. Duty, to the living and the dead, hemmed him in. His life, from the moment he opened his eyes – and whether he found Ailinn beside him or not – was a chain of rituals he could no more break than he could go without food or self-reprobation. Without obligation and repetition he was as chaff in the wind. If religion meant anything he could under-stand, it was this: doing again what had worked when you did it the last time, doing it because you believed you had to, remonstrating against the random, refusing to be tossed about the universe as though the universe had no use for you. That was the beginning and the end of reli-gious devotion to him, anyway. Not what you owed to a god but what you owed to the idea that you weren't arbitrary or accidental. And whatever you did more than three times a week, at the same time and with the same reverence, was another blow struck against the haphazard.

Densdell Kroplik had told him, the last time they met, that he was lucky to have been born in Port Reuben. *Lucky*? The thought that he owed anything to chance disheartened him. If he was only here by chance then he was indeed chaff in the wind and might as easily have been blown somewhere else. So where? *Absolutely anywhere*, was the answer, but how do you live a life that isn't random when the circumstances of your living it are? There had to be something between him and Port Reuben that was more than fortuitous; each had to have needed the other. All right, he accepted Kroplik's view of him as a child of aphids who were themselves children of aphids. No one can go all the way back to the beginning. Invaders, migrants, vagrants, came and went. He'd settle for ten generations. If he had to, he'd make do with even fewer. Soil was all he was after. Not real soil, God forbid, but the idea of soil. If not native soil then soil that at least was congenial to his growing. Bodies rejected implanted organs; some took but others the body found too alien. Why did he feel that the village of Port Reuben, in which his papers certified he'd been born, had always been rejecting him like an organ it didn't need or want?

This rummaging through his parents' papers was not going to help him find an answer. It never had before. Yet each time he did it he came upon something he hadn't paid attention to previously. A joke so acidic that it had burned through the paper on which his father had written it. The names of jazz records he intended to buy. Titles of books still to be read. A manila folder containing a few watery sketches, none of them remarkable, done by his mother presumably, of him as a baby, of his father as a younger but no less rancid-looking man, of a beautiful dreaming woman he didn't recognise but whom now, after Kroplik's description, he took to be his grand-mother, of the cliffs, of a sunset, and of hands – just hands – drawn so tenderly they had to belong to her butcher-lover. So they'd lived here at least, his mother and father – because bitterness and infidelity constitute lives.

He missed their lives for them, missed what he didn't remember, yearned for what he hadn't known. Can you be nostalgic for nostalgia, he wondered. His answer was yes, yes you could.

It was while he was again, ritualistically, going through drawers in his father's workshop that he came again upon a foolscap black notebook with scribbled entries in his mother's hand. It hadn't interested him the first time he'd found it, because it seemed to contain no more than lists of non-essentials his father must have asked for, sacks for rubbish, a new coffee mug, a fan heater, antiseptic cream. But he realised he should have wondered why it was here, in his father's space, among his

372

father's things. After the first half-dozen pages the book became something else. Sketches again, but not at all watery this time: strong charcoal portraits, in the manner of woodcuts – had she been thinking of actually doing woodcuts with her husband's help? – of people he didn't recognise, squatting careworn women in turbans, angular men in long beards, carcasses of slaughtered animals, executioners in bloody aprons standing over them, a child looking out of the barred window of a train, figures huddled in fear, and one of herself, he was sure it was her, with her mouth open and a hand, not hers, over it, pressing hard into her face. And then, at the back of the book, half a dozen small crayoned studies in a style so different he marvelled the same person could have done them – what they depicted he couldn't say for sure, cityscapes a couple of them seemed to be, whores, or were they birds, cranes or storks, standing under phosphorescent yellow lamp posts, their scarves or feathers blowing about their necks, their bodies rendered in patches of the most vivid colour, purple shoulders and breasts, vermilion bellies, attenuated lime-green legs, the stones they stood on as black as night. Two were more abstract still, mere blobs of violent colour, like pools of blood, and one a nude, somehow African in conception, primitive certainly, painted freely, her eyes orange, her skin a throbbing pink, her hands stretched out towards . . . towards whom?

Could his mother really have done these? They

were signed, simply but deliberately, in upright letters, as though she wanted there to be no mistake about it, Sibella.

He had always discounted his mother. Other than when he heard her calling to him on the cliffs, he rarely thought about her. It was his father he had grieved over, not out of love but out of sorrow. His father had made small beautiful things. Miniature ring bowls whose rims fell away like lace around wrists, mahogany trinket boxes with secret compartments so finely concealed that people who hid things in them sometimes never found them again, slender swaying single-rose vases carved out of 'whispering walnut' – his father's phrase, whispering this, whispering that, their whole lives lived in a whisper. How could such delicacy of work proceed from so frightened, unhappy and lumpen a temper? His mother too had been unhappy, but she was no artist and Kevern Cohen was sentimental about art. Now he had to revise his thinking.

His father had kept this folio of hers. Why? Did he secretly admire her gift? Did he ever tell her, Kevern wondered.

It even crossed his mind, for the very first time, that his father and mother might have loved one another. The idea, at least, of his father being proud of her, made him tremble with the realisation that he'd known as little about his family as he knew about the earth he trod on.

How good an artist was she? He couldn't tell.

Her hand was strong and sure, the colours piercing, but were the images hers? He felt he had seen some of them before, or at least that they gave off an atmosphere he had breathed before. Even had they been copies, they were good, for copies too are distinguishable by the feeling they show. But where had she seen such work to copy? He couldn't recall her ever having left the village. Nor did he remember her poring over art books. And if they were hers entirely, out of what depths of visionary dread had she drawn them?

He knew someone he could ask. Ailinn. But if he suddenly rang her to say he had unearthed remarkable art made by his mother she would smell a rat. *If you want to talk to me, just talk to me, Kevern,* she would say. *You don't need a pretext.* Besides, what if she didn't value the work? She wouldn't be able to say so. And thereafter there'd be a dishonesty between them. It wasn't fair to ask her.

Then he remembered someone else. Everett. Professor Edward Everett Phineas Zermansky.

iv

'And these were done by whom again?' the eminent professor asked.

He was nervous. Only nerves could explain such a question, given how clear Kevern had been about finding the notebook in a drawer in his father's workshop, how he recognized other entries in her hand, and how sure he was of her signature. Did

Zermansky feel he'd been compromised by Kevern's excitement because it showed that he wasn't only illegitimately hoarding heirlooms but hankering inordinately for something in the past? Surely not. Everyone knew that everyone else kept more than they should. Curiosity had not been altogether stifled anywhere.

'My mother. I told you.'

'And you never knew?'

'Never.'

'Never saw her do these?'

'Never.'

'So they might not be hers?'

'Believe me, that's her signature.'

Zermansky shrugged. In the world of art a signature was nothing.

'I can't imagine her signing what she hadn't done,' Kevern continued. 'Nor can I think of who else could have done them.'

'You?'

'Why would I be passing them off as hers?'

Zermansky scratched his head. Good question.

They were standing in Zermansky's studio, on his easel the beginnings of another golden sun setting like liquid gold behind St Mordechai's Mount. 'I am perhaps the wrong person to ask,' he said, nodding at the unfinished painting and laughing uncomfortably.

'You must be able to judge the quality of work even when it's unlike your own,' Kevern said. 'Your students' work, for example.'

376

'Oh, if any of my students were to do what your mother did . . .'

His voice trailed off.

'What?'

'Well, they just wouldn't. Couldn't.'

'Are you saying what my mother did would be beyond them?'

'Not beyond them technically. Not beyond the *best* of them technically, anyway. But beyond them – how can I best put this – emotionally and volitionally. They wouldn't know where in themselves to find such thoughts. And it wouldn't occur to them to try. Why would it?'

'Why wouldn't it?'

'Because that isn't how we see any more. To be frank with you, Kevern, that isn't how I'd like them to see any more.'

'That sounds prescriptive, Everett.'

'No. I don't mean it to. I don't run a dictatorship of the arts here. My students paint what they feel. But some things are no longer felt, and I am glad of that.'

'What is it that my mother felt that you are glad your students don't?'

'Kevern, I never knew your mother.'

'Neither, it seems, did I. But we aren't talking about her personally, are we. What is it in the work—'

'Kevern, look. I don't know when your mother did these. But they are of another time. Art has changed. We have returned to the primordial

377

celebration of the loveliness of the natural world. You can see there is none of that in what your mother did. See how fractured her images are. There is no harmony here. The colours are brutal – forgive me, but you have asked me and I must tell you. I feel jittery just turning the pages. Even the human body, that most beautiful of forms, is made jagged and frightful. The human eye cannot rest for long on these, Kevern. There is too much mind here. They are disruptive of the peace we go to art to find.'

'You make me proud of her.'

Zermansky took a moment to process a thought. *Like mother, like son – I bet she too had difficulty apologising.*

But he was quick to reassure Kevern of his motives. 'Good,' he said, 'because it's not my aim to make you ashamed of her. She was certainly gifted – primitively gifted, I'd say, in the way that a particular period of art was cerebral and primitive at the same time – but not every gift needs to see the light of day.'

'I wasn't proposing to mount an exhibition of her work.'

'Excellent, excellent. You enjoy looking at them, that's sufficient. I'd keep them as something between you and her.'

'Keep them hidden, is what you're saying?'

Zermansky made a pair of scales with his hands, weighing 'hiding' against . . . well, whatever he was weighing it against. *Keeping them as something between a son and his mother.*

Kevern was irked and puzzled. 'Anyone would think,' he said, 'that these little sketches could get me into trouble.'

Professor Edward Everett Phineas Zermansky threw him a weak smile. For the first time he understood to a certainty why he'd been asked to keep an eye on Kevern 'Coco' Cohen.

v

Coira grew up in St Brigid's Convent and Orphanage, ignorant of how she'd got there and knowing nothing of her mother and father. It was thought by many of the nuns that she had the ideal temperament to be a nun herself. She loved the ceremonials of the place – the sweet companionship, the daily round of repeated activity, the quiet of the church, the statuary, the incense, the music, the rhapsody. Convent orphanages were good for this. Over the years, as in many countries that had seen civil strife, children of other, not to say competing, faiths were secreted with the nuns of St Brigid's and countless convents like it, and there, without theological turbulence, willingly embraced beliefs alien to their own – that's when they knew what their own were. Occasionally some were delivered into the care of the nuns at an advanced enough age to notice the difference between the rituals of worship here and at home, but practised a gentle and compliant apostasy, relieved to be somewhere peaceful, away from rage and oppression, and grateful to feel accepted into a community. It could be confusing sometimes: the kind consideration they encountered from the nuns contrasting with the violence of the sermons to which they were subjected, in which many couldn't fail to recognise themselves as the children of Satan, doomed to be swallowed by the fires of hell for all eternity. But at least in St Brigid's no one tried to beat the wickedness out of those orphans who had been born into evil – the worst they did was to pray for their deliverance – and in Coira's case they had no knowledge of what she had been born into anyway. Whether she would finally take vows herself she wasn't sure, but she worked contentedly with the nuns she loved in a lay capacity until her sixteenth birthday when, with understandable reluctance, they handed over the letters her mother had left her. She locked herself away with them for many weeks, asked questions to which no one had an answer, requested the key for the convent library but found nothing there that helped shed light on why she had been abandoned, or what had happened to her mother or her grandparents. Her father she traced to his island parish, but decided, on the strength of sitting unknown through a sermon he gave on the subject of family love, that she had nothing to love him for. As she understood it, he had been instrumental in having her baptised and since, had she not been baptised, her mother would never have deposited her like unwanted luggage, he alone bore the blame. She had the wrong end of the stick, but her mistake was perfectly explicable. There was no one at the convent orphanage able to explain the ins and outs of matrilineality to her.

It was only after this that she became difficult to control, suffering bouts of anger and depression, making unconvincing attempts to end her life, resorting to petty thieving, staying away for days at a time and sleeping with local boys. Her natural sweetness of temper always won the nuns round in the end, however, and no moral disaster ensued. Soon she was back to her old self, not quite as cheerful as before, and no longer talking of taking vows, but reconciled, it seemed, to a life of only occasionally fractious usefulness. But in her thirty-ninth year, just as her hair began to turn grey and her existence seemed to be moving into a blessedly placid phase, she fell pregnant with a child whose father she either wouldn't or couldn't name. The nuns didn't judge her. Some felt that her failings were their failings, others that her mother's sins, whatever they had been, were bound to be visited on her in the end. She went away to have the baby and then returned with it, one early morning, as her gift to the nuns. They found the bundled child before morning prayers, in a basket outside the chapel with an identifying label tied around her wrist. This, Sister Agatha, who was old enough to remember the depositing of Coira herself, took to be a bitterly ironic reference to that event, a perpetuation of rejection. A bundle of letters tied with pink ribbon was in the basket together with a note asking that they keep them for the girl and give them to her only in the event of her asking for them, but whatever happened no earlier than her twenty-fifth birthday.

'Why would she ask for letters she doesn't know exist?' Sister Perpetua wondered.

Sister Agatha shrugged. 'Why anything?' she said.

In fealty to the memory of her own mother, Coira too disappeared from the face of the earth.

vi

'And thus does THE GREAT PISSASTROPHE,' Kevern mused gravely to Ailinn as they lay entwined like a pair of foundlings in each other's arms, 'claim another victim.'

She drew him close to her. 'It's more complicated than that,' she said.

He stroked her hair, pulling it back from her forehead. He loved the broad, clear expanse of her brow. Broad brow: capacious intelligence. Broad brow: magnanimity. Broad brow: intuition, compassion, sense of humour, sense of tragedy, vulnerability. He could stroke her brow for hours at a time. How glad he was to be soothing it again. How he'd missed it in the weeks he hadn't seen her. Broad brow: sorrow, longing, fidelity.

She hadn't told him everything. In truth – or rather not in truth – she hadn't told him very much. Not to start with. Long ago, in the mayhem of civil conflict her grandmother had abandoned a baby – what happened thereafter was a common tale of history repeating itself, one generation after another passing down its inheritance of shame.

He understood that, he the grandson of a displaced hunchback.

'But you have nothing to be ashamed of,' he said.

She wasn't so sure. 'It's not a pretty story,' she said.

He couldn't resist saying that she, though, was a pretty story in herself.

She shook her hair, as if to shake away the thoughtless compliment.

'It's hard to imagine what they must have gone through, those women, abandoning a child. Only think how desperate they must have been.'

'You are a child of sorrows,' he told her.

He turned his head momentarily to hide his tears from her.

They irritated her. They flowed too soon. Wait till he heard all she had to tell him. What would gush from his eyes then?

She knew him well enough to follow his emotional reasoning. He would be blaming himself for all that had befallen her, and not just her but her mother, and her mother's mother before her. Somehow or other he would be sheeting it all back to himself. His fault, everything his fault. Greedy for a share in her suffering which was no suffering when all was said and done. What had she been through? Nothing. It was those before her who had been in hell. And if it was wrong for her to appropriate what was theirs, how much more wrong was it for him. How ghoulish!

Everyone wants a piece of me, she thought, meaning Ez as well. They are thirsty so they drink of me.

Well, she had reason to be furious with Ez. Meddling on such a scale! Kevern, on the other hand, was only letting his sympathy for her overflow. Her irritation with him had its cause in her, not him, in her apprehension, in her dread of telling him all she had to tell him.

She submitted her brow to his stroking. She would have disappeared into him if she could have. Found safety inside his skin, turned back into the ribs from which irresponsible theological fantasy taught that she'd been fashioned.

But that was selfish of her. She should have been holding him. The helpmeet cradling her husband from all harm. She remembered a simple poem she had liked at school – *Grow old along with me, the best is yet to be*. Only it wasn't the best she was asking him to grow old along with her in, was it? It was the worst. Not for her, for him. For him, not for her, she was full of dread.

'So was Ez aware of your history all along?' he wondered.

'That depends on what you mean by "all along". From the beginning of our friendship, or just

384

before, yes, it would seem so. I'm only just getting to the bottom of it. But don't blame her.'

'I'm not.'

'Leave it to me to do any necessary blaming. It won't help if you crowd me into anger.'

'I understand,' he said. 'But you can't expect me not to be curious. Did she befriend you in order to find the kindest way to tell you what she knew?'

'Something like that.'

'So how did she come to be in possession of those letters anyway? Is she some sort of social worker?'

Crowding, Ailinn, thought. Crowding.

'In a manner of speaking, yes,' she said. 'I suppose she is.'

'You are convinced she meant well, at least?'

She hesitated. Now it was her turn to avert her head. 'It's all more complicated even than I've told you,' she whispered, not looking at him.

In her chest, her heart was leaping like a frightened animal.

CHAPTER 11

DEGENERATES

i

Esme Nussbaum was also enthralled, the first time she clapped eyes on Ailinn in the book group, by the smooth beauty of her brow. Esme was not, as her father thought, a lesbian. His crude mistake was to suppose that everyone was sexually distinct – a choice for which, if you made it wrongly in his view, you would pay – whereas many people, Esme thought, are neither one thing nor another, by and large indifferent to the whole business of sex and gender. She numbered herself among the latter. She fell in love with people's natures not their bodies and wanted nothing in return.

Ailinn called out something in her at once which she was happy to recognise as motherly. The girl needed, if not looking after exactly, then direction. Esme was convinced she would have felt this, and acted on it, person to person, even had she not set out to meet her armed with a set of very particular intentions as to the direction in which she wanted – no, not wanted, *needed* – Ailinn to go.

She was surprised by the girl's beauty. It wasn't that she really expected to meet someone with drooping eyes and puffy lips and large ears like the handles of a coffee cup but it had been hard for her to dispel all expectations of ugliness or, alternatively, all expectations of exoticism. But other than in the profusion of her hair, Ailinn answered to none of the descriptions with which, over the years, Esme Nussbaum had conscientiously made herself familiar. Even the girl's lovely forehead – which certainly did not overhang – wasn't of a different ethnic order of foreheads.

Nonetheless, she found herself, throughout their early meetings, looking out for evidence of peculiarity – not in the pejorative sense, but with regard to unaccustomed and specific habits of utterance and thought. That she found none she attributed at first to the time Ailinn and indeed her mother had spent among the nuns. It was more than sixty years ago that Coira had been dropped off at the convent orphanage, and whatever characteristics of race or belief she'd inherited from her own mother would over that period have been eradicated in her daughter. Ailinn had been swept clean. Esme had read about the eternal reluctance of families such as Rebecca's to entrust their offspring to the care of convent orphanages and other religious charities in times of trouble, for fear that in the event of their ever being reunited with their relations they would be radically changed in outlook and theology. She didn't doubt that had Rebecca ever again encountered her daughter or her granddaughter she would have been struck – she could not with confidence say 'disturbed' – by the change. But as she got to know Ailinn better she didn't feel competent to distinguish what was natural to her from what had been acquired. And by the time the two moved to Paradise Valley she found herself thinking of Ailinn as essentially unexceptional – unusual for her beauty and the sweetness of her disposition, yes, and for her stubbornness, and maybe even her occasional moroseness, but racially – or did she mean religiously? or did she mean culturally? a young woman like any other, a young woman, indeed, in many ways similar to the woman she had been herself, at least before the motorcyclist rode into her and broke every bone in her body.

That thought, too, brought her still closer to Ailinn. They were both who they were, directly or indirectly, as the consequence of foul play. So while she wanted something 'from' Ailinn that Ailinn herself as yet knew nothing of, she wanted something 'for' her, too, that had nothing to do with her ambitious scheme to restore the nation's equilibrium of hate. Esme considered it a stroke of remarkably good fortune – particularly when she became privy to Ailinn's feelings for Kevern Cohen, and witnessed their evident reciprocity when she saw them together – that her professional scheme and her private hopes coincided perfectly in so far as they bore on Ailinn's happiness.

How long it was going to take before either could be realised depended, she understood – for all her impatience – on feelings and events beyond her control. It was not all in her hands, as it was not all in Ailinn's. But when the girl returned from her trip away with Kevern only to discover his cottage had been broken into – an action Esme very much deplored – and Kevern, as a consequence, began to say reckless things and make wild plans, Esme knew she had to intervene. 'It's now or never,' she told herself, although the time was still not right, at least as far as the clearing of Kevern was concerned. 'What you don't do yourself, is rarely done well,' was what she also told herself. But she couldn't be everywhere at once. She couldn't have researched Kevern 'Coco' Cohen as thoroughly as she had researched Ailinn Solomons. And besides . . .

Well, if she understood the logic of matrilineality adequately, the clearing of Kevern was of less consequence than the clearing of Ailinn. She wasn't saying Kevern was immaterial to her plans – far from it – but she could afford a degree of blurring around Kevern that she couldn't around Ailinn.

ii

Saturday 30th
Well what was I supposed to say? That I liked the stuff? Thank you, Kevern, I can't wait to show

it to my students as an example of that deviant, flagitious, vitiated modernism (as I've said, nobody dares go near the word 'degenerate') they've read about in their textbooks . . . He wouldn't exactly have thanked me for that, would he? No son wants to hear his mother described as deviant.

Which brings me to the real problem I was faced with when he bounded in (*bounded in* for him), looking as pleased as punch and flaunting that odious sketchbook – that he didn't know how much he was giving away about himself and I didn't know whether to tell him. 'If you're the son of that mother, fellow-me-lad,' I wanted to say, 'you're in a spot of bother.' Or not. This is the thing: never having been adequately apprised of what I'm looking for, I'm not only in the dark as to whether or not I've found it, I'm in the dark as to the value, good or bad, of what I've found. As to that – the latter – I have my own views. I like the man, as I've made abundantly clear, but that doesn't mean I have to like what it would now appear I must call his antecedents. The other way of putting this is that I detest the sin but love the sinner. But I am going too fast even for my own brain.

Why, I have to ask myself – taking a pause – am I not more *étonné* by what I have discovered? Did I suspect all along? Did I *know* all along? Well, whether I knew at the beginning or not I'd have had to be some sort of nincompoop not to have had a pretty good idea more recently that something of this sort was in the wind. The strange behaviour of a certain detective inspector was clue enough, and then the strange behaviour around him – their getting me to call him off, for example – was surely a clincher. I just didn't know what it clinched. And I still don't know what's to be done with what I now know, that's if I now know anything. There's a lot of knowing and not knowing here – knowing what you don't know and not knowing what you do – but then that's the secret service for you. Ha! Which is not to say I am amused. I am worried for him. My man Kevern, I mean, not the detective inspector about whom I have no worries whatsoever. And I must say I am the smallest bit worried for myself. Hurt might be a better word. Just because it's been my job to suss him out doesn't mean it's been his job to string me along. For how many months have I been declaring him clean? And all that time he's been posing as my friend, even bringing his poor girlfriend round to meet us. Does she know? That's supposing, of course, that he himself has known any more than I have. Does he even know who or what he is? The innocent way he presented his mother's wretched work – unaware that he was as good as handing himself in – doesn't suggest duplicity. Had he known what he was about, or had any inkling what it was necessary to conceal, he'd have gone out into his garden in the dead of night, dug a hole as deep as hell, and dropped those sketches of hers down it. Alternatively, given where he lives, he should have thrown them into the sea the minute he found them.

And here's another question I'm bound to ask myself: was there always a suspicion that these works existed, and that eventually it would be they – this little nothing of a notebook, this handful of neurotic prints and drawings done by a deranged, unhappy woman – that gave him away? Was that why I – a professor of the Benign Visual Arts – was given him to watch? Because the crime, if a crime is quite what it is fair to call it, was always going to show itself first and foremost aesthetically? I'm flattered, if that's the case, though there might be those who wonder why it took me so long. To which my answer is – Art Appreciation is a slow business.

'It's the look of him we want you to engage with,' was what I was told at the beginning. Words to that effect, anyway. 'How he dresses, how he decorates his home, his taste in personal and domestic decoration.' I had to report back pretty soon that he had forcefully resisted every hint I'd dropped about visiting him in his 'home' – ugh, that word! 'I make a point of not entertaining,' he told me. 'I can't cope with it. It makes me anxious. But let me take you and Demelza out for dinner.' I could, I suppose, have dropped round on spec, but wouldn't that have aroused suspicion? You don't just find yourself on the cliffs of Port Reuben with time on your hands. A shame, as I said in my report at the time. I like to read a man's soul in his kitchen. And I doubt anyone would have done it better. Though after what I have just seen I'm more than a little relieved that I never did get to see what hangs on his walls. What if his house is festooned with more examples of his mother's sclerotic primitivism? I could not have let things lie at that. There are mistakes of taste you can let go – I'd have winked at the odd porcelain shepherdess or picturesque rendition of the Damascus Gate at sunset, believe me – but an unambiguous depravity of taste has to be reported. There's a box for that very thing on my forms. Tick the following: ersatz Negroid art; obsession with the fractured body as reflection of tormented mind; excessive devotion to biblical themes not rendered pietistically; asymmetry, violent oppositions of colour or form, counterpart shapes, dread, menace, anxiety, expressive dualities, basketcase subject matter, and more in a similar vein. You see my problem – if his walls are decorated by his mother I'd have had to tick the lot.

And that's before we get to the father whom he once described to me as a glassblower in wood, but that might just have been to put me off the scent. What if his candlesticks were ironically discoordinated – a veritable attack on Hellenistic proportion – to their very wicks and tails? Is there not even, now I put my mind to it, a grotesquerie of misshapen elaboration in the figures with which Kevern himself decorates his lovespoons?

Just thinking about all this sends me into a

moral tailspin. I love the man. Like the man, at least. All right, all right – I don't mind the man. It's possible, then, that I'd have not minded one or two of his confrères. But I am reminded that on grounds of their aesthetic I'd have been tempted to pick up a stone myself had I been alive at the time. I don't say to throw it, just pick it up. But who's to say that the action would not have been enough to encourage me to do something worse. Having said that, I trust that my love of beauty would eventually have won out, stopped my hand and bade me turn my back.

PS And now here's more news. Detective Inspector Gutkind has been found with his throat cut in his own 'home'. His cat too. Both of them shrouded in white dust. Sounds like something Kevern Cohen's mother might have drawn. Speaking of whom – the son not the mother – isn't he now likely to be a prime suspect?

Not too good for me, all this. Not a good reflection on my acuity.

iii

She was impressed by how well Ailinn took what she had to tell her – or at least that much of it which, initially, was all she dared tell her. She read the letters that had come down to her, not with calm exactly, but with the fatalism of someone who expected nothing better and had half-dreaded something worse, and this omened well, Esme thought, for how she would deal with further revelations. But Ailinn was a slow burner. 'And your role in this?' she asked after a period of reflection.

'That of a well-wisher.'

'Please don't treat me like a fool.'

'You think I intend harm to you?'

'I don't know what you intend. But you have deceived me so far, so why shouldn't I think you will deceive me more? Who are you and what do you want?'

'You know who I am.'

'No I don't. I thought you were someone I just happened to meet at a book group and who needed a friend. But there was obviously no "just happened" about it. Don't look at me in that bruised way, Ez. You have lied to me all along. Are you a policewoman?'

'Do I look like a policewoman?'

'What do looks have to do with it? You looked like my friend.'

'I am your friend.'

'But it's clear from the way you say it that our friendship was a happy accident. What are you actually?'

'I'm your guardian angel.'

'There is no such thing. And even if there were, you aren't it. Why do you know so much about me? Why have you made a project of my life? Nothing better to do with your own?'

'That's cruel, Ailinn.'

'Yes it is. But what you've been doing is cruel. Did you think I'd be grateful when I discovered you'd been digging the dirt on me?'

'It isn't dirt.'

'That's a matter of opinion. But you can hardly deny you've been digging.'

'I stumbled upon you, Ailinn, that's all.'

'*Stumbled?*'

For a horrible moment Esme wondered if Ailinn intended to jeer at the way she walked. But that wasn't what had struck the girl. 'Stumbled upon me in the course of what line of work, Ez?'

'You could say I've been trying to right the wrongs done to your family.'

'Was that your ambition after you met me or before? It makes a difference. Did you know of me before you knew of my "family", as you laughingly call it, or were you aware of "family" before you'd heard of me?'

Esme Nussbaum made a gesture suggestive of weighing with her hands. On the one hand this, on the other hand that . . .

It was not a gesture that satisfied Ailinn. 'There is something you aren't telling me. You aren't my mother, by any chance, are you?'

Esme experienced a momentary pang. It would have been no terrible thing, would it, being Ailinn's mother? 'No,' she said, 'I'm not your mother. I would not have abandoned you had I been.'

Ailinn was not going to show she'd heard that. 'Did you *know* my mother?'

'I did not. I know none of your family. I only know of them. And what I know I've passed on to you. There's nothing else.'

She felt a fraud as she said these words. It wasn't that she knew more so much as that she knew less – next to nothing if truth were told. What had she exhumed other than the dry bones of a story of desperation and deceit that Ailinn might with reason have preferred to leave buried? It wasn't all that long ago she'd been scrutinising the girl's features for telltale signs of genetic depravity. Viewed from one angle she was no better than a specimen collector. Ailinn had reason to be angry without knowing the half of what Esme was about.

'So the point of all this is what?' Ailinn asked. 'Am I the inheritor of a fortune of which you believe yourself entitled to a sizeable percentage? Are you some sort of bounty hunter?'

Esme wondered if she dared risk saying, 'In a manner of speaking, yes.' But while she thought about it Ailinn read her silence. She was on the edge of the bed, swinging her ugly feet. 'Does this have to do with Kevern?' she asked. 'Is there something you require of both of us?'

'Oh, *require* . . .'

'Expect, hope for, want . . . Choose the verb that best applies. You brought us together, didn't you? That's the short of it. You promoted his cause with me from the very start. You looked worried

397

every time we were on the point of breaking up. OK, I accept you're not my mother. I think I'd know if you were. But it wouldn't surprise me, given your concern for his welfare – I *assume* it was because you wanted him to be happy that you did your best to keep us together – it really wouldn't surprise me now if you turned out to be his.'

Esme did not this time experience a momentary maternal pang. 'It's a funny idea,' she said, 'but no, I am not Kevern's mother. I am of the wrong – how can I best put this: persuasion, denomination, credo? – to be Kevern's mother.'

Ailinn stared.

'So you knew Kevern's mother?'

'Trust me. I did not.'

'But you know her "persuasion"? Does that mean you know something about Kevern's that he doesn't?'

'Trust me,' Esme repeated, taking the girl's hands between hers. 'Trust me on the generalities. The details I'll give you later. Kevern's mother was who he thought she was. Maybe not "what" he thought she was, but certainly "who". And I don't qualify. I'm not his fairy godmother, either, though I think fairy godmothers are not bound by the laws of matrilineality. But you're right that I wanted you for him. I wanted you for each other. I still want you for each other.'

'Why? Would you like us to have a baby for you or something?'

The question surprised Esme into giving an answer that surprised her even more. 'Yes,' she said, 'as a matter of fact I would.'

She was always going to have to come out with it, but not in that way, not quite so abruptly and callously. Not yet.

Ailinn caught her breath. 'If you've been wanting Kevern's baby so badly you could always have slept with him, you know. I'm not saying I wouldn't have minded but I think I'd have preferred it to this.'

'I haven't been wanting Kevern's baby.'

'So it's mine you want?'

Whereupon, because she had nowhere else conversationally to go, and it had to be told sometime, Esme told her that she wanted Ailinn and Kevern to renew the future of their people.

iv

'How would you feel,' Ailinn asked him, 'if you found out we are not together by an act of our wills alone?'

'Is anybody?'

She didn't want him to go philosophical on her. 'What if you didn't choose me?' she said. 'What if I didn't choose you?'

'I did choose you.'

'You've forgotten. The pig auctioneer chose me for you.'

'No, he didn't. He pointed you out, that was

all. An entirely redundant act, as it transpired. I didn't need you pointing out. I was already well aware of your presence. I was irradiated by it. The fact that his judgement coincided with mine didn't make it material to mine. If anything, he could have put me off you.'

'In which case his judgement *was* material to yours.'

'Negatively, but even then not quite.'

'I didn't know you had nearly been put off me.'

'Isn't there always a moment of hovering? Is this her or isn't it? Do I leap or do I wait?'

'I didn't hover. I leapt.'

'But then you leapt back when I told you your feet were too big.'

'Not for long, though. I was on the phone to you almost immediately, though it took you an eternity to pick up.' She remembered Ez, telling her to ring him. Ez sitting on her bed. Ez getting in too close and getting on her nerves. Ez playing with their lives.

'Then there you are,' he said, encircling her with his arms. 'We chose each other. But what's this about?'

'Ez.'

'Ez brought us together?'

'You knew?'

'Well I do now. I guess it makes perfect sense. Ez had something about your past she needed to tell you and feared how you would take it. As she saw it, you needed someone capable of supporting you, someone physically strong, unwavering and emotionally resolute, so she hired the pig man to look out for a likely candidate, and he found me.'

'*Someone physically strong, unwavering and emotionally resolute?*'

'Yes.'

'This the pig man saw in the middle of a field?'

'Why not? I saw who you were in the middle of a field.'

He's going to need all his unwavering emotional resolution now, Ailinn thought.

'There was something about me you didn't see,' she said.

He waved the idea away. There was nothing he hadn't seen.

'You didn't see what Ez saw.'

'Ez, Ez . . . why is there so much talk of Ez?'

They'd been lying down, looking at the ceiling, but now she swung her legs out of bed and went to stand by the window. It was quiet out there, no wind, no gulls, even the blowhole subdued. The sky was low, without colour or promise. 'God, it can feel dead down here sometimes,' she said.

He remembered his mother saying the same. 'It's like being in a coffin,' she said once. 'With the lid down.'

Was that before or after the free meat, he wondered.

'Look on the bright side,' his father had answered. 'At least there'll be no surprises when they screw you in.'

His light-touched father.

He liked watching Ailinn naked at the window. He'd often thought of carving her, not just in miniature on a lovespoon, but as a candlestick maybe. Would he be able to render the responsiveness of her flesh, the reserves of life that were in her flanks, the strength of her legs? The springiness of her that made him believe in life?

'While we're laying cards on the table,' he blurted out, 'my grandfather was a hunchback.'

She didn't turn around.

'You never told me that before.'

'I never knew before.'

'So how come you know now?'

'Kroplik told me.'

'How does he know?'

'He knows everything. Like your beloved Ez.'

'Does it bother you?'

'To know I'm from crooked stock? Yes. But Kroplik reckons I should be grateful. It was the hunchback who kept us safe.'

'Safe from what?'

'I don't know. Whatever.'

'And how does Kroplik say he managed that?'

'By scaring people and being lucky. Apparently you don't mess with a hunchback. Or at least you don't in these parts.'

'Do you ever wonder . . .' she started to say, then relented.

'Do I ever wonder what?'

'It doesn't matter.'

'Yes it does. Do I ever wonder what?'

'What you're doing here.'

'On earth?'

'In Port Reuben.'

'All the time.'

'Would you want to find out?'

He got up from the bed and moved towards her. He wanted to feel her nakedness pressed into his, the lovely resilience of her buttocks.

'There's a lot I want to find out,' he said. 'But then again there isn't. Mysteries are always so banal when they're solved. You're better off living in uncertainty.'

'You say that, but you couldn't bear not knowing who broke in here and straightened your rug.'

'No. And now I never will find out.' This was a silent allusion, that Ailinn was quick to pick up, to the murder of Detective Inspector Gutkind, the gory details of which were the talk of Port Reuben and beyond. Neither spoke about it. Kevern was happy to have him out of their lives, but he didn't want to put that relief in so many words to Ailinn. He didn't suppose she'd wonder if he'd done it, but then again there was no reason to plant further anxiety. Who knows what anyone will do in the end? Who would have thought he'd kiss Lowenna Morgenstern? Who would have thought his mother had a secret life? And now Ailinn . . .

'Certainty might be banal, but better that, any time, than the immeasurable stress of uncertainty,' Ailinn said, reading his mind.

'So you're pleased to know now how you came to be in an orphanage? You don't wish that Ez had never told you?'

'Hardly "pleased", but yes, I believe I am better off for knowing, banal though you consider it all to be.'

'I didn't say that what happened to you was banal.'

'Don't apologise. I'm not offended. It *is* banal. But I would rather know it than not.'

'And you'd rather know that Ez was instrumental in our meeting?'

'Rather it had happened some other way, but rather know than not know that it happened the way it did.'

'We should drink to Ez, then.'

Was he being sarcastic, or just slow to take the measure of what she was trying to tell him?

He went downstairs to open a bottle and returned with two full glasses.

'To Ez,' he said.

She still couldn't decide. Sarcastic, or unfeeling, or stupid?

And then he noticed that Ailinn's eyes were red. Not with weeping, more with the strain of looking.

'You look as though you've seen a ghost,' he said.

And that was when she told him.

What will it take? The same as it has always taken. The application of a scriptural calumny (in this instance the convergence of two scriptural calumnies) to economic instability, inflamed nationalism, an unemployed and malleable populace in whom the propensity to hero-worship is pronounced, supine government, *tedium vitae*, a self-righteous and ill-informed élite, the pertinaciousness of old libels – the most consoling of which being that they'd had their chance, these objects of immemorial detestation, chance after chance (to choose love over law, flexibility over intransigence, community over exclusiveness, and to learn compassion from suffering) . . . chance after chance, and – as witness their moving in scarcely more than a generation from objects of immolation to proponents of it – they'd blown them all. Plus zealotry. Never forget zealotry – that torch to the easily inflamed passions of the benighted and the cultured alike. What it won't take, because it won't need – because it never *needs* – is an evil genius to conceive and direct the operation. We have been lulled by the great autocrat-driven genocides of the recent past into thinking that nothing of that enormity of madness can ever happen again – not anywhere, least of all here. And it's true – nothing on such a scale probably ever will. But lower down the order of horrors, and answering a far more modest ambition, carnage can still be connived at – lesser blood-baths, minor murders, butchery of more modest proportions.

From an unwritten letter by Ailinn's great-grandfather Wolfie Lestchinsky to his daughter Rebecca.

BOOK III

Meet . . .
Merowitz, Berowitz, Handelman,
  Schandelman
Sperber and Gerber and Steiner and Stone
Boskowitz, Lubowitz, Aaronson, Baronson,
Kleinman and Feinman and Freidman
  and Cohen
Smallowitz, Wallowitz, Tidelbaum,
  Mandelbaum
Levin, Levinsky, Levine and Levi
Brumburger, Schlumburger, Minkus
  and Pinkus
And Stein with an 'e-i' and Styne with
  a 'y'

> Allan Sherman, *Shake Hands With*
> *Your Uncle Max*

CHAPTER 1

THE LEAST LITTLE BIT OF UMBRAGE

i

'So I was right all along to think it,' Kevern said after a silence that seemed to Ailinn to go on for a period of dark time that could not be calculated in minutes or hours or even days . . .

'Right to think what?' she asked at last before her own life ran out.

'That Ferdie didn't like me. Ferdie has never liked me.'

It was four o'clock in the morning, the time no living thing should be awake. There was not a sound from the sea where Kevern had looked for seals and not found any – drowned were they? drowned in some communal act of self-murder? – and where he imagined that even the fish, after eating well, must be now sleeping. They had tried talking in bed but Kevern needed to be able to pace about, so they had gone downstairs to the little kitchen. Ailinn sat at the table in her dressing gown, absent-mindedly banging her fists together.

Kevern made tea, walked up and down, and made more tea. They had toasted all the bread they had and eaten all the biscuits. Ailinn couldn't face sardines or pilchards so Kevern opened tins of baked beans, cherry tomatoes, tuna in olive oil, mushroom soup and sweetcorn. These he mixed in a large bowl to which he added salt, pepper and paprika. No thanks, Ailinn had said. He was not wearing any clothes. In response to Ailinn's concern that he was cold, and then that he would scald himself, he said he wanted to be cold and wanted to scald himself. How you see me is how I feel, he told her.

Vulnerable, she could understand, but she wanted him to know he wasn't – they weren't – in any danger.

'Can Ez be trusted?' he asked.

'To do what?'

'To keep quiet.'

It was a difficult question to answer. 'No one means us any harm,' she repeated.

He laughed. 'Don't forget Ferdie. Never forget Ferdie.'

She was not inclined to follow him into Ferdie territory. She knew that he was preparing to go through the names of everyone he thought had ever harmed him or meant him ill – a list that could take them through many more nights like this – and still at the end of it scratch his head and say he didn't understand what he'd done to offend them. It appeared to give him consolation

410

to go on saying 'I don't think Ferdie likes me,' and she feared he would repeat it and repeat it until she was able to direct him on to another course.

'There is no point even trying to make light of any of this,' she said. 'I know that you only joke when you are at your most anxious.'

'Joking? Who's joking?'

He no sooner said those words than he knew he had to cross his js no longer.

Could this be called a liberation, then? It was too early to say.

He was past the point of marvelling at how much made sense to him now. He had always known . . . that was to be his defence against the horrors of surprise . . . he had always known *really*, at some level, below consciousness, beyond cognition, he had always known *somewhere* . . . not everything, of course not everything, not the half of it, but enough, for the news to be as much confirmation as shock . . . though whether that was confirmation of the worst of what he'd half known, or the best, or just something in the middle, he was yet to find out. But he hadn't been to sleep and was wandering his kitchen naked, drinking tea and eating bean and tuna soup, so it had to be admitted he was not exactly taking it lightly.

By comparison, Ailinn, banging her fists together like cymbals, was relaxation itself.

'Ferdie didn't like you, either,' he reminded her.

411

'Darling, I don't give a shit what Ferdie thought.'

'You should. The world is full of Ferdies.'

'*Your* world is full of Ferdies.'

'So you're OK about all this, is that what you're telling me?'

She had put herself in a false position. No she didn't feel OK about *all* this, but then Kevern still didn't know the full extent of it. She couldn't hit him with more than she'd hit him with already. This was part one. Part two would come when she thought he was good and ready. Give me time, she'd told Ez. Wouldn't it be best to strike while the iron's hot, Ez had said, but the metaphor was too close to the literal truth. It would have been like branding and braining him. I'll need time, she insisted. As for what she did tell Kevern about – their sudden consanguinity – then yes, the revelation did feel more a blessing than a curse to her. But however their histories had converged, their antecedent narratives were different. To put it brutally, she had none. Ez had simply filled the blanks in for her. And something was better than nothing. Whereas for Kevern, well he had to set about reconfiguring a densely peopled chronicle, reimagining not just himself but every member of his family. And pacing the kitchen with no clothes, trying for jokes that weren't funny even by his family's standards of deranged unfunniness, he didn't appear so far to be making a good job of it.

'I'll be OK,' she said, 'when you're OK.'

He stopped his pacing and leaned against the stove. 'Be careful, for Christ's sake,' she warned him.

'What did they see?' he asked suddenly, as though addressing another matter entirely, as though he had just strolled into the room with an incidental question in his mind. 'I'm not asking what they thought – they thought what they'd been taught to think – but what did they *see* when my hunch-backed grandfather popped his nose out of this cottage to sniff the poisoned air? What did they see when my mother went shopping in her rags? Or when my father crept into the village to sell his candlesticks to the gift shops? Or when you and I, come to that, first went strolling arm in arm through Paradise Valley? What do they see when they see us now?'

'Who's "they"?'

He wouldn't even bother to answer that. She knew who 'they' were. 'They' were whoever weren't them. The Ferdies.

'What do we look like to them, is what I'm asking. Vermin?'

'Oh, Kevern!'

'*Oh, Kevern* what? *Oh, Kevern, don't be so extreme.* Do you think I could ever outdo in extremity those who did what they did? But to understand how they could ever do it requires us to see what they saw, or at least to imagine what they saw.'

'Maybe they didn't see anything. Maybe they still don't. Has it occurred to you that we just aren't there for them?'

'*Just*! That's a mighty big "just", Ailinn. I think I'd rather be vermin than "just" not there. And even if you're right, it still takes some explaining. How do you make a fellow mortal not there? What's the trick of seeing right through someone? An indifference on that scale is nothing short of apocalyptic – or it is when it comes to getting rid of the thing you don't see, going to pains to obliterate what isn't there. But I don't think you're right anyway. I think they must see something, the embodiment of a horrible idea, the fleshing out of an evil principle that's been talked about and written about for too long, mouldy like something that's crawled out of its own grave.'

'You are in danger,' she said, 'of describing the horror you see, not the horror they do.'

'Why should I see horror?'

'Don't be naive.'

'How am I being naive?'

'When Hendrie raised his hand and told me I had been with them too long, that I didn't belong there, that he wished they'd never rescued me from the orphanage, I saw what he saw. An outcast ingrate – with big feet – whom no one could possibly love. That's the way it works.'

'I'm sorry about the feet. I love your feet.'

He dropped to his knees and thrust his head under the table where her feet were, and kissed them. I could stay here, he thought. Never come back up.

But he did come back up. That was the grim

rule of life, one always came back up . . . until one didn't.

She was smiling at least. Gravely, but a smile was still a smile.

'Take my point, Kevern,' she said.

'I take your point. And I don't hate myself, if that's what you're getting at.'

'That's not what I'm getting at. I don't hate myself either. But criticism rubs off. How could it be otherwise? Sometimes the glass through which others look at you tilts and you catch a little of what they see. It's understandable that you wish you'd made a better impression.'

'*Impression*! You make it sound like a children's story – *The Little Girl Who Should Have Made a Better Impression*. I'm not that little girl, or boy. I don't crave anybody's respect – except yours. I'm not trying to understand what people see when they see me – when they see *us*, Ailinn – because I think I ought to improve my appearance. I've no desire to wear a better aspect. I want to understand what they see on the principle that one should know one's enemies. I want to know what they see so I can hate them better.'

She fell silent – not bruised by the vehemence of his words but because she wondered whether she was wrong not to feel what he felt. Was it feeble of her to reject resentment, even on behalf of her poor great-grandparents? This queer exhilaration she was experiencing – as though her life could be about to start at last and never mind where she'd been before – was it disloyal? Was Ez sending her on a fool's errand whose futility was the least of it? Was it wrong? Was it treasonable?

But no. Whatever she was doing, right, wrong, feeble, gullible, treasonable, Kevern's way was plain bad. Bad for him. Bad for his mental state. Bad for them. Bad for their future together. *Bad.* 'This is unhealthy,' she said at last.

'It's a bit late for health.'

'You are also not being honest with yourself. You say you need to understand how others see you, but your curiosity isn't dispassionate. It isn't divided equally between those who don't like you and those who do. You're only really intrigued by those who don't.'

'Hardly surprising is it, given what I've just discovered, if it's those who don't like me I'm interested in right now. My friends I can think about later.'

Friends? Did he have friends? His recent conversation with Rozenwyn Feigenblat – not a word of which he'd mentioned to Ailinn – came back to him. She saw him as friendless – worse than that, she saw him as courting friendlessness. And now here was Ailinn saying the same. Why was his nature quite so pervious to women?

'It's not right now I'm talking about,' she persisted. 'You've always paid more attention to your enemies.'

'Ailinn, I didn't know I had enemies until five minutes ago.'

'That's ridiculous. Who do you lock your door against? Who are you frightened of being invaded by? You have lived in a world of enemies all your life.'

'You can talk, you and Ahab.'

She waved Ahab away. 'Now he's found me I'll deal with him,' she said.

'It's as easy as that?'

'No. But it's good to confront him now he's out of the shadows. It's good to turn and face him. Look him in the eyes. Your point – know your enemy. OK, Ahab – do your worst. And it turns out he isn't even called Ahab.'

'No, he's called Ferdie – who frankly I find more frightening.'

'That's because you want to go on being frightened. You know no other way.'

'Are you calling me a coward?'

'No. I'm sure it takes bravery to live with fear as you do.'

'That's patronising. I don't "bravely" live with fear. It's not something I choose. I have no choice.'

'You do – you have the choice not to wallow . . .'

'You think this is wallowing?'

She did, yes she did, but declined to answer. She dropped her head between her fists, and this time beat the cymbals against her ears.

He wondered if he ought to get dressed. The first squeeze of narrow light was showing out to sea. He wasn't ready for day, but if it had to come he should go and greet it. The cliffs would be a good place to be, on his bench, side by side with Ailinn, looking out to the dead, consoling sea. It wouldn't change anything but weather was preferable to the cottage, and the great sea justified his fears. The world was terrifying.

'Will you walk with me?' he asked, in his gentlest voice. She was right, he knew she was right, morbidity was his nature. So what was new?

'Of course I will,' she said, putting an arm around him. Not everyone was his enemy, she wanted him to know. But the gesture made them both feel isolated. They had each other, but who else did they have?

It was only when they were on the bench that she realised he hadn't double-locked and double-checked that he'd locked the door of his cottage. Had he kicked the Chinese runner? She didn't think he had. She should have been pleased but she wasn't. What was he without his rituals?

There was rain in the air. That squeezed sliver of light had been an illusory promise. Below them, the blowhole was clearing its throat in readiness for a day of tumult. A couple of gulls threw themselves like rags into the wind.

'What now?' he said suddenly.

'Do you want to go back in?'

'No, I meant what are we going to do with the rest of our lives?'

She knew but couldn't tell him. 'We can do whatever you'd like to do,' she lied.

'Well we can't just carry on as though nothing's happened.'

'Why not? How much has changed really?'

'Everything,' he said. 'Absolutely everything.'

'You'll feel differently in a few days. You'll get back into the swing of things.'

'What swing of things? I never was in the swing of things. I was waiting. Just waiting. I didn't know what I was waiting to happen or find out, but I now see that the waiting made for a life of sorts.'

'*Of sorts*! With me? Is that the best you can say of our time together – *a life of sorts*?'

He put his arm around her waist but didn't pull her to him. 'Not you. Of course not you. I don't mean that. We are fine. We are wonderful. But the me that isn't us, that wasn't us, when all is said and done, before I met you – before the pig auctioneer – that solitary me . . . where do I go with it from here? I waited and I waited, scratching away at bits of wood, and now I know what I was waiting for and it's . . .'

'It's what?'

He didn't know. Above him the raggedy gulls screamed desolately. Was it all just thwarted greed or did they hate it here as much as he did? He looked up to the sky and cupped his ears as though the birds might tell him what to do with himself from this moment on.

'Nothing,' he said at last. 'What it is is nothing. In fact it's worse than nothing.'

'You could try feeling pride,' she said.

'What?'

'Pride. You could decide to wear it as a badge of honour.'

'What do you suggest I do? Change my name back?'

'That's a black joke, Kevern,' she said.

He agreed. 'The blackest.'

'Then why did you make it?'

He shrugged. 'Why did you speak of pride and honour? Where's the honour, please tell me? You might as well ask this ant which I am about to tread on to view all the previous years of his ant life with pride.'

'It's not to his shame that you stamp on him.'

'I disagree with you. It is his shame, his fault, for being an ant. We have to take responsibility for our fate. Even an ant. What happens to him is his disgrace.'

She was shocked to hear him speak like this. It felt like a blasphemy to her. Perhaps he needed to blaspheme. Perhaps that was his way of working the shock of it all out of his system. Nonetheless she couldn't let his blasphemies go unchecked. 'You aren't saying what you really mean,' she said. 'You can't honestly think that your mother's and father's life was a disgrace.'

'They were in hiding for the whole of it. Yes, it was a disgrace.'

'And what about those who had nowhere to hide? Their parents and grandparents? Mine?'

'The trodden generations? A disgrace.'

'Then it's up to you to restore respect.'
'Me? I am the greatest disgrace of all.'

ii

Esme Nussbaum sits at the window of her room and watches rain drip from the ferns. Even when it's not raining anywhere else it rains in Paradise Valley and even when it doesn't rain in Paradise Valley the ferns go on dripping.

There is nothing more I can do, she tells herself. It's no longer in my hands. But it's in her brain, and with that she wills them on, the harbingers of her bright new equilibrium of hate.

Senior officials from Ofnow are on the phone to her every day. They want to know how it's proceeding. The population is still tearing itself apart – why, in her very neck of the woods there has been another brutal murder, a double murder, a policeman and his cat, for God's sake: what maniac would kill a cat? – so they need good news. She tells them this thing must run its course. Yes, she has other irons in the fire, but this is the best bet and, trust her, she won't take her eye off it for a moment. But she has to remind them that the complex structure of conflict that was Rome wasn't built in a day and that there'll be no imme-diate visible effect even if all does go well. They don't agree with her. They think the country will feel a different place the minute it learns that WHAT HAPPENED, IF IT HAPPENED was only, after all, a partial solution. They don't expect a uniformity of response. After years of saying sorry there's no knowing how the public will react but, by Esme's own analysis, the news itself – a few well-judged publicity photographs, the odd teaser interview, not giving too much away, in celebrity and gossip magazines – should begin to restore the necessary balance of societal antagonism. 'Just give us some tidbits we can definitively leak,' they tell her, meaning that the wedding, the conception, and the birth can wait. The child of course is crucial – *For unto us a child is given* – but even the promise of it should suffice for the moment.

I'm on it, Esme tells them.

There is one among the importunates whose excitement at the prospect of a cultural rebirth – musicals with wit, reject-rock, hellishly sardonic comedies, an end to ballads – is so intense he can barely express it in coherent sentences. So frequently does he call her that Esme is beginning to wonder whether he isn't himself one her scouts had missed. I have to tell you, she tells him, that reigniting popular culture is not high among my objectives. He baulks at 'popular'. The serious theatre, too, needs a shot in the arm, he reminds her. Imagine hearing complex, warring sentences on the stage again. Imagine paradox and bitterness and laceration. Art as endless disputation, bravura blasphemy – Oh, the bliss of it, Ms Nussbaum! Alternatively, imagine the *Herzschmerz* of a violin and piano sonata, played as only they can play it, as though for the final time. She warns him against premature recidivism. You know about things you shouldn't know about, she says sternly, and you make unwarrantable assumptions about my politics. I have no desire to restore a status quo from which so many suffered. To regret WHAT HAPPENED is not to throw the baby out with the bathwater. Something needed to happen, even if what did exceeded decency and proportionality. But nor must we force those who have been providentially spared back into demeaning stereotypical patterns. *Herzschmerz* indeed! I repeat, I am indifferent to the entertainment implications of this project. Not dismissive, just not engaged. My concern is not bebop but the physics of societal mistrust. You cannot have a one-sided coin. If what I am seeking comes about, we will once again enjoy the stability of knowing who we're not.

Her importuner laughs, optimistic despite what she has said to him, imagining he has heard irony. But he is wrong. Irony is not something Esme Nussbaum does.

It has occurred to her, of course, to worry for Ailinn should things not come about as she intends or, indeed, should it come about too well. What if the years of saying sorry have bred an antagonism even deeper than before? Could Ailinn find herself the object of violent suspicion long before the desired equilibrium has time to take hold?

But Esme is in the grip of a passion to do good, and all other concerns, including Ailinn's safety, are subjugated to the more immediate task of bringing that good about.

There is still some way to go. The problem is Kevern. Not the facts about the bloodline. The facts are fine. So easy of confirmation, in fact, it is a wonder the Cohens were able to go on living for so long in Port Reuben unmolested. The problem is the flakiness. She isn't any longer sure that he is suitable. She puts this down to poor preparation. Those who have been making him their study have not done their job well. They have not adequately assessed his character. They have been looking through him, or past him, not *at* him. But it's her fault too. When she came down to Paradise Valley it was with a view to scrutinising them both. So what went wrong? Ailinn went wrong. Or rather Ailinn went too right. Esme wonders if her vile father had her number after all. Was she indeed a lesbian? She didn't think so, but without question she'd found the girl engrossing. And while she was engrossed in the one she failed to keep tabs on the other. Perhaps Kevern had been exercising the same magic. Perhaps he too had blinded those charged exclusively with watching him. Is that their inherited gift, Esme catches herself asking. Are they charmers? Do they beguile? She stills her thoughts. If she's not careful she'll be understanding too well why WHAT HAPPENED happened.

Kevern is not her last throw of the dice. Neither, come to that, is Ailinn. Little by little, fragile shoots of hopefulness have shown themselves in remote corners of the country. Nothing showy, naturally, no salt-rose or topaz, but here and there, a violet by a mossy stone, a dark thing between the shadow and the soul, wasting its sweetness on the desert air. And these will certainly be significant when it comes to procreative negotiations further down the line. But they are not her first choice. Ailinn and Kevern remain her first choice.

There is another consideration when it comes to Kevern. Esme has given voice to this more than once, in private while watching the ferns drip and when irked by all the problems associated with his character. Who needs the little prick, she has wondered, surprised by her own violence. Expletives came to her often when she lay in her coma, but they haven't visited her much since.

What she means by this is that while Ailinn must be the real McCoy, and must, short of a miracle, have a father for the child, it might not be absolutely essential to that child's being the real McCoy that the father is the real McCoy as well. She has been hampered by having no one to ask and very few intact books to consult but she has beavered away and believes she can now confirm Ailinn's grandmother's understanding of the law of matrilineality: yes, it is indeed the case, as Rebecca thought when she defied her husband, that the McCoys, as it amuses her to call them while she bites her fingernails, look only to the mother for transmission of authenticity. Thus, though there's no knowing who Ailinn's father was, and though her grandfather Fridleif was unacceptable in every possible regard, the fact that she is in direct, unbroken line of matrilineal descent from her grandmother, who appears to have ticked all the boxes herself, is sufficient to make her what Esme wants her to be. That being the case, who needs that little prick Kevern Cohen?

No, no one *needs* him. That's the point to which Esme's rough scholarship has brought her. But still and all it will be better in every way if he can be roped in. His presence as Ailinn's agitated, unsmiling consort will help Esme to the composite effect she is looking for. Kevern does not, she is confident, photograph well. There are many aspects of character the camera can lie about, but stand-offishness is not one of them. A man so aloof that he accepts no kinship with the human race looks exactly that when he's photographed – an unquiet thing, displaced and determined to stay that way. Furthermore, if she can sell him the whole box of tricks, or at least keep the pairing to the degree that he will buy into engagement, marriage and the rest of it, she will be able to arrange them a traditional wedding – she will officiate herself if she has to – whose antiquated self-absorption will enrage as many as it pleases. Including, she has no doubt, Kevern Cohen. He will not behave well at his own wedding. She has come across the ritual of the bridegroom breaking a glass. Kevern, she is confident, will stamp it to smithereens. He will make a sardonic speech, compromising his love for Ailinn (she doesn't doubt its genuineness) with savage jokes that no one will enjoy. Yes, the more she thinks about his studied prickliness, the more she wants to keep him. Ailinn is a woman of immense charm. What no one wants is for people to fall in love with her to the degree that no equilibrium of hate is re-established. Kevern, on the other hand, even should he somehow succeed in not being wholly detestable, will not inspire devotion. In Kevern the people will have no difficulty recognising their own antithesis.

iii

Black Friday

Demelza has left me. My mistake – though in the course of our final argument she told me I had made more mistakes than she could count – was to leave my diary where she could find it. Unless my mistake was to confide quite so many sexual secrets to its pages.

Wrong again, she said, when I confessed to that. Your mistake was to have *had* so many sexual secrets.

She says there's no other man. Do I believe her? No, I do not. My money's on Kevern 'Coco' Cohen. I can't say I ever did care much for him but now I know him for what he is I suspect he has been scheming to squirm his way between

427

Demelza's legs all along. The metaphor of the reptile, by the way, is not mine. There was man, there was woman and then there was the all-knowing snake. I can't be blamed for the theology of that parable when it was they who told it about themselves. Enter knowledge into the paradisal world of love and innocence – in other words enter them with their obscene obsession for knowing everything – and that's happiness gone for ever. No wonder they shunned the human form and painted abstract robotical horrors.

Well, we thought we'd scorched that particular snake, but here it is again writhing between my wife's legs. And the crazy thing is that I've been instrumental in its rebirth. Had I seen what he was about years ago, before the Wise Ones rewrote the manual, I could have penned a damning report and that would have been that. There were enough clues, God knows. The never saying sorry. The never being out of the library. The furtive tap-turning and hand washing – what was he trying to wash off, I'd ask Demelza. Now it's clear: his own snake slime. Slime that is now inside my wife. No wonder she was evasive when I tried to talk to her about him. And no wonder, come to think of it, she suffered Credibility Fatigue. I know now just what was fatiguing her.

It's a good job I am civilised. I count to a hundred. I pat Petroc, pat a couple of students in the same spirit, take out my sketches of St Mordechai's Mount and remember when my mind was last given over to the contemplation of unsullied loveliness. I have an idea for a new series of watercolours – Eden. The Garden before the introduction of the snake. Just Demelza and I doing as we are told, unaware of our nakedness, alone under the trees, except maybe for Petroc. Speaking of whom, should I not have smelt a rat when he was snarling around Kevern 'Coco' Cohen's feet smelling something worse? 'Petroc!' Demelza used to cry, calling him off. 'Down, Petroc. Naughty boy. Down! I'm so sorry, Mr Cohen.' Mr Cohen! *I'm so sorry, Mr Cohen.* I bet she was. Poor Petroc. Disparaged for expressing his nature and keeping us safe from harm.

I wouldn't put it past him – the snake, not the dog – to have made her offerings of lovespoons. Portraits. Full-length. Top to toe. The pair of them entwined in lime wood. Not exactly likenesses. He doesn't do likenesses. A likeness is not primitive enough for his depraved aesthetic. They prefer a touch of the ape to show through. But likeness enough to be compromisingly recognisable. Probably shown them to our students, too, while lecturing on the intricacy of their carving – *intricate* all right! – hoping they would make out Demelza despite the monkey features and scoff at me. Where did they do it? Here, when I was teaching? Or did she go over there on days when she said she needed to do some shopping? On the floor of his workshop, would it have been? On a bed of sawdust? If only I'd been less trusting. I should have smelt her hair when she returned. Should have gone searching for shavings in her underwear drawer. Or better still should have had my way with that wild-haired piece of his while he was otherwise engaged. It must be assumed – forgive the fancy talk: I'm preparing my defence – I must assume that she too is to be numbered among the degenerates, though the flowers she made were beautiful enough. Veering on the odd, as you'd expect, even the macabre, but still close enough to nature to be lovely. So what would she have been like, that bird-woman of his with the hawk face? Sharp claws she'll have, I bet. A tongue wet with blood and little nibbly teeth. Mandibles – is that the word? *Rotten juice and mandibles* – who said that? *The shitty magma of rotten juice and mandibles* . . . blah, blah, blah . . . ring a bell? . . . *the passion of the termite* . . .

. . . it must, methinks, have been one of those resurrected samizdat pamphlets from before WHAT HAPPENED that did the rounds of the country's common rooms not all that long ago, probably as a medical corrective to our periodic recrudescences of unseemly guilt. All very well saying sorry sorry sorry sorry sorry – I have always been at the forefront of the apologising party myself, so long as we aren't apologising for anything we have actually done – but a little puncturing of the windpipe of our dutifulness is no bad thing, as many of us felt, hence the reappearance of

430

these short samizdatty things, if that's the right expression, inflammatory trifles, anyway, from those on the front line and who knew the problem of termite infestation for themselves, that brightened our lives for a while before we grew dutiful again.

When a thing is heartfelt it stays with you. '*Ich hab' im Traum geweinet*' . . . '*Où sont les neiges d'antan*' . . . You don't forget sentiments like those. They express the quintessence of regret. But quintessence of scorn can melt your bones as well. Like those lines about shitty magma . . . the termites being everywhere, selling everything, keeping everything, destroying everything, weaving their web, was it, yes, *weaving their web in the shadows* . . . then eliminating, dissuading, pursuing whoever might cause them the least little bit of umbrage – that's the phrase – to a final bloody course of reckoning, tee-dum tee-dum . . . *The least little bit of umbrage*. Can there be a more telling description of the disproportionality of Kevern 'Co-co-cocksucking' Cohen and his kind, can there be a better atomisation of their crazed thin-skinned sensitivity, than that? *The least little bit of umbrage*. That imagined sliver of a slight in retaliation for which they'd have shaken the whole planet to its foundations . . . if we'd let them.

It would come as no surprise to learn the snake believes he's been caused the least little bit of umbrage by me, though where and how I can't imagine, and deny all charge and knowledge, but believes it anyway, I bet he does, in return for which he deposits his slime in my sweet, gullible and far too forgiving, not to say slime-receptive, Demelza. He will treat you as he's treated me, I tell her. They are incapable of gratitude . . . But she denies all knowledge of him. You think I'd want to be with another man after you, she says. You think I'm that big a fool? But my mind races with suspicions of them both and that's enough for me. On my hands and knees I pursue the spattered trail of rotten juices to my bed.

That I have no recourse, short of a private feud which, as the older and more easily hurt party, I am sure to lose, has been made plain to me in a communication from up there. They don't exactly confirm my suspicions as to Demelza (though they blaze them forth as to everything else), but the warning is unequivocal: stay away. It's actually even blunter than that. You have made a balls-up, move aside. No mention of Mrs Snake but I take the injunction to include her. Stay well clear of them both. Pretty much what I told Detective Inspector Gutkind. So you could say that in death he must be enjoying his revenge. As for when I will be enjoying mine, God alone knows. I am not, anyway, to have the consolation of confronting either of them. Not a cold word into his ear, not a warm whisper into hers; no bite from those mandala mandibles; no last sniff of her paper flowers.

My hand is forced. I will away to beauty . . .

No, not Rozenwyn Feigenblat. The beauty of natural things – tidal flats, sunsets, unsullied by all the subtle demonism of life and thought . . .

iv

Ailinn Solomons, looking at the moon, and listening to her jumping heart, wondered at what was happening to her. She had returned, briefly – she didn't want to leave Kevern on his own for too long – to Paradise Valley where there were still things to find out, sort out, have out, and was sitting on a cold mossy bench, hugging herself against the chill damp, listening to Ez clattering about rather obviously in the kitchen. 'Do I feel any different?' she asked herself. Ez had been lending her books relevant to that question, or at least fragments of books, dog-eared, singed, defaced, some of them crayoned over as if by a class of three-year-old delinquents. Although they purported to have been written – whenever it was they were written – from the inside, by those in the know, or at least by those who knew others in the know, each work, no matter how little of it there was, contradicted the one before. It was her forebears' austerity of conscience, according to one writer, that had always troubled humanity and explained the hostility they encountered wherever they went. They demanded too much. They set too high a standard. A second writer understood their defining characteristic as a near irresponsible love of the material world, and it was this that had landed them in hot water. Offered the spirit, they chose matter. Offered emotion, they chose reason. This one said they were deeply pious; that one found them profoundly sacrilegious. They were devoted to charity, yet they amassed wealth regardless of how they came by it. When they weren't consumed by self-regard they suffered a bruising sense of worthlessness. They saw the universe as a reflection of the God that loved them above all people, but moved through it like strangers. When she came to the alienation they felt in nature she recognised herself at last. She had never been comfortable on a garden seat in her life. She disliked the damp newsprint smell of vegetation, detested snails and worms, felt threatened by the icy indifference of the moon, and feared the irregular rhythm of her heart which also, surely, was a thing of nature. So while she didn't feel any different after reading all Esme had given her to read, she at least understood why she felt the same.

Esme called out to her from the kitchen. She had, since morning, been making chicken soup to an ancient recipe she'd found in a cookery book that must have been as old as creation and wondered whether Ailinn wanted to eat it inside or out. Ailinn didn't want to eat it at all, so reverentially had Esme prepared it, with so much sacrificial ardour had she dismembered the chicken, so full of spiritual intention was her dicing of the carrots, so soulfully did she look at her through the steam rising from the pan, but decided that as she had to eat it somewhere she would eat it out. Compound the discomfort.

They ate silently for a short while, balancing the soup plates on their knees. Esme sneaked looks at her.

'Are you enjoying it, my love?'

My love!

'Am I meant to?'

'Well I've made it for you in the hope you will.'

'No, I mean is it part of my preparation?'

Esme winced.

'Will it count against me,' Ailinn continued, 'if I don't? Will it prove I'm a fake?'

'Well I won't tell,' Esme said.

'Forgive me, I am not able to finish it,' Ailinn said at last, putting the plate on the ground between her ugly feet. 'There is something more pressing than soup.'

Esme started in alarm. It irritated Ailinn how easily she could worry her. She had only to express the slightest disquiet for Esme's entire system of defences to be activated. She's too close to me, she thought. There's more of her inside my skin than there is of me.

'What is it that's more pressing?' Esme asked. She could have been asking how long Ailinn had known she only had an hour to live.

'Matrilineality,' Ailinn said.

'Could you explain that?'

'Matrilineality? After all you've said to me on the subject! My love' – take that, Ailinn thought – 'it's you who are the authority.'

'No, I meant could you explain what bothers you about it.'

So, Ailinn, shivering under the cold moon, did.

If fathers bore so little responsibility for the defining characteristics of their progeny, as Esme said they did, in what sense were they their progeny at all? There seemed to be a carelessness here that belied the otherwise strict code of kinship into which Ailinn had now been drawn. Had it really mattered not at all what sort of seed her father had put into her mother, and her grandfather into her grandmother? Was it merely incidental? She felt the pull of contradictory impulses: pleased to be incontrovertibly what she was, but disappointed she had got there, so to speak, so easily, with so few caveats as to fathers. In an odd way it devalued her new-found affiliation. 'I would want a child of mine to be validated on both sides,' she told Esme.

'I want that for you too,' Esme assured her.

Fearing that Esme intended to embrace her, Ailinn moved her chair away, pretending she was trying to make herself more comfortable.

'But . . .?'

'But we don't always get what we want.'

'You moved heaven and earth to keep us together, Ez,' she reminded her. 'You wouldn't let me walk away from him. "Ring him, ring him," you urged me. My soulmate, you had the nerve to call him when you knew nothing of my soul. And when I told you he was walking away from me you turned as white as your blouse. What's changed?'

Esme Nussbaum was relieved that Ailinn couldn't see her blush. 'Nothing's changed. I care about your happiness as much as I ever did. More. But you've taken what I've had to tell you remarkably well – far better, truly, than I dared to hope you would. I couldn't imagine you ever dealing with this on your own, yet you have.'

'Not have, *am* . . . I'm a work in progress, Ez.'

'I understand . . .'

'And I'm not on my own.'

'Are you saying that Kevern is with you on this every inch of the way?'

'I never said *I* was with me on this every inch of the way. I haven't chosen this, remember. And I haven't seen through to the end of all it means. You have to face the fact that I probably never will. I can't give you a guarantee for life.'

'I know that and I'm not pressuring you. If you and Kevern can work this out together there's nothing I'd like more.'

'Matrilineality notwithstanding?'

'Matrilineality is not my invention. It just happens to be the way it works.'

'And the way it works makes Kevern redundant?'

'Not at all. The future I envisage requires mothers and fathers.'

'For the look of the thing.'

This time Esme would not be denied. She leaned across and stroked the girl's arm. 'Ailinn, this is all about the "look" of the thing. You are no different today from who you were a year ago, a month ago even. What's changed is how you appear. How you appear to yourself and how you will appear to the world. It's all illusion. Identity is nothing but illusion.'

'I shouldn't worry in that case that I don't like chicken soup?'

'I'd like you not to worry about anything.'

Ailinn wondered why she'd made a joke. Was it Kevern's doing? 'If it's all illusion,' she continued in a different vein, 'why has it caused so much misery?'

'I've had a long time to think about this,' Esme said, pausing . . .

'And?'

Ailinn marvelled at her own impatience. She had lived in ignorance of just about everything for a quarter of a century; now she needed answers to questions she could never have imagined she would ask, and she needed them at once. The pity of it was that the person in the best position to answer those questions seemed to have all the time in the world. In fact Ailinn was wrong about this. Esme, too, was a cauldron of impatience, but did not want to frighten Ailinn off with her intensity. So both women sat with frayed nerves, listening to the clocks furiously ticking in their brains.

'We are dead matter,' Esme continued at last, 'indeed I was very nearly dead matter myself when I realised this – we are dead matter until we distinguish ourselves from what's not dead. I was alive, I told myself as I was lying there. Very nearly dead, but alive. And it made me more alive to realise that. I wasn't the me I'd been, but nor was I the me they wanted me to be, which was no me at all. Only when we have a different state to strive against do we have reason to strive at all. And different people the same. I am me because I am not her, or you. If we were all red earthworms there'd be no point in life. Identity is just the name we give to the act of making ourselves distinct.'

'So you're saying it's irrelevant what our identities really are? As long as we assume one and fight against someone else's.'

'I'd say so, yes. Pretty much.'

'Isn't that a bit arbitrary?'

'Perhaps. But isn't everything? It's just chance that we're born to who we're born to. There's no design.'

'So why fight for who we are?'

'For the sake of the fight itself.'

'Then isn't that a bit violent, as well as arbitrary?'

'Life is violent. I had to fight death to be alive.'

'But if "who we are" is arbitrary, and if we fight for whatever cause we just happen to be to born to, for no other reason than the fight itself, then it didn't have to be me you picked for this . . .'

'I didn't pick you, Ailinn.'

'All right. Describe it how you like. But if there is no identifiable me then it doesn't matter whether I am it or not. I don't have to be the real deal because there is no real deal. You could have hit on anyone.'

Esme bit her lip. 'You'll do it better,' she said.

They fell silent. Something crawled across Ailinn's feet. She wondered if it was Esme's red earthworm, that made life meaningless. She shuddered. Esme offered to go inside and fetch her a shawl. Ailinn shook her head. She could have been shaking Esme off her.

'If you're asking me to do this without Kevern,' she said suddenly, 'I'm afraid I can't. No, it's feeble of me to put it like that. If you're asking me to do this without Kevern, I'm afraid I *won't.*'

Esme felt as though all her splintered bones had been crushed a second time. She remembered what it took to distinguish herself from the dead.

'In that case we will have to make sure you do it with him,' she said.

CHAPTER 2

SHAKE HANDS WITH YOUR UNCLE MAX

i

It was Hedra Deitch who was the first to congratulate him.

'On?'

'Don't be like that,' Hedra said, wrinkling up her nose.

Kevern had dropped into her souvenir shop to see if her stock of lovespoons needed replenishing. She didn't sell many. Painted earthenware garden statuary, pressed-flower pictures, and Port Reuben tea towels and coffee mugs accounted for most of her trade. 'Cheap and cheerful, like me,' was how she described her business. But she thought a small selection of Kevern's lovespoons lent her shop a more upmarket feel, and she welcomed the opportunity his visits gave her to be suggestive with him. He wasn't like the other men in the village. You had to work a bit harder with him. She had snogged him once that she could remember, at the end of a wild night in the pub, when they were both drunk. She had done it to enrage Pascoe but she had enjoyed it too, after a fashion. He had a softer mouth than she expected. No biting. And no slapping. On his part, that is. So she was glad enough to return to Pascoe's rough indifferent gnawing later.

But Kevern was one of those men who got under your skin by not adequately taking you in. So he remained a challenge to her.

It was Ailinn's idea that Kevern do something practical such as checking on his outlets, no matter that there was no pressing financial reason to do so. He had not been down into the village, not seen a living soul since she'd told him the first part of what she had to tell him, and that was two weeks ago. He had gone into a decline, rapid even for a man who declined easily. He agreed to Ailinn's suggestion only because he knew it would make her, at least, feel better. He wasn't expecting to feel better himself. He didn't want to feel better. He owed it to what he'd been told to feel worse. That was what living a serious life meant, wasn't it, honouring the gravity of things by not pretending they were light? Rozenwyn Feigenblat had told him he was an ethicist, not an artist. He agreed with her. An artist owed a duty to nothing except his own irresponsibility. It was OK for an artist to frolic in the water, no matter how bloody the waves or how high the tide rose. An ethicist had an obligation to drown.

Just go for the walk, Ailinn had said. Just go for the exercise. See someone who isn't me. 'There isn't someone who isn't you,' he'd said. Whereupon she'd pushed him out of the cottage.

He meant what he'd said. There wasn't anyone who wasn't her, and if there were he didn't want to see them. And even she, since she'd become the bearer of bad news, was not always a welcome sight to him now.

But most of all he hadn't gone out because he hadn't wanted to be seen.

Was that because he believed he suddenly looked different? No. He trusted he looked exactly the same: the man he had always been, in decline as he had always been. The difference today was that he understood what they'd seen when they'd looked at him in the past.

He exchanged stiff greetings with people he barely knew. He had lived here all his life, in a village of fewer than two thousand souls, and yet there were still people who were lifetime residents themselves whose names he didn't know. His parents had taught him well in one regard. Remain a stranger to the place, they had said. Say nothing. Ask for nothing. Explain yourself to no one. But they had also cautioned him to go unnoticed, and in that he could scarcely have fared worse. Everyone knew who he was – Kevern 'Coco' Cohen, the man with the sour expression who sat on his own bench above the blowhole, saying nothing, asking for nothing, explaining himself to no one.

And now here was Hedra Deitch, coming out from behind her counter to look him up and down, surveying him in that hungry way of hers, wondering if he'd do for whatever her itchy nature needed at that moment, something or other that her shot-beast of a husband couldn't provide. Shame he wasn't an artist. He'd have provided it and painted her later.

But why the congratulations? Was she being sarcastic, welcoming him to a knowledge of himself the whole village had possessed for years? Was she applauding his cottoning on finally – Kevern, the last to know about Kevern?

'Don't be like what?' he said.

She put one hand on her hip, as though to answer his coquettishness. 'Don't be pretending you aren't proud.'

He was not a man who ever asked people what they meant. He would rather puzzle over their words for months, and still not get to the bottom of their meaning, than ask them for a simple explanation. Did he not want to know or could he not bear to appear uncomprehending? This was a time to wonder whether he'd ever in his whole life understood a word that had been said to him. Clearly he hadn't ever understood his parents. Could it be that he had missed the point of what Ailinn had been saying to him too?

If only . . .

But when the news was bad . . . then he understood.

And Hedra? He prepared his face to pretend to get her meaning – a half-smile and a philosophic widening of the eyes that would cover every eventuality: from a declaration of undying to love to news that she had a terminal disease.

'I'm not pretending anything,' he said. 'And I'm certainly not pretending I'm not proud. I have nothing to be proud about.'

She moved a step closer. Was she about to kiss him? *Then be proud of this, my lover . . .*

Funny how often, for a man who didn't consider himself lovable, he thought a woman was about to kiss him. Was it hope? Was it dread? Or did he think of himself as the unsmiling princess, waiting to be kissed back into warm life by a frog?

'I don't reckon your missus would be pleased to hear you got nothing to be proud about,' Hedra said.

He increased his half-smile to a three-quarter smile and opened his eyes a little wider. 'My missus . . .? What's Ailinn got to do with this?'

It was then she made a cradling motion with her arms, beaming like the Virgin Mary, rocking a little one to sleep.

'Come on!' she taunted him. 'You don't have to be coy with me. I know you're proud. Daddy!'

There, in the middle of the shop, with people watching, he snogged her brutally.

ii

Ailinn barely recognised him when he returned.

'My God, what's happened?' she said.

445

He felt that his face had grown to twice its length. He couldn't bear the weight of his jaw or control the movement of his tongue. He pointed to it. I have no words, the gesture meant. There are no words . . .

She put her arms around him and he remained enfolded in them. But he was unresponsive. This wasn't the first time she had held him, drained of life, but never before had she felt she couldn't at least thaw him back to something like good humour.

She made him tea which he drank without waiting for it to cool, almost in a single gulp.

'You are carrying our baby,' he finally said.

Now it was she who couldn't speak.

He waited for her to drink her tea. She could take all the time she liked. Time was not their problem. Then, looking beyond her, he repeated his words, without anger, without feeling. 'You are carrying our baby.'

'How do you know?'

'It's the talk of the village.'

She didn't believe that. The village had better things to talk about.

'What do you mean?' she asked. 'What do you *actually* mean?'

'I mean that it's known in the village that you are carrying our baby. I presume it's ours.'

'That's a low blow,' she said quietly.

'Yes. It's a low blow.'

Among the thousand things that hurt her at this

moment was the knowledge that he wasn't looking for reassurance and so there was nothing she could reassure him with – not tenderness, not devotion, nothing. Yes, it was his baby, and that only made it worse. There would not now be a moment when suspicion could dissolve in mutual delight. That joy was lost to them.

'It isn't just,' he said, 'that the village knows before I do.'

'I understand. I'm sorry. I have told no one.'

'No one?'

'I have told no one in the village.'

'Which means you have told someone?'

'Yes.'

It wasn't necessary for either of them to speak the person's name.

'And it isn't just that either,' he said. 'Though that is no small thing.'

'I know. I am so very sorry.'

He was listening to the logic of his thoughts, not the progress of her apology.

'We had an understanding.'

'I know we did, darling.'

'We had an understanding that no child would "come along" to surprise either of us. We both, I thought, were taking the necessary precautions.'

She wondered whether she should remind him that accidents happen, that no precaution was ever foolproof, but she couldn't bear even to essay a lie. 'We were,' she said.

'And then you weren't . . .'

She could find no extenuating explanation. '. . . And then I wasn't.'

'Did you think I would *come round eventually*?'

She heard the banality, heard how insulting to him it was to think it, but yes, she had thought precisely that. *He would come round . . .* At the far reaches of sanity she still thought it.

'I hoped.'

'And you didn't discuss it with me *why* . . .?'

She said nothing.

'Given your *hope* for me eventually,' he persisted, 'why didn't you at least try me initially?'

There was no way back from this. 'I couldn't risk it.'

'Couldn't risk my saying no?'

'Exactly.'

'The risk being?'

In a gesture of desperation, she ran her hand through her hair. He could hear it crackle. He used to love stirring up an electrical storm in her hair. Combing it through with his fingers and watching the sparks fly. Now it was a site of desolation. Her desperation was more than he could bear. He thought his chest would break apart – not for himself, for her. For himself he felt only sullen anger. It was dark, where he was. A black corner of stoppered fury. But it was worse for her. He was that kind of a man: he thought everything was worse for a woman. Especially a woman he loved. Was that a form of contempt? He didn't know. He simply thought the pain for her was greater, perhaps because for her there was still hope mixed up in it. And there wasn't for him. He had flattened out; there was nothing now he could reasonably hope for. Only her to be all right, not to suffer, and she was distraught beyond the point of help.

'The risk,' she said, reading his thoughts, 'was that you would express your refusal so vehemently that there would be no going back from it.'

'And then?'

'And then we would lose the future I wanted for us.'

'The future you wanted for us, or others wanted for us?'

'Both.'

'But the future you wanted for us was once the future I wanted for us, and that didn't include – Ailinn, as I recall it positively excluded – a child.'

She hung her head. 'It did.'

'So what changed?'

'*I* changed.' It wasn't a good enough answer. She heard its inadequacy hang in the air between them, the way a lie can be detected on a phone line, in a crackle of silence.

'This baby,' he said – and in that phrase she heard his final disowning of it – 'it isn't just any baby, is it?'

'I don't know what you mean.'

'You do. It isn't just a future for you and me, is it? It's *the* future.'

'Is that so terrible?'

'Yes, if that means what I think it means.'

'Well it's your choice of words, Kevern.'

'But not my choice of future.'

'And what's your choice of future? To die out?'

'I've died out.'

That was the moment, with a clarity and sadness that all but made her poor arrhythmic heart stop, when she saw her life without him. 'Well I haven't,' she said.

There was, to the dismay of both of them, vigour in it.

Kevern remembered the box his father had made him promise he would open only in the event of his being about to be a father himself. He was sure he knew what it would contain. The word DON'T. But he didn't open it to find out.

iii

They did have one last conversation. He begged for it. A final night wrapped around each other.

'It promised so much,' he said, waiting for the dawn to break. 'We promised each other so much.'

She'd been over it and over it with him. Didn't *this* promise so much?

She could have killed him – would have killed him had she not cared deeply for him – so perverse were the words he chose. What was she offering him if not a future? What was she carrying if not promise?

'What was our promise?' she asked him. Not looking any longer for a fight. Just wanting to hear him say it. One more time. What would it have been?

'The promise of not knowing what it would be,' he said.

'Kevern, that's just a riddle.'

'Ah, then . . .'

They said nothing for another hour, simply held on to each other. But she was not prepared to give up without a fight, no matter that the fight was lost. She had told him all there was to know, all that she knew anyway. But she still wanted him to see he didn't have to commit as she was committed. Couldn't he come along for the ride? Be her consort? Look on from the sidelines . . .

'At the misery you're preparing for our child?'

She wouldn't let him get away with that. 'You can't have it both ways,' she said. 'You can't disown the child *and* call it yours.'

Was she right? He lay, listening to the quivering of her atria. Would she bequeath the child her troubled heart, he wondered. If she did, she did. Better that than what he had to bequeath.

'I'm simply saying you could stay out of whatever you want to stay out of.'

All of it, he thought. But he said, more gently, 'That being?'

'The politics.'

'The politics?'

'The journey . . .'

'Oh come on, Ailinn. I never expected that of you. *Journey*, for Christ's sake.'

'Then what word would you use?'

'I wouldn't. But I'll give you "mission" if you must have a word. A misguided mission to change what can never change. And actually, you know, it's even worse than that. It's a mission to repeat what should never be repeated.'

'And why are you so sure it will be repeated?'

'Because that's the law of it. Your heart, my love, is a live, tumultuous thing. Most human hearts are stone. And the immutable law I speak of is engraved on all of them.'

'You let them win once you decide it's immutable.'

'They have won already. They won a long time ago.'

'We could do so much to change this.'

'I don't want to change this. I want it to go on being. It's the only vengeance we have left – our refusal to stay around. Hand them the victory, I say, and let them see how empty it is.'

'And that's the future you say you promised me?'

'I thought it was the future we promised each other.'

'Don't you see how empty that would be for us too?'

He thought about it. For a long time, stretched out beside her, lying on her shoulder, bringing her on to his, kissing her face, her ears, her eyes, he thought about it. It was morning when he spoke.

'At least it would have been an emptiness of our deciding,' he said.

She was back in Paradise Valley by the time he rose. He breathed gently on the vase of paper flowers she had brought him as her moving-in present, barely daring to touch them, then he walked out on to the cliffs. He looked down into the great mouth of the blowhole. It was sucking so hard he needed to stand back from the edge. He felt it could reach up and gulp him down whole, like Hedra Deitch subjecting him to one of her snogging kisses.

But he didn't have to submit, even to Hedra. A life was owned by the person who lived it, he believed. What happened didn't always happen because you wanted it to, but what you made of it was your responsibility. Help there was little and gods there were none. We are the authors of our own consequences, if not always of our own actions.

The credo of a serious man. You could be too serious, he didn't doubt that. But his birthright was his birthright. No one can make me, he thought, feeling the spray on his cheeks.

Though even that turned out not to be entirely true. Distinct from the sucking of the sea and the screaming of the gulls he heard his mother calling to him. Her old, frayed, faint, reproachful cry.

'Key-vern . . . Key-vern . . .'

He put his ear to the wind. He had always been a good boy. When your mother called . . .

'Key-vern,' she called again.

He smiled to hear her voice.

'What is it, Ma?'

'Jump,' he heard her say.

Not feeling he should make her say it twice, he put his fingers to his lips, as though blowing her a kiss, and jumped.

Ailinn felt her heart crash into her chest. Esme Nussbaum heard it from the other end of the room and turned to look. She scowled.

They both knew.

'This is not a good way to start,' Ailinn said, 'with anger between us.'

'On the contrary,' Esme said, 'this is the best possible way to start.'